BEST NEW AMERICAN VOICES 2000

BEST NEW AMERICAN VOICES 2000

GUEST EDITOR

Tobias Wolff

SERIES EDITORS

John Kulka and Natalie Danford

CONTENTS

PREFACE

Best New American Voices 2000 launches a new series dedicated to the art of the short story. What distinguishes the Best New American Voices series from the many annual story anthologies on the market is its commitment to new writing by *new* writers. Rather than cull stories from literary quarterlies and general interest magazines, we dig one level deeper and solicit nominations directly from writing programs, arts organizations, and community workshops. Many of the contributors to *Best New American Voices 2000* are publishing their work for the first time in these pages.

The Best New American Voices series draws from an annual story competition. Included here are stories by some of the best emerging North American writers—as determined by many teachers, by workshop directors, by prize committee judges, by the series editors, and of course by our distinguished guest editors. Literally hundreds of readers have helped to shape the current volume.

The focus of our competition is the writing workshop here and in Canada. Why the workshop? The reason is simple. It's our belief that most of the good new writers can be found honing their skills in workshops, whether those writers are working toward graduate degrees at universities or polishing short stories during briefer stints at summer conferences. We solicit nominations from community-based workshops like the 92nd Street Y in New York City and Woodland Pattern in Milwaukee; from summer conferences like Bread Loaf and Sewanee; from the PEN Prison Writing Committee; as well as from the hundreds of MA and MFA writing programs associated with North American universities. We ask directors to send to us the best stories workshopped during the previous year. In this, the first year of our competition, we received about three hundred such prescreened nominations. Guest editor Tobias Wolff has selected twenty stories for inclusion in our debut volume.

As you read the twenty stories chosen by Tobias Wolff, you will find that these writers have diverse concerns and writing styles. They come from all walks of life—and they represent a wide spectrum of ages. Some stories are comic, others tragic, and still others both. Their settings range from Karuizawa, Japan, to the punk underground of New York City to the African desert. It would be impossible to generalize about topics, styles, or themes, but the quality is uniformly high. These are stories by writers at the beginnings of their careers. Awfully good stories. More than that, we cannot say.

We would like to extend thanks to Tobias Wolff for his careful reading of the manuscripts, for his dedication to this project, and for his excellent editorial suggestions. To the many writers, directors, teachers, and panel judges who helped to make this book a success we extend heartfelt thanks and congratulations. To name just a few others: We thank Bell Chevigny and Hettie Jones of the PEN Prison Writing Committee for their interest and participation in this project; Chuck Wachtel for his sage advice and encouragement; Wyatt Prunty for his suggestion to include summer conferences in our competition; our editor André Bernard for his patience and understanding; Meredith Arthur at Harcourt for her constant attention to details; Lisa Lucas in the Harcourt contracts department for the obvious and maybe not-so obvious; and our families and friends for their support.

—*John Kulka and Natalie Danford*

INTRODUCTION

Tobias Wolff

I was thirty years old when I first sat in a writing workshop. I'd been awarded a Wallace Stegner Fellowship at Stanford, thirty-six hundred dollars after taxes, not a fortune even in 1975 but enough to deliver me from the tedium and frustration of working for a living like every other poor stiff and also trying to get something written now and then. The fellowship was a devoutly hoped-for but truly unexpected gift of time; and that's all I thought it was. As for the workshops I was supposed to attend with the other fellows, I figured I could get through them if I had to, but wished I didn't have to. Why couldn't they just give me the dough and let me write? What was this workshop baloney anyway?

I really didn't know. Where I went to university, at Oxford, they weren't offered. In fact, the only time I let slip to one of my tutors that I was working on a novel he treated me exactly as if I'd cut a fart—the same vaguely discomfited look, the same icily polite refusal to speak of the offense. Friends of mine, other writers in the bud, had the same experience. We were there to study literature, not to indulge the risible fantasy that we could produce it. The curriculum in English Literature ended at 1914. After that—well, things *had* rather gone downhill, hadn't they?

I didn't mind this arrangement. I liked it. Whatever its limitations, the course of study was coherent and purposeful, unlike the hopscotch played by English majors in this country. It held us accountable for a historical, rigorous scrutiny of English poetry and prose and made no allowance for our own special interests in comic books or science fiction or, God forbid, "creative writing."

Of course I wrote anyway, but always with the sense that I was stealing the time, that I was engaged in something unauthorized, even subversive. This was the way I'd always written—in the back of a classroom while pretending to solve math problems, on guard duty, at work. The sense of writing as a renegade act was part of its appeal. I developed patterns of work that shadowed like a kind of black market my official, licensed schedules and duties, and showed my work to no one except now and then my brother, but only now and then—very seldom. Books—at least the books I loved—got written by men and women in solitude, and I accepted solitude as the essential condition of my own efforts. Secret, unsanctioned, and isolated—that was the writing life as I had always known it.

So the whole idea of a workshop was foreign to me, and I was suspicious of it—especially of its official, institutional status, and its communal character. I was most afraid that it would be mendaciously "supportive" and emotional, a gooey hugfest. Ha! Fat chance. From our first meetings, it was plain that there were deep fissures in our group of twelve—between the four Stegner Fellows, who had a free ride, and everyone else, who had to pay to be in the workshop, and resented it, most acutely when one of the Fellows brought in a weak story; between the men and the women, who were outnumbered and generally disgusted—not altogether unjustly—with the way we men wrote about women; between self-consciously postmodern narratologists and no-nonsense genre writers, one of whom was writing a novel about his high school football team; between women who didn't shave their legs and women who did; and between lovers whose affairs went sour. The atmosphere was so crabby that it always astonished me to hear that any of us had managed to get to the point of sharing a kiss, let alone a bed.

Crabby. Tense. Dour. And yet this turned out to be the single most important year I'd had as a writer. Working alone, hoarding my work, I didn't know how it looked to other people. I quickly learned that it looked different to them. Not everyone in the workshop had useful things to say—useful to me, that is. In the end I found myself listening to two or three voices. Much of what they had to say made me squirm, not because it was mean but because I could feel the truth of it—certain tics of language, habitual poses and attitudes. By seeing my work through their eyes I began to take a less forgiving view of it, and though this did not always feel like a gift at the time, it was a gift. Being made familiar with my own mannerisms, to the extent that they were unconscious, made me less subject to them, and allowed me a wider field of play when I came to write the next story.

In less evident ways I learned from other writers in the workshop, especially those who provoked me to define myself by contrast or refutation. One day somebody said about a work under discussion, Oh no, not another priest story, you can't write about priests anymore, J. F. Powers has used that stuff all up. The piece in question wasn't mine, but this crack irked me so much that I immediately started writing a priest story of my own. A similar comment about hitchhiking stories launched me on a hitchhiking story. And after reading a great many self-reflexive "fictions," and hearing the theories that proved them brilliant espoused at length, I found myself more and more interested in writing stories that did not unravel themselves and that concerned people whose reality I would not mock my readers for believing in.

And finally there was the pleasure of spending a year with other people who cared about writing. The world at large does not; the world at large is indifferent to Babel's proposition that "no iron can pierce the heart with the force of a well-placed period." What a joy it was to be excused for a time from that colossal indifference. Cross-grained though we were, we all loved books and urged our darlings on one another and argued their merits. Not always with the best will in the world, but to generally good effect, we tested and honed each other.

This is not an apologia for creative writing workshops. How could it be? Each is different, even within the same program, and programs themselves vary dramatically. In one, Kafka would no doubt be given a sharp talking-to for failing to create in Gregor Samsa a character with whom we can identify; in another, Mary McCarthy would be brought to account for the masculinity of her politics and the cheerful cruelty of her wit. Some workshops really are orgies of affirmation, others stupidly vicious and destructive. But on the evidence, it's hard to believe they're doing too much damage. Here in no particular order are a few of the fiction writers who've passed through just one program, Stanford's: Robert Stone; Raymond Carver; Evan S. Connell; Tillie Olsen; Larry McMurtry; Ernest J. Gaines; Ron Hansen; Ken Kesey; Scott Turow; Thomas McGuane; Alice Hoffman; Allan Gurganus; Wendell Berry; Harriet Doerr; Al Young; Michael Cunningham; Blanche Boyd; N. Scott Momaday; Vikram Seth; Dennis McFarland; Stephanie Vaughn. This is a very thin slice of a very long list, which, added to Stanford's poets (including the last two poet laureates), would make up a creditable national literature all by itself. And it should be noted that all of these writers work in different forms and voices and are animated by different concerns. The supposedly homogenizing effect of the workshop is nowhere in evidence here.

Nor will you find it in this anthology, drawn from hundreds of workshops across the country, some community-based, others in universities, still more at summer conferences, and even in prisons. What you will discover here is an extraordinary display of inventiveness and variety within the story form. You'll read a cool, measured piece, then find one whistling with steam. You'll go from the fabulous to the realistic, taciturn to lush, experimental to traditional, sober to funny. But none of the writers is just fooling around, making a show of expertise; they're all dead serious in some way that sharpens our sense of the world.

In reading the many fine stories from which I selected these twenty, I detected no "school," no signs of any herding instinct. These writers are all over the map, in every sense. And they're good. Are they good partly because of their workshops, or in spite of them? Who knows? Who, in the end, cares? The point is the work, not the workshop, and the work in these pages is a gift in itself and a generous promise of more gifts to come.

ANA MENENDEZ

New York University

In Cuba I Was
a German Shepherd

The park where the four men gathered was small. Before the city put it on tourist maps, it was just a fenced rectangle of space that people ignored on their way to office jobs. The men came each morning to sit under the shifting shade of a banyan tree, and sometimes the way the wind moved through the leaves reminded them of home.

One man carried a box of plastic dominoes. His name was Maximo, and because he was a small man his grandiose name had inspired much amusement all his life. He liked to say that over the years he'd learned a thing or two about the physics of laughter and his friends took that to mean that good humor could make a big man out of anyone. Now, Maximo waited for the others to sit before turning the dominoes out on the table. Judging the men to be in good spirits, he cleared his throat and began to tell the joke he had prepared for the day.

"So Bill Clinton dies in office and they freeze his body."

Antonio leaned back in his chair and let out a sigh. "Here we go."

Maximo caught a roll of the eyes and almost grew annoyed. But he smiled. "It gets better."

He scraped the dominoes in two wide circles across the table then continued.

"Okay, so they freeze his body and when we get the technology to unfreeze him, he wakes up in the year 2105."

"Two thousand one hundred and five, eh?"

"Very good," Maximo said. "Anyway, he's curious about what's happened to the world all this time, so he goes up to a Jewish fellow and he asks, 'So, how are things in the Middle East?' The guy replies, 'Oh wonderful, wonderful, everything is like heaven. Everybody gets along now.' This makes Clinton smile, right?"

The men stopped their shuffling and dragged their pieces across the table and waited for Maximo to finish.

"Next he goes up to an Irishman and he asks, 'So how are things over there in Northern Ireland now?' The guy says, 'Northern? It's one Ireland now and we all live in peace.' Clinton is extremely pleased at this point, right? So he does that biting thing with his lip." Maximo stopped to demonstrate and Raul and Carlos slapped their hands on the domino table and laughed. Maximo paused. Even Antonio had to smile. Maximo loved this moment when the men were warming to the joke and he still kept the punch line close to himself like a secret.

"So, okay," Maximo continued, "Clinton goes up to a Cuban fellow and says, 'Compadre, how are things in Cuba these days?' The guy looks at Clinton and he says to the president, 'Let me tell you, my friend, I can feel it in my bones, any day now Castro's gonna fall.'"

Maximo tucked his head into his neck and smiled. Carlos slapped him on the back and laughed.

"That's a good one, sure is," he said. "I like that one."

"Funny," Antonio said, nodding as he set up his pieces.

"Yes, funny," Raul said. After chuckling for another moment, he added, "But old."

"What do you mean old?" Antonio said, then he turned to Carlos. "What are you looking at?"

Carlos stopped laughing.

"It's not old," Maximo said. "I just made it up."

"I'm telling you, professor, it's an old one," Raul said. "I heard it when Reagan was president."

Maximo looked at Raul, but didn't say anything. He pulled the double nine from his row and laid it in the middle of the table, but the thud he intended was lost in the horns and curses of morning traffic on Eighth Street.

Raul and Maximo had lived on the same El Vedado street in Havana for fifteen years before the revolution. Raul had been a government accountant and Maximo a professor at the University, two blocks from his home on L Street. They weren't close friends, but friendly still in that way of people who come from the same place and think they already know the important things about one another.

Maximo was one of the first to leave L Street, boarding a plane for Miami on the eve of the first of January 1960, exactly one year after Batista had done the same. For reasons he told himself he could no longer remember, he said good-bye to no one. He was forty-two years old then, already balding, with a wife and two young daughters whose names he tended to confuse. He left behind the rowhouse of long shiny windows, the piano, the mahogany furniture, and the pension he thought he'd return to in two years' time. Three, if things were as serious as they said.

In Miami, Maximo tried driving a taxi, but the streets were still a web of foreign names and winding curves that could one day lead to glitter and another to the hollow end of a pistol. His Spanish and his University of Havana credentials meant nothing here. And he was too old to cut sugar cane with the younger men who began arriving in the spring of 1961. But the men gave Maximo an idea and after teary nights of promises, he convinced his wife, she of stately homes and multiple cooks, to make lunch to sell to those sugar men who waited, squatting on their heels in the dark, for the bus to Belle Glade every morning. They worked side by side, Maximo and Rosa. And at the end of every day, their hands stained orange from the lard and the cheap meat, their knuckles red and tender where the hot water and the knife blade had worked their business, Maximo and Rosa would sit down to whatever remained of the day's cooking and they would chew slowly, the day unraveling, their hunger ebbing away with the light.

They worked together for seven years like that, and when the Cubans began disappearing from the bus line, Maximo and Rosa moved their lunch packets indoors and opened their little restaurant right on Eighth Street. There, a generation of former professors served black beans and rice to the nostalgic. When Raul showed up in Miami in the summer of 1971 looking for work, Maximo added one more waiter spot for his old acquaintance from L Street. Each night, after the customers had gone, Maximo and Rosa and Raul and Havana's old lawyers and bankers and dreamers would sit around the biggest table and eat and talk and sometimes, late in the night after several glasses of wine, someone would start the stories that began with "In Cuba I remember."

They were stories of old lovers, beautiful and round-hipped. Of skies that stretched on clear and blue to the Cuban hills. Of green landscapes that clung to the red clay of Güines, roots dug in like fingernails in a good-bye. In Cuba, the stories always began, life was good and pure. But something always happened to them in the end, something withering, malignant. Maximo never understood it. The stories that opened in sun always narrowed to a dark place. And after those nights, his head throbbing, Maximo would turn and turn in his sleep and awake unable to remember his dreams.

Even now, ten years after selling the place, Maximo couldn't walk by it in the early morning when it was still clean and empty. He'd tried it once. He'd stood and stared into the restaurant and had become lost and dizzy in his own reflection in the glass, the neat row of chairs, the tombstone lunch board behind them.

"Okay. A bunch of rafters are on the beach getting ready to sail off to Miami."

"Where are they?"

"Who cares? Wherever. Cuba's got a thousand miles of coastline. Use your imagination."

"Let the professor tell his thing, for God's sake."

"Thank you." Maximo cleared his throat and shuffled the dominoes. "So anyway, a bunch of rafters are gathered there on the sand. And they're all crying and hugging their wives and all the rafts are bobbing on the water and suddenly someone in the group yells, 'Hey! Look who goes there!' And it's Fidel in swimming trunks, carrying a raft on his back."

Carlos interrupted to let out a yelping laugh. "I like that, I like it, sure do."

"You like it, eh?" said Antonio, "Why don't you let the Cuban finish it?"

Maximo slid the pieces to himself in twos and continued. "So one of the guys on the sand says to Fidel, 'Compatriota, what are you doing here? What's with the raft?' And Fidel sits on his raft and pushes off the shore and says, 'I'm sick of this place, too. I'm going to Miami.' So the other guys look at each other and say, 'Coño, compadre, if you're leaving, then there's no reason for us to go. Here, take my raft, too, get the fuck out of here.'"

Raul let a shaking laugh rise from his belly and saluted Maximo with a domino piece. "A good one, my friend."

Carlos laughed long and loud. Antonio laughed, too, but he was careful to not laugh too hard and he gave his friend a sharp look over the racket he was causing. He and Carlos were Dominican, not Cuban, and they ate their same foods and played their same games, but Antonio knew they still didn't understand all the layers of hurt in the Cubans' jokes.

It had been Raul's idea to go down to Domino Park that first time. Maximo protested. He had seen the rows of tourists pressed up against the fence, gawking at the colorful old guys playing dominoes.

"I'm not going to be the sad spectacle in someone's vacation slide show," he'd said.

But Raul was already dressed up in a pale blue guayabera, saying how it was a beautiful day and smell the air.

"Let them take pictures," Raul said. "What the hell. Make us immortal."

"Immortal," Maximo said like a sneer. And then, to himself, *the gods' punishment.*

It was that year after Rosa died and Maximo didn't want to tell how he'd begun to see her at the kitchen table as she'd been at twenty-five. Watched one thick strand of her dark hair stuck to her morning face. He saw her at thirty, bending down to wipe the chocolate off the cheeks of their two small daughters. And his eyes moved from Rosa to his girls. He had something he needed to tell them. He saw them grown up, at the funeral, crying together. He watched Rosa rise and do the sign of the cross. He knew he was caught inside a nightmare, but he couldn't stop. He would emerge slowly, creaking out of the shower and there she'd be, Rosa, like before, her breasts round and pink from the hot water, calling back through the years. Some mornings he would awake and smell peanuts roasting and hear the faint call of the manicero pleading for someone to relieve his burden of white paper cones. Or it would be thundering, the long hard thunder of Miami that was so much like the thunder of home that each rumble shattered the morning of his other life. He would awake, caught fast in the damp sheets, and feel himself falling backward.

He took the number eight bus to Eighth Street and Fifteenth Avenue. At Domino Park that first day, he sat with Raul and they played alone, Maximo noticing his own speckled hands, the spots of light through the banyan leaves, a round red beetle that crawled slowly across the table then hopped the next breeze and floated away.

Antonio and Carlos were not Cuban, but they knew when to dump their heavy pieces and when to hold back the eights for the final shocking stroke. Waiting for a table, Raul and Maximo would linger beside them and watch them lay their traps, a succession of threes that broke their opponents, an incredible run of fives. Even the unthinkable: passing when they had the piece to play.

Other twosomes began to refuse to play with the Dominicans, said that Carlos gave them the creeps with his giggling and monosyllables. Besides, any team that won so often must be cheating, went the charge, especially a team one-half imbecile. But really it was that no one plays to lose. You begin to lose again and again and it reminds you of other things in your life, the despair of it all begins to bleed through, and that is not what games are for. Who wants to live his whole life alongside the lucky? But Maximo and Raul liked these blessed Dominicans, appreciated the well-oiled moves of two old pros. And if the two Dominicans, afraid to be alone again, let them win now and then, who would know, who could ever admit to such a thing? For many months they didn't know much about each other, these four men. Even the smallest boy knew not to talk when the pieces were in play. But soon came Maximo's jokes during the shuffling, something new and bright coming into his eyes like daydreams as he spoke. Carlos's full loud laughter, like that of children. And the four men learned to linger long enough between sets to color an old memory while the white pieces scraped along the table.

One day as they sat at their table, the one closest to the sidewalk, a pretty girl walked by. She swung her long brown hair around and looked in at the men with her green eyes.

"What the hell is she looking at?" said Antonio, who always sat with his back to the wall, looking out at the street. But the others saw how he stared back, too.

Carlos let out a giggle and immediately put a hand to his mouth.

"In Santo Domingo, a man once looked at—" but Carlos didn't get to finish.

"Shut up, you old idiot," said Antonio, putting his hands on the table like he was about to get up and leave.

"Please," Maximo said.

The girl stared another moment, then turned and left.

Raul rose slowly, flattening down his oiled hair with his right hand.

"Ay mi niña."

"Sit down, hombre," Antonio said. "You're an old fool, just like this one."

"You're the fool," Raul called back. "A woman like that..."

He watched the girl cross the street. When she was out of sight, he grabbed the back of the chair behind him and eased his body down, his eyes still on the street. The other three men looked at one another.

"I knew a woman like that once," Raul said after a long moment.

"That's right, he did," Antonio said, "in his moist boy dreams, what was it? A century ago?"

"No me jodas," Raul said. "You are a vulgar man. I had a life all three of you would have paid millions for. Women."

Maximo watched him, then lowered his face, shuffled the dominoes.

"I had women," Raul said.

"We all had women," Carlos said, and he looked like he was about to laugh again, but instead just sat there, smiling like he was remembering one of Maximo's jokes.

"There was one I remember. More beautiful than the rising moon," Raul said.

"Oh Jesus," Antonio said. "You people."

Maximo looked up, watching Raul.

"Ay, a woman like that," Raul said and shook his head. "The women of Cuba were radiant, magnificent, wouldn't you say, professor?"

Maximo looked away.

"I don't know," Antonio said. "I think that americana there looked better than anything you remember."

And that brought a long laugh from Carlos.

Maximo sat all night at the pine table in his new efficiency, thinking about the green-eyed girl and wondering why he was thinking about her. The table and a narrow bed had come with the apartment, which he'd moved into after selling their house in Shenandoah. The table had come with two chairs, sturdy and polished and not in the least institutional, but he had moved the other chair by the bed. The landlady, a woman in her forties, had helped Maximo haul up three potted palms. Later, he bought a green pot of marigolds he saw in the supermarket and brought its butter leaves back to life under the window's eastern light. Maximo often sat at the table through the night, sometimes reading Marti, sometimes listening to the rain on the tin hull of the air conditioner.

When you are older, he'd read somewhere, you don't need as much sleep. And wasn't that funny because his days felt more like sleep than ever. Dinner kept him occupied for hours, remembering the story of each dish. Sometimes, at the table, he greeted old friends and awakened with a start when they reached out to touch him. When dawn rose and slunk into the room sideways through the blinds, Maximo walked as in a dream across the thin patterns of light on the terrazzo.

The chair, why did he keep the other chair? Even the marigolds reminded him. An image returned again and again. Was it the green-eyed girl? And then he remembered that Rosa wore carnations in her hair and hated her name. And that it saddened him because he liked to roll it off his tongue like a slow train to the country.

"Rosa," he said, taking her hand the night they met at La Concha while an old danzon played.

"Clavel," she said, tossing her head back in a crackling laugh. "Call me Clavel."

She pulled her hand away and laughed again. "Don't you notice the flower in a girl's hair?"

He led her around the dance floor, lined with chaperones, and when they turned he whispered that he wanted to follow her laughter to the moon. She laughed again, the notes round and heavy as summer raindrops and Maximo felt his fingers go cold where they touched hers. The danzon played and they turned and turned and the faces of the chaperones and the moist warm air and Maximo with his cold fingers worried that she had laughed at him. He was twenty-four and could not imagine a more sorrowful thing in all the world.

Sometimes, years later, he would catch a premonition of Rosa in the face of his eldest daughter. She would turn toward a window or do something with her eyes. And then she would smile and tilt her head back and her laughter connected him again to that night, made him believe for a moment that life was a string you could gather up in your hands all at once.

He sat at the table and tried to remember the last time he had seen Marisa. In California now. An important lawyer. A year? Two? Anabel, gone to New York? Two years? They called more often than most children, Maximo knew. They called often and he was lucky that way.

"Fidel decides he needs to get in touch with young people."

"Ay ay ay."

"So his handlers arrange for him to go to a school in Havana. He gets all dressed up in his olive uniform, you know, puts conditioner on his beard and brushes it one hundred times, all that."

Raul breathed out, letting each breath come out like a puff of laughter. "Where do you get these things?"

"No interrupting the artist any more, okay?" Maximo continued. "So after he's beautiful enough, he goes to the school. He sits in on a few classes, walks around the halls. Finally, it's time for Fidel to leave and he realizes he hasn't talked to anyone. He rushes over to the assembly that is seeing him off with shouts of 'Comandante!' and he pulls a little boy out of a row. 'Tell me,' Fidel says, 'what is your name?' 'Pepito,' the little boy answers. 'Pepito, what a nice name,' Fidel says. 'And tell me, Pepito, what do you think of the revolution?' 'Comandante,' Pepito says, 'the revolution is the reason we are all here.' 'Ah, very good, Pepito. And tell me, what is your favorite subject?' Pepito answers, 'Comandante, my favorite subject is mathematics.' Fidel pats the little boy on the head. 'And tell me, Pepito, what would you like to be when you grow up?' Pepito smiles and says, 'Comandante, I would like to be a tourist.'"

Maximo looked around the table, a shadow of a smile on his thin white lips as he waited for the laughter.

"Ay," Raul said. "That is so funny it breaks my heart."

Maximo grew to like dominoes, the way each piece became part of the next. After the last piece was laid down and they were tallying up the score, Maximo liked to look over the table like an art critic. He liked the way the row of black dots snaked around the table with such free-flowing abandon it was almost as if, thrilled to be let out of the box, the pieces choreographed a fresh dance of gratitude every night. He liked the straightforward contrast of black on white. The clean, fresh scrape of the pieces across the table before each new round. The audacity of the double nines. The plain smooth face of the blank, like a newborn unetched by the world to come.

"Professor," Raul began. "Let's speed up the shuffling a bit, si?"

"I was thinking," Maximo said.

"Well, that shouldn't take long," Antonio said.

"Who invented dominoes, anyway?" Maximo said.

"I'd say it was probably the Chinese," Antonio said.

"No jodas," Raul said. "Who else could have invented this game of skill and intelligence but a Cuban?"

"Coño," said Antonio without a smile. "Here we go again."

"Ah, bueno," Raul said with a smile stuck between joking and condescending. "You don't have to believe it if it hurts."

Carlos let out a long laugh.

"You people are unbelievable," said Antonio. But there was something hard and tired behind the way he smiled.

It was the first day of December, but summer still hung about in the brightest patches of sunlight. The four men sat under the shade of the banyan tree. It wasn't cold, not even in the shade, but three of the men wore cardigans. If asked, they would say they were expecting a chilly north wind and doesn't anybody listen to the weather forecasts anymore? Only Antonio, his round body enough to keep him warm, clung to the short sleeves of summer.

Kids from the local Catholic high school had volunteered to decorate the park for Christmas and they dashed about with tinsel in their hair, bumping one another and laughing loudly. Lucinda, the woman who issued the dominoes and kept back the gambling, asked them to quiet down, pointing at the men. A wind stirred the top branches of the banyan tree and moved on without touching the ground. One leaf fell to the table.

Antonio waited for Maximo to fetch Lucinda's box of plastic pieces. Antonio held his brown paper bag to his chest and looked at the Cubans, his customary sourness replaced for a moment for what in a man like him could pass for levity. Maximo sat down and began to dump the plastic pieces on the table as he'd always done. But this time, Antonio held out his hand.

"One moment," he said and shook his brown paper bag.

"Que pasa, chico?" Maximo said.

Antonio reached into the paper bag as the men watched. He let the paper fall away. In his hand he held an oblong black leather box.

"Coñooo," Raul said.

He set the box on the table, like a magician drawing out his trick. He looked around to the men and finally opened the box with a flourish to reveal a neat row of big heavy pieces, gone yellow and smooth like old teeth. They bent in closer to look. Antonio tilted the box gently and the pieces fell out in one long line, their black dots facing up now like tight dark pupils in the sunlight.

"Ivory," Antonio said. "And ebony. It's an antique. You're not allowed to make them anymore."

"Beautiful," Carlos said and clasped his hands.

"My daughter found them for me in New Orleans," Antonio continued, ignoring Carlos. He looked around the table and lingered on Maximo, who had lowered the box of plastic dominoes to the ground. "She said she's been searching for them for two years. Couldn't wait two more weeks to give them to me," he said.

"Coñooo," Raul said.

A moment passed.

"Well," Antonio said, "what do you think, Maximo?"

Maximo looked at him. Then he bent across the table to touch one of the pieces.

He gave a jerk with his head and listened for the traffic. "Very nice," he said.

"Very nice?" Antonio said. "Very nice?" He laughed in his thin way. "My daughter walked all over New Orleans to find this and the Cuban thinks it's 'very nice'?" He paused, watching Maximo. "Did you know my daughter is coming to visit me for Christmas? She's coming for Christmas, Maximo, maybe you can tell her her gift was very nice, but not as nice as some you remember, eh?"

Maximo looked up, his eyes settled on Carlos, who looked at Antonio and then looked away.

"Calm down, hombre," Carlos said, opening his arms wide, a nervous giggle beginning in his throat. "What's gotten into you?"

Antonio waved his hand and sat down.

A diesel truck rattled down Eighth Street, headed for downtown.

"My daughter is a district attorney in Los Angeles," Maximo said after the noise of the truck died. "December is one of the busiest months." He felt a heat behind his eyes he had not felt in many years.

"Feel one in your hand," Antonio said. "Feel how heavy that is."

When the children were small, Maximo and Rosa used to spend Nochebuena with his cousins in Cardenas. It was a four-hour drive from Havana in the cars of those days. They would rise early on the twenty-third and arrive by midafternoon so Maximo could help the men kill the pig for the feast the following night. Maximo and the other men held the squealing, squirming animal down, its wiry brown coat cutting into their gloveless hands. But God, they were intelligent creatures. No sooner did it spot the knife, than the animal would bolt out of their arms, screaming like Armageddon. It had become the subtext to the Nochebuena tradition, this chasing of the terrified pig through the yard, dodging orange trees and rotting fruit underneath. The children were never allowed to watch, Rosa made sure. They sat indoors with the women and stirred the black beans. With loud laughter, they shut out the shouts of the men and the hysterical pleadings of the animal as it was dragged back to its slaughter.

"Juanito the little dog gets off the boat from Cuba and decides to take a little stroll down Brickell Avenue."

"Let me make sure I understand the joke. Juanito is a dog. Bowwow."

"That's pretty good."

"Yes, Juanito is a dog, goddamn it."

Raul looked up, startled.

Maximo shuffled the pieces hard and swallowed. He swung his arms across the table in wide, violent arcs. One of the pieces flew off the table.

"Hey, hey, watch it with that, what's wrong with you?"

Maximo stopped. He felt his heart beating.

"I'm sorry," he said. He bent over the edge of the table to see where the piece had landed. "Wait a minute."

He held the table with one hand and tried to stretch to pick up the piece.

"What are you doing?"

"Just wait a minute." When he couldn't reach, he stood up, pulled the piece toward him with his foot, sat back down, and reached down for it again, this time grasping it between his fingers and his palm. He put it face down on the table with the others and shuffled, slowly, his mind barely registering the traffic.

"Where was I? Juanito the little dog, right? Bowwow." Maximo took a deep breath. "He's just off the boat from Cuba and is strolling down Brickell Avenue. He's looking up at all the tall and shiny buildings. 'Coñooo,' he says, dazzled by all the mirrors. There's nothing like this in Cuba.'"

"Hey, hey, professor. We had tall buildings."

"Jesus Christ!" Maximo said. He pressed his thumb and forefinger into the corners of his eyes. "This is after Castro, then. Let me just get it out for Christ's sake."

He stopped shuffling. Raul looked away.

"Ready now? Juanito the little dog is looking up at all the tall buildings and he's so happy to finally be in America because all his cousins have been telling him what a great country it is, right? You know, they were sending back photos of their new cars and girlfriends."

"A joke about dogs who drive cars, I've heard it all."

"Hey, they're Cuban superdogs."

"All right, they're sending back photos of their new owners or the biggest bones any dog has ever seen. Anything you like. Use your imaginations." Maximo stopped shuffling. "Where was I?"

"You were at the part where Juanito buys a Rolls Royce."

The men laughed.

"Okay, Antonio, why don't you three fools continue the joke." Maximo got up from the table. "You've made me forget the rest of it."

"Aw, come on, chico, sit down. Don't be so sensitive."

"Come on, professor, you were at the part where Juanito is so glad to be in America."

"Forget it. I can't remember the rest now."

Maximo rubbed his temple, grabbed the back of the chair, and sat down slowly, facing the street. "Just leave me alone, I can't remember it."

He pulled at the pieces two by two. "I'm sorry. Look, let's just play."

The men set up their double rows of dominoes, like miniature barricades before them.

"These pieces are a work of art," Antonio said and laid down a double eight.

The banyan tree was strung with white lights that were lit all day. Colored lights twined around the metal poles of the fence, which was topped with a long loping piece of gold tinsel garland.

The Christmas tourists began arriving just before lunch as Maximo and Raul stepped off the number eight. Carlos and Antonio were already at the table, watched by two groups of families. Mom and dad with kids. They were big—even the kids were big and pink. The mother whispered to the kids and they smiled and waved. Raul waved back at the mother.

"Nice legs, yes," he whispered to Maximo.

Before Maximo looked away, he saw the mother take out a little black pocket camera. He saw the flash out of the corner of his eye. He sat down and looked around the table; the other men stared at their pieces.

The game started badly. It happened sometimes, the distribution of the pieces went all wrong and out of desperation one of the men made mistakes and soon it was all they could do to knock all the pieces over and start fresh. Raul set down a double three and signaled to Maximo that it was all he had. Carlos passed. Maximo surveyed his last five pieces. His thoughts scattered to the family outside. He looked to find the tallest boy's face pressed between the iron slats, staring at him.

"You pass?" Antonio said.

Maximo looked at him, then at the table. He put down a three and a five. He looked again—the boy was gone. The family had moved on.

The tour groups arrived later that afternoon. First the white buses with the happy blue letters WELCOME TO LITTLE HAVANA. Next the fat women in white shorts, their knees lost in an abstraction of flesh. Maximo tried to concentrate on the game. The worst part was how the other men acted out for them. Dominoes was supposed to be a quiet game. And now there they were shouting at each other and gesturing. A few of the men had even brought cigars, and they dangled now, unlit, from their mouths.

"You see, Raul?" Maximo said. "You see how we're a spectacle?" He felt like an animal and wanted to growl and cast about behind the metal fence.

Raul shrugged. "Doesn't bother me."

"A goddamn spectacle. A collection of bones," Maximo said.

The other men looked up at Maximo.

"Hey, speak for yourself, cabrón," Antonio said.

Raul shrugged again.

Maximo rubbed his elbow and began to shuffle. It was hot, and the sun was setting in his eyes, backlighting the car exhaust like a veil before him. He rubbed his temple, feeling the skin move over the bone. He pressed the inside corners of his eyes, then drew his hand back to his left elbow.

"Hey, you okay there?" Antonio said.

An open trolley pulled up and parked on the curb. A young man, perhaps in his thirties, with blond hair stood up in the front, holding a microphone. He wore a guayabera. Maximo looked away.

"This here is Domino Park," came the amplified voice in English, then Spanish. "No one under fifty-five allowed, folks. But we can sure watch them play."

Maximo heard shutters click, then convinced himself he couldn't have heard, not from where he was.

"Most of these men are Cuban and they're keeping alive the tradition of their homeland," the amplified voice continued, echoing against the back wall of the park. "You see, in Cuba, it was very common to retire to a game of dominoes after a good meal. It was a way to bond and build a community. Folks, you here are seeing a slice of the past. A simpler time of good friendships and unhurried days."

Maybe it was the sun. The men noted that he had seemed odd. The tics.

First Maximo muttered to himself. He rubbed his temple again. When the feedback on the microphone pierced through Domino Park, he could no longer sit where he was, accept things as they were. It was a moment that had long been missing from his life.

He stood and made a fist at the trolley.

"Mierda!" he shouted. "Mierda! That's the biggest bullshit I've ever heard."

He made a lunge at the fence. Carlos jumped up and held him back. Raul led him back to his seat.

The man of the amplified voice cleared his throat. The people on the trolley looked at him and back at Maximo, perhaps they thought this was part of the show.

"Well," the man chuckled. "There you have it, folks."

Lucinda ran over, but the other men waved her off. She began to protest about rules and propriety. The park had a reputation to uphold.

It was Antonio who spoke.

"Leave the man alone," he said.

Maximo looked at him. His head was pounding. Antonio met his gaze briefly then looked to Lucinda.

"Some men don't like to be stared at is all," he said. "It won't happen again."

She shifted her weight, but remained where she was, watching.

"What are you waiting for?" Antonio said, turning now to Maximo, who had lowered his head into the white backs of the dominoes. "Shuffle."

That night Maximo was too tired to sit at the pine table. He didn't even prepare dinner. He slept and in his dreams he was a blue and yellow fish swimming in warm waters, gliding through the coral, the only fish in the sea and he was happy. But the light changed and the sea darkened suddenly and he was rising through it, afraid of breaking the surface, afraid of the pinhole sun on the other side, afraid of drowning in the blue vault of sky.

"Let me finish the story of Juanito the little dog."

The men nodded, but did not speak.

"He is just off the boat from Cuba. He is walking down Brickell Avenue. He doesn't know what to expect. He's maybe a little afraid." Maximo cleared his throat.

"But when Juanito sees an elegant, white poodle striding toward him, he forgets all his worries and exclaims, 'O, Madre de Dios, si cocinas como caminas—' The white poodle interrupts and says, 'I beg your pardon? This is America, speak English.' So Juanito pauses for a moment to consider and says in his broken English, 'Mamita, you are one hot doggie, yes? I would like to marry you, my love, and have gorgeous puppies with you and live in a castle.' Well, all this time the white poodle has her snout in the air. She looks at Juanito and says, 'Do you have any idea who you're talking to? I am a refined breed of considerable class and you are nothing but a short, insignificant mutt.'" Maximo stopped to look at the others before continuing.

"Juanito is stunned for a moment, but he rallies for the final shot. 'Pardon me, Your Highness,' the mangy dog says. 'Here in America I may be a short, insignificant mutt, but in Cuba I was a German shepherd.'"

Maximo turned so the men would not see his tears. The afternoon traffic crawled eastward. One horn blasted, then another. He remembered holding his daughters days after their births, thinking how fragile and vulnerable lay his bond to the future. For weeks, he carried them on pillows, like jeweled china. Then, the blank spaces in his life lay before him. Now he stood with the gulf at his back, their ribbony youth aflutter in the past. And what had he salvaged from the years? Already he was forgetting Rosa's face, the precise shade of her eyes. Carlos cleared his throat and moved his hand as if to touch him, then held back. He cleared his throat again.

"He was a good dog," Carlos said, his lips thin.

Antonio began to laugh, then fell silent with the rest. Maximo started shuffling, then stopped. The shadow of the banyan tree worked a kaleidoscope over the dominoes. When the wind eased, Maximo tilted his head to listen. He heard something stir behind him, someone leaning heavily on the fence. He could almost feel the breath. His heart quickened.

"Tell them to go away," Maximo said. "Tell them, no pictures."

KATE SMALL

San Francisco State University

THE B-ZONE OPEN

"Rods will fly when the algae dies off," Gary says. Pavel and Gary are lifting driftwood in the rain, pretending they are men. Gary is eleven, Pavel nine. Gary knows how to talk about fishing. He knows about trolling crank-bait and back-bouncing roe in the Barge Hole.

"Hardware is the way to go," Gary says, putting down a branch. "You want your Super Dupers, your Kastmasters. Maybe some Blue Fox Spinners."

The boys stand in a brown tidal pond to the side of the Columbia. Dead canneries cut their spaces in the skyline, but aluminum owns the river now. Mills and dams block the shoals and sandbars at the end of the Oregon Trail. Pavel bends down to right starfish on their backs. Storms toss them gut-side up.

"Look." Gary points at an Alaska tanker nudging toward Portland's Swan Island dry dock. Pavel lifts his eyes.

"So you're in your boat," Gary says. "Start trolling as soon as you clear the five mph buoy, but be careful! They're connected by a cable that snags tackle hanging twenty feet down." Gary exhales like he's smoking a pipe. Pavel has discovered that people here like the way he listens without talking, especially men.

"Let's get some hot dogs," Gary says, driving a stick into a pink starfish core. "You seen my new bow? These starfish are weeds."

Pavel looks at Gary's lips, unchapped by the hard K's of underground Serb. Gary withdraws his stick and mimes the pulling of a bowstring. An invisible arrow arcs and lands in the back of some phantom prey twenty yards down the beach.

"Kick ass," Gary says, throwing a rock after it. "My dad bagged the turkey in one shot." He heads home to his father. His mother has moved away.

Sea bass and snapper wash up in blistered pieces. It's the poison runoff from the pike eradication project. Pavel's stepfather would fish the dam after it slammed shut in October on thousands of salmon, but the Indians get the first two hundred yards past the locks. Fish and Game says it'll replant the lake but never gets around to it.

"Takes ten years to replace a trophy fishery after a chemical kill," Rick complains. "Used to be, you'd hoop up a sturgeon, seventy, eighty pounds, with nothing more than a glow-bug." Rick says he's going to write to the authorities about the lake, the U.S./Canada fish treaty, the Oregon Salmon Plan, and habitat restoration, but he hasn't gotten around to it.

It's a minus tide, but the pools are clean. Hundreds of minnows point in the same direction. Pavel snaps his fingers over the water and they all turn ninety degrees. There's a hard wind but the surface is taut. It's a good time to catch them for bait, but Rick doesn't use bait. When Rick casts a line, tie and leader shoot sixty feet. The fly lands like the real thing. Rick knows how to make mice and moths out of the belly-hair of a white-tailed deer. Fish shock into the light, yanked by a feather with industrial teeth. Then Rick lets them go.

Jalanta is knitting when Pavel gets home.

"Itissa lovely day," she says. She's talking to an English language tape from the library. "It," Pavel says. "Is." Jalanta speaks with too many Z's and *shushes*. Pavel has gotten rid of them.

Her head snaps up. "You look cold," she says in Serb, in a careful Kosovar way, as though they've just found themselves in the street during a cease-fire. People feel their way out and blink. No wind, no shelling. A person could be overheard.

She holds the knitting to his chest. Rick's TV flashes at the couch. The remote is on the floor.

"To that man speak Cakavian," she'd say on a train moving over scarred perimeters. Gray blurred past, studded with black. Nobody printed maps anymore. "To that one over there," she'd say, "speak Kajkavian." He couldn't see how she knew.

"I'm hungry," Pavel said once, the wrong way, too loud. Jalanta put a hand over his mouth. They were en route to Belgrade. "You will be assessed for a widow's pension by an officer of the bureau," the letter had said.

"Slim possibilities on thin paper," the old neighbor who accompanied them had said. He had his own letter. They would wait six hours. They would be interrogated.

"No Bread." Pavel said into her fingers, reading the newspaper headlines stuck to the floor. The consonants expelled his mother's hand.

The old neighbor wore a large brown coat. He leaned down. "Put a question in everything," he said.

Pavel looks around Rick's condo. He can see the heat in the air clinging to the windows. "I'm not cold," Pavel says in English. He can smell the lanolin in the yarn. Everything was plastic before. Everything they had you could melt with a candle: the chairs, rug, rope, the table. A woolly elbow dangles in his face. "Stop making parts," he says. He pushes the needles away from his chin. Jalanta used to finish things: resiny gloves with long fingers, synthetic socks that bunched in the boot. One birthday there was an onion, a can of pudding, and a polyester muffler. When Yugoslavia stopped making everything else, it still made nylon. All you need is coal, air, and the hydroelectric dams of the shit-filled rivers. The last thing she finished was a rough blue scarf for the old neighbor in the brown coat. Now she begins thick one-limbed sweaters but abandons the single arms. Jalanta hates knitting. She used to have a microscope. She used to dance.

"Excuse me, where is the travel agency?" the English tape asks. "Where is the ticket window?" Jalanta snaps off the machine in the slot of silence that follows. Pavel can smell burnt flour. The house is hot, but Jalanta's makeup holds fast. Before there was only yogurt and lard for the skin, and black-market lipstick filled with paraffin. Now her eyes are rimmed in kohl. Her mouth is creamy and meat-colored. Rick is in the shed. The needles click for a long time after Pavel goes to bed.

Jalanta found Rick in a magazine called *Alaskan Men,* worn copies of which appeared in train stations of the former Yugoslavia.

"Don't speak at all," Jalanta would say to Pavel, before she and three friends from the Kosovo Blood Clinic gathered to read the personal ads in a closed and broken beauty shop.

The women toasted each other in the dark. "Have a drink of the Morava," they'd say, "the cleanest river in the world." The power plant went off without warning. They couldn't heat-treat the plasma at the lab, to kill the hepatitis. They raised their stained cups.

"Blue-eyed man," Lisle read in English. "Fifty. Looks thirty-five." The F's stuttered. The S disappeared.

"I own my boat. I own my home. I own my satellite dish," Anik read. "Tell me a bit about yourself."

"Handsome pipe fitter," Saskia said, "seeks, petite nonsmoking female."

"Bit?" Anik repeated. The T cut. She held her finger to the print.

"I am a vampire," Lisle replied in bleached, clinical Serb. "I am a Slavic tradition," Lisle said in a dialect stripped of residue. It sounded like acid. The women developed a strange sarcasm. The Communists were gone but you still couldn't say things.

Pavel watched them move through their childhood folk dances without music. They'd stand in a line, arms raised, the tips of their fingers lit yellow by a crack of high transom light. There were pauses. There were silent questions about variations. Raised elbows betrayed a childhood in Novi Sad. A pair of crossed arms pointed to Pristina. Pavel watched the feet. The steps were the same. The sweat was indistinguishable, moisture from one river system. Salt perched on each woman's lips before draining back to a watershed of race. Pavel knelt, stacking curlers. He could see their breath. They'd rest in the ripped seats of the hair dryers and drink Coca-Cola doused with laboratory alcohol. He'd inhale the hard, sweet scent as Saskia tried to write back to a bachelor in English, her elbows propped on a manicurist's table.

"I am," she said over a piece of paper. "I am," but the pen never moved. Without so much as a hand mirror they saw their bodies, in each other. The anemia, the pallid hair, skin pulled over bones grown from powdered milk.

Someone would hum the song about the crow and the hunter. Someone would supply the words: "His hawk watched that doe heavy with young. She lifted the man's head and kissed bloody wounds." They'd stand. They'd twist when the rhythm pushed them forward, face to face. "Ha ha! The crow laughs at the hawk." They'd kick the floor and clap.

Lisle lifted her skirt to examine her ankles. "I can smell it," she said to Anik, who considered the back of her own hand. Pavel knew what they meant: a faint scent of human decay, mixed with a harsh, Czech-brand detergent. They would look for it later, that home-smell, in the lining of their suitcases, in an American garage, an attic, a porch.

"How do you do?" Anik said in English. She straightened Lisle's collar. They would each take away scarves of the same nuclear blue. You could get only one color of yarn.

The women laughed, but they meant something else. They bent their knees and spun. Their hems flared a little. They shook hands, their poise wasted in morgues and cemeteries. Batteries and razor blades passed between them. They traded peroxide and sugar and surgical gloves. They saw their own arms, extended with the stopped-time grace of antique statuary reaching to complete its gestures, even after it's been bombed and cut off at the knees. They mailed off wordless missives, black-and-white passport photos, names inked on the back. Two weeks later these landed in an Anchorage post-office box like delicate spoils of war.

When Pavel wakes up it's Thanksgiving.

Rick is already in the shed. "One hundred and twenty sorties on the Ho Chi Minh trail," he says to no one as Pavel opens the door. He's modifying a tiny Jeep by torching it with a butane lighter. Rick was an Alaskan Man for three months before he got laid off. He returned to the Oregon coastal town where he'd grown up with a new stepson and a wife who stores sacks of rice under the bed. Rick wants a new baby. Pavel can see it, spherical and hot, simmering in Rick's chest like a melon or a grenade.

Pavel pulls a stool to Rick's diorama. Village and army unit spread around a varnished river, propped on sawhorses. Pavel pulls straw from a broom for bamboo hootches; he mixes soil with glue. Rick makes a bag of plastic soldiers into snipers. He slices out the strips between their feet and paints on black pajamas and red headbands.

Rick's brother Charley bursts in. He's come from the kitchen, having left the turkey for Jalanta to clean and cook. "You gotta get that woman in the family way!" he says. "More horizontal mambo!" Steam comes off Charley's hands and face. Even though Rick is taller, Charley is too big for the shed.

Rick's neck cables with veins, but this time they go down again.

Charley tweaks the chipped breast of an old department store mannequin by the door. "Yessiree"—Charley winks at her—"things are looking up." For two years Charley has been about to get a promotion. He'll sell product over the phone. "Sheet and plate extrusions," he sings into the silence which sucks up his brother. "Foil, wire, rod and bar, tube and pipe, forging stock."

Rick's arms engulf a helicopter with small moving parts. He keeps making more, but there's no way to suspend them over the village. "You think about that land idea?" Rick asks. He reaches for a bar of soap carved into the shape of a water buffalo. The helicopters lie on their sides in a box.

"Prefab bus shelters," Charley says. He's not done with his song. "Press-apply road dividers, aluminum speed bumps." He lists the things on his fingers. Charley's skin is pink all over, like a giant baby.

"A bird sanctuary with your name on it," Rick says. "People would pay to see it." He wants Charley to preserve his inherited property as marsh, maybe attract some unusual species.

Charley shakes his head. No matter what, Charley smiles like an infant. "You gotta stop playing with dolls, man." He beams at a tiny figure of a woman with outstretched hands. He beams at the beers in his lap like they're bright plastic spoons. Charley is Gary's father.

"It'd be tax exempt, too," Rick says, "and EPA subsidized." He arranges moss around a hut.

"I prefer *large* game myself," Charley says, "but I say: dig the hell out of it, flood it, and pack it with stock, reservoir style."

"But it's peat and good groundwater. It's wetland."

Charley smiles like an angel. "Fish and Game says, when you've got twenty-five acres and you take a hundred trout out, that's like a thimble of rice. They've got studies. The lake would reproduce that many fish before you could weigh the first ones in."

"Those kind of fish are weeds."

"Swimming food. Money in the bank." Charley cracks open a beer. "Personally, I can afford an ex-wife." Charley got Rick his job. Five days a week Charley tells Rick and a row of women cutting screws at the extruder how to do it faster. The workers are mostly Filipina and Vietnamese. Charley doesn't care who is which and they don't talk to him or each other. His ex-wife Daisy used to work on the assembly. Now she works at the Sea Galley Buffet. One of these days, Charley says, he's going to win Daisy back. Daisy is Gary's mother.

"Hatchery fish choke out the salmon and kill the green food," Rick says.

"When there's a perch die-off in the reservoir, just grease those up and float them by a big hole. They're like cheeseburgers for bait." Charley cups the mannequin again.

"But maybe we'd get something rare," Rick says. "Like the Saurus Crane in Tram Chim. Big white birds. Presumed extinct in the Mekong Delta. Six years after the war, they came back, behind the DMZ. Gray hatchlings. Huge wings." His palms are printed with petal-sized scars.

"You gotta forget about that place," Charley says.

Rick sits down. He nests sweet grass around a thatched house. He attaches a tiny paper lantern for the festival of the moon. Rick sold his own portion of the property to pay for Jalanta and Pavel.

Charley puts a beer in Rick's hands and pulls him out the door. Pavel hears them move down the street, punching each other, their voices blending as they exchange gun advice over malt liquors peeled from Charley's six-pack. Fog encircles the strip's inhabitants. Thermos steam yokes them together like the chain-link around their backyards, filled with fenders and crab traps, all nudging the east end of the reservation. "You still driving that thing?" Charley's voice floats up. "This outboard got any kick?" From a distance, the white men's trailers and crumbling cars blend with the moss-eaten canoes and rusted ski mobiles of the Indians. The sun frames the brothers, then a garage, and finally a finger of the Interstate.

Pavel sets a bundle of toothpicks in a tea-bath. In Kosovo he built paper churches, with salt on the steps for snow. Pavel likes the things Rick has. In the corner there's a tray of lures like the wings hatched from gill nymphs in May. When the larval husk breaks, the fly floats up to dry. "Gossamer bribes," Rick calls them, but Pavel always hears the word *bride*. Rick knows where the fish are and what they want to taste.

"Club the Eskimos and the seals, same difference!" Charley blusters, on the way back into the shed. Pavel picks up one of the helicopters. They look like insects caught in shellac.

At first Pavel listened to the footfalls of his mother's new marriage through the wall, their socks soft and clumsy on the linoleum. They brushed their teeth politely. They stretched for lamp switches with the intimate formal choreography of the Kosovo blood workers. For months they met in the long grassy yard, drinking coffee. They'd stare at the posts of the low wire fence and the Erector set flight towers beyond it.

"I will wear that," she said one night, pointing at the cloth on Rick's chest. Rick looked at Jalanta the way he would a trout moving over the bottom of a pool. Pavel watched through the curtains. Rick pulled off his coat, then his T-shirt.

"This one from Slovenia," Jalanta said. She wrapped his T-shirt around her head and took three serpentine steps to the left. She tipped her chin up. Her neck lengthened. It remembered the weight of a heavy bleached kerchief. Rick's chest and shoulders gleamed. Pavel saw the veins in his neck come up, but then there was the thing on Rick's face when he holds a fish in his hands. Rick's mirth is quick and rare, like fish falling home.

"You can only dance this with other people," Jalanta explained. She danced by herself. She shut her eyes, gesturing to partners not there. Rick stepped aside for her. She inclined her head to a vanished companion. She spun in the space he had made.

"Like a feather lure," Rick said.

She stopped moving, her head splashed white by the tower lights. She shrugged. They finished their coffee. He put on his shirt.

"I want my own baby," he said.

"I am not understanding," she said, but she did. Pavel tried to transmit it to her, the message he gets from the bird by the underground lake. *Hide your will, hide your will.*

"No," she said. She handed Rick his shirt.

"I made bread, but it wouldn't rise." Jalanta says. Pumpkin pie and glossy yams sit on the counter like exotic diorama props. Pavel can see Rick's legs on the couch. Charley's voice comes toward them, rosy with beer and football. A cylinder of cranberry jelly shivers for its can.

"Hey, li'l gal," Charley says to Jalanta at halftime. Charley chucks Pavel under the chin and sways a little. Pavel follows his eyes to the shy new fat trembling from the thigh of his mother's arm. She opens the oven door and jams a syringe into the bird.

"You can inoculate me anytime," Charley says, but Jalanta doesn't get the joke. She has tried to explain that she's a research hematologist, but she doesn't have the words for it, so Charley thinks she's a nurse. "Uncertified here," he says, "but she sure knows how to cut and clean a bird."

"Or," Charley says, "I could inoculate you." Jalanta turns up the oven to five-hundred degrees. She leans into the heat but her makeup stays dry. A light covering on her neck continues beneath her collar.

When the turkey comes out charred with the insides running wet, Charley pretends to take the blame for it. "Now I know, the reality is, a fat, farm-fed Butterball beats the hell out of a skinny acorn-eating turkey. But what can I say? I like whacking one of these suckers with my bow."

Pavel looks at the vein on the side of Rick's jaw. Charley does his shooting at a stocked preserve, its hatchlings supplied by a nursery in Taiwan.

"They can be either sex," Charley says to Pavel. "Which means you can shoot a hen, jake, or gobbler."

"See, gobblers will respond instinctively to sudden noises," Gary says. "Which is what your so-called shock calls are for. These would be your crow calls, your predator calls, your coyote howlers." Gary and Charley are wearing identical baseball hats, and vests with small, zippered pockets. Pavel knows he and Rick are supposed to mirror one another like this, but he can't reconcile bright belt-buckles and big gestures with invisibility. Pavel used to watch his old neighbor cross the street in Kosovo. The man always wore gray pants and a brown coat. But once when he saw Pavel near the window, he waved a bright blue mitten, and a grenade came. Pavel drew from his neck a scarf of the same yarn and dropped it over the sill. It landed near a small green cabbage that had rolled from the man's right hand. Red filled the coat like foam. Pavel wants to blend, but by fading into the background.

"Most hunters miss a turkey because they shoot too high," Charley says. "What you do is, just bust up the flock and call them within range. *Boom.*"

Jalanta pushes her food away.

"Yearlings are suckers for a kazoo," Gary says. "But put camouflage tape on your shotgun. And don't move an inch. Turkeys see eight times better than humans."

Jalanta gets up to clear the table.

"I know you like the rare ones," Charley winks at Rick. "But you don't bring them down, somebody else will."

Rick swallows something. "You should plant marsh crops instead of bulrush," he says.

Charley's smile sags.

"Plus there's that new bill passed," Rick says. "Makes some bog areas exempt from federal taxes."

Charley puts his face in his hands. "Look," he says. "It's getting rezoned."

"You should plant milo," Rick says. "And swamp timothy."

Charley looks up. "I'd make more money with a parking lot."

"What about your lake?" Rick says, turning to see him.

"I don't need a lake."

"But fishing?"

"There's enough fishing. If it continues to rain, I'll get my steelhead explosion. One good storm, I'll get my flood of landlocked fish." Charley stands up, smiling.

Rick stands up, too. "Half the wetlands in the U.S. are gone." Rick says, gesturing to a room larger than the one they occupy. Behind him Jalanta's face fades into the white of the refrigerator door. The first package Rick sent to Kosovo was filled with Maybelline. For about a minute it meant that everything here would blush with color. "Half," Rick says again. "That equals the combined area of Massachusetts, Connecticut, and Rhode Island." He lifts his palms awkwardly, like the brown plastic woman in the diorama.

"I've got more than enough food to fill up my freezer."

"Your freezer," Rick says.

Charley sighs and settles in front of the TV with a plate of leftovers. Rick drops his hands and heads for the shed.

Gary and Pavel lie on the floor with Rick's photo album. On the first page there is a child and six dead fish. The boy gets bigger and so do the fish.

"There aren't any deer in this book," Gary says.

There aren't any pictures of Rick throwing them back, Pavel thinks, or the bright empty space between his hands.

Charley stirs around. He cups his hand to his mouth. "Dad had a 20-gauge Browning. He'd line up dolls and apples on the fence. Kick us if we wussed."

"Rick got kicked a lot," Gary whispers.

The album is open to a picture of Pavel. His knees are pale in the boat. His rod bends at an absurd angle. Food is getting away. He turns to the camera, white-faced. The picture was snapped before the unexpected laughter, escaping from Rick in a voluptuous stream.

Charley leans closer. "Rick's never brought down a forked horn buck, not even a mule deer. And those are exploding like rodents." Charley has infrared binoculars, a three-wheeled ATV, and a 130-

grain Sierra boat-tail automatic. Charley has a forty-thousand-dollar credit card debt.

"When's mom coming home?" Gary asks. He sits on Charley's feet and throws Doritos into his mouth.

"Pretty soon I bet," Charley says.

Gary starts to cry. Charley pats him on the head.

Pavel carries Charley's dishes into the kitchen. He drops a half-eaten drumstick and a bunch of grapes into the garbage. Jalanta stares at the food, stares at Pavel.

"No," she says in Serb.

"Speak *English*," Pavel says.

"You got more chips?" Charley yells from the living room.

"Speak Serb," Jalanta says.

"*Which* Serb?" Pavel asks.

"*Ours*," Jalanta says.

"Well?" Gary yells. He's not crying anymore. Brisk gadgets on TV have perked him up.

"Sorry Charley!" Jalanta calls back in English, too bright. It's a joke Gary taught her. Charley laughs. Jalanta puts her face close to Pavel's. "It is a fucking lovely day," she says.

Rick surges from the doorway and knocks Jalanta to the floor. She won't learn it herself, what not to say.

One night when Jalanta finished work too late to come home, Saskia stole Jalanta's diary. Saskia lived downstairs. Sometimes she'd come up and look in on Pavel, but this time he was sitting between the blackout curtain and the wall, staring at the moon and two helicopters. Saskia turned the pages for ten minutes.

"Welcome to the Kosovo Hepatitis Factory," she read out loud, testing the weight of the words. "We specialize in septicemia. Those injured in the street are graciously killed at the hospital."

Saskia stared at the door. In the apartment above, someone had dropped a boot or shoe. Someone stumbled over an empty box.

"'We are Albanian,' the corpuscles cry on the way into the general's arm. 'Arrest us for pan-Islamic activity.'"

The blade sound faded over some other district. Saskia looked up to some motion in the curtain. "Pavel," she said.

They stared and waited, like dancers before the music starts. They made tea. She gave him a hard green lemon. The next day she traded the diary for a government apartment in a safer part of the city. Jalanta was dismissed, her own apartment ransacked.

"Just like old times," Jalanta said when the policeman hit her. She tried to make ends meet by cleaning slaughtered rabbits for the old neighbor, who raised them in the cellar. The salon group disbanded. The old neighbor disappeared beneath a grenade. Jalanta looked with determination to her American correspondent. Pavel hid his lemon until it rotted.

The day after Rick hits Jalanta, Charley takes the boys out and wins them the pick of the fairground trophies at the All-Welded Aluminum Boat Show.

"Anything you want," he says beaming, as though he could shoot that from the sky. There seems to be everything: cap guns, water pistols, decals, erasers. Charley is a crack shot at flattening cardboard ducks and things that don't move. Pavel picks something small and plush: a deep red poodle with a tiny vinyl tongue. Gary picks a Styrofoam glider, but melts it on the heater when they get to Rick's shed.

The diorama is gone. Rick cleans the old Browning on an empty table.

"What's up? Shooting blanks, big guy?" Charley knows Rick wants a baby. Charley's lips are curvy and wet.

"We need a road closure system," Rick spits. "Keep the Portland yuppies off the ridges in their fancy-ass Jeeps." An old yellow map is spread on the floor. Lakes are crossed out. Ponds and streams are slashed with ballpoint ink.

"What are the X's?" Gary asks.

"Malls," Rick says. He jams pushpins into the frail brown paper, balkanized by parking lots.

Pavel shuts his eyes. An American boy now, his mouth has learned to water for Pop-Tarts, crackers, and frosted breakfast cereal. He only ever eats fish after it's shipped out and back, frozen or packed in a can. Pavel holds the dog against his chest and inhales its bright synthetic smell. When he opens his eyes, he sees on Rick's face a blushing sneer, and newly focused suspicion.

Jalanta snaps on the radio and cleans a bloated quail. Rick has been taking target practice at an indoor/outdoor range. Now he's shooting at a sporting preserve where they breed slow, fat fowl. Pavel watches Jalanta sharpen her blade to transparency toward the edge. They listen to a call-in show for enraged hunters. Rick has brought home a few birds to eat, but he hasn't told his brother.

"I could give a goddamn about some goddamn owls," a man says as Jalanta cuts a hen down the middle. Stomach and lungs tumble out. Jalanta folds the wings out from the slit. The oil animates the meat. "If a guy's kid is stupid enough to *need* a childproof lock," a voice surfaces as Jalanta turns down the flame. "Because, the Boy Scouts already *are* fags," he adds, apparently finishing his thought. Pavel has heard most of it before: complaints about the Feds, gun control, poaching forensics.

"*Hunt* the goddamn Boy Scouts," the next caller suggests, sounding feebler than intended because he's holding the phone away from his mouth.

Jalanta lets the flesh char when the talk gets around to the bodies of bear and elk piling up for analysis at the national wildlife lab in Ashland.

She looks at Pavel. "Why are these animals not being eaten?"

Pavel shakes his head, at the question, and at the private language which clings to their throats like fingers in a gas chamber, like verbs crawling from a mass grave.

"There are ways of catching people for endangered kills," a state examiner says. "Flies like to clean an open wound. We measure the larvae. Their size and stage of development will determine the time of death, we—"

"And remember," the radio host interrupts. "One drop of blood on a hunting knife will reveal the slaying of a listed critter, *so you boys need to soak your gear.*"

"Where is the travel agency?" Jalanta whispers in English. "Where is the ticket window?" Fat burns at the edges of the fryer. She wipes her hands and writes something down.

"Just like old times," Pavel thinks in Serb.

"Where's Rick?" Charley asks, a couple of weeks later. His promotion has come through and he wants to celebrate. "I'll cook you a spread," Charley says. "Lobster and the works." His eyes circle Jalanta's arms and hips. Her hands are greased. There's dough rolled on the table.

"Just go," she says. "Get Gary."

"Barefoot and in the kitchen," Charley stage-whispers to Pavel. "That's the way I like them." Jalanta is rounder now, but Pavel looks back at her shoes. He imagines the bones within, flimsy as the heads of snapped goslings.

On the way to pick up Gary, Charley and Pavel stop at the Sea Galley Buffet. Charley keeps the engine running and hands Pavel a hundred-dollar bill. He always sends the boys in with hundred-dollar bills because he wants to impress Daisy.

"What's the occasion?" Daisy asks, tired, but Pavel can tell she doesn't really want an answer. Her hair is a stiff straw color, her face smoked and puffy. She lowers the lobsters into a paper bucket. They are half dead and flown in from somewhere else, though silver-dollar-sized crabs scudder the beach at night by the thousands. The Vietnamese eat them whole. Charley jokes about this and says they eat cockroaches, too.

"Wait a minute," Daisy says. She follows Pavel out of the restaurant, and waves Charley from the truck. The wind is blowing and she's not wearing a coat. Pavel gets in the cab and watches through the windshield. The lobsters shift in their bucket. Daisy holds herself while she talks. Her fingers are white. Charley's hands hang at his sides. Daisy goes back into the restaurant, and Charley turns toward the car. His smile is fixed, like he's been shot in the chest and can't feel it yet. He takes Pavel back home without talking. His eyes are milky and pinkish.

"Where's my dad?" Gary asks on the phone, later.

"Call Daisy," Jalanta says.

Rick takes Pavel duck hunting in a closed, stocked range. Pavel wakes to the fussing of ravens and creeps from his bag at dawn. He follows the birds a half mile to find a female blacktail, just gutted. It's an illegal kill: the season hasn't started and the doe is out of zone. Sometimes a deer jumps the electrical perimeter and can't jump back. Pavel kneels. The big-muscled flanks are cut away, the neck and torso steam. He can see himself in the upturned eye. By the time Rick crunches over, the cornea has frosted.

"It's a doe," Pavel says.

"I want a buck," Rick says.

Rick shoots an endangered teal that afternoon, stumbled away from wild flock outside their range.

"This is so little," Jalanta says. Rick is holding a small, mutilated bird. Pavel has never seen one before. The feathers are green-tipped, the breast crested white.

"We're not eating it," Rick says. "We're hanging it on the wall." He lays the bird on the washing machine and steps into the bathroom.

"It is a rare thing?" Jalanta asks Pavel. Rick hands out his bloody watch for her to clean.

Pavel shrugs.

"That Browning is useless," Rick says through the shower doors.

Jalanta removes the leather band from the watch, wraps it in plastic, and places it in the back of the freezer. Pavel can hear Rick vomiting in the stall.

"You won't get one," Charley says, smiling sadly. Rick has applied for a deer tag.

He pokes Rick's stiff glazed teal. Rick has glued it to a block of wood. "This is tiny," Charley says.

"Proof," Rick says. Charley's eyes are still smeary. His dog barks in Rick's yard. Jalanta's head snaps toward Pavel. "Is that the mail?" she asks.

"And the deer will go there," Rick says. He points to an empty wall.

"It won't make any difference," Charley says.

The letter is in Pavel's pocket. It's addressed to Rick, from Oregon Recreational Management. Pavel knows it's an official insignia. He'd open it if he could read it, but the alphabet won't settle into English.

Letters reverse and cough like they're trying to decode themselves back into another language. The envelope is plain, windowless. These are the delivery systems of a state poised to punish and coerce. He'll take it to the beach. He'll drop it into the pool where the minnows suspend, like drops of mercury, or lead. Charley and Rick drive away.

The house recedes into a smear of vinyl siding and blackberries. The dog follows, then quits. Pavel cuts through 160 acres freshly ploughed under, rezoned for commercial use. There were nests there last week, pheasant and chukar, their eggs vanished beneath tractor wheels the size of small houses. Pavel passes the junior high, a church, a bait stand. There's a six-pack of Eagle-claw fishhooks under the bench at the bus stop. There's an inept swastika sprayed on the sidewalk. Pavel changes his mind. A Fred Meyer shopping cart noses the shelter.

Two hours later Pavel finds Charley's dog leaning on a car outside the Northspit Lounge. Pavel knows they'll come out together, Charley and Rick, that they'll go up to Charley's place and watch Charley shoot things off the fence. He throws a stick, but Charley's dog has given up on all that and slumps to the ground with a sigh. Thunder and lightning start. Car alarms go off in the Fred Meyer parking lot. It's the newer trucks, waxed and ready for repossession. Pavel opens the back door to the lounge just a crack and makes out their shared glum shape, clamped to the counter, backlit by a ball game. They throw back their beers and stretch from their stools.

Rick sees Pavel but keeps talking. "If your Sump 1-A was planted right, the ducks would come and so would the hunters."

Charley's cheeks go flaccid.

"If a guy sets out a decoy he'll bag a pair of mallards in no time flat," Rick says. "A guy will pay good money for the opportunity." Jalanta has replaced Rick's watchband with something smooth and stainless.

"Daisy's going away." They get in the truck. Charley hasn't shaved in a few days.

"Greenheads'll hit newly flooded fields with less than six inches of water, guaranteed." Pavel sits between them.

"I didn't apply for tags," Charley says. Pavel watches the dog in the mirror, hunched by the wheel-well.

"And a guy would need a scull boat," Rick says. "So we'd have to get a bunch of those for renting."

"She's leaving town. Won't say where she's going."

"We could do something, Charley. Wing shooting."

"Shooting?" Charley says.

"Ducks, geese, honkers, white-fronts."

"What about your rare birds?" Charley says.

"People love animals they can eat."

Charley's dog jumps the tailgate and slinks to the woods.

Charley is famous for his outdoor hunter's trophies, things like the bones of a deer in a curled, nested position, bordered with sea and gun shells arranged to spell "Can do!" A stretch away from his garage, behind it, is the skeleton of a human woman, pelvis propped higher, limbs spread open. One hand is folded against the wrist, fingers piled under the elbow. There's refrigerator insulation arranged around her skull and a plastic hula lei at her throat. Charley mail-ordered it from a chiropractic catalogue one Halloween for Gary, but always spins a yarn about ultimate bow-hunting and the perfect double-lung shot. "Because she was down for the count," he says now, "and that's why we call Oregon the Beaver State."

Charley goes into the house and leaves the front door open.

In the middle of a joke of their own, Gary and two other boys tumble out of the garage. It's about Amber Platt who wasn't at school yesterday because her hair got sucked up by a Dirt Devil, so they pretend the skeleton is Amber Platt. They're all drinking cartons of chocolate milk and carrying them like beers. One of Gary's friends says something about the guy who allegedly cut off his own head with a chain saw. They break out in buzzing and gagging noises, spewing milk on each other. When this subsides, Gary tries to establish pack dominance near a mound of sawed-off elk antlers.

"If those gun control losers want to get their paws up my ass," he begins, but he can't figure out where the sentence should go. He swigs his milk and another boy takes over.

"Yeah," this boy says. "Fed fags come in and yank our dicks, then hang around to catch a couple of stupid stocker rainbows."

"Hey," the third boy leaps in on a tangent. "You can scoop those weenies easy with Sierra Gold or a tube-jig and mealworm trailer." The other boys nod.

It's Pavel's turn to speak but his mouth is dry, his gaze fixed on the lichen creeping into the hollows of the skeleton's plastic hipbones. Spelled out in beer caps between her knees is the phrase "I been had!" Some of the caps have been kicked away so that the two parts of the exclamation point are parted, pressed into the ground by the heel of a boot. Pavel's eyes move from this to the gape in the jaw, the eye sockets, the empty bottle pointed at the place where her legs meet. Pavel feels past the unopened letter to the ribs under his coat. He sees his mother, peering at the diagram in *The Joy of Cooking* for trussing small game—duck, pigeon, pheasant—struggling to translate the instructions for the American way of tying and peeling, but she already knows how; she doesn't want to do it anymore. She wants a quiet cupboard full of cans, six deep, their watery taste bloodless on the tongue without the whiff of anything slain, though a death smell creeps from the wet edges of pigless American ham.

Gary forgets about Pavel and begins karate chopping an invisible assailant. His friends join in, kicking and leaping. Pavel locks eyes with Rick over this clot of boys who eat so much. Soon they'll be strong enough to jerk stumps out of the ground. For a while they'll stand under streetlights and watch cars. There will be no more welders among them. They will be engineers. They will belong to associations. They will pelt each other with sheet and plate technologies. They will argue about aluminum yield-strength and corrosive resistance. They will oversee coil coating facilities in Mexico. They will marry women smooth as fiberglass. They will reproduce quickly and disperse widely, like weeds. Sheet Metal Local 20 will drain from their blood and they will wonder about aluminum and Alzheimer's, only insofar as it applies to their fathers.

From the house comes the sound of a square thing being rolled. The kitchen freezer appears in the doorway. Charley is behind it, pushing. The boys stop moving. Charley's face clots red. They can see his teeth. Charley topples the freezer out of the house. It dents a railing and lands on its side in the dirt. The door flops open. Pavel can see dates inked on the tops of chili containers. The boys stare at the empty doorway. Charley comes out with his new gun, a Marlin 30/30, as Rick appears from around the side of the house. Charley closes the freezer door and hikes up the rifle. He backs up. Everybody backs up. Charley shoots the freezer three times. The holes smoke.

Daisy pulls up in an old, mossy station wagon. The boys look at the freezer, then Charley, then the car. Daisy honks the horn. The boys get in the car. Daisy waits while they buckle their seat belts. Pavel, Charley, and Rick watch her brake lights go away.

"I don't want this," Charley says. He hands the gun to Rick. It wavers up in Rick's hands. It's so much lighter than the Browning. "I'm giving it to Daisy," Charley says.

"The gun?" Rick says.

"The land."

"Daisy? What will Daisy do with it?"

Charley shrugs. "I don't know. I don't know what Daisy will do."

Pavel gets in the truck and Rick drives fast. It's hard not to run over a lot of rabbits in Northspit, and after the first few, nobody stops to pick them up for pelts. From Nehalem to Mist, their pink-streaked bodies lie to the sides of the road that wends through flooded brush and lay-down trees. Pockets of reeds lift through the marshy ground, spread from pond and river plantings gone all wrong, choking the waterways, where hungry hatchery-planted trout move in behind the native salmon, slurping up the eggs. Rick knows the land is worth its weight in condos and Charley will cave to it. Charley's frontier is the transit corridor squeezing the river. He'll find a new girl when he feels better. He'll tame the bar, tunnel the channel, and blast past the rapids. The watershed will be paved. Any nesting refuge left will owe its existence to the very men who shoot the eggs, bedfellows like the barbwire around the birds in the Mekong, like the blanket of land mines sleeping between North and South Vietnam. Rick knows that hunters will move indoors, that they'll shoot at paper targets dyed black with a fan of concentric rings, footless and hung by the crown on a clip-line, fluttering a little, like plastic bags in trees.

A few miles before the turnoff, Rick points at a half-fallen scarecrow dressed like a woman in an empty field. "Bang," he says, and Pavel tries not to flinch. Pavel shuts his eyes and wills the deer down from the high summer ranges toward mid-elevation, past the legal borders of the B-Zone, where Rick can get to them.

Jalanta is staring into the empty mailbox when they pull up, her hands hanging at her sides. Rick slams the truck door and heads for the shed. Pavel goes around to the front door where Jalanta is waiting for him. Sweat beads up through her heavy white makeup. Eyeliner marks a blue shadowed place, the look of Yugoslavia.

"Was there any letter today?" Her hands make the shape of an envelope. Pavel pans up to the new-fixed gaze of the wall-mounted teal. In the corner of his mind he smells the rotting pinecones at Charley's and moves toward the kitchen, where the fake pine scent will cover that up. Jalanta stands behind Pavel as he opens the freezer. He moves around blocks of meat, ice-cube trays, frozen peas, but the watchband is gone.

She has mailed the watchband to the wildlife lab for analysis, together with an accusation of poaching. Pavel is sure the letter he carries begins the machinery of government punishment and intrusion. Pavel sees his stepfather shifting and grinding in its gears, his mother caving in under quantities of laundry detergent, fabric softener, bleach and spot remover—all the things they married this man to get. She has been saving this thing, *informing,* and the bricks, glass, and beams which came down around them in Kosovo didn't warrant it. A better apartment, a car, a visa, more food, a transfer, study abroad hadn't, didn't, nor his father lying on his back in the schoolyard, his hands stretched above his head with his jacket yanked up because someone had been dragging him by the feet, his body leaving a long dark trace in snow that didn't melt for a week. Where he sleeps now, Pavel has his own room. There are three blankets on the bed, and a door. There is a window he can leave open, and a light. At night, his room marks the house like a bomb target, but nobody cares.

They stare, but Jalanta might as well be at the wrong end of a telescope, her outline oscillating with squares of yellow linoleum. To the left is the sound of the freezer humming, farther away, the roar of the freeway, which rattles the windows of Rick's prefab house.

"Give him a baby," Pavel whispers in Serb.

"No," she says in English.

Rick comes into the kitchen, reaches between Pavel and Jalanta, and pulls a beer from the refrigerator. Pavel pulls the letter from his pocket.

"Get on dinner already," Rick says. He tears the envelope with his teeth, draws out the letter, and reads. Jalanta and Pavel watch his forehead crease, the left to right motion of his eyes. Pavel imagines himself swimming with the tide-pool minnows, each like every other, no reason to be singled out. Rick explodes into a shout and slams down his beer. It foams over the lip, onto the counter, and into a drawer filled with coupons, twist-ties, and sandwich bags.

"Fucking A!" Rick bellows. "Get the fuck out." He grabs his own hair, rubs his eyes, then punches the wall. He takes a breath, refolds the letter, and clenches his teeth. He reaches for Jalanta, grips her shoulders, and kisses her hard on the lips. "The tag lottery," he says, swinging her around. "The B-Zone."

She stares at his mouth, then Pavel.

"My goddamn hunting license," he says, pulling her face back to his, yanking her chin. "Charley didn't get one," he says, grinning at his wife. "Charley doesn't have it anymore." Rick high-fives the air in front of Pavel's face and hurries back to the shed, to his guns, knives, and fishing flies.

Rick's fingerprints pulse on Jalanta's jaw. She dumps flour on the counter. "The Adriatic Sea," she says, slicing a map through the dust. "Republics, provinces, zones." She stamps a circle at the edge with the rim of a glass.

"We. *Us*," Jalanta says in English.

Pavel covers his ears.

"It doesn't matter how we sound, which way we *say*, everywhere there is always someone who will be the Jew." She wipes away the contours of a country about to disappear.

Pavel hears Rick calling him and spins into the cold night of the yard. Rick leans close as Pavel's eyes adjust in the dark.

"Look," he says. There's something propped on the fence post, the torso of the department store mannequin Rick keeps in the shed. Rick hangs his hats on its arms, initials nicked into its dented plaster, its pinkish tan. On top of the cocked, smiling head are the crooked ears and winky eyes of Pavel's fairground poodle.

"Easy shot," Rick says. "Fish in a barrel." He places the Marlin in Pavel's arms. The gun is too long to fit in the crook of his collarbone, the way it will in Rick's. Pavel shifts in the sling and settles his shoulder up to the butt. The barrel presses away from Pavel's palms in the precise weights of food rations—150 grams of bread, a potato, four grams of rice—the gun's heft like the cross Pavel carried at a wake for a body not there.

"Don't look," she had said, and he won't.

"Put yourself in the jungle," Rick says. "You're a tunnel rat, a gunner on patrol."

The trigger is brass, the wood around it flush with the skin of his hands. Pavel puts his eye to the sight. He thinks of bright places called convenience stores, crammed with food in nice packages, no lines, the smell of hot coffee, gum, chocolate, gasoline, Xerox, endless plenty. She can be the Jew.

"I don't care if you miss and blow its head off," Rick says, but Pavel doesn't. There's a burst of tiny Styrofoam beads, and then Rick's gorgeous laughter. Rick reaches to shake Pavel's hand like a man, but Pavel is still stumbling back from the shot.

DAVID WOOD

PEN Prison Writing Committee

FEATHERS ON THE
SOLAR WIND

A heavy winter rainstorm drummed the buildings of Hesiod Correctional Institution the night Daniel Martin Pinkston finally died in the AIDS Dormitory. It was two A.M. when four corrections officers in protective clothing wheeled him out the iron door for the last time on a gurney. Kenneth "South Philly" Johnson and Willie Norton looked up from their card game. John Mohammed "Deathrow" Rollins spared one last glance at the closing door before he began his cleanup duties.

"That's two we lost since midnight," Willie said as he began shuffling cards. "First Parker Calloway, now Pinkston. You know when it goes like this there'll be a third."

"Third time's a charm," Johnson said. "I'll put up a pack of Lucky Strikes that Morgan will go next."

"Be quiet, man," Deathrow snarled. "You don't respect death and you don't respect God." He was stripping off Pinkston's soiled sheets and double bagging them in red contagion bags. "And keep it down! These sick men are trying to sleep!"

"Sorry, man," Willie said. "We just can't sleep."

Deathrow looked up as he scrubbed the waterproof mattress with bleach. "I can get you some sleeping pills if you want."

"No need, brother," Willie said. "I'll just play with South Philly here and let him tell me his life story. I'll be asleep in fifteen minutes." He nodded at Johnson, who'd spent most of his life in South Philadelphia before coming to Florida and landing a bid for armed robbery and kidnapping. Now in his midforties, he was an animate human skeleton, his neon-white skin spotted by Kaposi's sarcoma. Willie, at fifty, was just as thin—his black skin dry and flaky, most of his graying hair gone.

"But if you need something, you tell me!" Deathrow said, pointing his thumb at his chest. "You got a problem, I'll take care of it."

He returned to his duties, and the older men watched him for a moment. Like them, Deathrow had HIV, but he was still big and black and muscular, his voice deep like James Earl Jones's, his energy and patience endless. At nineteen he had killed two police officers and then he'd spent twelve years shooting one writ after another into the courts from death row, doing all he could to keep from making that last walk to Old Sparky, Florida's electric chair. He'd finally got his sentence changed to life, but after one year on the compound he had contracted the virus.

After six months of bitter denial he converted to Islam, and though he could have spent years on the compound until full-blown AIDS set in, he volunteered to live in the AIDS dorm to work as a nurse's aide. He humbly performed all the duties shunned by the doctors and nurses, who visited the dorm as little as possible. He emptied the catheter bags, changed soiled linen, gave bedbaths to men too weak to bathe themselves. He held men up and fed them, checked them for bedsores, and his muscular killer's hands massaged sore spots to keep them from becoming bedsores. His prison job duties required him to work eight hours a day, five days a week, but he never stopped working as long as he wasn't asleep.

"I wish I had that kind of energy," South Philly said, watching Deathrow carry the contagion bags to the laundry.

"You got plenty of energy," Willie said as he dealt the cards. He noticed Jimmie Long across the dorm climbing out of bed into his wheelchair. "Look at you, up all night partying and playing cards. You're as lively as a feather on the wind."

"Give me three cards," South Philly mumbled. "And hold your sarcasm. You're full of shit and bad jokes, and your farts stink like roadkill when they float over my bunk." He examined his cards and bet two tailor-mades—Lucky Strikes—while he puffed a cigarette he'd rolled himself. "Deathrow had to slide my locker between our bunks so we could play. My strength is draining."

"At least you don't have to wear diapers," Willie said, reaching for his Chesterfields. "I'll see your two and raise you three. Now, when you ask me if I'm going to wear briefs or boxer shorts tomorrow, I answer 'Depends.' Jimmie's coming for a visit."

"What got you up?" South Philly asked, nodding at Jimmie. "You're usually sawing logs about now."

"Can't sleep," Jimmie mumbled, stopping by their bunks.

"Deal you in?" Willie asked.

"I'll watch," Jimmie said. Though he looked healthier than the two older men, his legs were quickly growing weak. The doctor couldn't figure out why. His face looked as if it had a rash under the red ceiling night-lights.

"I call," South Philly said, setting his cards down, two queens, ace high. Willie showed him three deuces, scooping up his cigarettes. "Damn."

"You never traveled enough to play against good players," Willie said.

"Well, I won't get a chance to travel now."

"Oh, you are, in a way," Willie said. "The earth is twenty-four thousand miles around, and it spins like a sonovabitch. You're going about a thousand miles an hour and don't even know it."

"Who gives a shit," Jimmie mumbled.

South Philly looked at him. "Homey, you in a bad mood or something?"

"I know what it is," Willie said, putting on his state-issued glasses and gazing at Jimmie. "Pinkston died tonight, and he's the one who gave you AIDS, isn't he?"

"Man, I'm no fag!"

"You two were cellmated," Willie went on. "You can't tell me you didn't get some mud on your turtle."

"Man, just shut your fuckin' mouth!" Jimmie yelled, his cheeks redder than normal.

"Watch your mouth, bro," South Philly said, scooping up the cards. "We didn't invite you over here, so if you want to cop an attitude, take it back to bed."

"And don't get defensive," Willie added. "None of us got in this dorm by sharing a needle or getting a blood transfusion."

"Man," Jimmie shook his head. "I just don't want to die like this. This place stinks like a busted meat locker, people dying every other day, we're fenced off from the rest of the compound, and all we can do is wait to die. I don't want to die like this, I want to die like a man!"

"Shut up, punk," South Philly hissed, rising up on bony legs hidden in nylon pajama bottoms. "This *is* how a man dies. Look at me. My mother writes me every week, but here I am, I got myself locked away from her and dying. You think she's proud of me? You think I'm proud of myself? My father has Alzheimer's, and she's trying to take care of him, and she probably wonders every day who's going to die first, me or my father. But this is how a man dies, with the Ninja or Alzheimer's or cancer. If you wanted to throw yourself on a grenade and save your buddies and die a hero, you should've joined the Marines."

"South Philly, stop running your jaw," Wyman Reed said, walking through the maze of bunks toward them. "If Deathrow comes back and catches you waking up his patients, he'll gag you and tie you to your bed."

"You guys are waking the dead over here," Carl "Smokey" Dukes said. "Can't you keep your voices down?" Both men wore their blankets over their shoulders. Like Jimmie, who had on a sweatshirt over his pajama top, they couldn't put up with the cold air in the dorm. The heaters were in the ceiling instead of the floor, and the slow-turning ceiling fans couldn't quite get the warm air down. Willie and South Philly both had fevers that night and sat on their bunks shirtless, their ribby chests like washboards.

"I'm sorry, Smokey," Willie said. "We won't holler and hoot again. This was supposed to be a quiet party. Go ahead back to sleep."

"Hell with that," Wyman said. "Deal me in." He held up a pack of generic cigarettes.

"You up to a game this late?" South Philly asked, shuffling the cards. Wyman nodded. "Smokey?"

"I'm all out, homey. I'll just watch." He pulled an empty wheel-chair closer as Wyman sat on the bed next to South Philly. Wyman was a tall black man who hadn't yet shown signs of the virus, but three long bouts of pneumonia had weakened him. He couldn't live in open population anymore. Sometimes he'd go outside and stand by the fence, watching inmates play basketball in the distance. He never stayed out long, because it was only a matter of time before he'd be noticed and become the target of insults and catcalls. This irritated him no end: At least a third of them were also infected, though outwardly healthy, and they, too, would be landing in the AIDS dorm.

"You know they took Pinkston and Calloway out tonight," Willie said, rolling a cigarette.

"Hospital?" Smokey asked.

"Morgue," Willie answered.

"Two?" Wyman whispered. South Philly nudged him to cut the cards. "Jesus Christ, that's not good."

"Don't take the Lord's name in vain, man," Smokey said.

"Save your church for Sunday," South Philly snapped.

"Philly thinks someone else will go before the dawn comes up," Willie said.

"This is too morbid," Jimmie whispered.

"Why three?" Wyman asked.

South Philly began dealing. "It goes in threes, Wyman. If two die during the week, it's a sure bet a third will go before that week is up. Just listen." He held up his hand for silence. The sounds of snoring men, mixing with the whirring of the fans and the steady tattoo of rain on the roof, but behind it was the rattling, deep breath of several men struggling through pneumonia.

"You hear that?" South Philly whispered. "We got Death waiting in the wings. It's that kind of night."

"Man, you're getting a bad attitude," Smokey said. He was feeling uneasy, as were Wyman and Jimmie. "You're not psychic."

"I don't know," South Philly said. "But that's the way it goes, people die in threes. I used to work in a nursing home in Pennsylvania. Weeks would go by, and then three old people would go in one week. It was strange, no reason for it, but there you are."

"C'mon, man, let's play cards," Wyman said. "Your talk's getting too creepy. And I don't believe it anyway."

"What?" Smokey whispered. "That someone else will die tonight?"

"Far as I'm concerned, that's a given," South Philly said. "I propose we each bet on *who* will die."

"Man, you're sick," Smokey growled.

"Ashes to ashes, dustballs to dustballs," Willie said. "Even the Bible admits that, Smokey. I read my King James daily, too, you know."

"So we pick someone in the dorm?" Wyman said. "One of our sick patients?"

South Philly slowly set his cards down, his face serious. "No, that's too easy. Way too easy. I predict it will be one of us here." The other men gazed at him in silence. Even Willie looked shaken. "I say we bet one pack of tailor-mades each. We each choose a different one among us, place our bets, and wait for dawn."

A dreadful silence fell over them, a silence like an arctic night. Smells of the dorm wrapped around them, smells of sickness and sweat. "It's sinful," Smokey said.

"Sin got us here thus far," Willie mimicked, "and sin will lead us home."

"Don't try me, Willie."

"You fucked a punk like the rest of us," Willie said. "Don't give me any of your self-righteous crap, Smokey. South Philly has hit on something, I don't know what, but I'm game."

"You want to die?" Smokey asked. "Is that it?"

"No, it's not," Willie said. "But I'm going to die anyway, whether I like it or not. And if I gotta die, I might as well play one last game with Death himself."

Wyman nodded. "Yeah, maybe. But I don't think no one's gonna kick off in our little circle. What if it happens, Philly, and it's not one of us?"

"Then nobody wins, and we all keep our cigarettes, and die of lung cancer instead." South Philly looked from man to man. "In fact, the way I see it, winning and losing are both desirable. You win, you get the cigarettes. You lose, you get out of the goddamn dorm."

This time Smokey didn't complain. Jimmie was looking into his lap, gripping his wheels. At twenty-five, he looked like a little boy awaiting the whipping of his life. Wyman looked from man to man, intrigued but scared, as though he had just been invited to play a game of Russian roulette, and he knew he was too tempted to refuse. "All right," he said. "Let's go for it."

"It's not right!" Smokey yelled.

"Shut the fuck up!" someone yelled from across the dorm. "I'm sleeping!"

"You're a bunch of fools!" Smokey whispered. "No wonder you're in this mess."

"You're in the same predicament, my man," Willie said. "And you fall as short of the pearly gates as the rest of us. I know more about you than you might think."

"And what's that supposed to mean?"

"It means you don't have much leeway to complain about anybody else." Willie took off his glasses and stared at him. "Now, if you don't like what we're doing here, go back to bed, I'm tired of your mouth."

Smokey was silent, but he stared back until Willie looked at the others. "Boys, I don't know how real this all is, but I swear I feel spirits in the air. I've been scared of dying since I popped out of my momma's womb, but just tonight I'd like to look Death in the eye and prove I'm a good sport."

He put his glasses back on. "Now there's science and there's the spirit world. According to science, we are mostly made up of water, but we are what's known as a carbon-based life form. Carbon is that black stuff left over after you burn something, and a friend once told me that no planet naturally has carbon on it anywhere. Carbon comes from the sun and other stars."

"So what's your point?" Wyman asked, still holding his cards.

"My point," Willie said, examining his hand, "is that we are made of stardust. And when we are dead, our carbon molecules go into the soil and become part of other life forms. So you see, part of us goes on, just like the carbon molecules of other living things that are in us now, and all of it comes from the big burning stars in the sky."

"So there's bits and pieces of dinosaurs in us, too," South Philly said.

"Something like that," Willie agreed. "But now we're heading slowly back to our old carbon selves. I like to think we're heading back to the sun myself, that we're going back to be cremated into nonexistence, nothing but that damn stardust. And if I go, I might as well play over the sunspots, and this little bet is how we can do it, how we can be feathers on the solar wind for a while, floating and dancing on the music of the cosmos before the final incineration."

"Willie, you sure know a lot of big words and ideas for a black man," South Philly snorted.

Willie grinned at his old friend. "If it makes you too uncomfortable, Philly, I could talk like Aunt Jemima for a while."

"It's still a lot of bunk," Smokey said.

"If you think so," Wyman answered, "then you make the first bet."

Smokey opened his mouth, about to refuse, when he looked around. "A pack of smokes, you said?"

"Exactly," South Philly answered. "But you got to pick one of us."

Smokey stroked his chin. "Okay, I bet a pack of rip that old Willie here will die first."

The other men looked at each other.

"Man, that's slimy," South Philly said. "Just because he told you about your ass..."

"He done right," Willie said. "And he chose well, I look like I'm halfway to the crypt, the way I see it."

"And who do you choose?" South Philly asked.

"I place my bet on Wyman," Willie said. "No offense."

"None taken," Wyman answered, though he looked a bit shaken. The game was too real to him.

"Wyman's the healthiest one here, and I got the feeling too much health is not always a good thing," Willie explained.

"That's crazy," Smokey said.

"Yeah, it sounds sorta crazy, but I figger to go against the odds."

"And you, Wyman?" South Philly asked.

Wyman looked around from face to face. "I don't think any of us are going to die, leastways not tonight. And I'd hate to name someone and actually have them die and me win cigarettes on their body. I just don't know."

"Yeah, it feels a little dirty, I admit," Willie said. "But I feel the spirits kicking tonight, and me, I gotta dance with Death, just one slow dance. If you don't feel up to it..."

Wyman shook his head. "Philly, I put my pack on you. God knows, I hope I lose, but I'm gonna play this game."

South Philly smiled at him. "No hard feelings, brother. Tonight I don't feel afraid. I don't even care. But I put my smokes on Jimmie."

"Oh, no, man," Jimmie gasped. "Hell no, man! I'm not gonna die tonight!"

"Well, if you don't, then I lose. You got nothing to worry about."

"Change your bet, Philly. Change it!"

"You're my pick, bro. Now your turn."

"I'm not gonna."

"Smokey's left," South Philly said. "Though he looks like he'll live a good long time. Still, you can never tell."

"Back off, man," Smokey said. "The boy doesn't need any help."

"Man, I'm through with this shit," Jimmie said, and wheeled off.

"We scared him," Wyman said. "Maybe we shouldn't have done this."

"It's done," South Philly replied. "The boy needs to cope with what's happening."

Jimmie's wheelchair clipped a steel bunk as he turned and headed for the shower room. They watched him disappear through the door.

"Sirius is high in the sky tonight," Willie mumbled, "and the natives are restless. "

"Sirius?" South Philly asked. "What's that?"

"Sirius, the Dog Star, the harbinger of death. The brightest spot in the sky, if the moon isn't out."

"Putting out carbon molecules," Wyman said, picking up his cards. "Maybe if we get enough carbon molecules, we can all be made whole again."

The shower room was a long hallway illuminated by filthy neon lights. The walls and floor were covered by worn white and tan tiles. A chest-high wall ran along the middle, with sinks and mirrors on both sides. To the right were a dozen stainless-steel toilets and an equal number of metal urinals. To the left were a dozen showerheads, with two specially built showers to accommodate the handicapped.

Jimmie rolled his wheelchair through the meat-locker-cold room to the farthest sink. He looked into his own haunted eyes in the bent steel mirror, at his rash-covered cheeks. He turned on the cold water and let it run while he reached beneath his sweatshirt and pulled out two bottles of pills—Pinkston's pain pills, which he'd stolen before the officers had come to take Pinkston away. When he heard somebody come in, he quickly stuffed the bottles out of sight between his legs.

One of the showers came on. Someone couldn't sleep, he thought. He was shivering from the cold, but he got one of the plastic bottles open and poured six pills into his palm, tossed them into his mouth, and leaned over the sink, scooping water into his mouth. He had dumped six more pills into his hand when he noticed steam filling the room.

Something seemed out of kilter. He gripped the pills in one hand and with the other pulled himself up to a standing position. He gazed at the naked figure under the spray of hot water, and his weak legs nearly gave out. "Oh my God," he whispered.

"Give me two cards," Wyman said, setting two cards on the locker. "I know what you're talking about, us under the influence of that star."

"Sirius," Willie said. "Canis Major."

"Just a star," Smokey said.

"With stardust," South Philly added.

Smokey pulled his blanket closer around him, glancing at Deathrow, who was going from bed to bed, emptying catheter bags into a plastic urinal bottle, writing down the amount, then pouring the urine into a bucket before moving to the next bag.

"We'd be in a bad fix without Deathrow," Wyman said, following Smokey's gaze. "That man's a saint. If I could choose one person to survive this dorm, it would be him."

"Maybe in the parallel world, he's out free and clean of the virus," Willie said. "Erwin Schrödinger once mentioned that there might be a whole series of different dimensions where the same people were living different lives."

"That doesn't help me none now, does it?" South Philly said. "Maybe next time I'll try a different dimension."

Wyman looked over his shoulder. "Jimmie must be off beating his meat, he ain't come back yet."

"He's just taking a dump," South Philly said.

"He could've passed out," Smokey said. "Let me check on him." He rose from the wheelchair and stalked off, his blanket dragging on the floor.

"He needs to deal with things," South Philly said. "Maybe we all do. I'll see your two cigarettes and raise you two, Willie."

In the shower room, Jimmie stared over the wall at the naked inmate in the steam. The two bottles dropped to the floor. Pills fell from his sweaty palm. He was staring at Daniel Pinkston, very much alive, young and muscular as he was when they'd first met, not in his later emaciated state. Jimmie felt he was hallucinating, but Daniel stared right at him, smiling. The tiny metal ring pierced his left nipple, and above that was the team emblem of the Florida State Seminoles tattooed where it always had been.

"But you're dead," he whispered.

"What does a small thing like that matter to anyone?" It was Daniel's voice.

His mannerisms, his movements, everything; Jimmie felt sick. "I never even tried to say good-bye."

"I never did like that word," Daniel said.

"My God, Dan, do you forgive me?"

"For what?"

"For every way I wronged you. For ignoring you in this dorm while you were lying there, dying and pissing in your bed, and you wanted to talk, I could see it in your eyes . . ."

"There's nothing for me to forgive," Daniel said. "It's you who must forgive yourself." He turned, and Jimmie followed his gaze. Smokey stood in the doorway, his mouth open, his eyes wide. Steam filled the room in billowing clouds. "Only you can forgive yourself. Nobody else." He said this while staring at Smokey.

South Philly picked up the cigarettes, his winnings from the last hand. Wyman shuffled the cards. They turned their heads when Deathrow gave a yell, stepping out of Jimmie's way as he wheeled into the room. "Next time you run over my foot I'll pour this bucket of piss on your damn head!" he shouted before continuing to the shower room.

"I saw him!" Jimmie banged against the bunk, gripping Wyman's arm. The cards fluttered to the floor. "I saw Danny's ghost. Danny Pinkston!"

"Brother, what got into you? Willie asked.

"Danny didn't give me AIDS, I gave it to him!" Jimmie cried. "I swear! It wasn't his fault! I was punked out when I first came to prison. When I started doing Danny I didn't even know I had the virus! I should've died first, I had the virus first!"

"The truth comes out," South Philly mumbled.

"Easy on the boy, Philly," Willie said. "I believe he really did see a ghost. I told you the spirits were restless tonight."

"I asked him to forgive me," Jimmie gasped, his voice trailing. "But he said I had to forgive myself."

"That's the first thing you said tonight that makes sense," South Philly said.

"Wyman, I need your help."

Deathrow stood silhouetted in the doorway. His voice was soft, almost a whisper, but the authority in it carried over the roomful of snoring men. "After I tell the bosses." He nodded at the two officers sleeping on chairs in the Plexiglas-enclosed officers' station. "After I tell them, I'll need you to help me with the body."

"Body?"

"Smokey—he cut his throat with a razor blade," Deathrow said.

Jimmie stared after him, dumbstruck, as he went to wake the officers. Wyman gazed sadly at the empty shower room doorway. South Philly angrily picked up the cards. "Third time's a charm," he mumbled.

"Why?" Jimmie whispered.

"He had a little dirty secret," Willie said. "Parker Calloway told me before he died. Smokey turned state's evidence on his brother, got his brother the chair, when it was him who did the killing. When you saw Daniel Pinkston's ghost, he probably saw his brother's ghost. Only he wasn't capable of forgiving himself."

"You shoulda took that bet," Wyman said bitterly. "You'd have scored a few packs of cigarettes." He rose and headed off to help Deathrow.

"That could've been me," Jimmie said, feeling tears well up, remembering Daniel when he first met him. He leaned over, weary. Willie, suddenly cold, pulled his blanket over his bare shoulders. South Philly shuffled the cards.

LISA METZGAR

Colorado State University

CAT AND MOUSE

Marcy first sees the mouse on Wednesday, October third, the day after she has her last two wisdom teeth out. When the mouse appears, Marcy is sitting at the kitchen table, swimming in the slow, pink haze of Percodan, staring at a bowl of oatmeal and wondering—very, very slowly—about the mechanics of lifting the spoon to her mouth. At the edge of the haze there is a little shuffle along the baseboard by the trash can. When she looks, a tiny, gray racecar of a mouse is looking back at her with round, black eyes. Marcy blinks, and then the mouse is gone. For three days, until the Percodan is used up, Marcy thinks of the mouse as a hallucination.

"Nope," Tom says. "You have a mouse." It is late Sunday morning and he has just finished making her French toast, her first solid food in days. He is down on his knees, peering behind the trash can.

He stands up and holds out a finger with three black rice grains of mouse poop stuck to the tip. He is grinning the same kind of grin Bobby Thompson grinned at her in third grade when he pulled an earthworm out of his pocket at lunch in the cafeteria, then swung it around his head like a lasso. Marcy wonders if it is the idea of marriage in general that terrifies her or whether it is the specific idea of marrying Tom that does it.

"I'll get some traps and kill it for you," he says, brushing off his finger on his jeans, still grinning.

"I can do it," she says—it is, after all, her house.

The next morning, on her way to work at the hospital, Marcy stops at the store. She looks up and down the shelf of rodent control products. Super snap traps, disposable snap traps, the absolutely number one guaranteed better mouse and rat trap. They all look like tiny guillotines, and Marcy thinks about the swift, sharp arc of the bar, the bone-crunching whack. She decides on poison.

Back at the house she reads the package of little, greenish brown pellets. HANDLE WITH GLOVES! it says. PLACE ALONG BASE OF WALL IN AREA FREQUENTED BY MICE. It seems rude, she thinks, for them to assume that she has more than one mouse. She sticks her hands inside sandwich-sized plastic bags, rips open the package, and places the little pellets around the pantry floor.

The problem with poison, she realizes, is that you don't know when the mouse is dead. Later, when Tom calls, she asks him.

"When the little turds stop appearing," he says without sarcasm. "Then it's dead." She spends the evening in a turd eradication program, cleaning shelves and scrubbing the floor. She thinks of the mouse as she cleans, its little gray body curled tight into some warm corner, sleeping, perhaps for the very last time.

Her father calls when she is down on her knees, wiping the floor around the trash can. "Why didn't you ever teach me how to deal with mice?" she says.

"You kill them." She cannot tell whether he means it as a joke. "I called to tell you something," he says. "I met a woman."

Marcy is standing with the phone tucked between her shoulder and her ear. It is dark outside and she can see her reflection in the window looking rumpled in jeans and sweatshirt, her hands and lower arms encased in bright yellow rubber cleaning gloves. "Where?" she says.

"The singles' club," he says, as if it were obvious that a fifty-five-year-old man, seven and a half months separated but not yet divorced from his wife, would have joined a singles' club.

"Who is she?"

"Her name's Helen."

"Is she nice?"

"You'll like her." His sentences are absolute, imperative. She wonders if he used such sentences to tell her mother that he was leaving. She wonders if he speaks to this Helen woman in such sentences.

Later, Marcy's mother calls. "I've got a mouse," Marcy says.

"Oh dear, they have those awful, naked tails."

"Those are rats, Mom."

"I'm sure mice have those kinds of tails, too. And aren't you afraid it will escape and then you'll find it God knows where—in your bathrobe pocket or in the toaster—"

"What do you mean escape?" Marcy says.

"You know, get out of its cage." Sometimes when Marcy talks to her mother, she has a spinning feeling that makes her want to sit down and close her eyes for a very long time. "You should get a nice dog or a cat or something."

"Mom, it's not a—"

"I need to tell you something, Marcy. I don't want to burden you but I have to tell someone and there's really no one else—your father's met a woman." The words come out in a great rush like water out of a burst pipe.

"Oh," Marcy says. Her mother sniffles.

"Deborah saw them," her mother says, "playing golf. Deborah says she's got awful, bronzy dyed hair and long, red fingernails and huge, fake eyelashes and a handicap ten strokes better than mine."

"How did Deborah know her handicap?" It's the wrong thing to say, but Marcy feels like a small Dutch boy jamming his finger into a hole, words rushing by, spraying out like water.

"At least," her mother is saying, "at least in all these years I've never looked cheap." Marcy knows she is supposed to say something, but a sharp knot of ache coalesces at the back of her skull. She stares at the package of Oreos Tom left open on the kitchen table the night before, the Oreos she bought three days ago which are now half gone though she hasn't touched them. She thinks of how it feels to twist them apart, to have, suddenly, two separate cookies where before there had been just one. "I just want you to promise me that you won't speak to her, Marcy. That's all I ask."

"I'm sure it won't be a problem," Marcy says.

The mouse is not eating the poison. Along the pantry walls, up on the shelves, among the cans and packages and boxes, the little turds keep appearing. Some mornings the poison pellets have been pushed away from the wall, dismissed. The mouse chews its way into two boxes of cereal, a bag of popcorn, and the cherry Pop-Tarts Marcy has been saving for some quiet morning by herself.

When Marcy thinks about the mouse, she cannot help thinking about all the other things that are wrong with her life. When she thinks about it sneaking around the pantry, nibbling through boxes and packages, she imagines her father cavorting around the golf course with some big-haired floozy with bright red nail polish, spider veins, and gold lamé golf shoes. When she opens the cupboard and finds tiny turds perched on cans and boxes, she thinks about how every time Tom is with her for more than ten minutes she becomes petrified that he will propose to her. Looking at the chewed corner of a muffin box, Marcy thinks about how yesterday she ate not one, not three, not five, but eleven and a half Oreos while watching a *Seinfeld* rerun. She goes to the store, buys two more packages of poison, and lines the pellets up along the pantry shelves.

Near the end of October, Marcy's father calls. "I want you to meet Helen," he says. "We'll take you to lunch."

The three of them end up in an Italian restaurant, sitting around a red and white checkered tablecloth, fishing meatballs from heaping plates of pasta. "Will tells me you have mouse troubles," Helen says, leaning toward Marcy and smiling. For a second, Marcy wonders who Will is, then realizes that Helen means her father. Helen lays her hand on Marcy's arm. Her fingernails are a perfect plum color and though her hair is certainly dyed, it's not brassy at all, just a nice, deep brown that glints in the light when she turns her head. Marcy looks across the table at her father. He is bent over a piece of bread, spreading butter.

"The poison isn't working, Dad," she says, as if Helen were not there at all.

"It rarely does," Helen says. Marcy wonders what this woman could possibly know about mice. "I grew up on a farm," Helen says. She is still smiling, showing beautiful, perfect teeth. "The problem with poison is that you can never tell whether they're still alive or not."

Marcy looks over at her father, who is winding pasta around his fork. She looks back at Helen. "So, how did you get rid of them?"

"Mostly cats. Do you like cats?"

"No. Not so much."

"I don't either." Helen laughs. It sounds like a fine-tuned instrument. "I guess I like them better than mice, though."

Tom loves cats. Unfortunately, on their second date just over a year ago, Marcy told him she liked them, too. "It's funny," he said then, "that we both work in the same field, that you're a nurse and I sell pharmaceuticals." And they had the same interests, too, he said. They both liked jazz and bicycling and tropical vacations; they hated tuna fish and loved Italian food. "I'm sure you like cats, too," he said, reaching across the table to take her hand. Because he seemed so happy, because it was easier than saying no, and because she was sure that it would never get serious with him, she nodded and said yes, yes she liked them very much.

Tom has a very fat, caramel-colored cat, Xavier, who likes to sleep in the corner of the couch where the sun comes through the window in the morning. "You should borrow Xavier for a couple of weeks," Tom says when she tells him about Helen. "I don't know why I didn't think of it before." Marcy looks at Xavier. It is late on a Saturday morning and they have just gotten up. The cat is still fast asleep in his spot on the couch. She thinks of her very, very dark blue couch that is upholstered with something like corduroy.

"He doesn't look like the kind of cat that catches mice," she says.

"He's a cat," Tom says. "Of course he'll catch mice. Besides, it'll be a kind of trial period so you and Xavier can get to know one another."

"I'm not sure," she says, but already he's gone into the spare bedroom and she can hear him digging through the closet.

When he comes back, lugging the cat carrier, he says, "Think about it as a step toward living together."

Driving home with the cat carrier buckled into the passenger seat, Marcy imagines living with Tom, but all she can think about is Xavier eating, getting fatter and fatter, spreading out across the entire couch, making it impossible to sit down.

Twice a week Marcy's mother walks from her job as a bank teller over to the hospital where Marcy works so that they can have lunch together. On the first of November they go to a deli across the street from the hospital. The special is turkey and cranberry sandwiches. Her mother sighs. Lately, everything is about Thanksgiving—"the first Thanksgiving," as her mother says, "since your father left." The sight of pumpkin pie in the dessert cooler makes her weepy.

"Your father always loved my pumpkin pie," she says. They sit down with their sandwiches. Marcy can see a line of tears building up along the bottom of her mother's eyes. "I'm just afraid," her mother says, "that you'll think marriage is a terrible thing because, well, you know." She picks up a spoon and stirs her diet soda.

"Mom, I'm not even engaged."

"But then," her mother says, brightening, "Tom is so different from your father. You get along with him so well." It's true, Marcy thinks. Tom is romantic and funny. He brings her breakfast in bed, and she can't remember them ever really having a disagreement. Her mother gives a heroic sniffle and dabs her eyes with a napkin. "We'll have dinner later this year. At four." She means Thanksgiving, of course, but it is only after saying, "That's fine," that Marcy realizes her mother has never asked, has just assumed they were coming.

Marcy buys Xavier a catnip mouse. He doesn't play with it. He doesn't play with anything. He curls up in the corner of her dark blue couch and moves only to eat, drink, and use the litter box. When he gets up, he leaves behind a caramel-colored puddle of hair.

The mouse thrives. It chews through a bread bag and eats a narrow, mouse-wide tunnel halfway into the loaf. It crawls into the Oreo bag and nibbles off all the remaining cookies. Marcy imagines it rattling around inside the cellophane, giggling. "Xavier just lies on the couch," she tells Tom after a week.

"Give him a while longer. He's adjusting."

All too well, Marcy thinks, but she doesn't say it because Tom is bent over, regrouting the corner of her bathtub, doing a much better job than she imagines she would do.

"Besides, even if he doesn't catch mice, he's nice to have around," Tom says.

Marcy goes into the kitchen. Xavier's bowls are on the floor. Tom's coat is hung over the back of one of the chairs. His briefcase and papers are spread across the table. Sometimes his things seem like an invasion, like foreign troops advancing through her house. Other times they make it seem as if her house has become a home where people live together, love each other, have pets.

"Marcy dear," a woman's voice says through the phone. "This is Helen. Your father and I want to invite you and Tom for Thanksgiving. We're having an early dinner at my house."

"Thank you," Marcy says. "But I think . . . I think that—"

"Oh here, your father wants to speak with you," Helen says, and Marcy knows that the invitation is about to become an imperative.

"Marcy," he says. "Helen told you about dinner."

When Marcy talks to her father, there never seems to be time to figure out what she wants to say. "The thing is I already told Mom I'd—"

"That's fine," he says. "That's why we're eating early."

———

"How am I supposed to be in two places at once?" she asks Tom.

"Let's go to Barbados or Hawaii or something," Tom says. When she rolls her eyes, he says he is serious. He would look good there, she thinks, strolling down the beach in his swim trunks. He would be telling funny stories about Xavier, or doctor jokes, and she would be laughing, having a good time. She imagines them eating dinner—candlelight, a warm breeze blowing through open windows. "I want to ask you something important," he would say, fishing in his pocket, and she would go cold, her mouth open, gaping and speechless.

"I need to spend the time with my family," she says.

"It would be easier if you went away for the holiday. Besides, we've both been wanting to do something like this for a long time."

"Tom, I just don't know."

"I'll look into tickets," he says.

Two nights later, when Tom is in L.A. on business, Marcy wakes to the sound of Xavier yowling. She can hear him thrashing around in the kitchen. "Gotcha," she thinks. The cat is still struggling when she gets to the kitchen, but when she turns on the light, she sees it's not with the mouse. He is flailing wildly around the floor, frothing at the mouth, his thick, caramel legs working in the air, a high, thin wail emanating from his throat.

She calls the first vet she finds in the phone book. He tells her to wrap the cat in a towel and come immediately to the office. When she picks Xavier up, he is still, but his body is hot to the touch, and though he is still breathing, he feels somehow rigid.

"Poison," the vet tells her. "Probably rodent poison."

"Oh God," she says.

"We can probably nurse him through it," the vet says. "But I'm not sure you want us to."

"Please. He's not my cat. Do whatever it takes."

The next night when Tom calls, Marcy is sitting in the living room, looking at the puddle of hair on the couch, thinking of Xavier curled up in his cage at the vet's office. She doesn't answer.

"Say hello to Xavier for me," Tom says to her answering machine.

"I almost killed your cat," she says when he comes back three days later. Xavier is spread out on the couch. "The vet said extensive nerve damage."

"He looks fine to me," Tom says. He goes to the couch and reaches out to touch the cat. Just then Xavier gets to his feet, tilts slightly to the left, and rolls onto the floor. He gets up and walks, almost in the direction of the kitchen, his hind end jerking out of sync with the front, his body listing first left, then right. "Oh," Tom says and sits down on Xavier's corner of the couch.

"I'm so sorry," Marcy says, and that's true, but at the same time, even though she knows it's wrong, it seems that maybe all this will buy her time. Tom is staring at the floor.

"You know," he says finally, and Marcy listens for his sentences to get short, clipped. "I'm very serious about you, Marcy." He looks up at her. His eyes are wide, glistening. "This seems like a big deal now. But the way I feel about you is more important." He reaches out and takes one of her hands. "When we're married, it won't seem so important." The word *married* makes Marcy feel as if the mouse has gotten into her head, like something small and gray and skittery is running around between her neurons.

"Tom," she begins, but then Xavier stumbles sideways into the doorframe. Tom looks over at the cat, then turns back to her.

"Marcy," he says. "It was an accident. It's okay." There is no scene, no yelling, no anger, no nothing. Tom just sits there, stroking her hand, and Marcy feels swept aside by the wide-open look in his eyes. It doesn't seem possible for her to say what she means; she is not even sure what she meant to say in the first place.

––––––––––

A week later, Tom leaves on another business trip, this time for Boston. Marcy comes home to find, just inside her front door, a bag of cat food, eight snap traps, a single long-stemmed red rose, and a note that says, "Peanut butter makes the best bait. I love you and I'll see you in a week. I have something important to tell you when I get back." Marcy is setting the traps along the shelves and the pantry walls when her mother calls.

"I was hoping you'd come help me cook Thanksgiving morning."

"The thing is," Marcy says. "I think I have to go—"

"Your Aunt Betty and Uncle Fred can't come this year. And your Uncle Joe and Aunt Charlene are going down to see their kids and that means it's just going to be you and Tom and me for dinner. I thought that morning would be, you know, a mother-daughter kind of thing."

Marcy has been making a list of the things ruined by the mouse. She stands in front of the refrigerator, the phone against her ear, reading it. Two and one half packages of spaghetti. One quarter package of Oreos. Three boxes of cereal. One bag of popcorn. Two Pop-Tarts. Pancake mix. Poppy-seed muffin mix. The brain of one cat. "I'm feeling so much better about the holiday," her mother is saying. "It's no good moping. You and I will have such fun. We can make that special kind of stuffing you like so much." There is something in her mother's voice right then, Marcy thinks, that sounds like excitement, almost like happiness. She thinks about how quiet it will be in her mother's house, cooking that dinner alone.

"Okay," she says. "We'll cook that morning."

Marcy calls her father. She wants to ask him what kind of traps to use and how many to set and whether peanut butter really works. She wants to tell him that she is sorry, but she cannot come to Thanksgiving dinner because while he at least has Helen to spend the day with, her mother, his almost-but-not-quite ex-wife, has no one at all but Marcy. She picks up the phone and dials. The phone rings and she is getting ready to say all those things when Xavier steps on the edge of his water bowl. A puddle of water spreads across the floor, and she has to tuck the phone underneath her arm to grab towels. Very far away she can hear a woman's voice saying, "Hello? Hello?" Marcy picks up the phone again, moving the towels around on the floor with her foot.

"Helen?" she says. "Helen, this is Marcy. I want to talk to you about Thanksgiving." No sound comes from the other end of the line. With a horrible, empty feeling, Marcy realizes that she has, from twenty-eight years of habit, just dialed what used to be her parents' number but what is now just her mother's number. "I was calling to cancel," she explains. "We were eating early. I thought it would work out, but then I decided to just—" At first she thinks her mother is laughing, then she realizes that the sounds are a kind of crying, a high, hysterical sound.

In a minute, the crying turns to hiccups. "You do whatever you want to do," her mother says. "If you want to go to that woman's house and just come over here for a bit, that's fine."

"Mom, I want to come." Marcy leans back against the refrigerator, waiting for the rest of it, about how sad it is to be alone, how terrible on a holiday like this when you are used to having family. But it doesn't come. There is a long pause and one or two sniffles.

"Well then. That's fine," her mother says, and her voice wavers, but doesn't break. She starts to tell Marcy about shopping, and it is as if Marcy can hear her pulling herself together all the way through the phone lines. "I found the perfect tablecloth," she says. "It's a kind of orange and yellow flowery thing, but not ugly like it sounds."

Later, Tom calls from Boston. "There are tickets to Jamaica on sale. We could leave Tuesday and come back Sunday."

"I can't do it," Marcy says. "Things are too crazy." Xavier stumbles by. He is shedding more every day. Wherever he goes he leaves a caramel-colored fog of hair behind.

"It'll be warm. And it'll be just the two of us." Marcy watches a little raft of five or six hairs rise off of Xavier's back as if they were lighter than air, then drift gracefully along above the carpet. "You've been trying so hard to make everybody happy," he says. "You deserve a break." Marcy thinks about bright white sand and big waves rolling up the beach. She thinks of warm, sweet breezes and palm trees and of tropical drinks with little paper umbrellas—a place where they probably don't have Thanksgiving at all. A place where Tom would certainly ask her to marry him.

"What about Xavier?" she asks.

"We could ask your mother to take him. She'd like the company."

Marcy thinks of her mother in the kitchen with Xavier on Thanksgiving. Sure, she wants to say, he could help whip potatoes and chop chestnuts and drink wine and tell divorce jokes. "I think she wants my company," she says. "I can't go."

"I'm going to reserve the tickets. So you can change your mind." They say good-bye. Marcy stands by the phone for a long time watching Xavier who, in some herky-jerky imitation of his previous self, is bumping again and again into the cupboard where she keeps his food. Maybe Tom is right, she thinks. Maybe she needs to marry a man who is willing to drag her off to Jamaica, away from all this. But thinking about it makes everything muddle together, and she cannot separate marrying Tom from the silence in her mother's house, cannot separate Tom wanting to take her to Jamaica from the cat hairs she found in her toothbrush this morning.

Marcy moves Xavier aside to get the food. When she turns around, a small, gray pointy nose and two black eyes are looking at her over the back of Xavier's bowl. She screams and flings the cat food. Pieces rain down and scatter everywhere. She wants to cry, but it seems like she can't remember how.

That night Marcy barely sleeps. When she does, she dreams of the sound of traps snapping—a sharp, echoing sound. In the dream, she gets up to check the traps. There are mouse carcasses everywhere, two and three to a trap. But in the center of it all, a single, grinning mouse is wearing a dark gray tuxedo, tap-dancing between a box of Triscuits and a chewed-open package of Fat Free Fantastic Fudgies. When she really does get up to check the traps, they are empty, but one has been licked shiny-bright clean, and a single, black rice grain of a turd has been left on top of a soup can like a thank-you note. She hates the mouse. She wants it dead. She wants it lying broken-necked in one of the traps, gray and stiff.

When she finally goes back to sleep, she dreams of marrying a giant, caramel-colored cat and of her mother saying over and over again that she's just glad Marcy is finally happy. In the morning, there is still no mouse in any of the traps, but there are, she sees, three new tiny black turds around the base of Xavier's food bowl.

The next morning, Marcy's doorbell rings. When she opens the door, her father and Helen are outside. "We were in the neighborhood," he says. "We thought we'd stop by."

Helen is holding out a little bag as they come in the door. "We brought you something." Marcy looks in at five or six mouse traps. "What a perfect house," Helen says. She walks around, looking at the books on the shelves, at the plants lined up in front of the windowsill.

"Where's the mouse?" her father says. He takes the traps and heads for the kitchen.

"Well," Helen says, looking down at Xavier on the couch. "You got a cat."

"It's Tom's," Marcy says.

"No wonder you've got mice," her father yells from the kitchen. "You've got cat food under the fridge and your traps are all turned around backward."

Her father helps her push the fridge and the oven away from the wall, and Helen gets down on her knees, sucking the cat food up with the Dustbuster that Marcy's father keeps in his car. She watches Helen leaning over, slim and fit, unruffled even when she's Dustbusting cat food and mouse poop. She's perfect, Marcy thinks. It's impossible to hate this woman. Later, when her father goes out to put the Dustbuster away and to get gas, she and Helen are left sitting alone together on the couch. "So, tell me about this Tom," Helen says.

"He's very nice." It doesn't seem right, she thinks, to tell Helen anything that matters.

"What does he do?" Helen is leaning forward, looking at Marcy closely.

"He sells pharmaceuticals." She intends to stop there, but she doesn't. "He wants me to marry him."

"Is that what you want?" Helen asks.

"That's the thing," Marcy says. "I don't know." She doesn't want to, but she can't help herself from talking. She tells Helen everything, how a year ago, when they'd started dating, she hadn't intended to get serious, how she'd lied to him about liking cats, how everything she told him seemed to be at least a sort of lie. "He's coming back in three days, and I know he's going to ask." Marcy looks down at Xavier sleeping, at the way his ribs rise and fall as he breathes. "I just don't know if he can make me happy."

"I think we have to make our own happiness," Helen says, and she puts her hand on Marcy's arm. A minute later, Marcy's father comes back in.

"Ready," he says. Marcy wants to say no, to put her hand on Helen's arm, to ask her to stay. She doesn't, of course, and Helen stands to put her coat on. "Well," Marcy's father says. "We'll see you on Thanksgiving." He and Helen turn and go out the door, then her father turns back. "At around two," he says, and they are already in the car, already backing out before Marcy realizes that it was supposed to be early, not at two, because if it's at two there is no way, even if she rushes and drives very fast and lies a little on each end, that she can be in both places.

When Tom returns, he comes in the door grinning, carrying a dozen long-stemmed roses, and without thinking about it Marcy knows that somewhere in a jacket pocket he has a little velvet box containing a gold ring with a diamond. All of it makes her want to run very far away. "They're beautiful," she says about the roses. "Tell me about your trip."

"I never stopped thinking about you." He can't stop grinning. "I have something important to tell you."

"You've figured out how to get rid of this mouse?"

"I want to ask you . . . I want to—"

"Tom, I don't think that now—"

"I've thought a lot about this."

"Hold on," Marcy says. "I think Xavier's out of food." She stands up.

He takes her hand and pulls her back down onto the couch. There's no stopping him. He reaches into his pocket and pulls out a velvet box. He gets off the couch and down on one knee. He looks up at her. There is a tiny quiver in his lower lip, and he is holding the box out on the palm of his hand as if he is a waiter. "I want you to be my wife," he says. At that moment, Xavier walks by, listing to one side, his legs out of sync, his head drooping. Maybe if something were different, she thinks. Maybe if it hadn't been this way of saying things so sincerely that she had liked about Tom in the first place. Maybe if he had made it a question instead of a statement, maybe if she could conceive of saying anything to him that wasn't at least partially a lie, maybe if Xavier hadn't eaten that poison, she could do it.

"Yes," she says.

Marcy is lying awake, listening to Tom breathe when she hears the snap—not a sharp echo like in her dreams, but a dull thud. Walking into the kitchen, she hears the mouse before she sees it, and she thinks that certainly this is a dream, because otherwise the mouse would be dead and still. She imagines opening the pantry door to find the mouse walking around, setting off the traps with a toothpick, wearing a top hat, dancing, and singing over and over again, M-I-C-K-E-Y M-O-U-S-E.

For a moment, right after Marcy opens the pantry door, she sees that the mouse is dancing with the trap. But then, because she is fully awake, she sees that it's not dancing at all but instead is backpedaling furiously, trying to get away from the trap that has latched down on its nose. It hits the corner of the pantry, but its feet keep going, pushing uselessly against the floor. Somehow, Marcy sees, the bar has not hit the mouse's head or neck, but has come down smack-blam onto the space between its eyes and the tip of its nose.

"Tom," she says. She can't bear to watch it anymore so she shuts the pantry door, but she can still hear the feet skittering fast and furious. "Tom," she says again, then walks back to the bedroom. He is still sleeping. She thinks of going back to bed, of pretending that this is a dream, knowing that by morning the mouse will have either gotten away or will be dead. But in the quiet between Tom's breaths, it seems like she can still hear the mouse's feet. "Tom?" She reaches down to shake him. He grunts and rolls over. She goes into the living room, puts on boots and a winter jacket, and pulls an empty shoe box out of the back of the closet.

Marcy has no idea what she'll do once she has the mouse in the box, but it seems as if that will somehow be an improvement. When she gets back to the kitchen, the mouse is no longer moving so much. Scooting the side of the box underneath it, Marcy tries not to look at the mouse's face, at the way the bar has come down and crushed the tiny, delicate bones in front of its eyes. She tries not to imagine how it is possible for the mouse to still be breathing. "Shhh," she says, the way one would to a noisy child, and she scoops the mouse into the box. Once the lid is on, the mouse begins to scamper around again.

She takes the box out back, still unsure what to do with it. Through the bottom, she can feel the tiny, tapping feet and the heavy movement of the trap as the mouse drags it across the bottom of the box. She could just put the box in the Dumpster as is, but she knows she won't be able to stop thinking about the mouse, still alive, struggling back and forth in the box with garbage all around. She has to kill it.

Out on the patio Marcy opens the box and, as gently as possible, tips the mouse onto the pavement in a rectangle of yellow light from the kitchen window. The mouse has slowed down, but Marcy still has to put one booted foot behind it to keep it from going backward. She puts the other foot over where the mouse's head and the trap come together, and she tries very hard not to think about what she's doing.

"I'm sorry," she says, pressing down, and then it is over.

Scooping the body back into the box, she makes a point of not looking at the head. The mouse is deep gray, a color that seems too perfect for such a small thing. She wants to reach in and touch the fur, but she is afraid of how it would feel.

She covers the box and sets it down. It doesn't seem like the kind of thing you just throw away. Just minutes ago, she thinks, this little gray wedge of a mouse had come pitter-pattering through the darkness of her pantry, sniffing along the walls. That's all, just this gray speck of breath that never had any intentions beyond the skimpy bit of peanut butter in the trap. She thinks of its breathless body there in the box, no longer moving, something very small and gray and somehow precious, a thing that until now, when it is much too late, she never really knew anything about at all.

She thinks about Tom sleeping inside her house, his breathing even and deep. She thinks about her father sleeping in his new house with Helen tucked against the curve of his body. She thinks of her mother sleeping, her breath rattling out into the emptiness of her house. She'll have to give the ring back tomorrow, she thinks. She looks down at the way it sparkles on her finger. Tom will say he loves her, and that he will give her time to think this over and make the right decision. Then there will be telling her father that no, she won't be coming for dinner, and he will say that he and Helen are disappointed, and his sentences, almost impossibly, will become shorter and more imperative. Then, at ten o'clock on Thursday, she will show up at her mother's. They will roast a turkey and bake pies and whip potatoes and drink red wine and maybe later, after dinner, watch a movie or even the football game. It won't be the way that either of them imagined it would be, but maybe it will be enough.

JENNIFER VANDERBES

University of Iowa

The Hatbox

National Geographic, **A Celebration of Discovery, 1950, The Recollections of Raymond Henry Gray: On Finding the Missing Link**

Since 1924, students and colleagues have asked me again and again: To what can I attribute finding Australopithecus? And I have answered, always: luck. For the successful paleontologist, there is no further requirement (as those who have persisted in its absence, and there have been many, will attest). Without luck a man becomes a casualty of this field. Men can spend months sieving every square centimeter of a riverbed only to have a visiting colleague discover a hominid molar on the first afternoon. The only difference between a man with a shovel and a paleontologist has always been and will always, simply, be this: what he finds.

When I set out to Africa in 1923, many were in search of *the* hominid fossil. Since Darwin's *The Descent of Man* and Huxley's *Man's*

Place in Nature, men like myself have been eager to find definitive paleontological proof of our ancestry. Where was the apelike creature we had supposedly descended from? What did this missing link between man and his simian ancestor look like? How old was it?

At the time, paleontology and archaeology were fledgling disciplines. Formal training, in the contemporary sense, did not exist. The first prehistoric man-made tools were found in France by a young customs official with an antiquities hobby. Heinrich Schliemann, a businessman with only a copy of Homer's *Iliad* to guide him, sailed to Turkey and unearthed the ruins of Troy. Hearing of these discoveries, many of us became eager for our own conquests and discoveries, setting off on ships and horseback to strange, inhospitable landscapes in search of great relics from the past. It seemed a major discovery might yield itself to anyone (with the financial means) who stuck his trowel in the right spot.

Finding the right spot, however, was a matter of great difficulty. There was much debate at the time over which continent had witnessed the birth of humanity. Asia—some of the first *Homo erectus* samples were excavated from Zhoukoudian, China, in the twenties— seemed promising. Africa, on the other hand, despite Darwin's insistence that it was the cradle of human evolution, had become an unpopular choice. After digging unsuccessfully in German East Africa for six years, Van Mannerling (an unfortunate example of a man without luck) renounced the continent as the home of man's early progenitors. Then, in 1914, Van Mannerling upset all previous geographical conjectures when he unearthed the now infamous skull of Dover Man in England. Suddenly it seemed hominid evolution had centered on the European continent. In retrospect, the immediate and near-unanimous support Dover Man received is an unfortunate and regrettable chapter in the history of paleontology. But neither Van Mannerling nor anyone in the scientific community knew the skull was a forgery. Why should they have suspected that somebody would file and stain an ape's jaw and bury it in the ground? Again, luck is key.

A question that has often been posed is: Did *I* believe in the authenticity of Dover Man? When Van Mannerling's Eoanthropus Doveri was unearthed, the whole world assumed it was the missing link. And yet if *I* had believed, why would I have traveled to Africa? My colleagues at the University of London strongly advised me against excavating in Africa. I was, in fact, invited to assist in subsequent excavations in the Dover area. Instinct, however, told me that the link between hominid and pongid *had* to be in Africa. I had simply never lost faith in Darwin's initial assertion. To what do I attribute finding Australopithecus in the same area where Van Mannerling had been digging for six years? Luck, luck, and nothing but luck. It is, even to a man of science, inexplicable.

For the next generation of archaeologists and paleontologists, undiscovered treasures still abound. To the young man who stirs ceaselessly in his bed, slave to that insomnia of ambition, I say, simply: *dig.* Another ruined Troy awaits the shovel of another Schliemann. Another Australopithecus waits beneath the soil of centuries to see sunlight again. Even as we exhaust all our geographical frontiers, the last frontier, the one we will never wear out, is the one beneath the earth. As we run out of mountains and valleys and continents to explore, we will take our trowels in hand, we will dig, and we will go back in time.

In the desert, on her honeymoon, Anna had a fever. Her knee—where she had fallen—was swollen. How long she lay wrapped in blankets on a cot in her tent, she did not know. Masai women poured milk on her torn flesh. They slipped sour berries into her mouth, sprinkled water on her face. Above her head their beads clicked loudly. *Msabu, Msabu,* they whispered, bathing her in their warm, meaty breath. Once, they pressed a clay cup against her mouth and poured something thick and slick down her throat—sheep fat—to make her vomit. Whenever she opened her eyes, they chanted. *Ah, Msabu, Msabu.* Anna thought, Who is Msabu? I'm Anna. Anna. They are talking to somebody else. Again, she would sleep.

Often, Anna had the sensation of being lifted, of her body bouncing and shifting in her sagging cot, of the sun's fierce rays burning her face. Several times a day, she awoke to the sound of prolonged words: *Bones? Yes? Bones.* The voice was a man's—her husband's? She opened her mouth to call to him, but she was too weak. Once, she thought she felt rain on her face and believed she was sitting in the Vrijthof without her umbrella. But it was not rain. It was sweat. Her fever was breaking.

Anna recovered in a new landscape. Limping from her tent, she saw shrubs and thorn-trees and brown soil where sand had been. It was no longer the desert. In the distance a wall of red ragged cliffs glimmered in the sun. Hot, she thought. It was still hot. *Ah Msabu!* The Masai—seven, more than she remembered—crouching in the shade of a tree, weaving sisal baskets, called and waved to her. Her husband, Kees, ran from his tent. He was sunburned and smiling beneath his Panama hat.

—Anna, he said, squeezing her shoulders, I think we're close.

—I'm so sorry, Kees, she said. It was stupid of me to just walk . . . I didn't know.

The fever had shielded Anna from her foolishness, but now her mistake came back to her—wandering away from the camp one evening, finding herself just meters from the glowing eyes of a leopard. She had wanted to look at the stars that night. Kees was in his tent with the Masai, once again mapping their course, trying to pinpoint the gorge. Anna—wasn't she supposed to have interests and curiosities of her own? wasn't that what he had told her?—strolled away from the camp to explore, with no gun. No knife. Kees, of course, had warned her about wild animals, but she had imagined the foxes and rabbits and pigs of Limburg. All she could do when she saw the leopard—she had never even seen an animal that big!—was scream and scamper back toward the camp. Only it was dark, and she didn't see the rock mound where they had cooked their dinner, and she caught her right foot, fell, and tore the flesh around her knee, exposing the bone. Now she was wounded.

—For next time, Kees said, handing her a gun.

From baobab branches and twine, Kees fashioned Anna a crutch. He showed her the map and with his blackened finger traced the course they had already traveled. Look! he said. I think we're approaching the Great Rift Valley. He placed his hand on her shoulder and said there were rocks ahead, and riverbeds and forests. It will be difficult, he told her. Difficult to walk. Despite the pain she still felt in her knee, Anna told him she could make it. From the beginning she had been determined to show Kees she had the strength for this journey. She had said nothing of the rats on the ship or the roaches beneath their bed in Zanzibar. She had endured, with grace, even with laughter, the mosquito bites marbling her arms and neck. And when the Bantu man in the bazaar shrieked at her, when he grabbed her arm, Anna had simply pried herself away and shaken her head. But now, this. She feared Kees was angry with her. Or disappointed? She could make herself walk, but surely she would slow them down. The adventurer's wife, he had warned her before the journey, before they married, had to prepare for a life of bravery. Already, she had failed.

They collapsed their tents and packed their bags and set off again behind their Masai guides across the dry grasslands, past patches of thorn-trees and baobabs, into the dust-filled bottoms of dried out rivers. In the heat, the air shimmered, waving and reflecting like water. When sluggish winds rustled a patch of dry grass, or briefly bent the thinnest of baobab branches, the caravan paused for a moment and Anna turned to face the breeze, swallowing a small sip of cool air before the wind surrendered to the hot stillness of the bleached land. On the plain ahead Anna often saw large glistening ponds, which, as she moved closer, disappeared, and then reappeared farther ahead. The first time Anna saw this, she shouted to Kees: *Look! A lake!* The Masai elbowed each other and laughed. Kees erupted in a momentary giggle. *What? I said there's water ahead.* Kees then explained the water mirage. So the water wasn't real. Only a liquid image. But when was the last time she had seen *real* water? How she missed the Maas River! It had been a month since she had walked along the canals of Amsterdam as Kees arranged their passage south. But how long ago had they been in Zanzibar? There, at least, she had seen other foreigners. She longed now for the boat ride across the Mediterranean, even the small creaking dhow along the Red Sea. It seemed they had been walking for weeks, or even months. What she wouldn't give to simply sit again. She faltered often on her crutch. Kees, despite her refusals, carried her over rocks. At times, she wondered whether this was a gesture of kindness or haste.

Whenever they passed a Masai or Kikuyu village, Kees assembled a crowd and began with his questions. With his thick sunburned hands he would carve a V in the air. *Ol-du-vai? Gorge? Bones?* He would point to his forearm, jab at his ribs. *Bones? Gorge?* The Masai or Kikuyu would shrug or giggle. They would point him back in the direction from which he had come. Once, a Kikuyu *huka* mistook Kees for a German official and wildly chased the caravan out of the village. But usually, Kees persisted. *Bones, gorge.* He would kick his thick boots in the dirt, dust rising and lingering with his frustration. He would begin again. He would gesticulate and shout until somebody—probably guessing, perhaps humoring—pointed vaguely toward the setting sun.

The days of walking were long and draining, and often Anna wished she were back in Maastricht. This was not the honeymoon she had imagined, not the romantic African adventure she had described to her friends at home, friends who squeezed her hand with happy jealousy: *Oh Anna! To leave the Netherlands! Europe!* The *silence* of the land she had not expected. Their caravan walked for hours, with nobody exchanging a word. She grew accustomed to the sound of their shoes crunching against the dry earth, the whispered yielding of parched grass against their legs. At dusk came a clanging through the silent land of their rocks hammering iron stakes. In the evenings, after they had pitched their tents and dined on ostrich steaks and milk and rice, Anna watched Kees by his oil lamp once again unfold the creased and weathered map. At these moments, watching her husband—yes, she reminded herself, he *was* her husband, her *future*—Anna was happy. Or believed she would soon be happy. Once they found the gorge. Once they settled. Kees, then, would certainly be happier. It had been two years since a British butterfly collector had traversed East Africa, returning to Europe with stories of a magnificent gorge littered with bones, two years since Kees had seized on the idea of finding the gorge—now *his* gorge, when he spoke of it—struggling to raise funds for the journey. He had even considered joining the army for the boat passage to South Africa. Anna was glad that, with her father's money, Kees would now be able to find what he was looking for. That they would. Together.

On the plains one day, they were joined by several Kikuyu who seemed eager to help lead the caravan. They walked ahead with the Masai, often looking back at Anna and Kees with broad and curious smiles. The orange and red of the Masai's *shukas* were the only colors in the landscape. As if they were the flames of a guiding torch, Anna followed the colors, mesmerized. She still did not know the Masai by name. From behind, she tried to tell the men from women, but their shaved skulls and elaborate jewelry confused her. Their coiled brass necklaces glistened in the sun, their beaded anklets clicked with each stride, heavy hoops swayed from their earlobes—what did these ornaments mean? But now, at least, she could tell the Masai from the Kikuyu. The Kikuyu were shorter, she noticed, and they braided their hair. The brown of their leather capes dulled beside the fiery Masai *shukas*. As the two groups walked together, there was a swell of excited conversation. Anna thought she heard the familiar word— *Msabu!* But the rest of their words were like laughter or singing, sounds with emotion, suggestion, emphasis, but no clear meaning. It made her uneasy that she could not communicate. If something were ever to happen to Kees, she would be in great danger.

As they came over a rise, the Masai ahead waved their arms in the air. *Msabu! Msabu!* Kees stopped in his tracks, turned to Anna and grinned. At last, Anna thought. At last we're here. *Msabu!* She hobbled quickly behind Kees to the top of the rise. But where was his gorge? The dry land spread evenly toward the horizon. Only a small Masai mud hut broke the expanse. Kees cursed. He pulled his map from his pack and threw it to the ground. But the Masai continued to shout, *Msabu! Msabu!* And then, from the hut, came a slender white woman in a red silk kimono with gold dragons embroidered on each panel. She wore sandals. Her hair was cut short like a man's. She tightened the belt of her kimono and walked toward Kees and Anna, shielding her eyes from the sun.

She laughed and said, So they've led you to the crazy white woman?

That is how my mother began the story.

She was dying. This was not what the doctors said, or what the doctors said the X rays said, but she believed she was dying. "You better get over here," she had sighed on the phone. "Your mother's on her way up the escalator." She arranged a schedule for my visits to the "home"—a nursing facility just six miles from where I lived. She wrote my name in the blank squares on her activities grid and taped it over her bed. "You're right in between Ikebana and pet therapy. Don't be late." This, I realized, was the beginning of our "sessions."

Years before, my grandmother, while dying, had arranged with my mother what she called "sessions." While my father and I played gin rummy in the waiting room of the hospital, my mother disappeared to my grandmother's room for an hour, sometimes two, emerging dazed and exhausted, walking straight through the waiting room as we gathered our cards. My father and I would eye each other and follow her to the parking lot. When I asked her what she and Nana had been doing she would simply say, "talking." She would fall silent for the car ride home and my father, driving with only his left hand, would rub her neck. When we got home, they would retreat to their bedroom. They would whisper. And I would try desperately—drinking glasses do, in fact, help—to catch any word or phrase about the mysterious sessions.

Despite my curiosity, I was happy to wait with my father during those visits. My grandmother's face had started to terrify me. Her nose had collapsed into a sea of shriveled skin. My mother, the first time she saw me flinch at my grandmother's bedside, dragged me into the hospital corridor and slapped me across the face. Had she raised her daughter to have no sympathy? No compassion? Years of melanoma removal and skin grafts, she explained, had changed Nana's face. She had once been beautiful, really beautiful! My mother began to cry. I'm sorry, I told her. But I was eleven and those words—*melanoma, graft*—meant nothing. All I knew was that there was something monstrous about my grandmother's face. Years later, I would realize that what had frightened me so much was not simply the sight of old age, but the suggestion that someone you loved, could, despite your resistance, despite your awareness that to feel such a thing was unfair, disgust you. At that age, I had known love and I had known repulsion, but I had never known them together, in the same room, in the same person. These two emotions fought inside me each time I looked at my grandmother. She was frail and helpless, a woman I had known my whole life, a woman dying, and I could do nothing but flinch.

My grandmother had been a high school biology teacher who spoke often of her involvement in the famous Scopes monkey trial. She had been one of a group of teachers who went to Tennessee to support evolution in school curriculums. Whenever she had guests, she led them down the hallway and into her study where she showed them the framed photograph of her and John Scopes on the steps of a Tennessee courthouse. She was shaking his hand and smiling, a look of celebration lifting her face—a look I rarely remember seeing.

My grandmother was both imposing and reserved. She read a great deal, always drank a glass of gin after dinner, and refused to stand still for holiday photographs. I remember her mostly, however, as a woman in the hospital. I visited her bedside for five months with my mother. And then, two days before Christmas, in the middle of a blizzard, she died in her sleep. But she returned to me often in name and spirit, invoked by my mother: *If your grandmother could see this . . . If your grandmother only knew.* And once, after my wedding, when I told my mother I would probably never have children: *Thank God your grandmother isn't alive to hear this.*

Now I was sitting beside my mother's bed, my hand resting on the cold guardrail. My mother had fallen and fractured her hip and looked fragile beneath the covers. She was only seventy-one, but years of smoking had added a decade to her face. Her voice was scratchy and severe, louder than her small body suggested. Even though she was one of the younger residents, she was quickly acquiring an *old* manner. She said coy, helpless things like: *Oh, why doesn't somebody open a window in here*—somebody meaning me. She complained about the poor machine weaves on blankets or the frustrating pump on the soap dispenser. *Who had problems with the soap bars, I ask you?* I felt guilty that I could no longer care for her, but she disdained my guilt. When I arrived that day, the first thing she said was: "Get that mopey look off your face. This is where I should be unless you want to stand beside me all day long and spot me like some gymnastics coach."

Now, she wanted to know if I would remember the story she was telling me or if I needed to write it down. I told her I thought I would remember, but if it made her feel better, I would bring a notepad next time.

"If you remember, you remember," she said. "It has nothing to do with me feeling better. I feel fine."

"I'll remember it," I said.

"Because I'm not done yet, you know," she said. "It might not be a bad idea to write it down."

"All right," I said. "I'll write it down."

"If you think you need to."

I told her I thought I needed to.

"You're probably right. When you come back tomorrow, bring something."

The woman's name was Dora Bickensdorf—a name Kees recognized immediately. She was the wife of the British butterfly collector whose reports of the gorge had lured him to this strange continent. Dora, however, had never laid eyes on the gorge. Two months into their African expedition, while her husband hiked farther inland, Dora built for herself a dung hut on the plains. When her husband passed through again, Dora told him she had decided to stay. That was two and half years before Kees and Anna arrived outside her hut. This they learned as Dora served them a picnic of ostrich meat (she had killed it that morning) and goat's milk beneath a large acacia tree. She sat cross-legged in her kimono, talking loudly. The ostrich is a terribly mean bird, she told them. It can fight like mad with its legs and wings. It can kick a dog to the ground. A lion attacking an ostrich? Hah! It's like those Saint Petersburg students trying to bring down the Romanoffs! Wait, they haven't succeeded, have they? Oh, how I miss a newspaper now and again. But I'm straying. The ostrich, yes. Ostrich *oil* is one of the wonders of the medicinal world. And you can drink it like water! After their lunch, Dora translated to Kees's Masai guides that he was looking for a place called the Olduvai Gorge, a place supposedly littered with bones. Kees told Dora about his search for the hominid fossil. Well, if you don't mind, Dora said, I'd be most interested in accompanying you newlyweds. I'm eager to see if our Mr. Darwin is a genius or a crackpot!

Within two weeks, the caravan, now led by Dora, made its way to a cliff, a steep cliff hovering above a great hollowing in the land. Olduvai Gorge. *Kees's* gorge. It was two kilometers across and eighty meters deep, higher than any building Anna had ever been in. It stretched farther than her eye could see—forty-nine kilometers, they would later measure. As she stood on the edge looking down, Anna's stomach tugged her away. Finally, she thought. Finally we are here.

It took them a day to descend, first lowering by rope their tents and bags and crates of rations, then easing themselves down the smoothest section of wall. Never had Anna seen anything like this. From the base for the gorge, the towering walls—striped in places by colored clay—rose around her like the edges of the world. And what a strange world—sisal trees speckled the landscape, but not a single shrub or patch of grass. The ground was covered with brown dust, rocks, and bones! Giant bones lay everywhere, like pebbles. Anna threw down her crutch and wandered from the group. Look, Kees! she shouted, lifting a large and heavy crescent-shaped fossil with both hands. Is this it? she asked. Be very careful where you step, dear, Kees shouted. If the world's first hominid fossil gets smashed under your shoes, I might just ask for an annulment. Then, sweetheart, she shouted back, I'm afraid you'd have no money for your digging. You're stuck with me, shoes and all, she hollered. Kees stared at her with astonishment, and horror. Anna quickly regretted what she had said. She had been joking! Surely he could take a joke! Kees turned his back to her and began to pry open one of the ration crates. Well? she said tentatively, after she had carefully made her way back to the group and handed him the crescent-shaped fossil. Just wonderful, my dear, he said, you're brilliant. We can all go home now that you've discovered the jaw of a very dead elephant.

They pitched two separate camps. One inside the gorge, just beside the south wall, and one above. Kees was concerned about water and animals and weather. He said they were probably safe from animals within the gorge, but it was far from water and shade was scarce. Dora Bickensdorf said she wanted to set up her tent above the gorge. If she was going to hunt, she should be near the animals. Besides, she said, she wasn't sure if she was going to want to listen to digging all day long. Isn't that what you're going to do? she teased. Dig, dig, and dig. Anna set up the tent for herself and Kees, while Kees staked and tarped a work station several yards away. Within a day they had arranged a "dining room," an "office," and several "chateaux." Dora named her tent Windsor Castle. That night, after both camps had been arranged, Dora invited them to celebrate with a bottle of English brandy. She offered a toast: To my new friends! And *not* just because you're the only white people I've seen in a year! Hah! And to the newlyweds!

Anna and Dora did become good friends. Each morning, Dora climbed down the gorge wall in khaki pants and a crumpled shirt, a rifle slung over her shoulder. Anna, who wore her long hair in a braided bun and whose lace-hemmed skirts dragged in the dust, found Dora strange, and fascinating. When Kees set out to scout the sunlit gorge, the two women sat in the shade of the mess tent drinking tea. They spoke about Europe, the journey across the Mediterranean, their husbands. And though Anna was at first shocked by Dora's candid description of her bedroom affairs, Anna, one day, at first timidly, then eagerly, offered the same.

—Frustrated, Anna said. I get the feeling he's frustrated with me. I think he wants me to try ... I don't know.

—Listen, some men are like that. Tell me, darling, you've got a cap? You know about that, right? Because we don't want you having a litter out here in the middle of nowhere.

—My mother gave me something, Anna said, blushing slightly. Before we left Maastricht.

—Because you must be careful, Dora said. I had a scare with Simon and another with Daniel.

—Daniel?

—*Before* Simon.

—You've been with ...

—Of course, darling. Did they lock you in the attic back in Maastricht?

Apparently, before her marriage, Dora had slept with other men. Anna—she had never even kissed anyone but Kees—was shocked. Dora even confessed she had gone to bed with a Kikuyu man at Lake Manyara the year before. No! Anna shrieked, looking around to see if the Masai were nearby. I can't imagine. ... They began to pass hours this way, Dora recounting adventure after adventure with different men, Anna laughing in disbelief. These stories, Anna knew, were *meant* to shock her. It was a game—Catholic morality versus unbridled sexuality. *No, you didn't. Dora!* against *Oh Anna, but then he did this thing where . . .* They each played their part to entertain and provoke the other. It was the same when Dora slipped unexpected profanity into her conversation. *Dora!* was Anna's line. Or when Dora flirted with Anna, *Darling, you Dutch women are divine,* Anna would laugh and blush. So what if Anna suspected Dora was lying, or at least exaggerating? So many men? Anna didn't think it was possible. But she never begrudged Dora the stories. She loved the stories. It gave them something to do, something to talk about in otherwise desolate days.

One morning Dora asked about Anna's knee. Anna, by then, could walk without pain, but she still limped slightly. Anna lifted her skirt just above her knee. The skin was still striated with scars.

—It looks worse than it feels, Anna said. It was early on in the trip. A leopard frightened me. It's so embarrassing. This place isn't like home.

—I can teach you to hunt if you want, Dora said. You could probably spear an antelope with those shoes of yours if you wanted to. No. I'm kidding you, dear. If you like, though, I'll help you make a pair of sandals. I can teach you all sorts of things. You want to learn to triangulate your latitude and longitude using the stars? I'll teach you. This is an amazing place, Dora said. Especially for a woman. Well, a white woman. She leaned close to Anna and whispered. You know, they circumcise the girls here. The Masai. Before they're married. Zip. Chop. It's awful. Can you believe it?

Though Anna accepted Dora's offer to make sandals—they made three pairs one morning from buffalo skin—she was hesitant to begin hunting, or dressing, like Dora. One night in their tent Kees had said Dora reminded him of a man. And he couldn't imagine any man, he said, being married to her.

Each morning of the first few months, Kees would set out to survey the gorge before any digging would begin. He penned an elaborate map, pacing out the distances, coding in blues and reds the areas where fossils lay loose on the ground. Meticulous and patient, Kees left every piece in its precise place in the gorge until his map was finished. But once it was finished, and once the various sections were staked out, at sunrise he raced off with an empty burlap sack. By sunset he had hauled over one hundred fragments back to the camp. Over dinner he passed them excitedly to Anna and Dora, who held the curious fossils up to the oil lamp. What is this one? He answered: I'm not sure, something large, maybe from a water buffalo? A rhinoceros? Kees was frustrated because he needed books, reference books, with pictures and diagrams. He had brought Sir Francis Galton's *The Art of Travel,* Darwin's *The Descent of Man.* But he had no need for theories. He needed charts. The variety of fossils in the gorge he hadn't anticipated. There were skulls and ribs and jaws of every size. With the larger animals, Dora tried to help, offering comparisons from animals she had hunted. But Kees knew it was nothing more than guesswork.

After months of waiting patiently, Kees now decided he would collect as many loose fragments as possible, and as quickly as possible, as if quantity might compensate for his unfamiliarity. He offered the Masai a bonus for each piece of fossil they could find, and soon, day after day, knapsacks full of fragments collected in the tent. In the evenings, the Masai—Rikuni and Ole—would count out the pieces in their bag for Kees. He was encouraged, almost amazed, by how many they were gathering. He told the women that at this rate, he should find the hominid fossil within a month or two.

After 742 fragments had been entered in the excavation logbook, on a day when Kees was working at the farthest end of the gorge,

Anna saw why the Masai were collecting so many fossil fragments: Everything they found they were breaking into smaller pieces.

Ikebana is now beginning in the main house.

The announcement boomed into my mother's room. "Come on," she said. "Help me out of this." I eased my arms under her thin legs and swung them over the side of the bed. I pulled the wheelchair from the corner. "I sure wouldn't mind having one of those motorized chairs," she said. "A little remote control. I could zip around like in a go-cart or bumper car. My neighbor has one." She lowered her voice. "But she's a paraplegic."

"The doctor said your hip would be healed within the month," I told her. "It might not be such a wise investment."

"No, no, you're right," she said. "Besides, I won't be alive much longer to use any new gadgets."

I had grown accustomed to this kind of talk and I gave her my usual response, an emphatic *Mother.*

I wheeled her down the corridor and outside and across the parking lot to the main house. A young boy was pulling a wagon in which a younger girl sat sucking on a lollipop. "It cheers me to see children around," my mother said. "At my age, they begin to seem like magical creatures."

"Magical creatures still shouldn't be playing unsupervised in the parking lot," I said.

At the entrance to the house she signaled me that she could take it from there. We said good-bye and I got into my car to return home.

The story she was telling me was about my grandparents. I knew that my grandfather had been an amateur paleontologist before moving to the United States and becoming an actuary. He used to ask special permission from the local zoning board to excavate any cleared area before they laid the foundation. And when Parkinson's palsied him too much to dig, he simply set up a chair whenever ground was being dug. He was an old man in a fedora, seated cross-legged, dignified, a notepad on his lap with a pen stuck through the wire rings, watching intently in case anything of value or significance tumbled out of the tractor's mouth.

I wasn't close to him. He was a serious man, quiet and severe, prone to bursts of extreme anger. Often, he frightened me. Nobody got along with my grandfather except for my grandmother. She had a language for him alone, a language that tolerated and soothed him, that indicated a deep understanding. She supported his petitions and excursions to wrecking sites. Whenever he lost his temper, she would appear by his side, rest her hand on his shoulder, and say *Okay, dear, I'm sure they'll think about what you've said. You're good to offer advice, but now let's let them digest it.* They were not an affectionate couple, rather, their closeness came from a mutual respect. They might have been longtime business partners. And when my grandfather died, my grandmother mourned with composure, with an air of thoughtful regret, as though the world itself had changed.

When I was nine years old and I learned about the time capsule that had been sunk at the World's Fair in 1939—the year I was born—my grandfather encouraged me to dig in our own backyard. "Not just time capsules," he said. "There are all sorts of great things buried all over the world." I set to work, secretly gouging my mother's azaleas and tulips, leaving holes and mounds of soil all over the lawn, until finally I found what I thought was a small bone. I remember how excited I was, imagining I had stumbled on the remains of a dead body, and that I might single-handedly solve a murder. When I told my grandfather about the bone, he hauled himself out back with me and told me to keep digging. After another half hour of digging I had finally extracted an entire skeleton. I handed him each piece and he held them up to the sunlight one by one.

"Well?" I asked. "What is it? They're definitely bones. I know it's a skeleton. Right? It's a skeleton isn't it?"

He dropped the bones on the ground, abandoned them on the mound of loosened soil. "You've found a cat," he said. "You just dug up somebody's pet." He shook his head and laughed. I simply stared at the ground. "Don't be sad," he said as he turned to go back into the house. "Do you know how good it is to know the worthlessness of what you find?"

I put the bones back in the ground and covered them with dirt as best I could, smearing my face with streaks of dirt as I wiped tears from my face. I had disappointed him. He had thought I might have really found something. My grandmother came out a few minutes later.

"My my, what did you find out here?"

"A cat," I grumped. "Just a cat."

"You found a cat! Dear! How exciting. You just started digging and found that? You might have a calling."

My mother, when I came back into the house, secretly christened the dead cat our "spirit pet." We named her Fifi (we never had any real pets) and whenever a strange noise traveled through the house, my mother would wink at me and say, *Fifi is up to her old tricks again.*

But after that I had no interest in digging or exploring. And I had no interest in impressing my grandfather or in asking him about archaeology. I turned to books. It was the one thing he openly disdained—fiction, novels, "make believe"—so it became the one thing I determined to pour myself into. Was it the beginning of my writing career? Perhaps. Defiance quickly turned to love. I loved stories. I have always loved stories.

From my kitchen window, I could still see the spot where, years before, I had unearthed the cat skeleton. I was again living in the house in which I had grown up. A year before my mother broke her hip I had moved back in with her, after my divorce. *Don't just run back to mother* was what I told myself at the time when I was weighing my options. *You're too old for this.* I could have moved anywhere—the Southwest, in particular, had always appealed to me. Or, I could have traveled. I had money. I had always wanted to see the pyramids and Machu Picchu and the Great Wall of China. With the divorce from Charles, my responsibilities vanished. I could go anywhere, do anything. I was no longer responsible for his children (I missed them, especially Madeleine, but understood, as he had said, that "things had to change"). I had no children of my own. I was successfully freelancing for several women's magazines. Freedom, in its own way, was becoming dizzying. But around that time my mother was beginning to complain of back pain, of migraines, and then, out of nowhere, she had a stroke. My father had been dead for two years and she was living alone. I moved in immediately. What else could I do? The fact was: I had no reason to be anywhere else.

For six years, Anna lived in the gorge. There were droughts and dust storms. Torrential rains pounded their tents. Caravans of migrating Masai visited their camp, eager to trade livestock. German missionaries passed through, offering news from Europe, seeking advice in dealing with the natives. Reports reached Anna and Kees of a railroad under construction in the south, of Germans establishing rubber and sisal plantations, of Masai discontent, of small revolts. At times they returned to their tents to find their sheets outside, wet with saliva and jagged with tooth marks. They slept with rifles beside their beds, carried pistols when they stepped out into the night to smoke cigarettes. But there was no defeating the animals. Jackals and hyenas snatched their rations, lions clawed at the sides of their tents. They built their camps over many times, then finally abandoned their tents for Masai *bomas*. These changes, the only events in their lives, were the moments Anna's mind returned to when she thought of those years, the only days that stood out from the daily routine of digging, of searching, to no avail.

Kees—now always "poor Kees," in Anna's mind—continued his efforts. At dawn he set out with his trowel and pick beneath his arm, a large sifter tied to his canvas pack. Rikuni, Tingisha, and Ole followed in procession with their trowels and empty burlap sacks, marching in a slow, familiar line behind Kees along the narrowest and lowest point of the gorge, then spreading out to different and distant survey points, until Anna could no longer see them from the camp. But she could hear them, the rough abrasion of a trowel cutting into the dry earth, the hammering of a pick against rock. Throughout the day, Kees called out to each one: *Rikuni?* The name would echo through the silent calm of the gorge. *Rikuni*—the only sound for miles. Then the echoed answer Anna dreaded: *No find, Meester Kees. No today.* And then, the next. *Tingisha?* It was always the same. Kees dug from dawn until dusk, breaking only at midday to nap in the shade of their hut. During these siestas, Anna would take a trowel and pick and explore the gorge. Kees—despite her arguments—had grown suspicious of the Masai. He said he feared they might steal fossils while he rested. He told her to oversee the site. So for two hours in the middle of the day, beneath the fiercest sun, alone in baked-brown sunlit land, Anna dug and sifted. She exhausted herself. This was her favorite part of the day.

Things had changed for Anna. Dora, on whom she had come to depend, left the camp for months on end. During the winter she returned to her highland *boma*. In spring she left to hunt fowl at Lake Manyara. Once, Dora had even traveled back to England (Anna had begged Kees to let her go with Dora, but he refused). And months later, when Dora returned, she brought books for Kees, new books from Europe on paleontology and archaeology, the books he desperately needed to make sense of his growing pile of fossils. But these books also reported the great discoveries being made in China. Kees grew discouraged. The crates he had built to protect the great fossil had now stood empty for six years. He cursed the gorge, himself. He cursed Anna. For Anna, it seemed, could do nothing to help him. In her attempts to comfort him, Kees suspected pity. After all, Anna had been there to witness his failure, six years of failure, and for that, it seemed, he could not forgive her. If she asked Kees about his day, he answered begrudgingly at first, *No, nothing,* and then with exhaustion, as though she were extracting a confession: *So I've wasted my life? That's what you think? Well, I know it.* And though she wanted to calm him, to ease his sense of failure, how could she believe the decision to come to the gorge had been a good one? With each day that passed, the idea that Kees would find the missing link seemed increasingly impossible. Every morning, watching him tug on his worn leather boots and fasten his Panama hat, Anna felt as though she were watching a gambler sit down to another round of cards; there was a defiant gleam in his eye, a look that said: *Today will be the day to erase all losses.*

The only one who could now buoy Kees up from his sense of failure was Dora. For her, Kees always played the role of adventurer, talking excitedly over dinner about the day's exploration, eager for the next morning's excursion. Oh, Kees, she would say, I admire your determination. She would toast him, ask him question after question about the digs, summoning an encouragement that Anna had long ago abandoned. At these times Anna sat quietly, wishing she had the same enthusiasm—but hadn't her enthusiasm betrayed her? Hadn't her enthusiasm stranded her in the middle of East Africa for six years? For Dora, enthusiasm was nothing more than a piece of candy or a good-night kiss, a gesture of politeness, offered easily and without repercussions. She gave Kees a pat of encouragement and then hiked off to the prairie. She had even been back to Europe! How easy it would be to admire the spirit of this man if his spirit were not my own tether, Anna thought. And how easy it would be for him to admire a woman who had never left behind her family and her country for his own doomed dream.

Without realizing it, they had both come to rely heavily on Dora. She was the audience for which Kees and Anna performed happiness, and with her around Anna almost believed her life was still all right. But whenever Dora left, all efforts at optimism were jointly abandoned, and the quiet and tense routines of digging and eating and reading returned. Without Dora around to encourage him, Kees sulked. Anna grew restless without Dora to confide in. So she occupied herself learning the landscape. In Dora's absence, she began hunting. She quickly mastered the bola and the rabbit stick for small game. In the evenings, she lined up rocks for target practice and within a few months became an excellent shot, better than Dora. She learned to cut a baobab trunk for water, to gather tinder, kindling, and fuel for the evening's fire. She knew to drink kerosene to kill parasites. The further she grew from Kees the closer she grew to the gorge. When Dora returned from England, she was shocked. Darling, she said to Anna, you're practically a native! And Anna then told her the truth: More than ever, she said, I want to go home.

But while home was still impossible, or asking Kees to give up and return home was impossible, Anna continued to make a life in the gorge. Dora had brought several new novels back from England, and Anna read D. H. Lawrence and Somerset Maugham. Both women were mesmerized by *Death in Venice,* which Anna had to translate for Dora. They read the novels over and over, memorizing sections, adding new sentences in certain places. Then Anna suggested they try writing a novel together, and so in the evenings, while Kees sorted through his office, the two women composed aloud the story of a young Dutch bride who comes to Africa.

Toward the end of her sixth year Anna was digging at Area Seventeen, a section of the gorge that Kees had excavated extensively in the first year, but, unable to come up with even a decent rhino fossil, had quickly abandoned. Anna adored the area. One of the lowest points of the gorge, the air there was cooler and held a hint of moisture. On occasion a slow breeze pressed through and unsettled her hair. She went there often. An area that Kees had forsaken, it had become her area, her own portion of the gorge.

That day Anna sat with her skirt hiked up above her knees, shoving her trowel into the ground again and again, scooping aside small piles of dirt and clay. The rhythm soothed her. Kees, as usual, was resting in the hut. Rikuni and Ole had gone to the water hole. Dora, who now sometimes accompanied Anna, had decided to stay inside. Anna was all alone. From where she sat, she could not even see the camp. She could hear only the sound of her trowel cutting into the dry earth, the short dry pants she made breathing the thick air. She was content.

Anna felt a familiar sweat gather above her lip like dew. Dew, she thought. I remember morning dew on a yellow tulip. A field of yellow tulips. When was the last time she had seen yellow? No, she thought. I must fight this. But there is no yellow here, she realized. I have not seen yellow in six years. Brown and green and blue, but no yellow. She closed her eyes and felt a hint of a breeze which she imagined was drifting toward her from a cool wet morning all the way in Maastricht. She could hear the clop of horse hoofs clambering on the cobblestones beneath her childhood window. Maastricht. Maastricht. What is this?

Anna's trowel had struck something hard. As she pulled the trowel back, she saw the chalky edge of what appeared to be a bone pro-truding from the dirt. She grabbed the whisk broom from her pack. She brushed the dirt off—was it a pelvis? Anna wedged her trowel beside it and carefully pried out a triangular piece, the size of her hand. She began whisking it off when she noticed something beside her foot. She inched aside. She whisked over the ground. One, two, three small pieces of bone. Four, five. She thought: vertebrae. Her heart jumped. Anna stepped back slowly and surveyed the ground. Be calm, she told herself. Watch where you step. She knew how easily a fossil could be trampled, crushed, lost forever—Kees had warned her a thousand times. Anna squatted, balancing herself on the tips of her toes, and leaned forward. Lying beside a flint stone, she saw what she had read about in Kees's books, what she had never thought she would see: a hominid tooth. It was a molar, a single molar clinging to the crescent remains of a jaw, a small jaw, too small to be anything but . . . And there was part of a skull. A skull the size of her own head, with hollowed eyes and nose. Anna carefully pried out each piece she found, dusted it off, and set it in the sack of her skirt. It was a fifteen-minute walk back to camp and she would have to go slowly. She thought of screaming to Kees, but what if she were wrong? What if he came all the way out in the middle of his siesta and she had made a mistake? No. It was best to bring the bones to him. She shoved her pick into the ground to mark the area and headed straight for the camp.

The sun was fierce. Sweat streamed down her forehead and dripped into her eyes. She couldn't wipe it away, as both her hands were bal-ancing the edges of her skirt. She blinked to ease the stinging. She stepped carefully, watching the placement of each of her sandals on the rocks, careful not to trip. If she dropped the bones, if something happened, Kees would never forgive her. Should she have left them at the site? No, she could be wrong. And he would think her foolish, making such a fuss over an animal skeleton. What would she say to Kees? *I've found it.* No. *You've found it.* Or: *We've found it.* Or maybe: *Have a look at this, would you?* At the doorway of their hut, Anna pulled aside the canvas and was surprised. Kees's bed was empty. Had he gone to the water hole with Rikuni? No, she thought. She stepped outside and looked up toward Dora's tent. How have I missed this? All this time. Of course he is with Dora. She went back into the hut, set the bone fragments down, and then began climbing up the side of the gorge. It was still possible she would find Dora alone, that Dora would simply tell her where Kees had disappeared to. Then she could confess to Dora what a ridiculous suspicion had seized her. But as she came over the edge, Anna saw beside the tent's entrance a pair of worn leather boots. Kees's boots. She sat for a moment on the ground; it was the same place she had stood the first time she had looked out onto the gorge. From within the tent came the sounds she knew from their own clumsy nights on his cot. No, was the only word that came to Anna's mind. No. Suddenly she felt tired from the climb, from the digging. Exhausted. But she remembered the bones she had left below. She had to get back to them. She crept away from the tent and made her way back down to the camp.

In the hut Anna spread the fragments on her cot. One piece— what she thought was the femur—had somehow broken in two. Now, in the warm shade of the hut, Anna fingered the broken pieces and tried to set them back together. Anna sat down on the cot and then stood up again. She could not leave them out for Kees to find. She could not bring them back to the site and leave them where they had been; he would find them. From beneath her cot, Anna pulled out a stuffed leather suitcase filled with clothing she hadn't worn since she arrived in Africa. Stockings, silk petticoats, lace-fringed knickers, a boned corset. She took each vertebra and wrapped it in a stocking, swaddled the jaw and broken femur with her knickers. The skull—the largest piece—she padded between two petticoats. Then Anna pulled from beneath her cot a lavender hatbox. It had been a wedding present. She removed the brown, feathered cloche she hadn't had occasion to wear since her wedding. Anna placed the wrapped fragments carefully in the hatbox and slid it under her bed. She went outside and looked up toward Dora's. Kees was nowhere in sight. He wasn't expecting Anna back for another hour. She was safe. She held the brown cloche in her hand and thought, There is nowhere to get rid of anything here. Anna grabbed her trowel and pack and headed back toward Area Seventeen to bury her hat.

Shortly after my divorce, after I had moved in with my mother, I began dating a man who had once defeated me for senior class president: Paul Freedman, former debate team captain, former shortest-boy-in-the-class, now successful (but, he reminded me, with alimony and two children to support) investment banker. Paul was recently divorced from Raina Korman, a woman who had also gone to our high school. It was a story we often told at cocktail parties—*to think, all the women in Paul's life were right there in Algebra with him!*—but in actuality, Raina had graduated eight years after us, so the three of us never had neighboring lockers or anything of the sort. And Paul and I had really only been mere acquaintances in high school. Nonetheless, we revisited that election, the campaign, the eager competition of our younger selves, until we had constructed as romantic a narrative of our past as any couple of divorcées.

Raina I knew only from photographs. Because they also had his children in them, early in our relationship Paul had shown me the family snapshots he kept at his house. Raina, with a child holding either hand, had black hair and large brown eyes. She was beautiful. I think I even said as much at the time. But Paul quickly footnoted my impression: She was a woman prone to frequent and unprovoked fits of hysteria. When he told me this, *Well, Raina is hysterical, you know,* he said it as though he were stating her nationality, some benign, unalterable fact. "It's not that I can't accept hysteria," he explained to me. "It's just that I don't understand it. Raina insisted I understand all her rages and fits. There's no getting past something like that." I'm sure there was more to their divorce than that, but I didn't press him. I wasn't ready to get into the details about Charles, so I accepted Paul's explanation. I even enjoyed it. Raina was bonkers. The end. I, however, was the sanest woman he had ever met. He said I had the antidote—stability, maturity. He fussed over my calmness as though it were some exotic sexual technique. "It's amazing," he laughed. "You're like a Zen garden. All serenity. I can feel my blood pressure stabilizing."

Had Paul somehow mistaken my aftershock for calm? That was a time in my life when I was often dazed and thoughtful. People mistook my daydreaming for the silence of a good listener. I spent half an hour getting through any hot beverage. I read the coupon section as if it were a novel. My life had taken an unexpected turn, and I was trying hard to absorb the meaning. Of course, in the end, there was no meaning to be found. Charles and I had divorced. I was supposed to move on. I *was* moving on, slowly. Paul, however, made me realize that I had become, to my surprise, incredibly serene. I had done one, great irrational thing in my life—marrying Charles—and in that act, I now realized, I had exhausted a lifetime of madness. Over our marriage there was so much commotion—between his ex-wife, the university, and my parents—I feared I would never shake the *naughtiness* of it. Did I decide to be as reasonable as possible from that moment on? Was I trying to compensate? I'm not sure. When Charles was offered the job at Duke, it seemed reasonable for us to go. When Charles explained that he didn't want more children, I flirted with the idea of a temper tantrum, or even having an affair (that would have brought things to a furious close), but in the end I calmly acquiesced. Of course, I really did want children. I had always wanted children. But why hadn't we discussed it before the wedding? Or at least before he left Kathryn? Why hadn't it ever occurred to me that he would say no? It was my mistake. I should have known better. And how ridiculous to cause such commotion to be together, to upset so many people, and then separate! Perhaps, Charles suggested, since I hadn't brought it up, it wasn't as important to me as I thought. He said David, Scotty, and Madeleine would also become my family in time. And they did. They were a part of our weekend ritual, a part of barbecues and Sunday brunches, of building model rockets and hiking up Bear Mountain. When Madeleine was diagnosed with scoliosis in middle school, I helped her adjust to her back brace, convinced her that boys would still kiss her and want her. Weekdays they spent with Kathryn in Fairfield, but on weekends I was Mom. Of course, when they left for college, things changed. Perhaps—I had always feared this—it was strange for Madeleine to reach the age I had been when I met her father. Did she imagine herself having an affair with one of her professors? Did it now seem awful to her? Did she say to herself *I don't understand how it could have happened?* It was hard for me to know. Aside from sporadic phone calls, a well-intended ex-step Mother's Day card, and a series of postcards from Madeleine's European trip, Charles's children had drifted from my life.

With Paul came Timothy and Sarah. They were kind and curious. Timothy, nine, with his buck teeth and passion for ant farms. Sarah, seven, with long red hair and a beautiful singing voice. With them, from the beginning, I could relax as I hadn't with Charles's kids, because I knew I couldn't rush their acceptance of me. I simply had to give them time and that, in turn, gave me time.

Paul commuted into the city for work and I would meet him at the train station in the evenings on my way back from visiting my mother. Since I usually needed to wind down after my visits with her, this worked out nicely. We cooked dinner and watched television. We went to parties. Sometimes, if we were giddy, we pulled out our yearbook and made fun of each other's senior photos.

Our sex was good. We discovered a playful kinkiness in talking about our senior year competition. (Once, I even imagined we were sleeping together the night after the election, that I was seducing him to compensate for my loss.) Though he never exactly said it, Paul hinted that Raina had been shy in the bedroom. Shy wasn't my problem. If nothing else, Charles had given me confidence in my sexual performance. Always the professor, Charles liked to discuss all aspects of our lovemaking—techniques, positions, reactions. At times I teased his academic approach, what I liked to call his "sexual revisionism," but in the end it left me comfortable with my abilities. I knew what worked. Of course, there was no reason to assume that Charles and Paul would enjoy the same things. But my desire for confidence outweighed correctness, so quite literally, I stuck to my old tricks. It also pleased Paul that I had had my tubes tied. He alluded to some mysteries involving Raina's diaphragm and a concern that she had been trying to "slip up" and get pregnant a third time. "I love Tim and Sarah," he said. "Don't get me wrong. But there's a time for children and there's a time for yourself. Now, finally, I think is the time for me."

These kinds of issues and discussions were helpful because I was still freelancing at the time. Paul provided good material for several of my Dating After Divorce pieces: "Getting to Know His Children" and "Did I Mention I'm Divorced? Talking about the Exes." Paul was a good sport about it all; even though he appeared with the name Joshua, most of our friends read my articles and recognized him. It

was a joke. A few drunken toasts were made to Joshua, and Paul's secretary, an avid reader of women's monthlies, started writing out his
phone messages to Mr. Joshua. It's difficult to say if he was support-
ing my career or simply enjoying a little extra attention. In the end,
I suppose it makes no difference, because I was happy and Paul was
happy and for a little while longer, at least, I had a career.

Anna said nothing.

After she had buried her hat, after she had returned to the camp,
she found Kees in their hut, lying on his cot with his boots beside
him. His eyes flickered open as Anna entered. Well, Anna? Good day?
Anna smiled, mustering a look of genuine sympathy. Strangely, she
did feel sympathetic. Nothing, she said. But maybe tomorrow, Kees.
Maybe tomorrow. He tugged on his boots, moodily she thought, and
went outside.

Anna made tea, lay down on her cot. She rubbed her feet—calloused and caked with dirt. She massaged oil into the skin on her
neck. Her skin no longer burned and blistered the way it had the first
year from the sun, but it had hardened, tensing as if petrified of the
sun. The oil, she thought, was a last effort to keep up her appearance.
There were no mirrors in the camp. That was what she wanted at
that moment. A mirror. What had six years done to her? Had she lost
all hints of beauty? She could ask Dora: *Tell me how I look.* But how
could she now trust Dora? More than Kees's infidelity, it was Dora's
betrayal that haunted her. She couldn't really blame him for falling in
love with her when she herself had fallen in love with her. But Kees
had taken from Anna the one true friend she had ever had, the one
thing that made this bleak landscape bearable. The thing she now
feared most was this: How to look Dora in the eye?

But when Dora later came down to visit, Anna surprised herself.
She *could* look her in the eye. Anna had feared some sign of sadness

would show in her face. But Dora carried on as usual, chatting casually about Thomas Mann and an idea that had come to her about *Death in Venice*. Something about art and homosexuality. Anna sat in the shade of the dining area, watching Dora across the table. Dora knew nothing. She thought Anna knew nothing. And Anna felt something strange and uncomfortable surge inside her. Was it power? Is that what the box beneath her cot gave her? She looked at Dora and smiled. She offered Dora a bowl of peanuts. What was the insult of her friend and husband hiding their affair compared to what she had done? In the end, she would win.

From the moment she looked Kees in the eye and said: *Nothing. But maybe tomorrow,* Anna had changed. Never before had she had cause to lie. She had thought herself incapable of deceit. Anna had been a woman who blushed when complimented, who bit her nails under stress. But now, Anna began to control her reactions. When at the table Kees said he was disappointed in his digging, Anna showed sympathy, offered him another glass of water. At noon she welcomed Kees back from his dig and set out for her usual two hours, her face trusting and kind. But this change in Anna's character was not sudden; it was the final stage of a transformation that had started when she arrived in East Africa, when she first began walking across the desert. How strange it would be if she ever went back home. What would her parents think? Her friends? *Our sweet Anna. Is that you?*

She did want to go back home. And only the box, she knew, could get her there. She thought about returning the fossil to Area Seventeen, or to another area, letting Kees find it for himself. She could pretend to find it on her afternoon dig. Or, she could leave it for Rikuni or Ole. Yes, if Kees had the fossil, he would be happy and they would be able to go home. Going home was now something within her control. Eventually, she thought, I will have to surrender the box. Eventually.

Anna began to wonder about the extent of the betrayal. There was, of course, the betrayal of Kees and Dora hiding their relations, of keeping things from her. A betrayal of omission. But would Dora—they had known each other six years now—actually look her in the eye and lie? Sitting in the *boma,* Anna said to her one afternoon: Sometimes I feel Kees and I are growing apart. That something is driving us apart. But Dora only threw back her head and laughed. Anna dear, you're both fine. Don't let the heat activate your imagination.

Well then, the box would be Anna's lie, her deception to match and one-up theirs. She held to the deception, nurtured it. She would say to Dora: I think Kees must really be close. She would say to Kees: It must be out there. It has to be out there. Whenever Kees was away from the camp, Anna pulled the box out, unwrapped one of the vertebrae and clenched it in her palm. Or she ran her fingertips over the smooth curves of the mandible. At first she checked on the fossil because she feared it might have disappeared. Then she began taking it out because she found it soothed her. As days and then weeks went by, she realized Kees wouldn't simply happen upon it. Absurdity was on her side. No chance of: *I wonder if there's a hominid fossil in my wife's hatbox.* . . . She did worry, however, that her hat might be unearthed at Area Seventeen. But couldn't that be easily explained through some kind of African heat hysteria? Menstrual dizziness? Or just plain silliness? *Well of course I buried my hat, sweetheart, I had nothing better to do with it* . . .

Anna now liked to imagine what would happen if she told Kees what she had found. Over and over in her mind, she played different scenarios—the best involved her showing Kees the fossil and then smashing it to pieces in front of him. All involved some form of yelling and taunting, Kees falling to his knees and begging forgiveness. But Anna emerged from these fantasies frightened, frightened of her own anger, the way her body tensed with excitement as she thought of hurling her own betrayal in the face of her husband's. Anger. Anger had grabbed hold of her mind and it would not let go.

Dora left again for several months, this time to Dar es Salaam, and Anna, to her surprise, felt no relief. She felt dread. In her mind, Anna had allowed them to couple off. She had surrendered Kees to Dora and kept the fossil for herself. Dora's absence unbalanced this. She had come to count on Dora to entertain Kees, to detract attention from herself. Now Kees's focus returned to her. She resented his nightly visits to her bed. One night disturbed her greatly.

—They say China is a pretty good spot, Kees said.

—Well, what's a good spot isn't so good once everybody has been there.

—China is enormous. Plenty of spots.

—Going to China will cost a lot of money.

—Yes, Kees said. Your friend Dora is quite rich, you know. Did she tell you? Loaded.

—I didn't know, said Anna. I suppose it never came up. I guess her husband didn't get her money in the divorce.

Anna turned to face the wall of the hut.

—Her money has nothing to do with us.

—No, Kees said. But she's lucky. Lucky she didn't have a child. She told me if she'd had a child they wouldn't have granted her a divorce. But I don't think that mattered much to her so long as she could stay here. She would have stayed in East Africa no matter what.

—Maybe, Anna said. *We've* been here a long time, you know. Sometimes I think about going home.

—I have to stay until I get it. It's here. I know it must be. Patience. I've been here too long to give up now. He leaned in toward her and kissed her neck, laid his arm across her.

Anna thought for days about what Kees had said. He would stay until he found his fossil. They would stay. That was it. If she wanted to go home, there was no other way. She would just have to show him the box. She resigned herself to the idea of it, no matter the consequences.

But in the end, their departure was not Anna's doing. Dora returned from Dar es Salaam sooner than expected, hollering for both of them as she approached the camp. She stood in khakis on the cliff above. In her hand was a piece of paper. Listen darlings, she yelled into the gorge. It appears that an angry young man has just killed the heir to the Austrian throne. There's going to be a war and the Germans are giving all of us the boot. Now. The party is over.

This news thrilled Anna. They were finally leaving. They would be sailing away from Africa forever. Only she didn't realize they would all be sailing straight for London, Dora's home.

My mother wanted to know how Charles was doing and I had to tell her that I hadn't heard from him.

"Sometimes a clean break is best," she said. "This Paul sounds very nice."

"He is," I told her. This was my mother's way of reminding me that I had not yet introduced them. But how could I bring him with me on my visits when he was in New York? And weren't these *our* sessions? Private sessions? My mother would never continue the story if Paul were in the room. Besides, bringing Paul to meet her would scream *serious relationship;* it would suggest I anticipated his permanence in my life. But Paul had children who were separate from us and I had a mother. Why couldn't she be separate from us?

"I'm sure you'd like him."

"Well, it doesn't matter whether or not *I* like him. I didn't like Charles and you were happily married to him for twenty years."

It was true. My mother had never particularly liked Charles. But I had never viewed this as a flaw in his character or in her judgment. It seemed reasonable. Charles was much closer to my mother's age than to mine and it was difficult for her to adopt a maternal attitude toward him. She saw him as a colleague or peer, not a son-in-law. He never fumbled around her when he came to pick me up the way I imagine most boys do around their girlfriends' parents. He was a man and he came and shook hands with my mother and asked what she thought of the House Un-American Activities Committee hearings. I think she liked him, or at least accepted him and tried to like him, until I told her we wouldn't be having children.

I met Charles in 1957 at Barnard. He was a professor of Romantic Literature. He was my professor. He was married. He had three children. The catalogue of obstacles is clear to me now, but at the time they blurred, disappeared. I was young. He was simply a man I thought I loved. Simply Charles.

I once had lunch with a woman my age who had married her former boss. It was strange and gratifying to hear her description of what had happened: innocent flirtation, flirtation reciprocated, a gradual exploration of the limits, and then, one superficially accidental moment alone that changed the course of everything. That's how it began with Charles, but not how or why I fell in love with him.

There was one ridiculous episode early in our affair in which my diaphragm (it was my first one) got stuck. It was a frightening incident and I will say, simply, that Charles behaved heroically. He was as calm and gracious as though he had lost a sock under my bed. Is this the way everybody falls in love? I had only been with two other men—Douglas Metcalf from high school (actually, I later learned, on the debate team with Paul) and a Columbia sophomore majoring in economics. They had been embarrassed and awkward, rough in their haste. So how could Charles, with his calm, with his kindness in the face of my embarrassment, fail to seduce me?

We were married the June after I graduated. The university asked Charles to resign. Kathryn, his wife, went to live with her family in Montreal. (Charles had once suggested that he and Kathryn had initially married because she needed citizenship, though it seems clear now that they really did love each other.) I have always admired and pitied Kathryn. She was a stoic woman, permitting Charles to carry on an affair with me because she believed in standing by him while he got something out of his system. How absurd it must have seemed to her, beautiful, gracious, strong Kathryn, that a young coed could take her husband. Even I didn't really think the relationship would threaten their marriage. She had me over for dinner, went for weekend walks with me and Charles as if I were a visiting niece or cousin. She believed courage and tolerance would win and I admired her for that, and perhaps wanted her to win.

But did I say things against her at the time? Did I tell Charles that maybe she allowed the affair because she didn't love him enough? Didn't love him the way I did? I remember how sorry I felt for her when Charles told me they were more like brother and sister than husband and wife, that friendship, not romance, was the essence of the relationship. At that time, loyalty and friendship seemed good, but somehow incomplete. A consolation prize. I was determined to have romance. But how often I have thought since then of what it would be simply to have a best friend. To rely on a man as if he were a brother. To tease each other about sexual failure, crushes on movie actors and colleagues, gray hairs and crow's-feet. I would think about these things constantly once Charles returned to Kathryn.

Kathryn had remained in our life. She returned from Montreal and bought a house in Fairfield. For the first few years, she brought the children on Fridays and picked them up on Sundays. She was always courteous to me, which, with time, made my sense of guilt accumulate rather than subside. Then, when the children left for college,

Kathryn called one day and said she had decided to move abroad. There was a prolonged and adventurous tour through Portugal, Spain, and France with a group of divorcées, and then she settled down in Switzerland. She sent postcards and telephoned early in the morning. She flew back for David's graduation and Madeleine's last back operation. But for the first time since Charles and I had been married, I felt her absence. She had moved away, disappeared. I believed something, a chapter in our lives, so to speak, had come to a close.

At first, Charles and I experienced the difficulties most May-December couples face. The gap in our ages was obvious to anyone who met us. Charles was already graying and developing a slight waist-bulge. I still had smooth skin, a loud, careless laugh, and a habit of wearing short skirts. People often imagined us in the act of sex. My closest friends confessed they couldn't help themselves. Even my mother wanted to know what it was like. Perhaps it was in defiance of this that Charles and I developed a certain ostentatious way together, an instinctive kissing and clutching in public, and an almost exaggerated comfort in private. Sex was frequent and furious. It was as if we were constantly reminding ourselves *This is normal. We are healthy.* It was at this time I started publishing my first articles. With Charles's permission, I wrote my first series, *The Younger Woman,* discussing the difficulties of our relationship. Of course, when I wrote those, I didn't understand what serious difficulties still lay ahead for us.

As Charles (and I) got older, I found I had to take great pains to let him know I still found him attractive. Little things—wearing negligees, stroking his thigh under the table at dinner parties, even hiding under his desk in one case—became a necessity. At times it seemed foolish, like some elaborate game of role playing. But I knew he was afraid I was no longer interested in him. He complained of balding, arthritis, bursitis. Once, he pulled a back muscle during our lovemaking. "Why don't you take a lover," he said, as he pulled himself from me in obvious pain. "You need a lover. I'm too old for you."

"You're being silly," I said. "Let me help you."

"You always wanted children? In a few years you'll have the equivalent of an infant."

"Stop it," I said. "I'm not going to take a lover."

"Well I'm not young, you know."

"You're still young."

"No, I'm not. And I can't pretend I'm young. I don't want to pretend. I want to get old and feel good about it."

"And I don't make you feel good about it?"

"You're still young," he said, almost crying. "Sometimes being around youth makes people feel younger. Sometimes it makes them feel old, old and wrong. You know "The Miller's Tale"? I feel like the gross old miller."

"No, you're not," I said.

"You haven't even read Chaucer," he said. "You've got to stop trying to please me."

We managed. Humor, temporarily, saved us. Charles always warned he was on the verge of life support or intravenous feeding or diapers. He began referring to himself as Old Man. He called me Little Girl. I described to him the young lover I would take. "He's got to be no older than fifteen. After fifteen the skin starts to sag. We can't have that." I admit, it *was* difficult watching him get older. He experienced pains I knew nothing of, feared crossing streets too slowly, tripping on things left lying around the house. But it did make me feel young. With Charles, I was always the baby. Young simply because I was younger than he was. It wasn't until we divorced and I was left with the rest of the world, with Paul, with people my age, that I realized suddenly, I myself had become old.

One night, Charles and I had a sushi dinner with Terrence and

Theresa Blakely—Terrence was a colleague of Charles's at the New School. Both Terrence and Theresa were young, much closer to my age than to Charles's, and Charles had become a sort of mentor to Terrence. This dinner was our first since the arrival of their baby— Theresa had had a difficult pregnancy and had been bedridden the last four months. I had stopped by once or twice to say hello, but this was the first time in months the four of us were out together. After dinner we sat sipping our green tea. When the waitress brought the check, Charles immediately palmed it. When Terrence offered to pay, Charles dealt out his usual jovial insults—"You might be given the boot any day now" and "Don't spend all your allowance in one place, young man." Terrence teased back—"So long as it's not all your Social Security money!" Charles laughed and slid his credit card on top of the check and handed it to the waitress. After the waitress returned with the bill Charles leaned into it and signed. He handed it back to the waitress. Our conversation had taken a quick turn to the issue of the stock market. "Anna has heard this a million times but I'll tell you both we're in for another crash. Not as bad as '29. But a significant crash."

Theresa shook her head. "They have all sorts of government checks on that now to prevent another crash. It might take a dip but I don't think it would be anything you could call a crash."

"You'll see," Charles said. "You can't have a popular knowledge attitude about these things. Talk to the economists. They'll tell you the same thing." Charles said this kindly, but I could tell it put Theresa off. Charles had a habit of always playing the senior professor, of treating any other opinion as though it were the opinion of a mere amateur. It was hard to talk him out of this behavior, because most of the time Charles *was* more informed on most issues than the people with whom he was speaking. I once asked him if there would be any harm in letting people think he respected their opinions. It might make people a little fonder of him, I suggested. He said he wasn't, at this point in his life, going to start humoring people. What Charles couldn't see was that people like Theresa were also humoring him.

"Well, I'm sure you're right," Theresa said, glancing toward Terrence in a way that suggested they would later have a recap of the evening and of Charles's domineering behavior. She smiled at Charles in a way that said: I am kind to you for the sake of my husband.

Terrence made peace. "Charles is always right. Haven't I told you that a million times? I've no doubt he knows who really murdered JFK. Right, Charles?"

As Charles was about to answer, the waitress came over and whispered something in Charles's ear. Then she set the check back on the table. Charles shook his head and said, "No." Our conversation fell quiet.

"I think you made a mistake," the waitress was saying as quietly as possible, "and I didn't want you to get home and be upset. See?"

"Problem, Charles?" Terrence said kindly. "I've got my Visa right—"

"No," Charles said.

"Really, Charles, I'd be happy to."

"We're fine." He turned curtly to the waitress. "We're all set."

"I'm sorry," she said. "I just thought you made a mistake."

At this point I leaned forward and glanced at the check. It was difficult to read upside down, particularly with Charles's handwriting, but I could see that Charles had written the tip amount in the wrong column and instead of $15.00, it was written as $150.00, and he had added it as that amount. I suddenly realized that he didn't have his glasses with him. Terrence and Theresa did their best to keep up a conversation that ignored what was happening with Charles: "Yes, I'd say the stock market is . . ."

"Sweetheart," I whispered. "Do you want me to fix it?"

He shook his head without looking up at me.

"I just think . . . it looks like the decimal is off."

"The decimal's fine," he said, handing the check to the waitress in a forceful way. "Everything is fine. If you don't want a tip, I'll start all over and I won't leave a tip."

"I'm sorry," she said. "Thank you, sir."

"Did you forget your glasses?" I asked.

"Let's go."

We said good night to Terrence and Theresa, who, in an effort to ignore the obvious tension in the air, offered the most jubilant good-bye I had ever seen. We hailed a cab and got into the backseat. I was silent, waiting for Charles to make the first move, to apologize for snapping, or to explain what had happened. Instead, he said: "The best thing for us now is a divorce. For all concerned."

And that was the end of it. Kathryn, who had been living in Switzerland for the previous four years making documentary films, suddenly came back to the States. It was as if for eighteen years she had simply stepped down the hall and lent me her husband. *Oh, thanks for looking after Charles, but we'll be fine on our own now.*

I said good-bye to Charles. I said good-bye to his children. I moved in with my mother. I met Paul.

I grew old myself.

Geachte Mevrouw Van Mannerling:

The telegram you sent to your parents has just recently been forwarded to my attention and I regret to inform you of what will no doubt, after your long absence, be some terribly shocking news. Your mother, after a prolonged and noble struggle against the consumption, passed on almost one year ago now. Your father nursed her with great tenderness and compassion that I feel privileged to have witnessed firsthand. He, however, passed on two months ago due to what can be described only as inordi-

nate sadness at your mother's death. In his final weeks your father expressed a concern at your absence and, in anticipation of his own death, I believe, arranged for my firm to inform you of their deaths and assist you with all necessary issues of property and estate. Unfortunately, at the time we had no way of reaching you. It was a great relief to learn that you are safe and healthy in London. Though this news will probably deter your plans of returning to Maastricht, in case you still intend to visit I should warn you that the war, as you must already know, has greatly interrupted ferry services from the isles to Rotterdam and even Zeebrugge. Any attempt to travel here in the near future I would consider inadvisable as well as unnecessary. As concerns your father's estate, I will soon telegram to this same London address (please inform me in the event of any change) all details for transfer which will be necessary to you. Per his request, we have already consolidated the estate and you need only supply us with the account information for transfer of assets. Do contact our firm if you have any questions.

> *Once again, my sincerest regrets,*
> *Mr. Pieter Noteboom*
> *Noteboom, Kastorp & VanDrooge*

The lavender hatbox now sat in the bottom of a closet in a London flat. It had been fastened with a piece of twine for the journey. It had been dented and scratched by Anna's suitcase, Kees's crates, and Dora's backpack as it was shoved into the crowded cargo bays of boats and carriages. Anna never looked in it now. She never unwrapped the vertebrae or the mandible, never fingered the fragments. She lay in bed, seized by sporadic sweats, chills, and dizziness. The change in weather had made them all ill. The London air seemed unbearably thick and wet to Anna. The rain—it had rained for weeks—was frightening. Anna had trouble sleeping with the sounds of the city. Having arranged a dig expedition in Dover, Kees was gone much of the time. He wrote a paper on the gorge, cataloguing the animal fossils he had found, but was unable to publish it. He read reports of the finds in Java and China and spoke of planning an expedition there as soon as the war subsided. Dora visited frequently, but was now living with her sister and sleeping with a geologist at the University. She rarely visited when Kees was home.

One evening when Anna was alone in the flat, lying on the divan, someone knocked at the door. She slowly pulled herself up and steadied herself before opening it. A man was looking for Kees. He was a young Australian with short-cropped brown hair and a reassuring smile. He wore an angled fedora. His name, he said, was Raymond Gray. He explained he was interested in digging in the East Africa or Kenya area. He was hoping to discuss with Mr. Van Mannerling where, exactly, he had been digging and what he had found.

—Kees won't be back until later, Anna said. Or tomorrow. Or maybe the day after. He's in Dover, digging. There's a site there now. Anna was seized by nausea and breathed deeply. I'm sorry, she said. I'm not well.

—Can I get you something?

—No, I'll be fine. It's just a little illness.

—Have you seen a doctor?

—It's the change in weather. Too much rain here.

—I don't wish to intrude, Mrs. Van Mannerling, but I've studied medicine. I'd be happy to look at you.

—I just need to sit.

Anna moved away from the door toward the divan and the man grabbed her arm to steady her.

—How long have you felt ill?

—Weeks.

—And . . . have you had your monthly menstruation recently?

Anna lay back on the divan and closed her eyes. She sighed.

—There are tests, right? To be certain?

—Yes. A doctor can tell you for certain. I'd be happy to fetch you a doctor. Your husband would want you to see a doctor.

—You can fetch me one, but not right now. Tomorrow. Yes. You can do me a favor and get me a doctor tomorrow.

—Absolutely. And you'll do me the favor of letting your husband know I'm eager to speak with him.

—I'll do you a favor, Anna said. You know I was there? For six years I was there with Kees. I can tell you what is there. I can help you, she said.

Anna turned on her side to face the man, and then she spoke.

She was pregnant. As promised, her Australian friend had brought a doctor and the doctor had confirmed it. When Kees returned two days later, she told him. To her surprise, he rejoiced.

—A baby! We're really going to have a baby?

—Yes. That's what the doctor said.

—This is good for us. Yes. This is what we need. A baby! My God. I need this. I need something to change. It's the stagnation of it all that's been killing me. Parents! We'll be parents! He hugged her gingerly. You must take care of yourself now. You have to ask the doctor what you're supposed to eat and you must rest as much as possible.

—At least, Anna said, I'm not dying. I thought I was dying.

Kees continued to make long trips to his excavation site. In his absence, Raymond made several visits to Anna. They became friendly. Now that Dora was busy with her geologist friend, Anna had only Raymond to talk to. They spent afternoons chatting over tea and biscuits. He was eager to explain all the China and Java discoveries to her, things that Kees, perpetually gloomy, had refused to talk about. Anna was interested. She asked questions. He brought her books, articles. She learned more about fossils from Raymond than she had in the six years in Africa with Kees. But she never told Kees about Raymond or his visits. She never told him that she spoke with anyone about East Africa and where they had dug. As Raymond visited more and more frequently, as he took her for short walks around the neighborhood for fresh air and exercise, as people smiled knowingly when they passed, Anna feared that Kees would grow suspicious.

The night Kees suddenly blasted into their flat she thought he had heard something, that he was about to accuse her.

—I thought you were staying at the site for a few more days, she said. What's wrong?

A grin, a grin such as she had never seen on him, spread across his face. She was looking at a different man. A happy man. A satisfied man.

—Anna, I'm going to be famous.

Kees had found the oldest hominid fossil. He made every headline in the world. Within days, he was invited to lectures and panels on paleontology and archaeology. He was *the* expert. He was a hero.

All those years had paid off, he told Anna. But more than anything, the baby, the baby growing each day inside of Anna, had brought him the best luck of his entire life. It was a sign, he told her. A good sign.

The rest, I think you know.

My mother was tired. She had talked longer than usual. Already it was dark outside—only five o'clock, but just weeks before the winter solstice. I offered to take her outside for air or even a ride in the car, but she refused. "It's freezing out there. Don't you watch the weather reports?" She had been in bed all day. Her hip had healed completely and she was able to walk, but now fatigue had grabbed hold of her and was pulling her down, limb by limb, back into her bed.

"Can I get you something? What about dinner?"

"Darling, I'm simply going to read. Read until I fall asleep. That's all I want right now." She insisted I leave, said she needed nothing from me, so I got into my car. I had called Paul at work two hours earlier—midtale, I could tell she was slowing down, that we would run late—to let him know I wouldn't make it to the station. He said he'd just call a cab. I told him then to wait for me and I'd fix dinner when I got home. But when I was finally sitting in my cold car, buckling my seat belt, I realized that the story had tired me as well. I was too tired to even think of boiling water. I drove straight to Reed's Deli, one of the few places in town with a hot counter for takeout. Others, it seemed, had had the same idea—there was a long line at the deli counter and I skimmed a magazine while I waited. The air was thick with the smell of grease and roast chicken. Soon I made my way up to the Plexiglas barrier and indicated to a boy in a dirty white apron the dishes I wanted. I was pointing to a vat of mashed potatoes when I heard Sarah calling me.

"Anna! That's Anna!"

I turned and saw that Timothy and Sarah, bundled like astronauts, had entered. Their cheeks were flushed from the cold air. Behind them came a slender woman with a black fur neck muffler and a black ski cap. She followed the children in and took a place at the end of the line. It was Raina.

I smiled at Sarah and returned my attention to the boy behind the counter. I picked out a whole roast chicken, a side of Caesar salad, some mashed potatoes. I made my way down the counter toward the register, with my back to Raina. I couldn't see Timothy or Sarah, but I was sure I could hear Sarah whispering, whispering to her mother. Was she telling Raina who I was? Did Raina already know? I couldn't decide if it was rude for me to ignore her or rude for me to presume she had any interest in meeting me. I paid the woman behind the register and decided on some sort of eye-contact, something friendly, honest. A smile that offered a simple hello. After all, I had nothing to hide.

I lifted the warm bag of food from the counter and turned to see that Raina was watching me with interest. She had removed her hat. Her hair—black and long and tousled—now framed her face. With one hand, she was stroking Sarah's head. Timothy was on her other side with her purse slung over his shoulder.

"Anna?" Her voice was softer and more timid than I had expected.

"Yes," I said, moving closer to her but maintaining my angle toward the doors. Did she want to chat? "It's nice to meet you."

"The children have talked about you. And Paul, too. It's really nice to meet you."

"You, too," I said.

"Paul has given me all assurances about you, but it's nice to be able to put a face on someone they spend time with."

She made it sound as though I might be a child molester. "Of course. I understand."

I glanced down at Sarah and Timothy and they offered me mild smiles. Even at that age they understood who I was, the position I held. They clutched their mother's hands and legs, knowing it was the same as telling her they loved her, of letting her know they had never betrayed her.

"I don't want to keep you. I just wanted to say hello. It looks like you've got some dinner to bring back to Paul."

"Good night," I said, offering slight waves to the children before I left. I sat in the car for a minute and breathed deeply. Hysterical? She seemed the furthest thing from hysterical. But I suddenly felt hysterical. I pulled the seat belt across my chest and buckled it tight as though it were the only thing that would keep me from floating away. I missed Charles. I missed the life I had once thought I would have with Charles. Where had that gone? When had it slipped away from me?

I started the engine, turned up the radio, and drove around town until I had exhausted myself. Then I went to Paul's house.

"What is all that damned buzzing?" I asked.

This was several nights later, at Paul's. It was a Saturday and Timothy and Sarah were sleeping down the hall. The bedroom was dark. I was curled beneath the blankets, on the verge of sleep. Paul had just turned off the bathroom light and slipped into bed.

"What's the one thing you have never tried?"

"You didn't."

"Just relax."

Yes, I had told him I had managed to go forty-five years without ever using a vibrator. I had meant it more as a joke—bragging about an absurd achievement—than a plea. Couldn't he tell I wasn't in the mood?

"Come on, Paul."

"I want your first time to be with me. This will be a first for both of us."

"But it sounds like a buzz saw."

"No buzz saw sounds like this."

"Like a buzz saw outside the house then. Or a lawn mower."

Paul flicked on the bedside light and examined the vibrator.

"It has different settings. There. See? Low. That's better."

"You'll wake Timothy and Sarah."

"They can't hear it from here. They're fast asleep."

"They can hear it if they stand outside the door."

"They're not standing outside the door."

"What if they get up to go to the bathroom?"

"Look, let me worry about my children. Come on. It'll be fun."

"You know what it reminds me of? It reminds me of your god-damned Interplak. I'm not going to make love to an electric tooth-brush."

"All right," he said, flicking off the power. The room was suddenly silent. He turned toward me kindly. "It was a bad idea. I'm sorry. Lis-ten," he said, settling his head on the pillow. "How's your mother doing? Do you want to talk about your mother?"

It was an honest mistake. Paul thought I was sad about my mother. And it was easier to let him believe that than to tell him the truth. How could I tell him that I didn't want to be a woman who makes love to a machine? That it foreshadowed aloneness, need? That I wasn't yet ready to concede to a future—did I foresee it or create it?—in which I lay in bed alone at night, longing for my past, for the selves I had lost along the way, hoping for one brilliant mo-ment in which my body could trick my mind into bliss. That it would make me cry.

"Did you know my grandparents spent years in East Africa?" This was the first time I had mentioned my mother's story to Paul. "That they were archaeologists? My mother has told me stuff about them I never knew."

"That's amazing," he said, readjusting his pillow. "I remember when I was twelve and I found out my grandfather had been a Mar-coni wireless operator. He was one of the first men ever to send out the CQD. I thought he was the greatest man in the world."

"Well, do you ever think that our lives would disappoint them? When you think that they had so much to fight against? Wars and famines. Disease. Everybody worked and saved for the future, for the next generation. They crossed the whole fucking ocean to move to a place they had never seen, to make a new life, a better life."

"I think my grandfather would be proud of me. I'd like to think that. My parents are certainly proud of me."

"But it's so silly sometimes. Here we are, playing with vibrators in the middle of the night."

"Anna, I'm sorry."

"Don't be. It's not that." I turned my back toward him. "Do you know what my grandmother did? She stole, and I mean outright stole, one of the world's most important fossils." I was talking into the darkness now, to the night, to some empty space beyond me. "She just packed it up in some stockings and skirts and tucked it away for years."

"You're kidding me."

"No, I'm not."

"What did she do with it?"

"I don't know. She kept it. She threw it out."

"That's awful," Paul said. "You can't just steal stuff like that. The government has a right to it. They keep track of stuff like that. There are commissions. Committees. You know. Hhmm, Anna?"

I felt a sickness tugging inside me. I had surrendered the one thing I had that still felt like a secret, one of the few things in my life that belonged to me. I wanted it to be something wondrous and shared between us, a common knowledge of something bigger, something beyond us. But how could I expect him to understand what it meant to me?

"Go to sleep," I said. "I'm just kidding you. Sometimes you're too gullible."

The famous Dover Skull, the skull the whole world thought was the missing link, was actually the jaw of an ape, stained and filed and placed near a relatively young human head. It was buried in the ground in northern Dover. It was thought to be over one million years old. My grandfather, Kees Van Mannerling, found it. After all his years of fruitless digging, he found the one thing in the world that could bring him unparalleled success, and eventually, even greater shame. The publicity of the find was doubled, three years later, by the publicity of the hoax. This failure would change him forever. Always, people would suspect him. Did he know the truth? Did he plant it himself? He, in turn, would suspect everybody. And for reasons he would never understand, he would always, shamefully, be suspicious of his wife. Of course, it was the most ridiculous thing in the world to imagine! Anna was in London. And pregnant! Whenever his mind was drawn to this strange suspicion of her, he would reason himself out of it. Years later, in the United States, when she was a schoolteacher, and he had a job studying actuarial tables, he would, for the first time in years, bring up the Dover Man incident. He would mention it to her only so he could mention, finally, this bizarre fear. *Anna, did you . . . ?* He would laugh when he said it and try to pass it off as a joke. But she would know. Would understand that he meant every bit of suspicion toward her. But this, of course, would seem the funniest thing in the world to her, growing funnier each year, because she was suspected only of the thing she had not done.

To this date, nobody has determined who was responsible for the hoax of the Dover Skull.

On January 16, 1980, my mother died in her sleep. I had visited her the day before and it was clear she knew she wasn't well. She lay in bed and stared out the window. She squeezed my hands every few minutes. After I brought her a glass of water for her pills, she said: "Your grandmother's hatbox is still in the attic. I've never opened it. But it's still up there. It's yours."

I rubbed her hands and said, "Fine, fine. If I find it, what do you want me to do with it?"

"You'll find it," she said. "And I don't know what you should do with it. I never knew what to do with it. Now it's yours to do with what you like."

As I kissed her forehead before leaving, she said to me: "It's very hard to live without your father."

Paul came to the funeral with me. Strange as it sounds, that was one of our last good days together. In my need we connected better than ever. Loss, I suppose, brought out the best in us. He loved me. I let him love me. I feared nothing between us. We exalted in those last moments, hoping they might sustain us. But after another few months we parted.

It wasn't until the spring that I made my way up to the attic to sort through my mother's belongings. I had been busy with the logistics of settling her estate. Also, the attic was too cold to move around in during the winter. But now it was warm and damp. The smell of mothballs cut into my nostrils. Old cobwebbed weather vanes sat propped against the walls. Boxes labeled and relabeled, sealed with four different brands of tape, one representing each decade. Folding chairs for parties that were never thrown or for those last few guests that never arrived. An open box of the Most Improved trophies they always awarded me for being so clumsy. In the corner, by the window, a round box that would fit a hat.

I expected something grander, perhaps a combination lock on the latch or a warning sign. But it was just an off-white (I suppose the color faded) silk hatbox. This was it, though. Nearby sat a box stuffed with dusty books: *The Origins of Humankind, The Magic Mountain, Lady Chatterly's Lover, Fossil Evidence, A Beginner's Guide to Paleoanthropology, The Dover Forgery, Morphology and Anthropology, The Collected Works of William James, In Defense of Women.* On top of the pile sat a torn copy of a 1950 *National Geographic* with the line "A Celebration of Discovery," and a photograph of a man identified as world-famous paleontologist Raymond Gray on the cover. I wiped the dust from the hatbox with my sleeve. On top of a bundle of withered fabric was a piece of notebook paper that looked like an abandoned grocery list:

Australopithecus—Olduvai Gorge, 1913
1) femur
2) tibia
3) mandible
4) skull
5) vertebrae—4

I carefully unwrapped the largest, and heaviest, bundle. A yellowed lace petticoat, a red scarf, and then an embroidered napkin. In my hands I held a partial skull. It was smooth, almost oily to the touch. The hollowed out eyes and nose disturbed me. I quickly covered it again with the napkin and the red scarf and then folded the petticoat around it. I pulled out several of the smaller bundles and in each one there was small piece of bone.

When Kathryn died four years ago, I got a letter from Charles:

> *Anna:*
> *I realize late in my life that I have never known the right thing to do. I have simply done what I had to and hoped that it never hurt anybody. But I did hurt you. I stole things from you I could never return.*
> *I have no answers. Only love for you.*
> *I ask not for your forgiveness, but for understanding.*
> *   —Charles*

I wrote:

> *Charles:*
> *I am not the same person you once knew and you are not the same man I married. But somewhere I'd like to believe those two people, if not us, are still together.*
> *Is it safe to send them a blessing from us?*
>
> *—Anna*

Charles died one year later.

There is a part of my grandmother's story that I think about often since my mother's death. It is this:

One day, perhaps while she is still in England, Anna wakes up, she puts on her robe, her slippers, she steps out of bed, and she thinks to herself, *I have made a mistake.* The fossil, the skeleton that she has been hiding for months in her hatbox, has become a statement she can't find a way to retract. She will carry this secret from England to the United States, for the length of her entire life. She forgives her husband. Yes. She forgives him. She cannot hate; it is too tiring to hate. But now, more than ever, she cannot tell him what she has. Her silence is not to punish but to protect. If he knew what his own wife had taken from him! She thinks of the baby. At this point I imagine it is still growing inside her. Boy or girl, she doesn't know. She only knows that if she can protect this baby, raise this child, she will have an ally. She will have someone to tell her story. It will be a long time, but she will wait, wait until the time is right. Anna feels her hard, swollen belly. She whispers into it: *I will have something tremendous to tell you . . .*

I am now living in a managed care facility. (Not the same one my mother lived in—the manager there was sued for embezzlement and the facility declared bankruptcy ten years ago.) I had a stroke last year—a mild one—but I decided it would be best to be in a different community and finally to get out of my mother's house. My childhood room had started to depress me. My mother's belongings were like shadows, following me everywhere. So I called a realtor and sold the house. Before I moved out I took care of the bones.

In the backyard of the house, near the spot where I once, years ago, found the remains of a cat, I buried a box. In this box I placed the skeleton my grandmother found in Africa along with some of her letters, her original list from the hatbox, the *National Geographic* I found in the attic, and several pages describing the history, as my mother told it to me, of the fossil. On the top of the box I wrote *For a child.* Some would criticize my choice, argue that the fossil needs to be in a museum, or with the proper scientists. But it will always be in someone's possession, always passed from hand to hand, generation to generation. I have simply chosen a set of imagined hands, the hands of a younger me whose whole life might have been different if I had really found, beneath the azaleas and the tulips and mounds of dirt, something wonderful. The couple who bought the house said they plan to have children. In time, perhaps I will read in the paper of what an amazing thing a little girl found in her backyard. And I will know that I gave it to her.

I am thoughtful these days, perhaps because I have so much time on my hands. I wrote my last article, "Surviving a Stroke," and wasn't able to sell it. The editors told me as kindly as possible that the readership of their magazines is young and not really looking for reminders of what lies ahead. I don't need the money so I've stopped for now. I read a lot, more than I did even as a student. And, when I can, I talk to people. That is what's better about being here rather than still being at home. Here, there are always people around.

A large man named Hubbard cleans my room once a day. He also cleans vomit or blood or the wetted sheets for other patients (I am on the younger side of the curve here). He takes the train every day from Bridgeport, says he hates driving. He has three children at home and he moves like a father, attentive, in charge. I like to watch him walking through the corridors, moving slowly and serenely in his white pants and shirt, his thick black arms pushing his metal cart down the carpeted hall. Sometimes I can hear him when he's cleaning up someone's mess, shouting down the embarrassed apologies of the offender. He is a kind man.

Sometimes I think about Charles. I think about the night years ago when he helped me retrieve my diaphragm. I think about how I fell in love with him at that moment, how he seemed so good to me, good for me. He seemed safe. Could I have known then that every man, after fifteen years of marriage and three children, is simply more comfortable with his own body, and with a woman's body, than a seventeen-year-old boy clumsily trying to lose his virginity?

On occasion, I share thoughts such as these with Martha, one of the nurses: "I fell in love with my first husband because he helped me get my diaphragm out." It amuses her to hear somebody my age talk about sex. *Ms. Langely, you'll corrupt me!!*

Ikebana is out of fashion. Crocheting holds no interest for me. There are nice concerts and music classes, but they are poorly attended since many of the residents are hard of hearing. My hearing is still good, and my sight, too, thank goodness. I can read to my heart's content. I have finally made it through Herodotus and Marco Polo, though there is no one here to discuss them with.

A German shepherd named Teplo comes around twice a week to visit the residents and he is quite popular. I never thought I liked dogs, never thought I would enjoy having a pet of my own, yet this drooling furry creature is admittedly the best part of my week. He comes and sits beside me as if he belonged to me. He is patient with me as I learn to stroke his head and his ears, trying to understand what he likes. I suppose they have trained him to behave this way, taught him to play *loyal* as other dogs play *dead*. He is a professional, after all. No doubt they teach him those looks of love and devotion. But I don't really mind. I eagerly await his visits. At times I'm sorry that I never had a dog of my own. Or a cat. I can no longer remember why I never had one, but that may just be memory going. Anyway. Who has time for all these regrets?

Mrs. Ingersoll, one of the older residents, a woman originally from Norway, believes that Teplo is God. As far as most people here are concerned, Mrs. Ingersoll is pretty far gone. I don't really know if she believes this of all dogs or simply of Teplo. But she makes quite a fuss whenever she sees him. When she sees the dog leave my side, she shouts at me from her wheelchair, shakes her finger at me. "I hope you have shown respect! The Lord has just visited you."

What a mad and beautiful thing to wish for.

SCOTT ANTWORTH

PEN Prison Writing Committee

THE TOWER PIG

"Caine!" one of the East Wing hogs called after me through the crash and clamor of lunch release. I couldn't even see the guy, lost as he was in the flood of inmates surging past him for the chow hall, but from the tone of his voice he had to be a block officer. Rookie guards actually take classes: Speaking with Authority 101.

"Caine!" he barked again because I was acting like I'd not heard him, trying to be just another face in the stampede. "Stop by the SOC office. Captain Kruller wants to see you!"

Subtle, I thought. Tell me that when I've got two hundred cons packed around me to wonder what business I've got at the Security Operations Center on a Saturday afternoon. No one goes to the SOC office for good news. Standard convict paranoia—who's ratting who out—is enough to get at least some of them thinking.

"Spell my name right when you give your statement," my neighbor,

Hodgson, chortled from deep inside his walrus neck as he lumbered down the stairs.

"Sure." I sneered at his back. "You spell it how, d-i-c-k-h-e-a—," I began, but he was already gone.

Captain Kruller was six feet of spit-shine and razor-creased blues with a leathery hide looking like it'd been cut from a rhino's ass and superglued over an erector set. He kept his Marine citations and ribbons velvet-backed and under glass on his office wall to let everyone know he'd perfected his bearing on Paris Island and not behind the walls of Thomaston.

"Come in, Caine," he said. Before I showed up, he'd pulled up my file and glanced at my mug shot. "Take a seat," he said, to give us the illusion of familiarity. I'd been sitting on folding chairs and wooden stools for the better part of a decade. My ass didn't know what to make of Naugahyde and cushions.

"I've got some bad news," John," he said. Suddenly we were on a first-name basis.

"Who was it?" I asked.

"Your grandmother passed away yesterday morning," he said, his hands flat and precisely spaced on the blotter in front of him. "I'm sorry," he added as if such sentiments were foreign to him.

"Thank you," I muttered, only half believing I'd said it. Pleases and thank-yous pass between cops and inmates like bricks through a keyhole.

"You're taking it well."

I said that I'd known it was coming. She'd been sick for a long time. Truth is, I wasn't about to show him anything. Pain, joy, worry—whatever can be denied them—are shielded away until the cell doors slam and we're secured in our solitude. I'd weathered my first chunk of grieving for Nana when she was still mostly alive. For ten days in the hole, I had nothing to do but hate Strazinski, the

Tower Pig, for putting me there, and to mourn a grandmother, finally too sick to visit.

"I can let you call your folks," he offered, gesturing to the phone.

"Thanks anyway," I told him, figuring they wouldn't know what to make of me calling them. We had nothing to say.

"But they're letting you go to the funeral, right?" Hodgson asked, leaning against the bars of my house and trying to sound consoling. He could skip deftly from one prison heartache to the next as if they were footprints stenciled on a studio dance floor, but real world problems would always catch him short.

"Kruller told me I could," I said. "In full equipment."

"Are you shittin' me?" he whined. "Full equipment? You're minimum security, bro. They should give you a car to go up there, not chain you up like a, well, you know."

"That's what I told him. He just gave me his that's-just-the-way-it-is speech. Said it was up to me if I wanted to go or not."

I was sitting at the head of my bunk, my back to the wall, feeling like I should be doing something but not having a clue what. Hodgson's company with Nana's hands so firmly on my shoulders was intolerable. I wanted to be left alone but knew the minute he wandered off I'd be crushed by the silence.

"It ain't right, Caine, chaining you up like that when you're so close to getting out." He shook his head in disgust, warming to his subject. He was back in familiar territory: inmates treated like dogs, and pigs riding roughshod over us because they were the ones with the dime-store badges and the power-trip egos.

"Full equipment." He sneered, lighting another roll-your-own cigarette. "You know they're just busting your balls over Strazinski."

"Naw," I said quietly. "They're screwing with me because they can is all. The pigs like that friggin' Straz about as much as they do us.

Did you ever see him when he's off that wall? They damn near shake their drawers loose acting like he's not there."

He grins his best Hodgson smirk, the one that looks like it's been slashed with a rusty straight razor.

"It must be a stone bitch," he said, "to be a pig and have even your own kind think you're a piece of shit."

I figure that's why Strazinski stays up on the wall whenever he can, sequestered in North Post, the gun tower that commands the prison street from where the road arches inelegantly past the craft shop, from the cell house to the yard. The only time I've ever seen him among the living was when he's pulling extra shifts. He clings to the periphery when he's not on his wall, glowering disdainfully at the inmates and avoiding the knots of officers gossiping and playing grabass. He looks as out of place in a crowd as he must feel, pressing his back to the wall and trying to be invisible. Older cons will argue how long he's been the Tower Pig, but none deny he's been on that wall longer than most of us have been inside it. His brother officers, doing their eight hours in the towers and loathing their isolation, don't know what to make of him. He's a freak, just like the mental cases who stand in the middle of their cells for hours at a go, staring at nothing.

"You ever wonder what he's like at home?" I asked presently.

"All the time," Hodgson purred, waiting for me to bite. "The hell's the matter with you? I ain't thinking of him at all when I ain't got to. Besides, I don't figure he's any different there than he is here. Donnelson tells me his ol' lady ditched him years ago. He ain't got no kids. The friggin' guy must put in sixty hours a week. Might as well stick a cot in the tower and crash there."

"I didn't know he was married," I said.

"He ain't, at least he ain't been, long as I've been here. You're getting sentimental on me, Caine. Save it for your folks. All that guy's done for you is get you ten days in the hole."

Hodgson was hoping he'd get a rise out of me. He knew I was thinking of Nana again and he was doing his best to try and keep me distracted. "All I'm saying? You can go on thinking that their making you go to the funeral all chained up ain't got nothing to do with you and Straz, but they still thought enough of him to put you in the Seg Unit over it. You hear what I'm saying? Just because he ain't real popular with them doesn't change his being one of their own kind."

He was right, but I didn't want to be thinking of any of it: not pigs and inmates, not the last of my bridges over the wall collapsing with Nana's passing—things as unyielding as the metal bunk, bolted to the wall, on which I sat. I don't know how long he stayed there talking, jumping from one subject to the next. The more I listened, the more his voice dissolved into a drone. I offered monosyllables and halfhearted grunts to try to convince him I wasn't shutting him out completely. Finally, he drifted off with a "see you in the morning" and a sympathetic thump on my bars. I listened to the scuff of his footsteps and then I listened to nothing, already dreading the caverns of a Thomaston night.

I would not cry for Nana, but I would want to, wringing myself out through the hours after lockdown with all the recriminations and should-have-beens chanting in my head. I'd shed all my tears in the hole and in the weeks before.

Though Hodgson blamed Strazinski for my stretch in the hole a month ago, I'd gotten myself in that jam. It began the day Cassidy, the aspiring vegetable—who'd huff dry cleaning solvent if it was the only way to get high—stalked into my cell and pulled out a joint the size of his finger. "You want to burn this with me, just say the word," he said, tossing a book of matches down onto the table like a dare. Cassidy's the kind of refugee who ambles through life like everything's casual, drifting in unannounced at the oddest moments to flash enough dope to get us both an extra year as if it were a candy bar. He must have tried to get me stoned fifty times in the last twelve months, but that day I didn't want to brood any more about Nana wheezing from her hospital bed, those tubes in her arms, alone with the night. I didn't say no.

An hour later and on the way to the craft shop, anyone would have thought we were the best of buddies, telling war stories. I felt freer than I had in a very long time, bouncing down that road with a stoner jounce. I didn't feel the walls of Thomaston crushing me, leaving me unable to do more for Nana than wait for her to die.

Pausing at the foot of the craft shop stairs, out on the road and in the shadow of North Post, Cassidy was going on and on about this lady friend of his, a flaked-out hippie chick. I was digging it, and I was more interested in letting him finish than I was in getting upstairs to spend the afternoon acting like I was working. The river of inmates on their way to wherever had thinned to a trickle.

"You!" Strazinski roared from the wall above us, looking like he was having a raging hangover. "Yeah, you! How many times have I got to tell you people to get moving?!"

"Me?" I asked, my hands on my chest. I always play dumb with the pigs. It makes them nuts.

"Who the hell do you think I'm talking to, you moron?!"

"He's talking to us," I snickered, turning to Cassidy, but Cassidy had turned to vapor, bolting up the stairs when Strazinski started his tirade.

"What do you need, someone to hold your hand to get you upstairs? Or do you need to be locked in for the day? What's your problem, Caine?!"

"What's my problem?" I shouted back at the wall. "What's your problem? I'm the one that's going to work and you're the one acting like a headcase about it. Go on back inside your tower, Straz. You wouldn't know real work if someone rolled it in sand and shoved it up your ass!"

His face, chalky and time-furrowed, went the sweetest shade of vermilion.

"That's it! Goddamn it, that—is—it! Back to the blocks! You're tagged in!"

Seething, I managed to laugh as I turned back for the cell house with him still raging behind me.

"Have a nice day!" I yelled back over my shoulder while I snatched at the waistband of my sweatpants. I figured if he really wanted to see my butt headed back for the blocks, he might as well get the fifty-cent view. So I gave it to him. Both sun-starved cheeks and a vertical smile to remember me by.

Reviewing my case a week later, the chairman of the disciplinary board actually giggled when Straz's statement was read into the record. It had been months since anyone had mooned an officer. But amusement didn't prevent him from finding me guilty of a Class B Provocation charge and giving me ten days in the hole to contemplate my sins.

I didn't cry for my Nana the night before her funeral. Neither did I sleep. I rolled and tossed and jerked in disgust on a mattress little wider than my shoulders until, exhausted, I lay very still and watched the night pass on the bricks of the cell house wall. Across the way the steam pipe sputtered on, spitting hateful secrets to the twilight. I knew all the accusations, chapter and verse. I could already hear the hissing murmurs of the dozen remaining members of my family as they gossiped busily in the pews, darting glances over their shoulders at me, shocked that I'd been allowed to attend and not in the least bit surprised that I'd disrespected my grandmother by showing up handcuffed to a chain around my waist, with a guard hovering to make sure I didn't bolt for the door. I could even hear the bolder ones giving me their glad-you-could-make-its and offering me their insincere bests after the service, convinced I'd never amount to more than all the hardware hanging off me. I couldn't blame them. Junkie thieves are rarely prized seeds among those who have worked themselves to death for everything they own. Every last one of them had given up on me years before I'd managed to get myself thrown in Thomaston for a ten-year sabbatical.

Only Nana refused to surrender me to the void, for only she was too stubborn to let me go. She played ambassador right till the end, giving me all the family gossip—and browbeating my parents into their annual Christmas visit, although she had to keep the conversation going when the silences got so thick you couldn't hack through them with a machete.

The morning of the funeral began with my toilet plugging up with the first flush of the day and ended with the intake officer wrapping a belly chain around my waist and cuffing my hands to it. Between was the chaos of scrounging and making do. I finally got something of a shine on my weathered biker boots and spent half an hour pawing through the wardrobe of the prison commissary until I found a suit that was a close-enough fit. Having found no needle for the thread I'd managed to scrape up, I tacked up the hems of the trousers with an office stapler.

"Caine," Strazinski greeted me curtly as I was escorted into the intake area to find him not in his uniform but in a proper suit at least a size too small. "You're with me. Strip."

No inmate enters or leaves Thomaston without a thorough strip search. I've gotten naked for more cops than I have for former lovers. I stripped down mechanically, knowing the drill, all the while searching the room for someone else in civilian clothes, hoping this was some sort of joke. There were four officers in that room with me, and only Straz wore a suit. He'd pulled the short straw to be my escort home.

In the prison garage, he neither spoke to me nor looked me in the face. He held the car door open long enough for me to fumble into the back, then buckled the seat belt over me.

Strazinski wedged himself into the driver's seat, the wheel shoved into his starched white shirt, cleaving his belly. Growling and grumbling, he tried to adjust his seat, but the security mesh between us kept it permanently in place. He kept glancing into the mirror to see if I was amused by his predicament.

"It's going to be a hot one," he said, addressing me for the first time since I'd stripped for him in Intake. "When we get to where we're going, you might want to take that jacket off and carry it inside."

"I'll be fine," I told him. "It might get warm, but it still covers most of the hardware."

"Yeah, well," he said. "Kruller said full equipment, so you get full equipment."

I wanted to tell him to go screw himself as he pulled the Chevy into brilliant sunlight. By blaming it on the boss, he didn't have to admit he was loving it. I slouched against the door and rested my cheek on the glass, watching the cracked asphalt of Route 1 hurtle past with cars in the opposing lane racing east. We were better than two miles down the road before I realized it was me and not they who were moving so quickly, their rush amplified by my starved perceptions and by the years I'd been inside.

"I got a messed-up question," the Tower Pig said after we'd turned onto 17 and were torpedoing for Augusta and the places I once called home. "You do know where we're going, don't you?"

"You get us to Augusta and I'll get us to the church," I told him.

"Fair enough," he grumbled. "You've been away a long time, haven't you?"

"Eight years," I said, watching the trees whir past in kaleidoscope glimpses. Eight years, five months, and . . . eleven days, I thought.

"Long time," he announced, studying me in the mirror. "I bet it ain't changed all that much, has it?"

"Not much," I muttered to the window, still watching the trees and the undergrowth rioting in so many forgotten shades of green, green in a flood, all so impossibly thick and lush. They could not have been this dense when I bounded through them like a deer, the black earth and wet leaves like a sponge beneath ten-year-old feet. Through the hum of the Chevy I could hear the summer cicada scream, knifed through by the buoyant cries of half-remembered friends frozen in child-voices.

"No," Straz said presently, having thought it over. "Home never changes much."

I said nothing. My stare drifted from the window to the security mesh to the floor.

"I'm sorry about your grandma," he said.

I flinched. Back behind the walls, if he wasn't barking at inmates he may as well have been a mute. I didn't want him talking about her; I didn't want him talking. It seemed the farther we got from Thomaston, the harder it was for him to keep his mouth shut and leave me to my silence.

"I lost my mother last year," he said quietly. "This stuff's the worst, but what're you going to do, right? Get up, go to work, do your time. It gets easier someday."

"I'm sorry about your mom," I offered weakly, looking at him for the first time in miles. I stared at the back of his head the rest of the way to Augusta, watching the roll of fat at the base of his skull, pinched by the threadbare collar of his jacket, and waiting for him to speak.

Like every other city in Maine, Augusta bounds from the urban to the suburbs to the sticks in seconds. The broad wedge of St. Andrew's—the Roman Church meets seventies architecture—is shoved into the spine of a knoll wreathed in firs and hemlocks that wall out the erratically spaced lots and sagging roofs from the proper monotony of homes with identical floor plans and freshly mowed lawns.

I watched the church growing from its hill, remembering the masses I'd attended with Nana and how we'd go out for ice cream afterward. I scanned the faces of the mourners moving solemnly up the narrow asphalt path toward the rectory, recognizing none of them. Dumpy white-haired ladies in orthopedic shoes and old men in homburg hats despite July like a blast furnace. These were Nana's friends, I reckoned, pinochle players and retirement community denizens, all the faces who gathered for twice-weekly High Mass and for all the funerals as their members slowly fell away.

In the lee of the hill, in the broad oval of the parking lot behind St. Andrew's, Strazinski hid the Impala in among the hulking Buicks and salt-rusted Toyotas.

"So this is it?" he asked, and craned his neck to study the shingled cliff of St. Andrew's south wall.

"Funny-looking church," he said, glancing back at me when I didn't comment. "I guess I'm just used to them big stone Franco churches they got around here."

"I think that's why I liked this place when I was a kid," I told him when he opened my door. The heat hit me like a wall. "It wasn't like everywhere else."

At the base of the wall, ignoring the mourners drifting past them from the parking lot and hiding from the padre, two altar boys in black cassocks and white bibs pecked at a forbidden cigarette as if the filter burned their lips. I tucked my wrists to my waist and pinched the tails of my jacket in with my arms, hiding what I could of the chain. Straz stood off away from me, his hands parked on the roll where his hips should be.

"We going?" I asked.

"Give me your hands," he said presently, decisively, as he fished in his pocket for his key ring.

I flushed, exultant and trying not to show it, and shoved my wrists as far toward him as they would go, six inches from my waist.

"You shouldn't have to be going in there like this," he said as the cuffs popped free and he turned his attention to the padlock on the belly chain. The hot summer air chilled my wrists where the steel had been.

"I appreciate it," I mumbled as the chain fell away from my waist and Straz bundled it into the back of the car, leaving me standing there unfettered in my borrowed suit, like anyone else in the parking lot. For the first time in eight years I was on the right side of the walls of Thomaston and looking like a free man. Nana would have loved it.

"If you really appreciate it," Straz said, looking me in the eye, "you'll remember one thing: This never happened. If Kruller catches wind of this, then it's my butt that's hanging out. Still, no one should have to bury his grandmother chained up like that. Got it?"

"I got it. And, look, whether you believe it or not, it'll sure mean a lot to my family not seeing me like that . . . and maybe it means a lot to me, too, you know? Thanks."

His fleshy brow crinkled, not knowing how to take being spoken to like that.

"Yeah, well," he said, opening his jacket to show me the gleaming butt of his .38 in its cross-draw holster. "Just you remember that it's too friggin' hot for me to be running after you."

"I love you too, Straz." I grinned, stepping off for the path ahead of him.

Nana's casket was white and shone like ivory on its gurney before the altar. The priest had not yet made his entrance. There had to be a hundred people in there, massed in a semicircle around the coffin, lined up in the pews with their heads bowed. I could hear only the whispers of pages as the organist, hunched at her bench and hidden beneath her hat's broad brim, flipped through her hymnal, biding her time. Strazinski dipped his fingers in the holy water at the door and crossed himself.

"What?" he whispered, catching me watching him. "You figure I got to be French to be a Catholic? Hell, even the friggin' Pope's Polish." Then his hand was on my shoulder. "Go on and sit with your folks. I'll be back here by the door. Don't get lost now."

Taking a seat by himself, he left me standing in the aisle at the back of the church, scanning those gathered for a place to sit. My family was assembled in the pews immediately in front of Nana. My father, grayer and more railish than he'd been when I had seen him the Christmas before, was the first to notice me. The wrinkles of his crow's-feet pinched, his eyes hardening as he whispered in my mother's ear. Her shoulders trembled and sagged. I could just hear her sobs from where I stood in the rear. I watched the news of my presence ripple from them through the pews with quick glances and feverish whispers. My sister leaned more deeply against the husband I'd not yet met, the crown of her head in the ginger of his beard as he sized me up from over his shoulder.

Through the ride up from Thomaston, bouncing around in the back of the prison's Impala, I'd steeled myself to march right in, ignoring my chains, and impose myself on them because that's what Nana would have wanted. I barely acknowledged them before I turned from them and slipped into the pew beside Strazinski, knowing she'd understand. He tensed awkwardly as I sat, then nodded sympathetically. I watched his vast bulk relax from the corner of my eye. He shook his head and watched the altar, waiting on the organist and "Just a Closer Walk with Thee."

MERRILL FEITELL

Bread Loaf Writers' Conference

BIKE NEW YORK!

The ride was forty-two miles, covered five boroughs, and twenty-eight thousand people were expected to participate. The *Bike New York!* brochure said nothing about beer, but because he was getting married at the end of the month, lately everything Derek did with his buddies involved beer. Beer and lap-dancing. Beer and breasts.

The party plans for this ride purported merely to include pit stops at bars in every borough to celebrate the pending wedding—or was it to celebrate the last golden days of bachelorhood? Derek wasn't quite sure. At each prior bachelor event there had been a toast—a cheerful and heartfelt meeting of glasses—and then, emerging from behind the bar, under the table, beneath the sails on TJ's boat for Christ's sake, there were suddenly ladies peeling off panties, shimmying out of skirts, moving toward him.

And while Derek recalled feeling awkward and undone, shy at each celebration, his face in all the photos registered a grimace, a smirk—the face of a guy accustomed to the world performing for his benefit, the face of an asshole he'd never imagined himself to be. So despite his soft spot for the adolescent biathlon of sporting and drinking, he couldn't seem to get himself out of bed for the ride.

The rain, he reasoned, could serve as his excuse. Even from his bed he could see large drops plunking off the fire escape railing outside his window. The phone rang at 7:30, 8:00, and again at 8:15. He listened as the messages came in over the machine. *Hey, buddy!* and *Get up, guy!* and eventually: *Listen, man. At 8:30 we're gone.*

The sky was still gray and damp when, finally, at twenty past eight, he got out of bed and stood in the window of his second floor walk-up. Across the street, at the mouth of the Eighty-Sixth Street subway, he watched a clump of people and bicycles untangle themselves, making a calm, if slow, procession down the stairs. Derek imagined the awkward hoisting of bikes over turnstiles, the tired quiet of the riders, the good-natured quips about the rain. He had always liked the hushed camaraderie of a daunting expedition.

He watched a young woman in a yellow slicker stop just before the subway entrance. She rested her bike against her body and arched back, tilting her head to look deep and far into the sky. She turned in a circle, wheeling the bike around her as she spun, reminding Derek of street contortionists he had seen once in France performing with cups held out to collect thin, clinking change. In the last few years he'd traveled a lot—alone. At just thirty he was the last of his friends to get married, the holdout, the wild man. A ridiculous idea—his own parents had been past his age when they'd first met—but he played along. He'd always been wily and athletic, the first kid to scale the steeple, to dive from a treetop into a shallow bay. And now, as a last vestige of this, with a little encouragement and booze, he could still pull off the occasional act of sinew and charm.

Derek saw the woman outside smile as if discerning a hint of sun somewhere high, high above. Her neck was long and thrown back, stretching, and something tugged at him. Her forecast seemed charmed—he'd been looking forward to this ride. The friends who'd known him longest and best would be waiting for him. The day would be sunny; it would be sport. He decided to ride right then and there.

He opted out of the subway, choosing instead to course straight down Second Avenue, bouncing over potholes, checking over his shoulder before cutting around pokey buses. He slowed as he passed his fiancée's third-floor window—her blinds were open; she liked to wake to sunlight. He could go there later; he could sleep there tonight. His heart began to thump. Why hadn't he just gotten up in time?

He'd bought new brake pads for today, along with a case of Gusto Bars. He'd even had his tires trued. If he hurried, he reasoned, either he'd find his friends or just go it alone—meet his group at the message board at the Staten Island finish line. What was a little rain after all?

When he arrived at the meeting place under the scaffolding by Battery Park there was no one from his group, just a girl in a rain-coat—hood up and checking her watch, leaning against her bike. It was a twenty-one speed Panasonic road bike with souped-up compo-nents—the urethane rim liners, the lightweight suspension fork, the Z-back comfort arm brackets that shot up like a skyscraper from the horizon of the handlebars.

Derek was riding a twenty-one speed Hardrock Stumpjumper mountain bike that had seen trails in the White Mountains, the Smokies, the long wide highways of Montana. Both he and the girl wore yellow pullover rain jackets. They stood out from the dreary monochrome morning like unbroken egg yolks on a breakfast plate.

"Hi," said Derek, "Did you see a bunch of guys here? Four of them? I'm late."

"No. My people must have left, too." She looked up. Her hair was tucked back into her hood, but Derek could see that it was thick and dark, dyed somewhere between burgundy and red. She squinted from the rain as she searched the clouds, which were low and sinking down onto the city. She beamed as though she had, in fact, seen a promise of sunshine—of something—to come. Was she the same girl he'd seen from the window?

Derek looked around, past the trees of Battery Park dripping with rain and new spring green, past the oxidized copper lampposts, past the telescopes along the water that—for a quarter—could bring the Statue of Liberty into view. The girl brought a hand to her face, nibbled a cuticle, and looked up at him expectantly. "What do you think? Do you want to go anyway?"

Were his friends orchestrating this—were they behind the Dumpster up the path, huddled in back of the newsstand, under an awning across the street? They might be lunging out any moment, making lewd gestures, whisking Derek and this young girl away—bikes and helmets and all—to Bob's corporate law office just up Broadway, or to Mike's place on Church Street, or to an overpriced steakhouse near the Federal Building with a private room in back. "Fuck!" Derek huffed to himself, but there the word was, outside of his mouth and saturating the air along with the rain.

"What?" the girl turned her face up to his. At 6′2″ he had about eight inches on her. Her eyes were big and brown and wide open. "Fuck what?" she asked.

"I just should have been here earlier." He wiped rain from his face with his sleeve and the fabric caught on the reddish growth of his stubble. "I was supposed to meet friends."

"Me, too. I was supposed to meet people from school," she said.

"Which school?" Derek asked, assuming a college—NYU, Pratt, Hunter.

"Hudson High School," she said, laughing, glowing, unzipping her jacket to reveal the school name and the eagle printed on her sweatshirt, "I'm a junior. Almost done."

"Oh." Derek moved the word around his mouth in a drawn-out loop of sarcasm. Like a high school kid himself, he still used sarcasm when feeling insecure. How could he have guessed she was in high school?

"You know, I think I saw you this morning," Derek began hopefully, as though this coincidence would lend him some kind of permission. "Did you take the train here from Eighty-Sixth?"

"No. It couldn't have been me," she said. "I'm coming from somewhere else. But hey, I'm Serena."

"I'm Derek," he said, looking all around. If his friends were watching right now, they'd be laughing at him.

"I think we should just go," she said, and Derek looked at her, trying to determine if there was a come-on—a promise and threat contained in her words—but Serena just checked her tires, giving each a quick squeeze, a pinch between her thumb and forefinger.

"We can keep an eye out for our people," she continued, "but if we stick together we can have a buddy system, you know, watch each other's bikes when we have to stop and use the john."

It was so reasonable, Derek thought—exactly the kind of plan his fiancée Jill would endorse. Imagine if he was out somewhere in Queens and stepped out of a portable toilet to find his bike stolen. Or worse, what if—to avoid just such a heist—he got a ticket for taking a leak out on some street. "What were you thinking?" Jill would laugh and then shake her head, "Why didn't you team up with somebody, have some company? Or at least bring a lock?"

"Let's go," Derek said to Serena, shrugging and aloof, and he pushed off the curb without a look back.

They nosed their way through the other late-departing cyclists.

Derek scanned the crowd for his friends, even though he knew they'd be far past this last departing heat, largely composed of families with kids and training wheels and bicycles built for two. Here, the ride was rife with unfamiliar challenges: There were special bikes for the handicapped propelled by arm power; a pedicab towed a woman on crutches; a family stopped curbside and the dad hopped off his bike, took requests, and ducked into The Donut Hole.

"Look at that." Serena pointed to a rise far ahead up the canyons of Sixth Avenue, where the street clumped with the sloped backs of cyclists heading into Central Park. Even steering with one hand, Serena rode steadily, confidently, with the same ease Jill displayed coming in the front door after work, depositing the key on the hook, mail on the table, Tupperware in the sink, a hand on Derek's arm, his thigh—an unwavering flow of purpose and motion. "We're behind all the fun," Serena said.

"I know," Derek nodded. He knew that up ahead—in the thick of it—the crowd would be pulsing with hoots and enthusiasm. There would be team T-shirts, boom boxes, probably even a beer helmet or two.

She talked.

In the park she told him she was a Sagittarius and that she was saving up to get her chart done. She told him her friends would be irritated with her, that if she carried a pager like everybody else she would have been able to meet up with her group. "It's ridiculous though," she said, shaking her head and riding beside him, "You just waste a lot of time waiting around at pay phones that never ring. Besides, no one should be able to get a handle on you 24-7."

Derek laughed. It amazed him how difficult it was in New York to disappear completely. Once he'd escaped to Glacier National Park for a week, where he'd biked the Rockies, outsmarted the bears, and tented-up with a hiker named Lisette. He almost began a recount but stopped himself, afraid he'd sound like a geezer telling war stories, like a wash-up in love with his own reckless once-upon-a-times. Instead he said nothing, just listened to his tires picking up moisture, kicking mud and water up against his jacketed back. Vines hung down from overpasses, directing drops at his nose with the precision of a wand. They passed the carousel, the obelisk, the Harlem Meer, riding silently, legs pumping in quick, sure revolutions.

In the Bronx, across the Madison Avenue Bridge, they stopped at a rest area to eat quartered oranges and bananas just as the *Bike New York!* staff was cleaning up rinds and peels, breaking down the repair stand, clapping their hands and shouting out a call to get moving. Derek stood outside the portable toilets, both his bike and Serena's leaning against his hip. He eyed the broken blacktop of the streets, the gates pulled down over the row of storefronts, not a single thing open on a Sunday. He could see the backs of the billboards he'd long admired from the roadway on his route out of town, the steel lettering in reverse, the words backward. He hadn't been anywhere new in a while.

Now, in Brooklyn, twenty-eight miles into the ride, with the long carless strip of the Expressway before them, they rode past the three-story, two-family houses at roof level as though on some Disneyland monorail track. The gray road stretched ahead in a slight and steady grade upward. "So," said Serena, growing restless and impatient— they had been riding in silence for a while now—"next weekend there's a ride from Manhattan to Montauk. A hundred miles. How much GustoGranola is that?"

"Next weekend I'm getting married," Derek said. "At the Puck Building at seven on Saturday." He added the last information as though it were an invitation, as though Serena should consider, if she had nothing better to do, stopping by for a little champagne and dinner.

"Wow," Serena said, leaving Derek unsure of what she meant by the word. "Wow. Why aren't you riding with your girl?"

"Jill wanted to do it." Derek laughed, feeling proud. "She would have done it. Maybe we'll do it together next year, but this ride was supposed to be just one in a series of bachelor party events. Except that I woke up today and couldn't handle the idea of any more bachelor party anything."

"That's who you were meeting?"

"Yeah. My buddies. They kept calling all morning but I didn't pick up on the answering machine."

Serena looked at him steadily, her face turned toward him as they rode. Derek flexed his jaw and shrugged, laughing, convinced this generated light in his eyes. "I'm excited," he admitted. Serena bit her lip, looking curious. Or was it mournful? Derek considered the possibility. What if she was disappointed? It could be a look of jealousy, of longing.

"Do you have a cake yet?" Serena asked, using a forearm to brush hair from her eyes.

Derek just stared. "I don't know," he said breezily, "I haven't been that involved in the planning. Why?"

He had, in fact, spent hours tasting cakes and hearing bands. He'd even helped pick out the place settings. He'd been *very* involved in the planning, but more than anything else, he'd focused on Jill. He'd watched her in amazement—the way she kept the details all straight, the way she raised her eyebrows at a rip-off, how she threatened to take her business elsewhere. He'd known a lot of women in his life, but he'd never noticed any who had been so able. It most often rendered him silent, fascinating him, somehow filling him up. He'd been delighted even at the stationers and the florist, standing beside his lovely new life, but now this embarrassed him somehow—here in the damp gray of Brooklyn, with his heart pumping in sport, and his oldest friends whooping it up just around the next turn, or the next.

"You must have a cake if the wedding's next week," Serena said. "But I wish you didn't because my parents have this bakery and my mom makes the most amazing cakes. She really does. She's been in magazines."

"Oh yeah?" Derek asked.

"They're not far from here," Serena was eager, pedaling fast and close beside him. She had a beautiful smile, her cheekbones high and round. "We could go look. It'd be quick. We could take a shortcut later and catch back up with the ride."

"You want to go back to your parents' place?" he asked, a small tickle of disbelief stirring in his throat. This had to be some kind of joke. He looked all around and then back to Serena. He noticed the broad, pink flesh of her lips.

"C'mon," she said. She seemed so earnest and determined. It was still possible to discover a truly great cake, to pay extra and have it made in time. He could do that, call up Jill and say, "Honey, you've gotta come see this."

Derek followed Serena down the service road, which ran abreast of the B.Q.E. The roadside scrub grass was littered with glass shards and faded soda cans, but its new spring green shoots nearly glowed amid the trash, showing a color too tender for exposure, like new skin under a scab. He'd grown up around Manhattan money and always felt a guilty determination to know the whole city, to bike New York in its entirety, to pedal every bit of it both scary and safe. He worried briefly about getting hurt, or mugged, ending up with a lot of explaining to do, but these worries soon dissolved into a greater concern: When had he become so neurotic? Since when had he become so accountable?

He yanked up on his handlebars to jump over a pothole and he concentrated on the sound of his wheels grabbing at the pavement, the slight suction of the spinning treads. This was okay, he reasoned. He knew it was braver to be Serena, stepping off course with a strange man. He could feel the muscles in his thighs expand, pumping with blood and filling his skin.

Serena turned back to him, right hand still on the handlebar, left arm dangling behind her seat. "We're almost there." She urged Derek on. "I can point out local highlights or we can just ride."

He just nodded, imagining a pit stop at one of the bars they passed. What if he ran into his friends gathered around a pitcher of Budweiser? He'd say good-bye to Serena, say, "Thanks for your company. Good luck. Take care."

They turned right onto a small street and he followed Serena's hop onto the sidewalk. Two girls hula-hooped before the bakery storefront, blue and orange Knicks shirts cascading like dresses down their legs. Serena dismounted her bicycle and leaned it against the building facade. "Can you watch these? Will you two watch these bikes for me?"

"Nuh-uh, Serena. Not if you don't introduce us to your friend," said one, sway-backed and challenging, cocking her head.

Serena stepped back, allowing Derek room to dismount and lean his bike against her own. "This is Derek. He's about to get married, and I'm going to show him my mother's cakes. Derek, these are my cousins," she said and then gave a light laugh. "Welcome to munchkinland, right?"

The girls giggled. Derek held his broad palm out to them. They scanned the lines of fingers dumbly until he realized a handshake wasn't the standard greeting for a little girl. How did you greet a girl so young? He had no idea.

Serena tugged at the neck of her sweatshirt, awkwardly extracting a key on a string. She bent to unlock the door, and Derek stepped into the bakery, toward the rich, sleepy smell of bread, of chocolate, of yeast. Above the entrance an overhead fan thwacked flies away. The room was hot and loud as a heliport but Serena waved him on and, with two more steps, Derek hit a cool quiet pocket of air, as if he'd swum to a perfectly temperate spot in a lake.

A Formica counter connected to make an L shape with the line of bakery cases, which ran the depth of the storefront. Beyond the glass panels were gold-tinted trays arranged neatly with doilies and tiny desserts—tarts topped with single strawberries, mounds of raspberries, kiwi slices. The next shelf up flaunted tiny napoleons, palm-sized cheesecakes, miniature eclairs, cream puffs drizzled with nuts and drops of green frosting. There were cases of desserts in their standard sizes and then, toward the back of the store, a tall case hosted a wedding cake five tiers high and decorated down one side with a cascade of pastry-tubed peonies, flouncy and complex as prom dresses. Behind the counter was a stretch of table with cardboard sheets designed to fold into boxes and a spool of red-and-white string, the end of which snapped and tricked intermittently in the current from the fan. "We don't open till four on Sunday," Serena said.

Derek ran his fingers up and down the seams of his nylon shorts, in a nervous and futile search for pockets. Serena hopped up onto the countertop near the register, spun neatly on her ass, and jumped off the other side. She was nimble, he thought. She was quick.

She walked the length of the counter and pushed past a swinging door into what Derek presumed was the kitchen. "Mo-om," Serena called out. "Mom!"

Along the storefront window was a row of small, square tables for two. Opposite the display cases, the wall was lined with clean booths—except for one with a cup and saucer and a copy of the *Post*. Derek sat on the edge of a red padded chair with his legs parted, elbows on his knees, staring down at the gray flecks on the red linoleum tile. His calves ached. He could feel the blood hot and shifting through his muscles. The last thing he felt like doing was chatting up some girl's mom. He should have stayed home, should have slept late and then driven out to Jersey with Jill to find ivy at Plant Land. He should have gone out to Long Island to pick up cuff links from his father.

Cuff links? Was that all that had become of his desires? He heaved a great aggravated sigh, and a flutter developed in his stomach. He was nervous suddenly, suddenly excited.

What if there was no mom in the back, no dad. What if the back room was filled with his people, his friends waiting to catch him off guard. Derek knew—it was true—that this was all part of his friends' party plan. They would be coming out of the kitchen any moment, and Serena herself would be stepping from a giant cake. "Ha ha!" they would laugh. Serena would sit on Derek's lap, eat frosting off his lip, draw her quick, lithe tongue along the edge of his ear. "Gotcha" Steve-O would exclaim. He'd give a big belly laugh, crack open a beer.

"I was stewing a minute there, how I would handle this one," Derek would admit, snickering.

"Oh, you!" Serena would coo and wiggle about on his lap, take his broad hand in her delicate ones and walk him through the kitchen and up the stairs of the two-family home. Undoubtedly she wasn't in high school, but older, playing jailbait just to complicate things. He should have known—his friends wouldn't have left him alone for this ride. He could be so insecure. It was shocking that still, even now, as an adult, as a man on the brink of marriage, he could feel as abandoned as a teen.

Derek laughed and sighed at once. Still seated, he placed his hands on his knees and dropped his head, like a runner trying to regain breath, regain composure.

Noise came from the kitchen. Derek could hear it even above the fans—the clanging of pans, the squeaking of a wheeled cart in need of oil. Outside, the hula-girls leaned their hoops against the bicycles. One pressed her face against the bakery window—thumbs in ears, pinkies tugging at the corners of her eyes. She pushed her tongue against the glass before joining the other who, standing beside Derek's bike, patted the seat, squeezed the right brake, flicked on and off the rear red blinking light.

Derek watched the hot breath disappear from the glass, leaving a blot of saliva and the smudge of a lip print. What if those two saw Serena come from the kitchen, wheeled out by his buddies in a giant whipped cream cake? He could picture Serena done up sexy, laughing, and then looking to the window mortified.

"Hey, uh, Serena!" Derek called out toward the kitchen and stood to lean up against the counter, "Serena!"

"I'm coming," Serena drew out the words and they grew louder, like a drum roll. He kept his eyes from the window, fixed straight ahead instead. There was a two-dollar bill taped to the wall, a framed photo of Frank Sinatra, an etched mirror that Derek began to read: *There is a time for everything we will, a time to speak and a time to be still.* Maybe he should go, just turn and leave.

"They're not here." Serena pushed open the swinging kitchen door with a kick at the base and then a slam of her back against it. Her arms were full of binders, photo albums stacked just to her chest, Derek noticed, as if shelving her breasts. She dropped the books on the counter before him. "My parents must have already left for my uncle's on Staten Island. They're barbecuing there so they can pick me up, so I don't have to ride all the way home."

"That's nice," Derek said, unsure whether he felt disappointed or relieved. He was a little embarrassed, a little angry, and in the confusion he grew condescending. "That's a nice parent thing to do."

"Baby will be tired." Serena made her voice a high singsong, pouted her lips, and pinched her own cheek. "Bring these to a table and I'll get us some snacks. What do you want?" She studied his face for a moment and laughed. He knew his features were slack, stunned and confused. "The mini cheesecakes are the best but I'm afraid they'll make us cramp when we get back to biking. Maybe we should split one of those and then just stick with sugar. Go all chocolate and tarts."

She reached beneath the counter and pulled out a large white plate with which she walked the stretch of cases, expertly sliding open the doors, reaching onto the trays and extracting pastries without fumbling or looking, without hesitation. She dropped the full plate on the counter, ducked under the hinged section, and delivered the plate to the booth Derek had selected.

"Wow," he said, at once shy and delighted. He wasn't used to not knowing how to act around women—or girls. Maybe, he considered, in this distinction lay the problem. "What a spread."

Serena plucked a glazed kiwi slice off a tiny tart, popped it in her mouth and poised her fingers above a halved strawberry. "Yum," she said.

Derek contemplated the heaping plate, selected a mini mud cake, pulled back the wrapper and took a bite, wincing at the bite of sugar on his gums. Serena slid deeper into the booth, turned to lean against the wall, and stretched her legs down the bench seat. She broke a mini napoleon in half and inspected the layers of filling before taking a bite, as though she might have discarded the pastry had she not been pleased with what she saw.

"You must win a lot of friends with this place." He imagined the booths filling with her friends late at night, a picket fence of skateboards propped up by the door, the dessert trays raided by stoned kids with the munchies. He imagined weekends with her parents out of town, how the jukebox must play all night and couples must make out leaning against the cool cases.

"Puh-lease," Serena said, tossing half her napoleon back onto the plate. "Only the teachers care. They just want me to bring stuff for the holiday parties."

"Even with your folks out of town?" he baited, wanting to prove he knew the score.

"Even then," she nodded. She made a point of meeting Derek's eyes, but he noticed that her lips were tightly closed, as if containing a giggle. She was lying, he knew, and this was rejection—he wasn't a guy worth trying to impress. But he wasn't angry. Rather, he went sad somewhere in his throat, behind his ears. "So." He drummed his hands on the table, unsure where conversation could go next.

"So." Serena pushed the white plate out of the way and slid the stack of photo albums into place before Derek. "Since the family's all out at my uncle's I can just show you the wedding catalogues and you can see if there's anything that might interest you and you could either order now, or go home and discuss it with your, with your Jill, and come back or call or, uh, whatever." Serena giggled and shook her head, rolled her eyes, knowing she had broken her professional tone.

"What do you do, anyway?" she asked casually, flipping open an album.

"Law," he said, knowing it was enough of an answer but continuing anyway. "A lot of copyright stuff, patents. I always thought I'd do advocacy though, lobbying. But you never know how it'll go."

"Oh," she said, frankly bored. It was a little boring. But that was the funny thing about finding your way in the world. There was a place laid out for you, he thought, and you stepped into it happy for the chance to rest. It was like the small miracle of finding a New York apartment: You found one that would do—finally—and short of marriage or lottery-winning vowed never, ever to leave.

Serena turned the album sideways so that she and Derek could lean in to share a view. She began a slow turning of pages. Under the cellophane of each sheet was an eight-by-ten black-and-white photo of a cake—some on display at actual weddings, some just shot atop the bakery counter. Derek dully watched the pictures pass, anxious for the show to be over, until he found himself reaching out a hand to stop the pages from turning.

The photo that grabbed him was of a wooden picnic table—the slats disappearing off the lower left side of the print, the grain of the wood spotted with sunlight through trees. To the right was a tall, full cake, four tiers high atop a bed of ivy. It, too, was dappled in sunlight, and to Derek the spots of brightness and shadow made the cake look illuminated, like stained glass, as though it were shining from within. He turned the book to face him.

"That was my sister's wedding," Serena offered, "It was upstate. It was summer. It was nice."

"Your sister's wedding?" Derek asked, though he had heard perfectly. He was just unsure what to say but knew something was required of him, "Did everyone go? Did your family close the store?"

"For the weekend." Serena smiled. "I took the pictures. It was all on me."

"You took this?"

"Yeah. I take all the cakes." She winked at him—a businesswoman in the know. "I get forty a photo and I print them in the darkroom at school. The wedding, I let them give me money for supplies, but I just did it free. You know, family."

"Of course. Wow." Derek flipped through the album. "These are good. Have you always taken pictures?" He felt a little funny; it was the kind of question he might once have asked on a date.

"I guess. That's what I want to study. That's what I want to do at college." Serena got up and walked to the cooler near the counter. She filled two paper cups with water and brought them back to the table.

"That's good," he said, as if he truly knew. "This is all good stuff."

"You want to see my real stuff?" she asked, already running into the kitchen and coming back with a slick gray pocket folder that she slid before him. "Look at these."

Derek opened the folder and flipped through the heavy, curling prints. He, too, had done a lot of high school photography, striding through the hallways, confident with props—long lenses, flash bulbs, cigarettes. Girls would pose, huddling close, curls colliding. He remembered their bracelets, how at picnics, at the beach, smoking on the steps, the silver bands would catch sunlight and shine.

Serena had all the standards he remembered. There were night shots up Broadway, with headlights streaking across the dark. There were trees and storefronts around the neighborhood. And a Chinatown series, featuring dolls in windows, pagoda phone booths, a dense crowd bursting forth from small subway stairs. There was also the requisite fish on ice.

He was unsure what kind of fish they were but each was about a foot long. They lay stacked high in a pyramid atop a bed of ice. The eyes were perfect circles—wide and nearly lifeless. On the right side of the frame one fish hung just below the rest of its row, looking as though it was about to slide from the pile and escape off the bottom of the page. *Whoops!* Derek felt like exclaiming.

"Everyone likes that one. Why does everyone like that one?" Serena knitted her eyebrows together. "I keep trying to get one that good again but I can't figure out what I did right."

"Well," said Derek. The picture was printed poorly, underexposed. The focus was clear though: the drying scales, the light catching the ice, the eye that seemed—even as you looked—to slip farther down the pile, heading for the floor and a dangerous getaway. *Whoops!*

"Well," he repeated. He was about to say something thoughtful and profound, something about distinguishing yourself from the heap, about how the world loves a good renegade. But when he looked at Serena's expectant face, how eager she was, how demanding of counsel, he didn't feel like saying anything at all. This was his bachelor party, for God's sake. He could be anywhere in the five boroughs right now. He could be talking stock tips with TJ; he could be biking hard and fast, a little buzzed and hot after some personal best. He gave his neck a rub and crack. "It's good," he added dismissively. "It's all right. It's fine."

"Oh," she laughed quickly, high and forced. "I didn't mean to make a big deal." She grabbed the photos and slid them back into the folder, which she placed primly out of sight on her lap. She was blushing. He watched her skin spread pink up along her cheeks and under the fine hairs that had slipped from her ponytail to hang by her ears. "We should probably go soon." She wouldn't look up. She yanked a napkin from the dispenser to give a quick wipe across the table. Then she snatched up their white plate and carried it quickly behind the counter to the sink.

Why hadn't he just given her an answer? All she wanted was a little encouragement, a quick flurry of attention and awe. Could he not stand that—for a second, for a kid?

"Hey, Serena?" he called out. She ignored him, pretending not to hear. She left him there, sitting awkward and empty-handed as she turned on the water, pumped the soap dispenser, and began washing the single plate. Could he be such an ass? He couldn't wait to move, to slip out of the booth and get away. He got up without thinking, unsure where to go, so he turned in a circle before heading to the door marked GENTS.

Inside the cramped bathroom Derek leaned against the door and peered into the small mirror. His eyes looked lined and sorry, but that didn't surprise him: He'd caught himself looking old before. What struck him now was the awkwardness of his face. He wasn't at all sure how to hold it. His winning party-boy smirk looked small and tight on a man—and he was a man. After all, he was about to get married, to become part of man and woman, husband and wife.

He took a moment to close his eyes. He thought of Jill, of his in-laws arriving on Tuesday. He thought of Serena and her cousins outside. He considered how Serena might one day describe him: some cake-eating freeloader who just pedaled away. "I'm sorry," he said, watching his face in the glass. "Look, I'm sorry." He tried again, moving through a series of expressions as though warming up for a huge performance, a whole life of expressions to come. He shifted from tight smirk to wide-eyed wonder; from dull distraction to doting smile. He found his father's lightness in his own eyes, his mother's amusement in the right corner of his mouth, and a mischievous giddiness all his own as he thought about finishing this ride, this day, and heading home.

Outside, he watched Serena lock the door, give a cookie to each of the cousins, and then mount her bike. How could he begrudge her that little show-and-tell? He watched her now pedaling ahead, leaving him just the view of her backside and her shoelace. He watched the right lace drag along the ground and snap behind her foot as she rode, threatening to catch and tangle in her gears. It dragged and snapped, dragged and snapped. She was just a kid—a very pretty, athletic, bubbly kid—star of her own show, out to sell him a cake. "Wait," he called out. "Stop."

When she stopped, Derek got off his own bike and walked to her, kneeling beside her pedal. He picked up her right foot, rested it on his knee, and tied her shoe, holding his palm over the laces for a moment after he finished. "Thanks for the cake," he said. "Thanks for the show."

"C'mon," Serena said lightly, flirtatiously, giving her leg the smallest kick. She smiled coyly down at him.

Jill, he'd say, *what an amazing day.*

"All right," he said, "Let's get moving."

They caught up with the ride on the long stretch of the dull gray Gowanus. To the right was steely water and wire fencing clogged inches high with trash blown from the highway. To the left was a clot of deciduous trees and scrub grass that reminded Derek of his road trip back from Montana, the way the land lost splendor and offered nothing but the simple familiarity of a return home.

He slowed, his thighs growing stiff and bulky. The Verrazano-Narrows Bridge went on forever, never seeming to crest. Three times Serena shot past him and then waited ahead until finally she zipped off toward a peak on the horizon he couldn't seem to reach.

Inevitably, he knew, he would remember this day no matter what had happened. It was, after all, the last weekend before his wedding, a wedding for which, even as he rode, he was becoming more and more excited.

He wished for a moment that he had stolen the photo, asked for a copy. Why hadn't he? He could have slipped it into the back of his shorts to lie under his jacket flat against him as he rode. He could have cut out that single slipping fish and kept it in his breast pocket at the wedding ceremony, placed the wide-eyed head poking out instead of a pocket square. *Whoops!* He could say it with a lilt as he lifted Jill's veil. She might think he was joking, feeling clumsy with the delicate tulle, but only he would know he was recalling something he'd felt today: a shift in lighting, a realignment of composition, a moment when he slipped from the point of focus in his own life.

As he rode on he contemplated the lever of his legs—how each move they made cranked the pedals, advanced the chain, turned the wheels, and propelled him forward, displacing air and creating wind. Far ahead, light seemed finally to be breaking through the clayey clouds, and Derek was pretty sure he could see Serena marking a crest to the bridge. She had her yellow jacket back on, and it billowed around her as she pedaled into the wind. She seemed nearly to be floating on the pillow of her radiant jacket. Light shone through the fabric, harnessing the glow around her like a lantern's shade. "That was you once," he encouraged himself, pedaling steadily. "See that, friend? That was once you."

LADETTE RANDOLPH

University of Nebraska, Lincoln

THE GIRLS

Becca liked dogs. She might even have called herself a dog person, but she couldn't quite figure out why Professor Blakely had asked her to watch his dogs while he was in Italy for a conference during the week of fall break. Only later did she realize she hadn't been his first choice. Of course not. What had she been thinking? Everyone on the small campus of Pilgrims' College knew how much Professor Blakely loved his dogs. They were his children. Some of the guys in the fraternities liked to joke that they were more than his children. Professor Blakely was so closely associated with his dogs that he was known around campus, when the students talked among themselves, as Dog-boy. As the dog-sitting gig got closer, Becca heard from others who had done it before. "Wow. You sure you want to do that?" a guy in her Advanced Theater Design class asked. "You'll be cooped up in that house, and..." He didn't go on. It was like this with everyone, a strange reticence just at the moment they were about to give her details. When she pressed for more, they all shrugged. "You'll see," was the reply. All Becca knew was that she needed a letter of recommendation from Professor Blakely if she wanted to get into graduate school.

Becca went to Professor Blakely's house on the Thursday before he was scheduled to leave so she could meet "the girls," as he called them. From the first moment she saw them, Becca was put off by the behavior of the dogs, a large boxer named Desdemona and a pug named Hetta. They seemed more like naughty children than the well-trained animals she had expected of a true dog lover. When she first entered the house, the pug barked wildly and the boxer sniffed at her crotch and then, having apparently found her acceptable, jumped on her, large paws resting on Becca's shoulders.

She was put off by the house as well. There was a weird violence at work in most of the rooms—both in color and in the choice of decor. The closer she looked, the more troubled Becca felt. If the images weren't violent they were pornographic, shocking. She surreptitiously looked at several small prints in the den to find they were a black-and-white series of pornographic postcards—not anything like the burlesque, titillating, slightly humorous postcards she had found in her grandfather's desk the summer she was ten, but explicit photographs of what seemed like every sort of sexual activity possible. She turned away, flushed and disoriented, afraid Blakely had noticed her discomfort. He moved about the room in a businesslike manner, explaining that she must make herself at home. He acted as though there were nothing strange about the fact that a large, erect, stone penis served as a paperweight on the desk next to the phone.

Blakely invited Becca to stay for tea after he'd shown her around the house. He talked as he put the kettle on to boil, giving her a complicated explanation of both dogs' personalities and preferences. He set a plate in the middle of the table. "Would you mind putting out the cookies?" he asked and handed her three boxes.

"Hetta is very intelligent," Blakely said as he filled a tea ball. "She's very affectionate but not above withholding affection for her own manipulative purposes." He looked down at Hetta, who stood at his feet watching him. "Isn't that right, you little vamp, you?" Hetta opened her mouth and sneezed loudly. Blakely laughed. He looked at Becca. "She's such an actress."

While Blakely tended the teapot, Becca looked more closely at the kitchen. Like the rest of the house, it was eccentric and crowded with things. A riot of colors—tangerine seeming to dominate—the kitchen was filled with the same violent details found in the rest of the house, from the little pewter pistols that served as handles and the machete-like hinges on the cabinet doors, to the serving dish on which she was now placing the cookies—a large open mouth, like a close-up of a vintage Hollywood scream. Teeth lined the top and bottom edges while the center of the plate featured a ridged palate and a slimy-looking tongue.

Blakely poured tea into cups shaped like fish, their open mouths forming the lips of the cups. He gestured for her to sit down across from him. Suddenly, sitting across from Blakely, Becca panicked at the need to carry her end of the conversation. She was not someone who felt comfortable hanging out and chatting with her professors, and Blakely was more imposing than most. He wore his white hair cut short. It was always the same length, which led Becca to believe he had it barbered every week. Although he wore the customary uniform of the humanities professor—corduroy trousers and tweed jackets, wool vests and cotton or linen shirts—he did not go for the rumpled, just-slept-in look. He was immaculate. His shoes always shone; his watch gleamed; his skin and teeth gleamed as well. Even with all of its eccentricities, the house, too, was spotless. She had noticed this especially in the only room where there were no violent or pornographic images. In the back of the house, overlooking the flower garden, was a room that contained nothing but a perfectly white rug that matched the white walls and ceiling. Recessed lights shone on the room's only object—a white orchid in bloom, in a blue ceramic pot. Becca knew it was an orchid only because Professor Blakely had told her so when he gave her the detailed watering instructions—only once while he was away and then only from the bottom. If the plant looked strange for any reason, she was to call immediately a man named Vic Epperly. Under no circumstances was she to touch the plant. Already Becca had a reverent feeling toward the orchid. It was a rare variety, Blakely had told her, given to him by a grower in Florida. There were only a handful of this particular species left in the world.

Almost as soon as Blakely had sat down at the table, inviting Becca to help herself to the cookies, he said, "Treats," and the dogs bounded up from where they had been resting near the cabinets. Hetta was the first up to the table, leaping into the chair to the right of Blakely. Without interference from him, she proceeded to remove a cookie from the mouth plate with her teeth. Becca drew back in surprise and felt herself cringe involuntarily, awaiting the inevitable irate response from Blakely. Instead Blakely laughed and patted the dog's head.

"Hetta want some tea with the big people?"

Hetta wagged her hooked tail and seemed to grin and nod. Blakely was delighted. While Hetta was being indulged, Desdemona stood up on her hind legs and placed her large paws on the table. She, too, stuck her enormous head over the plate of cookies and snatched one with her teeth—rather daintily for a large dog.

No way, Becca thought. No way does he let her get away with that. But Blakely laughed again. "Mona, you beautiful thing, you. Are you starving? Are you starving, girl?" Desdemona also seemed to smile at Blakely as she swallowed the cookie in one big gulp.

"I allow the girls one treat each day," Blakely said to Becca, smiling in satisfaction. "Only one. Anything they want."

As he let Becca out the door a little later, Blakely gave her a spare key. "I'll leave the important numbers for you—the vet, the plumber, Vic. My friend Alan is available in a pinch. I'll leave his number, too. My one request is that you please not leave the girls alone overnight. They're quite terrified to be by themselves at night. It's why I have someone sit with them."

"Okay," Becca said.

"So you'll be here early Saturday morning?" he went on. "Eight o'clock? I'll want to know you're here with the girls before I leave for the airport."

"All right," Becca said. Hetta and Desdemona crowded around Blakely's legs as Becca opened the door to go.

"Say good-bye to Becca," Blakely instructed the dogs. As she walked toward her car, Becca heard both dogs yipping and howling. When she turned around to look, Blakely was laughing, his head thrown back just like the dogs' heads. She waved, though she wasn't sure any of them noticed.

On Saturday, after Professor Blakely left, Becca was alone with the girls. The "goyles," as she'd taken to calling them to herself. The dogs were silent and wary in Blakely's absence. They seemed depressed and slept together much of the day, Hetta curled between Desdemona's front paws. When they weren't sleeping they skulked along the walls. On a couple of occasions when Becca got up to get a drink from the kitchen or go to the bathroom, she startled the dogs from where it seemed they had been spying on her. When she surprised them like that there was a frantic scrabbling of claws on the wood floors—large claws and little claws—as they made their escape from her. Silly goyles.

That afternoon Leslie Ann came by to "check out the digs." She talked like that.

Leslie Ann snooped through every room responding out loud as Becca had silently. By now Becca had taken more detailed note of the strangeness of the house and she showed the most startling things to Leslie Ann as they went through every room. On two whole shelves in the library were books about torture: devices and techniques used throughout history. In the downstairs bathroom, the strange instruments hanging on the wall Becca now knew were torture devices. She'd seen them in some of the books. There was a large collection of books on human sacrifice, a series on mass murderers, and an even larger collection of pornography.

Leslie Ann giggled. "Oh no. He's such a pervert. Didn't you always know it? Everyone says he's a pervert—a closet pervert, you know. That's the worst kind."

"Is there a good kind of pervert?" Becca said.

"You know what I mean. There's the kind of pervert that you know is a pervert, so you can be prepared. You stay away from them. But the closet pervert, you never know what they'll do. Those are the serial killers and the pedophiles."

"You've thought about this a lot, haven't you?"

"Haven't you?"

"Not really," Becca said.

"He's a freak," Leslie Ann said. "This place is freaky. Aren't you going to be afraid to stay here alone at night?"

"I'll be all right," Becca said, though she had to admit she was a little jittery around all of the masks—horrific things, more like death masks than anything else she could describe. They had been arranged in such a way that she caught sight of them when coming around a corner or in the reflection of a mirror. Still, Becca felt she had to put on a brave front for Leslie Ann.

"What's this about?" Leslie Ann said when she discovered the white room.

"It's the orchid's room," Becca said. Already Becca had begun to think it was normal that a plant should have its own space.

Leslie Ann looked at Becca with a puzzled expression but didn't say anything as she looked back into the room again. Then turning to Becca, she said, "Don't you just want to have sex on that carpet?"

"No," Becca said, hoping she didn't sound as shocked as she felt.

"You're kidding. You didn't think about having sex on it?"

"No. It's the last thing I would think about doing."

Leslie Ann appeared slightly put out with her. "What's wrong with you?"

"What's wrong with me? What's wrong with you? You and your elaborate theories about perversion."

They left their argument as they moved to the upstairs where there were more marvels. Behind them the dogs crept like shadows... freezing in a crouch if Leslie Ann and Becca stopped and looked at them. Leslie Ann thought it was hilarious and deliberately stopped and turned a number of times. "Quit tweaking their wee brains," Becca said, but Leslie Ann was having too much fun. Finally, she turned once and ran toward them with a fierce cry. The dogs yelped and clattered down the stairs.

"Those are mutant dogs," she informed Becca. "They aren't normal."

When Leslie Ann left, Becca fed both dogs. They seemed to warm to her after that, creeping up to sit beside her where she had sprawled on the living room rug to watch TV.

"Hey, goyles," she said and reached to stroke their heads. Hetta initially pulled away, but then leaned into the caress. Eventually, her snubbed nose wheezed into Becca's face. Desdemona responded immediately, her perky ears moving even farther forward than usual. She studied Becca closely, and finally licked her hand.

"You rascals," Becca said. "You want a treat?" At the word, they were off, racing for the kitchen—Desdemona leading and Hetta's little legs trying to catch up.

"Won't it be strange if you aren't there? It's your birthday party after all," Leslie Ann was saying on the phone. She had arranged a party in Omaha with some friends from the university theater department that happened to coincide with Becca's birthday. "Your twenty-first birthday party," she added as though that would make their discussion more meaningful.

"It's hardly my birthday party, Leslie Ann."

"It won't be as fun without you," Leslie Ann said.

Becca felt irritated by the exaggeration. "I'm sure the party will be a great success even without me."

"Don't be sarcastic."

"I can't go, Leslie Ann. I have to be here with the girls. I can't be out late like that."

"Those dogs will be fine for one night. Besides, honestly, we'll get you home. Chad and I will personally ensure you'll be home by midnight at the latest. We'll leave early."

"No you won't. You won't. You're kidding yourself but you're not kidding me."

"My, aren't we little Miss Rejoinder today," Leslie Ann said. "I'm not going to quit bugging you, you know. I'm not going to quit until you give in."

Becca had been in this predicament with Leslie Ann more times than she liked to remember. Leslie Ann's powers of pestering were legendary. Becca both liked and detested Leslie Ann.

"Those damn dogs will be okay. They're dogs, not children."

"To Blakely they're children. I promised him I wouldn't stay away overnight."

"Grow up, will you?" Leslie Ann was using her put-out voice again. "We'll be there at six o'clock on Friday to get you. I told you we'll get you home. Remember to wear a Halloween costume. Oh, yeah, Chad's bringing a friend."

Becca sighed. "Don't bring anyone on my account, please."

"Oh, no problem," Leslie Ann said brightly, realizing she had won the argument, that Becca was relenting. "His friend Stephen is in town, high school buddy. You'll like him. He's a riot."

"Oh great, a riot." When Becca hung up the phone she realized she didn't feel as bad about going as she thought she would. She felt the teeniest bit excited having something to look forward to for the weekend. Maybe Leslie Ann knew her better than she knew herself. Maybe she was one of those women who said no and really meant yes.

When Becca woke up the following morning, Hetta and Desdemona acted as though she had always been there. They no longer sulked around the house. New day, new attitude. They knew who was feeding them now. That was good. Becca felt better, too, not having to deal with their depression.

That morning Professor Blakely called. He had rushed back to his hotel after the conference so he could call at exactly 9:00 A.M. Checking up on her, Becca figured, making sure she was there in the morning.

"How is everything?" he said.

"Things are fine." Becca didn't elaborate.

"The dogs are okay?" He sounded a little frightened by her reticence.

"Oh sure, the dogs are great. They're great," Becca said. "Hetta is standing here at my feet watching me talk to you, and Desdemona is by the sink. I think she's wanting more water."

"I'll wait while you get it for her," Blakely said, sounding happier now that she'd given him a few details.

Becca carried the phone to the sink and filled Desdemona's bowl. "Okay, that's done," she said. "She's drinking now, can you hear?" She held the phone away from her slightly.

"No, I can't hear it." Blakely sounded disappointed. "I can just see her, though. Is she looking up and smiling at you?"

She wasn't, but Becca said, "Yes, now that you say it, she is."

Blakely laughed again. "The orchid's okay?"

"Perfect. I haven't touched it. I'll water it day after tomorrow."

"Great. I'm so glad you remembered."

"How's the conference?" Becca asked, not knowing how one talked to professors about things like conferences. She wasn't even certain what Blakely was doing there. He hadn't mentioned it.

"Splendid," he said. "It's always lovely to get together with a bunch of people who despise one another's research and loathe one another's opinions. We're having a lovely brawl after each session. Very invigorating. We'll all leave battered and better off for it."

Becca didn't know if he was serious or sarcastic. "That's nice," she said.

Blakely laughed again. "That's one way of putting it. I must try to take a nap and sleep off some of my jet lag. Hugs and kisses to the girls from me."

"Sure," Becca said, looking dubiously at Hetta and Desdemona. Hugs and kisses? Not likely. After she hung up she said. "The big guy

called. He says hi and hugs and kisses." Both of the dogs looked up
at her. "What are you looking at me for? What am I supposed to do?
Entertain you, too?" Becca thought for a while. "Do you want to go
for a walk?" At the word *walk* both dogs grew animated. They ran
back and forth between her and the door, barking, until she'd managed to find and hook onto their collars both of their leashes. When
Becca opened the door, Desdemona took off in a bounding rush,
Hetta scampering and wheezing in her wake. "Wait up, Desi," Becca
said. The dog flung herself to the end of her leash and strained, then
bounded back to Becca.

Fallen leaves scuttled along on the streets and sidewalks. A gusty
wind blew the balmy air. Many of the front porches in the neighborhood sported jack-o-lanterns carved for Halloween. She'd have to
come up with a costume for the party this weekend. Having a birthday on the thirtieth of October meant she'd spent more than her share
of birthdays disguised as a witch or a ghost. She wasn't optimistic about
her ability to be any more creative this year, not with the dogs.

That night Becca allowed both dogs to sleep on the bed with her.
She woke in the morning slightly disoriented and was greeted with
Hetta's nose in her face.

"Hetta, someone could die from your breath." Hetta seemed to
laugh at the prospect. Desdemona stirred at the bottom of the bed.
The paper was there on the stoop as she let the dogs out. A newspaper, a house, two dogs. She was almost a real adult human being. It
seemed strange and nice. She made a pot of coffee, filled the dogs'
bowls, and let them back in. The sun streamed into the kitchen
through the large back windows. In only a few days, Becca had become accustomed to the strangeness of the house. The violent decor
no longer bothered her. It was just there, a subtext, like a scream in
another room at the doctor's office, something slightly startling but
not entirely out of the question.

Later, Becca stood to clear the table. As she moved to fold the paper, the gesture caused a strange reaction in the dogs. Both of them stood, tense, waiting, slightly anticipatory. She rattled the paper again and they tensed further as though they were about to bolt. Becca shook her head, smiled quizzically. When she shook the paper once again they were off, running insanely through the house. She was flabbergasted. The dogs returned to the kitchen then hesitated, clearly waiting for her. Becca picked up the paper once more and noticed the dogs go tense again. She shook it and they were off once more. This time she understood it was a game and she dropped the paper and chased them. Desdemona clattered across the wood floors, her nails sounding like cups breaking, her long muscular legs loping, bumping into doorways. Hetta skittered and slid along the slick floors, sometimes sliding on her hind end. They huffed and panted and ran through the house with Becca chasing after. This went on for several minutes and then suddenly both Hetta and Desdemona, as if on cue, turned and began to chase her. Becca, though startled, ran. She giggled with the sheer joy of the chase, shrieking as she came to tight corners where she felt them bearing down on her. The dogs followed madly. They played this game far longer than Becca would have wanted to admit to anyone she knew. She laughed and felt like a little kid, completely herself. She was amazed, when at last all of them landed together on the living room rug where they panted in silence for a while, to find that they had been playing together for over an hour. "You squirrelly beasts, you. Does Professor Blakely play that game with you every morning?" Becca smiled to think of Professor Blakely chasing and being chased through the house every morning before going to class.

When all of them were rested, they went for a walk. Becca had figured out how to keep Desdemona in a little better check with the leash so that she wasn't forever being pulled between the two dogs. It was almost noon by the time they returned to the house, and Becca wondered where the time had gone. She hadn't once felt as though she wanted to see anyone.

In the late afternoon, as the sun began to set, the house felt cozy and warm. The dogs were napping and Becca wandered toward the orchid room to check. In the dying sun, the flower seemed to radiate. It was an amazing sight, and Becca sat cross-legged on the floor outside the room just to watch. Later, when she realized the house was very dark, she couldn't account for how the time had passed or what she had done in the duration. Her legs were stiff from sitting so long in one position. Becca felt slightly disoriented as she stood to feed the dogs. Both of them looked up from naps as she turned on the lights in the living room.

Remembering she hadn't given the dogs their treat that day, Becca cut up some cheese and crackers to set on the table. They sat together at the table, Hetta in one chair, Becca in another, and Desdemona standing on her back legs, like three friends, two with really bad manners. It was a trick, Becca realized, something that Blakely had taught them to do. And Becca saw the humor of it as she sat there with them.

Professor Blakely called again the next morning just as she was getting ready to take the dogs for a walk. They were leashed and ready to go, waiting with their faces toward the door as she ran for the phone.

"We're fine," she said in response to his query. "I was just getting ready to take them on a walk. They're standing by the door waiting right now. They keep looking back toward me and wondering why we aren't going."

"Terrific. So you're walking them, then?"

"Twice a day."

"Terrific. That's terrific. That puts my mind at ease. Did you water the orchid then, too?"

"Not yet. It was next on my schedule when we got back from the walk." Becca knew without him saying it that Blakely would worry all day if he thought the orchid might not get watered. "Would you like to wait while I do that right now?"

"Yes. Don't worry about the time. These calls are costing me a fortune. It's no problem. It'll be worth the peace of mind knowing everything's okay. Don't hurry through it, though, take your time and do it right. You remember how I showed you?"

"Yes. I'll just be right back." Becca filled the pitcher, kicked her shoes off, and entered the white room. As she walked in, she felt as though she were intruding in some way. She slowly watered from the bottom, careful not to spill any water on the rug. When the job was finished, she came back on the phone. "All finished."

"Excellent," she heard from the other end of the line. "I won't keep the girls waiting much longer for their walk. I know how they are." In fact, Desdemona had barked a couple of times and Hetta had yipped impatiently. "Could you, though, before I hang up put the phone to Hetta's ear, please," Blakely said.

"Sure." Becca knelt and called to Hetta, who walked hesitantly toward her. "Here, Hetta. Listen."

From the distance, Becca could hear Blakely's tinny voice through the phone lines. "Hettie. Sweetie, it's daddy."

Hetta whimpered and looked at Becca who patted her head. She barked then and Becca heard Blakely's tinny laugh across the phone. He was still laughing as Becca put the phone back to her ear. When he grew quiet, Becca said. "Did you want to talk to Desdemona, too?"

"I've got to go now," he said. "Next time, though. What did Hettie do when she heard my voice?"

"She looked confused."

"Oh," Blakely said. Becca knew she should elaborate, describe how cute Hetta had been as she looked around the kitchen for Blakely, but the moment seemed to have passed before Becca could find the words, and then he was hanging up the phone.

That afternoon Leslie Ann called. "You ready for the party?"

"As ready as I'll ever be," Becca said, sounding grumpier than she felt.

"What are you wearing?"

"I haven't had time to think about that."

"Haven't had time? You have nothing but time. What's the matter with you?"

"It just isn't a priority," Becca said.

"Well, since you're Miss Dog-person right now why not go as Cruella De Vil?" Leslie Ann ventured. "We could rummage through the wardrobe room at Master's Hall and find a fur coat and some weird costume jewelry, a cigarette holder. Doesn't that sound good to you?"

"It sounds fine," Becca said, knowing the effect her lack of enthusiasm would have on Leslie Ann.

Leslie Ann brooded. "You're such a wet blanket, Becca. I'm trying to help you here."

"Sure. I see that. Sorry. Let's plan to meet this afternoon and put together a costume. It'd do me good to get out of here for a while anyway."

"That's more like it," Leslie Ann said. "I'll get a key from Dr. Williamson, and meet you there at two o'clock."

Although Becca was a little early for the meeting later that afternoon, Leslie Ann had already arrived. The door was ajar, wedged by a rock. Inside, only the hall light was on, the building a little eerie and cold. Like all campus buildings when they weren't lit and filled with students, it felt unfamiliar now.

Leslie Ann was in the wardrobe room sorting through the racks of clothes. She looked up as Becca entered the room. "Hey," she said. "I've found some coats and I'm looking now for a dress. Why don't you look through the props for a cigarette holder?"

Becca held up a couple of the coats and turned slightly in the full-length mirrors.

"Any of those going to work?" Leslie Ann said, glancing up.

"There seem to be some possibilities." Becca left the coats and went to the boxes of props stacked by category on large metal shelves. She knew the inventory fairly well after working on productions for over three years and quickly came to a box that seemed promising. With a slight groan, she pulled it from the shelf.

"How are you getting along over at Blakely's? Are those dogs driving you crazy yet? They drive everyone crazy. Anyone who's ever watched them for him. He doesn't leave much anymore because of it."

"I'm doing all right," Becca said.

Once they had put together a costume for Becca, Leslie Ann made suggestions for makeup and hair. "It'll be perfect," Leslie Ann looked at Becca calculatingly. "It's probably a good thing you never considered being an actress," she said.

"What's that supposed to mean?"

Leslie Ann shrugged. "You've got the looks, the height, but you don't seem to have the passion to make a character come alive. Somehow even in a great costume, you don't seem to have what it takes to be Cruella," she said—as though Becca should be ashamed of herself.

Before Leslie Ann and the guys arrived, Becca had a talk with the girls. She carefully put out more than enough food to get them through the evening and made sure the dog door worked in case they needed to go out. Becca explained she was leaving and that she'd be back that night, but that it might be late. As she was talking both of them watched her intently and she never once doubted they understood what she was saying. "Use the doggy door if you need to go out, you hear that Desdemona?" she said, since Desdemona was younger and didn't always seem as bright as Hetta. Desdemona licked Becca's hand as if she thought she were being scolded and wanted to appease her. Becca patted her head. "You'll be good, won't you? You okay, Hetta?" Hetta looked at Becca with her runny eyes. Becca wouldn't get off quite so easily with her.

The dogs stayed close while Becca transformed herself into Cruella De Vil. They seemed to sense something was happening. They watched as she teased up her hair and streaked the front, put on the jewelry Leslie Ann had found, and then applied more makeup than ten women should wear.

Later, the dogs hid away when Leslie Ann and the guys arrived. Almost as soon as they walked into the house, Leslie Ann made Becca turn around in her costume. "Grab the cigarette holder," she instructed, and Becca picked it up. "No. Not like that," Leslie Ann said with a frown. "Hold it, you know..." She took the holder away from Becca, thrust out one hip, and cocked her elbow, the cigarette almost to her lips, in a posture full of attitude. "Like that. Now you."

Becca struck the pose Leslie Ann had demonstrated.

"Yes!" Leslie Ann shouted. "That's perfect. See? You can do it if you try," she said as though Becca were a child learning to tie her shoes. Leslie Ann's self-absorption was already getting on Becca's nerves and the evening hadn't even begun. After Leslie Ann had okayed Becca's hair and makeup, she pulled out a bottle of red wine she'd brought along to toast Becca before they got to the party. Becca found a bottle opener and four wineglasses. Chad poured.

"To Becca," Leslie Ann said, raising her glass. "A great set designer. May all of your productions be under budget." As she laughed at herself, it was clear Leslie Ann had already gotten a good head start on her drinking. If this party proved to be like every other party, Leslie Ann wouldn't be satisfied until she was completely loaded. Chad and Stephen didn't seem enthusiastic as they endorsed Leslie Anne's giddy toast: "Hear, hear." Becca sipped the wine. It tasted slightly vinegary.

She realized as she watched Leslie Ann that their relationship was what passed for friendship between people who didn't really know one another but thought they did. Her realization was interrupted by Leslie Ann's invitation to the guys to take a tour of the house.

They tromped through the house with wineglasses in hand, exclaiming, raising eyebrows over various things until they got to the orchid room. Leslie Ann, showing off for the boys, kicked off her shoes and walked into the room. Chad and Stephen watched from the doorway with Becca. Leslie Ann was in her element: a stage and an audience. She began to improvise. "You water this thing yet?" Leslie Ann said, careening slightly toward the orchid. Becca felt her palms grow clammy. She tensed every muscle but knew enough about Leslie Ann not to give her any material, certainly not to ask her to be careful. Even without encouragement, Leslie Ann now lurched forward—a mock stage trip. She appeared to catch herself and her glass of wine only inches before she crashed into the orchid and spilled the wine on the white carpet. Becca's heart pounded. She knew Leslie Ann was a skillful actress, but she found nothing funny about the scenario. Stephen seemed to find the whole escapade very amusing as he laughed out loud. Becca wanted to say, "Don't encourage her," but she kept her mouth shut. Finally it was Chad who intervened. "Okay, time to get on the road," he said and turned his back on the orchid room. He's good, Becca thought. He knows exactly how to manage her. Stephen followed. Though Becca stepped away from the doorway, she waited for Leslie Ann, who was visibly disappointed to have lost her audience and needed to pout a little. In a moment she bounded out of the room with a happy grin. After putting her shoes back on and expertly balancing her wineglass, she slid her arm through Becca's. "I'm so glad you're my friend."

Later, Becca felt bad that she hadn't gotten a chance to tell the girls good-bye properly. Even as Leslie Ann and the guys left to wait for her in the car, the dogs seemed remote and hurt by her betrayal of them. Was that true? Hetta had turned her head away as Becca moved to pet her. Although Desdemona hadn't turned away she seemed confused and suspicious.

As the car pulled away from the house, Becca could see both of the dogs watching from the living room window. "Mutt and Jeff," Stephen said. Becca wished suddenly that she were staying home with the dogs.

The party was everything Becca had feared. The hostess was a woman known only by her first name—Karinth. Tinkly New Age music played on the stereo and people bunched into corners watching the door critically for newcomers. Everyone seemed to know Leslie Ann. They hugged and air kissed her on both cheeks, then threw up their hands and exclaimed over her costume. "Who are you? You look like a space-age Mary Tyler Moore," one woman said. "Exactly." Leslie Ann gestured for her to keep going as though they were playing charades. "Jane Jetson," the woman finally volunteered. "Of course," everyone agreed. "But a very sexy Jane Jetson," Leslie Ann said. Was there a script? Chad and Stephen seemed subdued. At one point, trying to break the monotony of standing around not being introduced or welcomed, Becca hugged Chad and mimicked the air kisses. "You look fabulous. Who the hell are you?" She stood back to get a better look at his costume. "Hercules?" she said.

"No," Chad said, obviously not understanding Becca's attempt toward humor. "I'm a gladiator."

"And you?" Becca gestured toward Stephen. "What are you supposed to be?"

Stephen looked slightly disappointed. "I'm the Mad Hatter."

By the time Becca had lost interest in her parody, she looked around the room for Leslie Ann, to find that she had disappeared into the bowels of the party. She would be gone all evening. As though all three were thinking the same thing, Becca and the guys headed toward what looked like a basement door. They found the basement empty, though the light was on and ashtrays were set out. In the middle of the room was a pool table. Becca didn't really know Chad, and she didn't particularly want to get to know Stephen, but she was glad to cobble together some sort of evening with the two of them. Above them the party thumped. Not once did anyone interrupt them in their game.

By eleven Becca had lost three games of pool and told the guys it was time for her to go. It would take over an hour to drive home.

"We'd better get Leslie Ann started then," Chad said, looking dubiously toward the basement ceiling.

Upstairs, Becca approached Leslie Ann who was flushed with alcohol and attention. "Oh, it's the birthday girl," she said with a flamboyant hug.

"I need to be going, Leslie Ann."

"But your birthday cake. You can't leave until we've sung Happy Birthday. Karinth ordered a cake especially for you."

"She shouldn't have," Becca said, feeling irritated again by Leslie Ann's insistence that this be a birthday party.

"It's your birthday. We need to sing and watch you blow out the candles."

"You're drunk, sweetie," Becca said, deciding to change tactics. "I appreciate the effort, I really do, but you promised me we'd get home by midnight."

Leslie Ann's jaw set. "We'll sing first," she said. Becca watched each person's reaction as Leslie Ann approached everyone about the birthday celebration—they all looked at her in confusion and said, "Who?"

Finally, by midnight a cake was brought out and Becca was placed ceremoniously behind it. The candles were lit. Leslie Ann led everyone in a raucous version of "Happy Birthday" and a roomful of drunk strangers clapped and cheered as Becca blew out the candles. She had never had a more miserable birthday in her life. As she bent to blow out the candles, she was tempted for a second by the dramatic image of her fur coat catching fire in the candles. Leslie Ann had been right when she had pointed out earlier Becca was not an actress. She neither desired nor appreciated the stage. She thought, as she blew out the candles, that Leslie Ann was bad news. The worst sort of news. She knew how to *act* like a nice person. But she was just an actress. Her stunning beauty made Becca, and apparently others as well, want to believe she was a nice person. But she wasn't. Becca decided she was never again going to allow Leslie Ann to talk her into anything.

When 1:00 A.M. rolled around and Leslie Ann was still not showing any signs of leaving, Becca tried desperately to recall the last name of Professor Blakely's friend, Alan-Who'll-Help-Out-In-A-Pinch. She had intended to bring his number in fear of the very thing that was now happening, but she had left it on the kitchen counter in the confusion. She was genuinely worried about the dogs and couldn't get out of her head Blakely's comment that they were terrified of being alone overnight. Whether that was true or not, Becca couldn't help but picture them still by the big window in the living room, watching for her return. But an even greater fear, inspired no doubt by the reverence she felt toward it, was that something would happen to the orchid. An image flashed across her mind of Hetta lifting her leg against the plant, and Becca felt weak with anxiety. And the white rug. How easily one of the dogs could soil it instead of using the doggy door to go outside. There had been nothing in the dogs' previous behavior to suggest this possibility, but Becca sensed something intelligent in Hetta, and with intelligence came the potential for vindictiveness.

As Becca had predicted, they did not leave the party until after 3:00 A.M. During the car ride home, Leslie Ann passed out in the front seat. Becca and Stephen looked out their respective backseat windows in silence as Chad drove. It was clear to the guys and Becca that there would never be any friendship between them, and it was clear to Becca that her friendship with Leslie Ann was over.

When the car stopped to let Becca out, Leslie Ann roused herself. "I'll call you later."

"Don't," Becca said as she pushed open her car door.

"Don't be mad at me, honey," Leslie Ann said. "After that nice birthday celebration."

Becca exchanged a quick, understanding glance with Chad and closed the door without responding to Leslie Ann.

It was 5:00 A.M. The dogs barked as she let herself in. After putting them out, Becca turned on the lights and went immediately to the orchid room, where she frantically searched the orchid for damage. When it checked out all right, she scanned the rug. She looked twice, got on her hands and knees, and inspected every inch. Finally, satisfied, Becca was so relieved she sank to the floor in the hallway and buried her face on her knees.

When she later let the dogs inside, it was clear Hetta was going to be slow in coming around. She turned her head away slightly from Becca. Desdemona was still confused, but Becca guessed she'd be fine once Hetta eventually forgave her. Becca understood Hetta's forgiveness could be counted on. That was the whole thing with the dogs. They wouldn't tattle on her. They were pure in that way, truly innocent. And the orchid was above emotion, the purest thing of all. Perfect.

In a day, Professor Blakely would come home. Even though nothing terrible had happened, nothing he could discern, she felt guilty. This was his family: the dogs and the orchid. She might have scoffed at that earlier, but not anymore. The dogs had taken her into their doggy world. She'd had a glimpse of transcendence in the presence of the orchid. She had endangered something precious to Blakely by not honoring his wishes. There were no excuses.

Hetta nudged Becca's hand with her little square head.

"Oh, Hetta," Becca said, overwhelmed by how quickly she had forgiven her. "Hetta." And seeing Hetta was okay again, Desdemona, too, came to Becca's side. The morning paper had just arrived. They all heard it at the same time as it landed with a soft thud on the front porch. Becca looked at the dogs. They followed her as she gathered the paper, and she performed the ritual for their game. Becca knew it was probably the last game of chase she would play with the dogs, and she ran with a giddy abandon through the house. She felt as though she had been given a second chance, and the feeling was not just about the white carpet and the orchid being safe, or the dogs' forgiveness. Becca couldn't say exactly what it was, only that she felt as though she had escaped something oppressive and dangerous and felt herself safe at home at last. When they had finished with the game, the girls and Becca fell together on the living room rug.

"Want a treat, girls?" Becca asked after they'd rested for a while. At the word *treat,* Desdemona was up and gone. She was there waiting when Becca and Hetta arrived in the kitchen. Her enormous paws were crossed slightly on the table, looking for all the world to Becca like they were folded in prayer.

MONICA WESOLOWSKA

Fine Arts Work Center in Provincetown

THE VIEW

They were arguing about deer when they rounded the bend and found one staring at them. Jim hit the brakes and threw an arm in front of Sandy, as if she were a child, and his forearm brushed against her breast. The deer paused, poised in a swirl of dust, one hoof raised, its head twisted back to hold them with its big, round eyes. Then it sprang. In the moonlight, everything shone silver—the trunks of the eucalyptus trees, the downed, decaying leaves, the furred flank of the bounding deer until it crested the hill and disappeared.

"Sorry about that," Jim said. He put his Jeep back in gear.

Sandy wasn't sure if he was apologizing for their argument, his driving, or brushing against her breast. At the party, he'd opened with a cliché about the weather, but now she could see that he'd meant it. The night *was* perfect, body temperature, and unusually clear for Berkeley. So what if he'd been arrogant in claiming that the best view in the whole Bay Area was from a boulder behind his house? The hair on his knuckles lifted as he slid the stick from gear to gear, and she wondered if big hands made for better drivers. Mateo drove so badly none of their friends would lend them cars anymore.

"Here she is," Jim said as they rounded the last bend.

Sandy giggled. "Wow." The house had been built against a steep hill, its front half supported by stilts, the area beneath the stilts cluttered with tools and tires and sporty-looking cars on blocks—a spider guarding its web full of flies. Only last weekend, she and Mateo had trekked into the hills to amuse themselves by mocking ridiculous houses like this. But then Mateo had accused her of secretly lingering beside someone's garbage cans for a slice of view, and he called her a view slut. They argued all the way home, Mateo claiming Sandy was destined to revert to her roots, to leave him for a yellow-haired yuppie, to settle down and have babies. There was no way. At twenty, Sandy knew she'd rather die than be a rich man's wife, knew Mateo was perfect for her, truly committed, as was she, to living as lightly as possible on this Earth. Still, sometimes she wished he weren't perfect, that he would match her weakness for commanding views with his own corrupt passion, something disgusting like fishing or, God forbid, golf.

They sat looking up at the house, the silence between them humming like a fluorescent bulb.

"Actually, deer aren't the real problem," Jim said. "I was reading this article." His arms felt light from the shock of the deer on the road. Although its appearance had proven his point about their abundance, almost hitting one felt like a bad omen. And the abundance of deer wasn't the point he'd been trying to make anyway. "During droughts, there are too many deer. That's a fact. The parks can't support them. They come out looking for food and eat my garden to the ground." When she said nothing, he was glad he hadn't specified that he grew roses. Roses would probably strike her as the ultimate symbol of excess. He opened the door of the Jeep and put one foot out. "But the point of this article I was reading was that, where the deer go, the mountain lions follow, which means, I guess, no one should go out unarmed. But don't worry, I've got my rifle handy."

He got the rest of the way out and lifted his arms high above his head, stretching, stretching, then dropping them, enjoying the rush of blood to his fingers. Bracing himself with his hands, he leaned toward the window of the Jeep to stretch his Achilles tendons and saw the look of shock on her face.

"Trust me," he said. "I'm an old pacifist." The stretch felt great after sitting all day; it refreshed him and he snapped up straight. "Be fair. We'd have to get someone to shoot them."

"Why?" she asked, her voice, high and pretty, sailing from the Jeep.

He laughed. "If I saw a mountain lion in front of my house..." He pictured the book he'd been reading to his kids, a neighborhood of wild animals in old-fashioned clothes, a lion in a top hat twirling his cane "...I wouldn't tip my hat to him and say How-dee-doo," and then he whipped an imaginary hat from his head and bowed profoundly.

"Why not?" she asked.

Still bent over he said, "Because they're dangerous."

"They don't usually attack," she said.

"So what are you saying? I mean, mountain lions stalk deer; that's nature." He leaned into the window of the Jeep and felt her lean away from him. "But what if I want to go jogging? Or take my kids out? You shouldn't have to be afraid to leave your own house."

"Ha!" she said.

Through the windshield, they saw the moon sliding up and glinting at the edge of the roof, deepening the dark face of the house, making it obvious that no one, no wife, no children, no one was home.

"Look," she said, with a high, breathless voice—as if she were scared, he thought, but then she went on with the argument—"Not only do mountain lions rarely attack humans but that's a *risk* you took buying a house next to the park. I mean, you get in your car, right? You accept that risk, right? Well, you're more likely to die from an accident than from a mountain lion."

"So what you're saying is you'd let a mountain lion attack and kill you before you'd attack or kill a mountain lion?"

"Maybe," she said, her voice still high but small now.

Thinking, *She's just being coy,* he smiled at her. "Look, do you mind waiting here while I run up . . ."

She stared up at him, then curled herself like a cat, or a fancy insect, tucking her hands tight between her legs.

Two steps at a time, Jim took the two flights of stairs to his front door. At the party he'd guessed at their age difference, confirmed now by their argument, but neither age nor argument quelled his excitement. Youth and idealism together were a turn-on. He saw himself young again, a starving student, surviving on principles and pasta. And sex. He saw again the length of her white neck, exposed to him at the party, as she threw back her head to laugh. They'd been talking drought-resistant gardens. She'd said she wanted to plant one where her garage now stood. He'd asked where she'd keep her car. "I don't even know how to *drive,*" she'd said, opening her eyes wide and leaning on him with her voice.

As he moved from keyhole one to keyhole two, the door swung open. He didn't usually forget to lock number two. Lucia—"the ex" as he had begun to call her with the divorce nearly final—did. He poked his head around the door and turned on the hall lights. The security alarm was off. He stepped inside, his footfalls echoing strangely, even now, weeks after Lucia had taken the Persian (out of spite, he was sure; he could imagine it rolled and standing upright in a corner of her mom's apartment). And then he saw the vase. It was a six-foot reproduction of a Ming vase. It had cost a fortune but somehow she'd convinced him they had to have it. And now in the center something was missing, a black hole the size of a fist, punched from the celadon. He spun around. Her mail was gone from the hall table by the door, where he had been stacking it, honorably, unopened, for weeks. He could feel her suddenly in the cold emptiness of the hall, could see her peach fingernails snatching the letters, smell her wild rose perfume, feel the hardness of her lips on his cheek.

"Bitch," he said aloud.

He took a deep breath and exhaled violently, something he'd learned to do late at night over legal briefs and depositions, Lucia in the other room doing what *he* wanted to be doing: feeding, helping with homework, brushing teeth, and sending to bed his kids, their kids, the ones she'd gotten primary custody over on the grounds that he'd been an absent dad. Goddamn it. He hadn't wanted the house; she had. He hadn't wanted the giant vase; she had. He hadn't wanted the Persian; she had. In fact, he hadn't even wanted kids, but, one by one, she'd convinced him to work for these things—and, one by one, they'd become essential to his existence. Now she was stealing them back. He hurried through the dining room, avoiding the windows. They'd bought the house for the view but ever since the ex had left, he'd felt queasy in the dining room, as though he were in the prow of a ship, heading out the Golden Gate to sea.

The first thing he saw in the kitchen was the fist-sized fragment of china set on a sheet of binder paper. His fury subsided as soon as he saw the handwriting. It was Sally's. "Dear Daddy, I am sorry I broke your vase. I was hiding from Daniel. He said he will help me get you a new one. I miss you." There was a P.S. from Lucia about how the kids really were sorry and how Lucia herself should be blamed (something about the edge of a box) and how they would do what they could to replace it. He slid the shard into the pocket of his shirt. He'd take it down to the garage. Maybe he could glue it back in. That could be a project with the kids. His eyes were stinging, and the inside of his nose was wet. He'd yelled at them so many times not to play around the vase but they loved that it was man-sized.

Nothing else in the kitchen seemed to have been touched, thank God. His dinner plate was on the table, where he had left it, beside the half-empty bottle of wine. Even the two roses the deer had spared were there in the sink, where he'd put them. He relaxed his hands from their fists. He would not let the ex ruin the night; he would not think any more about her, the house, the vase, the kids. He fingered a rose and considered opening a new bottle of wine. Then he dropped the rose and curled his fist around the neck of the open bottle; he didn't want to seem too eager.

The wineglasses hanging between the fingers of his left hand chimed as he walked. He was trembling. To calm himself, he counted off the things going in his favor: one, Sandy wasn't married; two, she loved views; three, she liked guys who liked views; four, she had *agreed* to come and see his view; five, she was too smart a woman to agree to things like that to be nice; six . . . He counted his way through the house and down the stairs and stopped at the bottom to confirm that, six, on top of everything else, she was sexy—even when she thought herself alone. She was leaning casually against the Jeep now, rocking slowly, her breasts loose beneath the fabric of her shirt. He hadn't touched breasts that young in years. It occurred to him that she wanted to look like girls had back then, in the seventies, with her Indian print blouse, her absent bra, her smooth hair hanging free, and he liked that. Beyond her, between two trees, was a view of the Golden Gate Bridge, and she was staring out that way, watching the winking lights strung sharp as diamonds across the velvet neck of the bay.

"You ready?"

He thought his voice had startled her, but then she turned slowly and calmly toward him. She even smiled. Beneath the smile, she was still considering what to do, how to escape, but she didn't want him to know. It seemed too late. She had been considering sneaking away while he was still in the house, running all the way downtown, taking a taxi home from there, but it was too late—he was back, looking bigger than ever, more alien, as if he might really be a man who carried a rifle. It was bad enough seeing him with a bottle of wine. What was he thinking? That she'd get drunk and pass out? And what about his wife? And Mateo? Hadn't they been explicit about having partners? She remembered, at the party, Jim leaning forward at her description of drought-resistant plants. Hadn't she mentioned Mateo at that moment, trying to make Jim back off? Yes, she knew she had because not only had she told him Mateo was a gardener, she'd also told him Mateo didn't own a car—which led to her stupid confession that sometimes she missed the romance of driving in the hills.

"Are you ready?" he said again.

"For what?" She smiled and turned to the slice of view between the trees. She hoped he'd take the hint, let her admire the view from here, where it felt safe, then drive her home.

"To see the view. The viewing boulder's up this way, around the house."

"Oh right," she said. She made her voice as hard and flat as she could but he still didn't seem to get it and now it was too late. She'd feel stupid saying "no" outright—now that they had come this far. And she couldn't let on she was scared of him. She could always say "no" up at the boulder if he wanted to do more than admire the view, right? But why didn't he get it? They'd argued the whole way to his house; they obviously had nothing in common. He was an old, rich guy who lived in the hills with his wife and children while she ... she was different. Keeping her hands in the pockets of her jeans, she shoved off from the Jeep with one hip. She would start yawning once they reached the boulder; surely he would get that.

Around the corner of the house, the ground was covered with round, white, sparkling rocks. A natural landscaping effect, he called it. In the moonlight, the rocks glowed and bulged bizarrely. He assured her this was the tough part.

Feeling her way along the wall of the house, she cursed her new sandals for being slick and feminine. Her toes kept sliding forward off the sole and into the shadowy cracks between the rocks, making the faux-leather thong bite deep. She wondered if he would have noticed her at the party if she'd been wearing her habitual boots. Finding him waiting for her at the back of the house, just beyond the rocks, slightly uphill from her, she sensed he was the kind of man who would offer a woman his hand at every rough part and she thanked God his hands weren't free.

"Okay?" he asked as she stepped from the final rocks.

When she nodded, he headed for a "path" she couldn't see, which he said led to the park. This part was supposed to be easier but, in fact, seemed more difficult with the ground steeply inclined and slippery with the decay of eucalyptus leaves. The heels of her feet slid off the backs of her sandals now, the occasional eucalyptus berry rolled underfoot, and the silver of the ground, striped black with shadows from the trees ahead, made her dizzy.

He was waiting at the edge of the trees. Again, he asked if she was okay.

From the way he asked, standing there jiggling one leg until the wineglasses clanged, she knew the boulder must be a long way off, deep inside the darkness of the trees. Days seemed to have passed since the party where she'd been charmed that he did push-ups on a boulder. Now it seemed creepy. With the moon behind him, she could see distinctly only the rim of one ear and the biceps of one fuzzy arm. Instinctively, she glanced back, assessing her chances of escape, how far she'd have to run, how many hours before Mateo, back from his wilderness retreat, would come looking for her. Telling herself not to be silly, she turned from the dark bulk of the house—and caught him taking a step toward her. She stared, trying to see his eyes, but the darkness furred his face.

Slowly, slightly she crouched.

He began another step, she was sure, a very slow step, like a giant cat preparing to pounce, and she could feel it on her skin, the hair there rising in anticipation of his snarl, his leap, his teeth at her neck.

If I had a gun, she thought, I would shoot him.

"What?" he said, stepping toward her.

She mumbled something about not doing this.

"Why not?" he said, still stepping toward her, forcing from her that high, breathless voice and a coy excuse—her silly, slippery shoes—hurled at him like a rock.

He stepped right past her.

Within seconds they were back at the carport. Under the fluorescent lights, everything—the red handles of his tools on the peg board, each fancy hubcap—seemed bright and separate. He felt her watching him, as if he might pounce, and he made himself small, eyes on the ground, as he passed her on the way to the Jeep.

"Where to? Your house?" he asked, opening the door for her.

When she hesitated, it occurred to him she belonged to a generation of girls who opened and closed their own doors. He abandoned her door for his own. Passing close again beside her he noticed the pores on her nose, big like the seeds on a strawberry, and marveled that she didn't hide them with powder. This pissed him off, having to prove he was nice, he thought, as, leaning into his side of the Jeep, he felt the weight in his pocket swing forward. He grabbed the porcelain and tossed it onto the dashboard. Seeing it trembling there like a severed hand, he knew he'd never fix the damn vase. He put his keys in the ignition and twisted to face her. He knew this made her nervous because she kept one foot out the door.

But he just had to get it off his chest first, he said, how much he resented her implication earlier that he was a monster for being honest enough to admit he'd try to kill a mountain lion before it killed him. He asked her what she honestly thought she'd do if her life were in danger. Ignoring the struggle clearly written on her face, he went on. He pointed out that most good, liberal, conscientious choices involved some ambiguity. As an example, he asked her to weigh the life of a mountain lion against the waste of gas driving up to admire his view. And he wouldn't let her bow out of this one, he said. "You were perfectly willing to let me drive you up here and you're perfectly willing to let me drive you home."

Sandy opened her mouth to say she didn't need a ride from him but then brought in her foot and shut the door.

He ground the gears into reverse, backed up so fast their heads hit the headrests when he braked. He felt the rush of control, gliding the stick into first, heading down his driveway. It hadn't been a very logical argument, he knew, but it was her kind of argument and if he could beat her at her own game, he would. He wasn't a lawyer for nothing. And if she tried to disagree, he had more for her: he'd remind her that deer once lived down in *her* neighborhood, too, and that tearing down a garage to plant a drought-resistant garden as a means of saving water was as dumb as buying bargains one didn't need as a means of saving money. Someday she'd learn that life was a series of compromises, a string of imperfect choices, and he refused to let her make him feel guilty.

They headed down, Jim taking the curves of the road with the same tight ease as before, the tires whimpering faintly.

With the moon higher overhead, the shadows of the trees had pooled beneath their trunks, and the road shone silver like a river down the hill. Sandy relaxed her grip on the door handle. She was, in fact, relieved and a little impressed that he had beat her on one point, that he had worried more about the waste of gas than she had. He was not such a brute after all, she thought, and then to keep the thing he'd tossed onto the dashboard from sliding about, she picked it up.

"Ming. Five thousand years old," he said with such arrogance that she had to challenge him.

"Really?"

"Well, a copy."

She smiled. Pale, silvery, blue green, and veined like the leaves of the yarrow she would grow in her garden, the pottery was soft against her thumb, curved, the white edges a nice rough change from its smooth, cool surface. "Still, it's beautiful."

"You can have it," he said.

Holding it up, she thought she saw through it the yellow glow of a streetlamp, blinking off and on, closer and closer, between the passing trunks of the eucalyptus trees.

"If you want it, take it."

"It's beautiful," she repeated, feeling guilty for liking it, knowing Mateo would use this as proof of something weak in her—her materialism, her reverence for things. But she liked it for what it represented, she argued with the Mateo-in-her-head. She was moved to think of Jim carrying such a thing in his pocket, as a good luck charm, or a worry bead, or, perhaps, as a reminder of the balance between human frailty and endurance. Still working the shard with her thumb, she sank back in her seat. She began to enjoy again the night air on her neck, the lifting of the yellow hairs on his forearm, the way he shifted gears, smoothly, taking each curve with the grace of a deer.

MARGO RABB

Wesleyan Writers Conference

MY MOTHER'S FIRST LOVER

The summer after my mother died, I dreamed about her first lover. In the dream I followed him, detectivelike, slinking through museums, coffee shops, libraries, subway trains, hoping he'd lead me to my mother. He strode like a movie star, confident and oblivious to the rest of the world; at dusk he wound his way through Central Park, down narrow paths along patches of forest to a small, secluded lake. There, drying off by the shore, stood my mother. She looked nothing like she had when I last saw her—her hair matted against the hospital pillow, her belly bloated with growths. By the lake her black hair gleamed like velvet; her stomach looked taut and smooth. At last you've found us, she said, reaching for my hand. I've been waiting.

The dream had started that summer in English class, when Ms. Poletti asked us to write a story about true love.

Groans all around. Felix Manquez sailed a spitball at the blackboard. "I don't *know* any love stories," whined Luisa Rodriguez.

Willy Silva muttered "Bullshit" through his gold teeth. Marisol Peters ignored the class altogether to doodle across her NO GUNS IN SCHOOL! bookmark—a gift we'd all received from the Board of Education. We were students in the Bryant High School summer program, who for various reasons had been unable to pass our classes during the year. I stared out the barred windows to the rolling pavement of Queens. My mother had died that January; the only spring semester class I'd passed was hygiene.

"Love is beauty," Ms. Poletti sighed, off in her own reverie. We'd just finished reading Elizabeth Barrett Browning in class; Ms. Poletti had recited each stanza in a Britain-meets-Queens accent, her flower-patterned dress dipping frightfully low as her bosom heaved. She was an anomaly at our school, flitting about like a robin, perching on our desks to impart to each of us seeds of hope. Rumors about her abounded: Luisa swore she'd seen Ms. Poletti adjusting her G-string in the girls' bathroom; Felix spotted someone on the subway reading a romance novel by a Madame Poletti. In the cafeteria and on the walk to the 7 train after school we made fun of her—arching our eyebrows, shrilling our voices—but the consensus was that she was an improvement over Mr. Gendler, the English teacher we'd all had that spring. He had been fired in May after recruiting on campus for the North American Man-Boy Love Association. Everyone was passing now—that is, everyone but me.

Failing English again was a particularly remarkable achievement, considering that I was the only native English-speaker in the class. I wasn't a terrible writer; my subjects were the problem. For the How You Overcame Your Deepest Loss assignment I'd written "Snuffy: Better Off Dead," about my recently departed overweight gerbil, who'd suffered a slow and painful demise after getting stuck in the Habitrail. Most recently, on a Topic of Great Social and Political Import, I'd completed "Plaid Pants: Should They Be Outlawed?" which had garnered a round of applause when I'd read it to the class, but received an N, Ms. Poletti's polite way of saying you failed.

She called me to her desk that day after class. She sat there like a magistrate escaped from Las Vegas, her sequined glasses slipping down her nose. "Miss Bloom," she said. "Are you familiar with the phrase *Attitude is everything*? She tapped a pink fingernail on my compositions. "There's a *tone* to these essays that's not suitable for the assignments. Good writing isn't about glibness. It's about *life*. Think Elizabeth Barrett Browning. Think 'How Do I Love Thee.'"

She smoothed the ruffled pages. "Now this Snuffy piece—I see things to admire here. Clear language. Solid composition." She removed her glasses. "Yet you haven't let your readers *feel* your triumph over this loss. What was your *connection* to Snuffy? What did he *mean* to you?"

I shrugged. I didn't know how to explain myself. All I knew was that after school and my shift waitressing at the Queens Burger, when I put my mother's old typewriter on the dining-room table and listened to my father snore in front of the TV (he liked to keep it on even while he slept, for company) the last thing I could write was something serious.

She surveyed the index card I'd filled in the first day of class. Under "In your own words, why did you not succeed in English during the regular school year?" I'd written, *My mother died.* It was strange to see it on the stark white card—name, address, Social Security number, grade-point average, dead mother.

"I know that other things have been going on in your life," Ms. Poletti said. "But if you fulfill the assignment just *one time,* you'll pass this class. I don't think you want to stay in high school an extra year."

I said I didn't think so either.

She sighed. "You shouldn't have trouble with this. It should be a pleasure to write about love."

That night my father wheezed on the couch while zebras leaped across the TV screen. The narrator droned on about mating practices as I settled in front of my mother's Smith-Corona. The first thing that came to mind was my parents:

True Love

On a cold rainy night in March, over a year ago, Simon Bloom gave his wife Greta their twentieth wedding anniversary present.

"Is it clothes?" Greta asked excitedly, clutching the huge box. "A case of wine? A crate of imported fruit?"

"Better," Simon said.

Greta ripped open the cardboard to reveal a glimpse of shiny red enamel.

"What is it? What is it?" shouted the Blooms' two charming young daughters.

The packaging fell away to reveal—a fire extinguisher.

"It was on special at Sears," Simon said, taking the extinguisher from her, stroking it lovingly. "Should we test it?"

Alex, the elder daughter, who was home from college, jumped up excitedly. "Yes! Yes!" she cried. The younger daughter, Mia, shook her head like her mother; neither of them was very interested in fire extinguishers.

"Simon," Greta groaned, "we don't have time to test it. We're supposed to be at the restaurant *now*. You *agreed*, for *once*, to go out tonight."

Simon didn't hear her. "I think that hooks there," he mumbled to Alex.

"*Simon,* will you listen to me?" Greta screamed.

Simon didn't look up.

"For *once,* will you just *listen* to me?!"

"Just a second—"

"*Simon!*" Greta lifted a plastic ashtray off the nearest shelf. She threw it at him. It missed and bounced off the floor. She picked up a candle in the shape of a turtle—a Chanukah present from her daughters years ago.

"Not the wax turtle!" the daughters shouted. "Not the wax turtle!"

I crumpled it up; this was not a love story. No matter what my parents talked about—the telephone bill, cleaning the gerbil cage, who bought the scratchy brand of toilet paper—they'd fight. Eventually Alex and I removed all fragile objects from their shelves, and at night I'd lie awake listening to the arguing, my sheet wound in my fist as they screamed. In the beginning Alex and I tried, in little ways, to repair our parents' marriage: we taped the praising *Queens Independent* write-up of my father's shoe repair shop to the refrigerator; we ordered two laminated oversized buttons made from their wedding photo. But soon my mother began to call her best friend, Fanny Gluckman, nearly every night (Fanny had divorced her husband, Irv, four years earlier) and whisper on the phone.

Fanny told my mother to give up trying to drag my father to restaurants and the ballet and to take me instead. I loved being my mother's date: Together at Lincoln Center we'd cascade past the outdoor fountain, through the main hall, amid the rustling taffeta and swishing silk of the finely dressed ladies, the sweep of furs, wafts of expensive perfume. I pretended we lived there, in this mansiony hall with marble banisters and chandeliers like explosions of glass. Afterward we'd linger at the Pirouette Café across the street, heavily under the spell of the performance, not ready to go home. Queens—our father and his stories of hammertoes and plantar warts, my sister shouting at her calculator as she practiced for math competitions—seemed like somebody else's life. For the first time, I began to wonder whether my parents should be married after all.

One night at the Pirouette, the summer before I started high school, my mother's mind seemed elsewhere. "I was talking to Fanny the other day," she said. "She invited me to come visit, for a little vacation. I was thinking you might like to come, too, and see Lucy."

I'd been friends with Lucy Gluckman since I was three; she and her parents lived four blocks away then. I hadn't seen her since the divorce. In her letters she said she liked Maplewood, in upstate New York, much better: the houses weren't attached, as they were in Queens—no more of crazy Mrs. Fonchette scratching the walls. And her father arrived for visits with presents overflowing from the trunk. Her boyfriend, Brad, was captain of the lacrosse team; in ballet class she was now en pointe. Not wanting to feel left behind, I'd embellished my own life: I invented a passionate affair with Luigi, the handsome cook at the Queens Burger; I told her that my recital at the Flushing Academy of Dance had received a standing ovation, when in reality I'd pranced across the floor twelve counts early, like an escaped jumping bean. But the embellishments never seemed entirely false—sometimes at the Pirouette, after a performance, a part of me actually believed that one day I would be a dancer, twirling around that huge stage, leaping into Luigi's arms.

"You'd like Maplewood," my mother said. "There's shopping, and forests and lakes—and the community center, where Fanny teaches folk dancing. You could even take ballet there, if you wanted."

"It might be weird seeing Lucy—it's been so long," I said, wondering how I'd explain my less-than-stellar ballet technique.

"Maybe at first. Then things'll be like before. Some of the people in Maplewood I haven't seen in years—old friends from Washington

Heights. People I've been wanting to see for a long time. Fanny said she's surprised how little they've changed."

Washington Heights: my mother and Fanny had both grown up there, when it was a neighborhood of German-Jewish refugees who'd narrowly escaped the Holocaust. Whenever we drove through it, my mother shuddered, remembering the stone-faced men and women shuffling from store to synagogue to their tiny, crumbling apartments, undecorated and bare—not like homes, my mother said. She told me once that her parents never hugged her; I couldn't even imagine it—our hugs were such an event. Even at fourteen I'd sit on her lap on the couch some nights, facing her, nuzzling my nose into her neck, talking as she kissed my hair—"huggies," we called these moments, like they were a pastime, a game, a performance.

"Why'd your old friends move to Maplewood?" I asked.

She shrugged. "I guess to be happier. To get away. To find a better life."

Fanny and Lucy met us at the bus stop in a yellow Volkswagen bug; Fanny lumbered toward us in her Birkenstocks. "Ya look gorgeous!" she told my mother.

"So do you!"

"That's what they tell me. I say leaving Irv took ten years off my age."

Lucy hugged me briskly. I didn't know what to say at first, we hadn't seen each other for so long. "How's Brad?" I finally asked.

"Oh good. You know. We're okay. And Luigi?"

"He's pretty good. Actually I haven't seen him much lately. He's really busy—making all those burgers and all."

"Brad's busy, too. You know—we kind of broke up."

"Really? Oh my God. I bet me and Luigi are going to break up, too."

"It's really not that bad. My mother says I'm better off."

We stared at our mothers, giggling like teenagers in the front seat. They gossiped on the whole drive and all the way up the gravel road to the house. It was a gingerbread bungalow, plopped in a sea of bright grass, the blades soft and cottony, whispering under my shoes.

"The block has a service that mows it," Fanny said. "Can you imagine if we had lawns in Queens? I'd have spent half my life getting Irv to mow."

My mother settled into the guest room while Lucy and I prepared the bottom half of her trundle bed. We dressed up for dinner at the Maplewood Grill: skirts and purses and high-heeled shoes. We sprawled out in our cushiony booth; our mothers lit cigarettes and poured us wine.

"I'm so glad you're staying two whole weeks—a week from Saturday is Summer Showcase," Fanny said. "The whole town comes out. My class is performing first—four versions of the hora. I'm hoping the girls will dance, too."

"*Ma*," Lucy groaned. "Not the *hora*."

"How are you going to get the boys to notice you if you don't shake your cute tush?"

"*Ma!*"

"These girls don't know how lucky they are—dinners out, dance classes. What did we have when we were their age? Boiled potatoes. Hopscotch. There was no music in our house. No dancing. No stomping around. No talking above a whisper. What did my father think—we'd be arrested by the Gestapo, lurking outside in New York?"

"Elsa became a dancer," my mother said. "Remember Elsa? Elsa Goldstone. I think she even made it to the Joffrey."

Fanny raised her eyebrows. "Then she danced her way out a sixth-story window. A little more graceful than Jack Cohen. You know I ran into someone who knew his wife—said she came home one night, found him dead on the couch. Pills."

I stared at Lucy, frozen in her seat. We had always frozen whenever our mothers' conversations turned to people they'd known—survivors or children of survivors who'd gone over the edge. The stories made me fear for my mother's life; it seemed suspended by a single thread. I couldn't make sense of her emotions: we had our nights out, the ballet, but she spent hours in bed, sleeping off an undefined illness, waking only to scribble in notebooks in her half-lit room. And there were the fights with my father, like sudden explosions, and her Wednesday night trips to Dr. Mallik, her therapist, whom Fanny had recommended. Fanny shared many of my mother's quirks: cupboards stocked with cans and cans of food, *just in case;* pocketbooks loaded with tissues, Band-Aids, a change of clothes, as if at any moment they might have to flee; the way they kept track of Lucy and me, wanting intricate details of our plans at all times, as if once they lost track of us for a minute, they'd lose us forever. And the way, when they said good night to us, they told us they loved us with near-desperation, as if they doubted that we'd still be there in the morning.

Our hugs and food and declarations of love—I knew how much these gestures meant to my mother, and this knowledge gave me an odd kind of power: I knew her happiness was inextricably entwined with mine. But I depended on her, too; I lived for her hugs, her food, I told her I loved her with her same intensity, as if to say, You have to live—if for nothing else, then for me.

My mother's attention to me, though, seemed to lag after the first few days in Maplewood. In the mornings Fanny deposited me and Lucy at ballet class, while my mother slept in; I didn't see her until dinner. She seemed quiet and distant then, but peaceful, even satisfied.

"What'd you do all day?" I'd ask her at dinner.

"Oh nothing—sat by the lake. Relaxed. Read some."

Fanny had given her a whole pile of books: *Fear of Flying, Heartburn, The Women's Room;* my mother pressed wildflowers between the pages. She was definitely enjoying life in this town, and I was, too— the clean, white sidewalks of Main Street, the wide, airy aisles of Stop & Shop, nights in bed beside Lucy, reading *Seventeen* out loud. Even ballet was better than I'd expected. Lucy did wear toe shoes, but she kept tripping over them, and the instructor, Jolée, didn't even notice me twirling off count.

"Think how good we'd be if we danced together all the time," Lucy said, nearly falling over from her arabesque. "We'd be like Baryshnikov and Gelsey Kirkland. Torvill and Dean without ice."

In Jolée's class we'd become a regular pair: Each day, for our improvisations, we invented a two-minute ballet and performed it as a couple. It didn't matter what we looked like; Jolée simply crooned, "Feel the *mooovement*, become the *mooovement*," and nodded with praise.

Out of the whole class, only one girl's mooovements seemed on target, even beautiful, and Lucy and I often stopped to gape at her with envy. She was sixteen, with black hair that swept to her hips, and breasts that made ours seem like walnuts. Jolée adored her. It wasn't until late in the week that I found out her name: Greta, just like my mother's.

"Isn't that weird?" I said to my mother at dinner that night. "Isn't that the craziest coincidence? Another Greta. I never met anyone else with your name."

My mother nodded and shrugged; she didn't seem fazed or surprised, but Fanny kept smirking at me and then glanced at my mother and said, "Honey, it's not a coincidence—Greta's father was your mother's old boyfriend. He's a widower now."

I gazed at my mother. Sometimes she would tell me about the men she'd gone out with before she met my father: Moshe the Israeli; Charlie the Navy sailor, whose whole crew stood up when she entered the room; Harry the Californian, with the red convertible. I always felt envious and proud that my mother had all these lovers, that she was so attractive and desirable, that she'd had this whole other exciting, romantic life, as I hoped I would someday.

"Greta's father is Moshe?" I said. "Harry with the sports car?"

My mother laughed. "No, no. This was the first boyfriend I ever had. Rolf—Rolf Stein."

Rolf. I peppered her with questions. She'd known him since she was my age, growing up in Washington Heights; unlike her family, who'd escaped to America at the beginning of the war, Rolf's had gone to Holland. His parents hid him in a Dutch orphanage, and he never heard from them again.

"We were engaged when I was eighteen," my mother said. "But before we could get married, he wanted some proof that his parents were actually dead. He'd had this hope, all those years, that they might still be alive. He left for Europe then—Germany, Holland, France, Russia. This long search. He found someone who'd known them in Amsterdam, someone who thought they'd been sent to Treblinka and survived."

He'd sent my mother postcards from across Europe for more than a year; suddenly the postcards stopped coming.

"What happened?" I asked. "What then?"

She shrugged. "Nothing. I married your father."

In bed that night, Lucy and I couldn't stop talking about it.

"Oh my God. It's so romantic. To name his daughter after your mother. He must have really loved her."

"I guess. I guess he did."

We recounted the story again and again. Drama, it was. Romance. *The Sound of Music,* starring my mother. In our minds Rolf grew as handsome and dashing as Christopher Plummer; my father became the balding understudy, with too-short corduroys and mismatched socks.

Lucy had seen Rolf only in passing; she couldn't remember what he looked like. "But I'm sure he's gorgeous. I bet you he'll be at Summer Showcase. Everybody goes. My God—we're really going to meet him."

As the showcase approached, Jolée told us that we could each perform a five-minute dance on stage. Lucy and I knew exactly what we'd do: We were going to dance the saga of my mother's first love. We choreographed it expertly. For the war we donned black leotards and galumphed across the stage; then we pulled on purple scarves and swept toward each other with elegance and grace; then we crumpled apart. We ended together in a passionate embrace.

As we rehearsed for Saturday, we decided that watching the dance would reunite my mother with her true love. She and Rolf would see the performance and recognize that their love had never ended; my mother would marry Rolf and we'd move to Maplewood; Fanny would marry Rolf's long-lost cousin, who'd suddenly appear, and Lucy and I would be related for real. We didn't even think of Lucy's father, my father, or my sister; in Maplewood the rest of the world seemed to disappear. It felt feasible, possible, that everyone could be happy.

On the morning of the performance I woke up feeling sick with a sharp, shooting pain around my stomach. I wasn't sure if the cause was anxiety or something concrete, but by the afternoon, at rehearsal, it hadn't gone away.

"I don't feel so well," I told Lucy.

"It's probably just nerves," she said. "You're scared of the responsibility. The pressure. It isn't easy, reuniting old loves."

I hugged my abdomen. "I don't know. Maybe—it could be my *friend*."

"Oh," Lucy said knowingly: my period. "Is she supposed to be visiting now?"

"She's early I think."

"She really makes you sick?"

"Yeah. Kind of." I'd rarely told anyone, aside from my mother, how sick my period made me. For most eighth-graders, cramps were the imaginary, convenient excuse for getting out of typing, math, or gym, but I was almost doubled over by the pains. I was embarrassed by how badly they affected me, how I missed school and threw up and ran fevers, spending all day in bed, writhing and crying, praying for the aspirin to set in. Even my father didn't wholly believe the pain was real; he seemed frightened of me then, averting his eyes when he asked me how I felt. And he wasn't unsympathetic just because he was a man—Alex didn't believe me either. We weren't like the sisters I wanted us to be, confiding all our womanly secrets; when she first got her period and surreptitiously popped the Kotex into our shopping cart, I was shocked and elated, expectant and jealous. "What's it feel like?" I'd asked her, eager to share in the delights of her budding womanhood. "Shut the fuck up," she'd said.

My mother was the only one who believed the pain was real. To her, any illness, menstrual or not, became an occasion. Out came the ginger ale, strawberry Jell-O, soup; sometimes she'd stay home from work, and when the painkillers finally set in, we'd paint with watercolors and play board games I was far too old for. She brought up trays of food for me to eat in bed—sandwiches with the crusts cut off, saltines spread with peanut butter and jam.

But now, all day, as rain poured down outside, we'd been practicing, decorating, and preparing for the showcase; I wouldn't see my mother till it was over.

"Once we start dancing you'll forget it hurts at all," Lucy told me. "You'll be fine."

But by evening my cramps were even worse. At six-thirty, half an hour before the performance, I pulled off my leotard in the bathroom.

Blood. Drips and gobs of it on my underwear; I recoiled at the sight. Shock it always was, and surprise, at seeing the redness; I never accepted that all this blood leaving my body could actually be a normal thing.

I felt dizzy and hot; I found Lucy backstage. "I'm *really* sick," I said. "My friend's *here*."

"Can't you just take care of it? No one will know." She glanced out at the auditorium. "You have to go on. The dance—we can't not do the dance. I can't do it without you."

She summoned Jolée, who suggested I try deep breathing methods, and Fanny, who procured aspirin from someone in her hora group.

"Do you know where my mother is?" I asked Fanny, my voice beginning to break. "I need to see her."

She looked around at the people filing into the auditorium. She seemed nervous. "I don't know. I haven't seen her since this morning. Maybe... she might be by the lake. But, honey—" She reached her hand out to me, but I started running, past Fanny, Lucy, Jolée, out the stage doors. I didn't know what I was doing. The performance, our rehearsals, our plans to reunite my mother and Rolf—suddenly none of them mattered. I had to see my mother now; I had to know where she was. I wanted not just her comfort but the assurance of her presence; for a moment I felt like the mother—worried about my daughter's whereabouts, needing the fact of her life to validate mine.

The rain had stopped. I ran the whole way to the lake, half a mile, the wet grass soaking through my pink ballet slippers, mud splattering onto my tights. Near the lake I paused, panting. My mother, her back to me, was sitting quietly at the water's edge. A man sat beside her, his arm around her waist.

"Mom!" I called out. "Mom!"

She turned and stared at me, standing there sopping wet and streaked with mud; she looked at me as if I were crazy.

"I'm really sick. I think—I think I need to go home."

I didn't get a good look at Rolf. In the rush all I saw was the dark form of his body, shaded angles of his face. My memories after that are shady, too, my brain trying to edit out my clumsiness, my humiliation at destroying my mother's love scene. I remember my mother taking me home to clean me up, and, later, apologies to Fanny for missing the performance, Lucy's silent disappointment, my mother's quick decision that we had better leave that night—that I'd probably feel better if I just got back to Queens.

On the bus ride home my mother showed no sympathy. I vomited in the bus bathroom; I sniffled in my seat. My mother hugged her pocketbook to her lap and gazed out the window, not listening. She seemed torn between Maplewood and Queens, angered by her decision, her obligation, to return home. In one instant she chose our old life over a new one, but that choice brought her no relief. Midway through the ride a woman tripped over my bag in the aisle. "Stop being so goddamn careless!" my mother screamed at me.

I gathered my bag to my chest. A month before, the last time I'd gotten sick from my period, we'd missed a ballet performance because of it. My mother had said it didn't matter, and she'd told me what she really felt about dancing then. In reality it's not a life, she said. You can't see it on the dancers' faces but underneath they're all in pain. Their bloody toes, their torn ligaments. They're all hiding tremendous suffering.

I cried that night on the bus, noiselessly, my face turned toward the aisle, buried against the seat so that my mother wouldn't see. I didn't cry because of the cramps or the sickness; it was guilty crying, over my own selfishness. That dancers hid their suffering seemed noble; they endured pain for something beautiful. And I'd been unable to make that sacrifice, or even come close. Self-absorbed, self-entranced, I'd embraced my pain, shouted it, flaunted it, as if it was something unique.

Little changed after we returned home: my parents' fights continued, my father still slept on the couch, my mother murmured to Fanny on the phone. My mother never spoke of Rolf to me, and rarely mentioned our trip to Maplewood. I didn't bring it up. I was grateful that our relationship seemed the same as it always had been: hugs, evenings at the Pirouette, declarations of love.

Then one night, two months after we'd come home, my mother said good-bye to Fanny on the phone and passed the receiver to me. "You have to watch out for your mother—it's bad news," Fanny said. "Rolf...he passed away. I can't believe it. I just...I can't believe it at all."

Passed away seemed the wrong choice of words when she told me what had happened: Greta had come home after school one afternoon to find him hanging from an exposed rafter in an upstairs bedroom.

That night I went to my mother's room to talk to her, to comfort her. I brought up milk and crackers, arranged on a tray. But she lay asleep in the darkness, surrounded by her open notebooks. I shut the door and returned to my room.

I didn't know what to make of Rolf's death. I blocked it out until three months later, when my mother was suddenly diagnosed with advanced melanoma. In the ten days between the diagnosis and her death—no one had expected it to happen so soon—Fanny sent packages of self-healing books, *Medicine & Miracles, Think Yourself Well.* The night after my mother died, Fanny told me on the telephone, "It was your mother's depression. She never came to terms with her history, with her parents. With the war. Really it's not so different from Elsa or Jack. Or from Rolf. I've seen it happen to so many people..." She trailed off and began to cry.

I didn't know what to say to her. I'd been devastated, stunned by my mother's death; everything, my whole life, seemed instantly gone. Part of me wanted to scream at Fanny that my mother could not have brought it on herself. She could not have wanted to die.

But perhaps my mother *hadn't* brought it on herself; perhaps we were to blame—my father, my sister, and I—in our inability to give her what she wanted. What if that night in Maplewood, I'd said, Stay with Rolf, Mommy! He's yours! You should be happy with your own life!

I didn't say any of this to Fanny. I just said, "Uh-huh. I have to go now," and hung up the phone.

The sun began to come up. My father still slept on the couch. Outside, a garbage truck groaned down our street. Our neighbors' bed rattled against their side of the wall.

"My Mother's First Lover" was all I'd typed on the page during the night. At some point I'd fallen asleep across from my father, at the other end of the couch. I'd dreamed of Rolf, and had trailed him to where my mother was, where she surely must be: in some other universe, alive and happy, with him.

For a few moments, in that hazy transition into waking life, a dream lingers as reality: Rolf's form strong and permanent, my mother lithe and healthy and satisfied. The peacefulness that surrounded them was what stayed with me the most in the seconds before I completely awoke—the rightness of it, of true love reunited. The perfect ending to this story, a story Ms. Poletti might write, one she'd certainly approve of.

But I'd barely become accustomed to that picture when it began to evaporate. Outside, the garbage truck creaked, car horns honked, a taxi driver screamed. On the dining-room shelf—the shelf off of which my mother had once tossed objects—lay one of the oversized buttons my sister and I had made of our parents' wedding photo. In that photo my mother smiled with the same satisfaction she'd shown in Maplewood. The same expression she'd had in the dream.

My father said to me once, not long ago, in the car driving over the bridge to Manhattan, one of the few times we talked about my mother after she died, one of the rare times we shared anything openly at all: "The problem with Mommy was that she never believed I loved her. I told her I did, but she never believed it was true."

At first I balked, not believing that any of my father's perceptions could be right. I had blamed him, along with myself, for her death, for not making her happier. But I knew he had loved her: His grief was as clear as mine since she'd been gone. And I thought about my mother, growing up without ever being hugged. Despite the lack of love she'd felt in her own life, she'd managed, somehow, to love me. The night we left Maplewood, after the long bus ride home, I awoke in the middle of the night to find a tray of ginger ale and sandwiches, the crusts cut off, and my mother next to my bed, her hand on my stomach, assuring me then and always that the pain was natural after all.

SHIMON TANAKA

University of Oregon

VIDEO AME

When I was ten, I prayed harder than at any time in my life. I prayed for a Commodore 64 every day, and for Ojīchan—my Japanese grandfather—every second or third day. This was backward, I knew, but I had not been to Japan since I was five and I could barely remember what he looked like. Even while she was sick, my mother told us to pray, not for her, but for Ojīchan, that he would become Christian. I wanted to be dutiful—to pray for him—but my mind wandered so easily, to the Commodore. When I remembered to include Ojīchan, I prayed with a fervor that I hoped would make up for my forgetfulness; my fingers, folded tightly, would end up blanched and sweating. "Father," I whispered, "open Ojīchan's eyes to Truth." Sometimes I prayed for my mother, too. But I didn't know what to say.

We didn't have a computer then, but we did have Atari. My sister, Ame, was a year younger but she was better at it than I was, better at Missile Command and Space Invaders—she would be the one, when the games ended and the screen went to pink and blue or green and purple, she would be the one slamming her joystick down, or else stretching her fingers slowly, working the knots out. I was usually killed long before and waiting for her to finish. When she did, I would stop reading computer ads or comic books to look at the screen, at the end of the world and its candy colors.

Ojīchan was baptized last month. I got the message from my sister in Tokyo. "It was beautiful," she wrote. "Ojīchan in robes, he bows and water sprinkle. all the days writes the verse on very long scroll, two hours. Obāchan happy time smile. love ame :)" Ojīchan is my maternal grandfather, Obāchan my maternal grandmother. I studied this e-mail at a desk that was not mine, behind the closed door of an office that was not mine. I was supposed to be fixing a Windows problem; that's my job. I have no desk of my own, strictly speaking. I'm a roving tech person, a problem solver.

I read the thing again. Ame knows English well, but she hates it so much she pretends not to sometimes. I replied: "ame: send pictures. love ken." I stared until the screensaver—the company logo, hurtling through space—came up, startling me.

We are all named Ken. What I mean is, there are many half-Japanese males with my name. It's popular because it's common in both Japanese and English. Your typical half-Japanese family has two children, a boy and a girl: the boy is named Ken and the girl, Emi. *Emi* is not quite *Amy*, but it is close enough for most Americans. My sister is named Ame, pronounced AH-may. It means rain. I've never heard of anyone else with that name, though now that she is famous, perhaps there will be more. I don't know why my mother decided to be different, naming her Ame. *Ame* is half of *America*, maybe that's why.

I rent an apartment in Fort Lee, New Jersey; not one of those high-rises above the Palisades, but a more modest one, along the water-front. It's slightly expensive but it's nice enough and I like being on the water. I can look across and see Harlem. The two-family where Ame and I once lived with my mother is close by, a few towns over.

In the kitchen next to my refrigerator—towering over it, actu-ally—is my PDP-11/45. Some people restore old cars; I have my PDP-11. It's got a reel-to-reel tape drive, expansion trays that slide out, black cabinet doors that open up on rows of circuit boards that can be con-figured in almost any way, and a front panel that's simple and clean with two knobs and one row of twenty-seven red rocker switches. Its programs are punched as holes on ticker tape five centimeters wide. There are people, the theologians of the computer world, who can ac-tually read and interpret these programs. In one of the trays, I've in-stalled a 224 megabyte Intergraph hard drive modification with a metal disk, hard like steel and with a diameter twice that of a vinyl record. In 1972 this thing did calculations faster than God.

Most people just don't see the point of it, though. There are few people I know well enough to have over, but every once in a while I get a chance to show someone the PDP. Nobody's really that im-pressed. Ame, especially, dislikes it—she visited once a couple of years ago and kicked it every time she went to the refrigerator. It's old, and I guess most everyone these days wants the fastest, the slick-est, the loudest.

My father left us soon after Ame was born. I don't know what the cir-cumstances were: he just disappeared. I have no memory of him. Al-though my mother's illness was a long one, she never really talked about what would happen after she was gone. The closest she came to saying anything concrete—to me at least—was near the end, when she called me to her bed. She lay under the covers and I knew how swollen her ankles were under them, filled with a mysterious fluid that I uncomfortably thought of as death. I imagined it thick and purple, dissolving tissue and bone and turning blood to oil.

She clutched my arm and pulled me closer. "You look American," she said, running her fingers through my hair. "You'll be okay. Different, but okay." I didn't know what she was talking about, so I asked her, but she didn't seem to hear. She said, "At least you know some Japanese," and then closed her eyes and settled into a thick snore.

Ame walked in then. Her hair was so black it was almost silver. It was almost blue. Her face was round. She looked like a doll. She walked into the room and when she saw me there she screwed up her face and walked out.

We stayed with the church pastor for a week after my mother died. "Wish we could keep you with us," said his wife, sweetly. I don't know if they tried to reach my father—or if anybody knew where he was. But my mother had made different plans for us. A week after the funeral, the pastor and his wife drove us to the airport, and we boarded a plane for Tokyo.

About a week after Ame's e-mail I get two more, right together. I read them at home on the PDP, which I have rigged for the Internet. The first has no message—just an attachment. When I click it open it tumbles out of my browser and into another window. It's a video of the baptism.

There is my grandfather, bowing. He stands straight and stiff. He still has the same bristled army haircut he had fifty years ago, only it is white now. The sounds are all wrong—I can hear people coughing, I can hear the squeak of chairs, but I can't hear the Japanese pastor and I can't hear Ojīchan's response. The water falls silently on his head, like raindrops. He turns to bow to the congregation and then the clapping starts and it is as sharp as thunder, before the camcorder mike recoils and smothers it. I can't see where my grandmother is, but I know she is weeping. She has been waiting a long time.

The second e-mail, directly after the first, is worded almost as an afterthought: "Job job job?" it starts. "come to tokyo, i can get you best computer job, drink pepsi and do web site. ken work with ame, call your sister for big yens." She's hinted before at things she has up her sleeve, cash in her pocket, and amazing, can't-miss opportunities. She has made a name for herself finally, and I can't help but read in this message a bit of gloating, a note of pity.

"Do you remember them?" I had asked my sister on that flight to Tokyo, years ago. From the window seat I saw us poised over a glaciered Yukon.

She shrugged.

"Well, do you?" I asked. I waited. "Do you think we'll understand them?" I was not sure—my Japanese was not good, and they did not know English. "Do you? Well?"

"Don't bother me," she said.

She was like that sometimes, so I chose to ignore her. I went back to what I was doing, looking at the map in the magazine, trying to figure out where we were.

A missionary friend of my grandparents met us at the airport, and led us onto the train to Karuizawa. Ojīchan and Obāchan greeted us at the train station. Obāchan took my hand and shook it continuously and profusely; all of the feeble strength in her body was directed toward my hand. She shook it, and it seemed she could not speak but only laugh, with tears that she wiped away using a handkerchief. I was embarrassed. Then she took my sister's hand, but Ame dropped it and hugged her; my grandmother uttered a short cry, of surprise and delight. Ojīchan stepped forward from behind her and immediately picked up a suitcase. He, too, smiled and laughed and remarked on how we had grown. I think he did not wish to submit to an American hug.

I noticed that Obāchan's breasts hung to her belly and I was suddenly mortified.

Their house was small and tightly fitted, with thin walls and square rooms. Ame and I were to share a four-mat room. In the closet were futons that we were to pull out each night, and fold away in the mornings.

"I thought that we should go for a walk," Ojīchan said, a phrase he would use often, *I thought that we would,* or *Now we shall do such-and-such.* But I was relieved that I had understood those simple words. Later, he confessed that he, too, had been relieved on that first day that we were able to understand. "We were both so nervous!" he exclaimed years later, remembering. "Obāchan couldn't sleep for a whole week, before you came."

That first walk was short. I remember being the first one outside, waiting for the others. It was early summer and there was an echo of tennis balls in the air. In front of the house I stood clutching the fence surrounding the tennis court across the street, the chain links digging into my knuckles and crisscrossing against my vision; and through it I saw the broad slopes of the volcano rising toward a gentle hump, and above that the wisps of smoke that trailed off, and after that the small, unmoored puffs, dissolving quietly into the blue sky.

"I can still picture it," said my grandfather from behind me, speaking slowly and clearly, "the last time it erupted. The stones dropped through the roofs of some houses like bombs. At night it was a pillar of fire." I turned around and he was staring intently at the mountain. He stood so still and straight with his hands clasped behind him. Then he said, "Okay," and we walked. We walked slowly and in silence, and I kicked the stones at my feet ahead of us, kicking them again and again as we went. Ame meandered along the road's edge. We stopped at the train tracks and rested on a log; my grandmother had brought plastic bags and we placed them on the log so as not to get dirty.

"Exercise is good for you," my grandfather said, looking at me. "We walk every day." He watched me and I nodded.

He asked Obāchan how she felt, and if she was ready, and then we walked back. This time Ame and I lagged behind a bit. As we walked I could feel her get closer and then her breath in my ear, and then she whispered, "I remember." She ran forward and before long she and my grandmother were laughing, Ojīchan chuckling alongside them.

It was apparent that my grandfather liked to talk. First he would say, "We will drink *ocha* now." Obāchan would pour the tea. Then he would talk. We had tea three, four, sometimes five times a day. Ojīchan was more interesting than any old man I had known, and I loved and trusted him immediately for that fact alone.

On the second night, after dinner, he explained things. In the summers, we would stay with them; for the rest of the year, we would go to a Christian boarding school in America. The American missionaries at their church were helping them with information and applications. In telling us this, he seemed so serious—and Obāchan so anxious—that from the first I understood that, in the matter of our schooling, he was bound to Obāchan's wishes.

"Next," he said, peremptorily, as if he were working from a checklist, which in fact he was, a short square of hand-ruled paper, dense with *kanji*. Mornings Obāchan was to teach us Japanese; three afternoons a week Ojīchan would drive us to the missionaries' house for English and math lessons. We were to watch television at least three nights a week, to help us with our Japanese.

"But Ame," he said mischievously as he was finishing. "But Ken. Want to see yourselves, as babies?" My sister and I looked at each other, and shrugged. He pulled out albums, reams of them, and showed us baby pictures and pictures from our last visit and black-and-white pictures of my mother at our age, Ame's age, looking just like her in fact. They had wedding pictures and he berated my father's photo as if it were my father himself. "You stole our child away to America," he scolded the blue-eyed groom, and Ame laughed and aped him, though I wasn't sure he was joking.

At the back of one album I found pictures of war, of horses and cannons and guns, and of Ojīchan in uniform, young and decorated.

"Tell me what it was like," I said.

He would not. "War is terrible," he said. "War is terrible and cruel." Obāchan shook her head. After the war they had nothing. After the war, Ojīchan told us, my grandmother took his uniform apart and sewed clothing for my infant mother with it. My grandfather tried to plant cabbage in his father's field, but the crop failed. He was no farmer, he said. He was a soldier. They ended up at the community center by the park where the town had pooled its rice supply.

We ate many new Japanese dishes. My mother's dinners had been simple: *soba, udon, okonomiyaki.* Obāchan cooked full meals every day. She always seemed embarrassed to be serving what she called "country foods," as if it showed she was clumsy, a simpleton. But the dishes were new to us, and exotic. I did not understand why she felt that way.

My sister has been sending me e-mails over the past two weeks, about visiting, and jobs. "ame misses ken, please call soon, write soon, visit soon. web jobs is waiting, you want?" Or, "Ojīchan-Obāchan ask, how is ken, when will we see ken? so old now, Ojīchan 86, so old!

visit japan, see them, see me, maybe see job?" She forwards me one job listing after another. She wants to twist my arm with question marks, to pull me along by the arm like I'm still eleven. "But no PDP in Japan," she says, "No place for big calculator box."

Before every meal, Obāchan would pray. *Inori.* She would bow her neck into her chest and her prayer would move quickly and quietly over the syllables that I could not pick up, that even Ame couldn't understand. She'd run through the sentences hardly pausing for breath, until she ended with a longer pause and a deep breath and the one word of English, *Amen,* that was almost not spoken but sung, and broken into two head-nodding syllables. *A-men.* Many times I kept my eyelids parted slightly, so that I could look across and watch Ojīchan sitting quietly and staring up at the ceiling. I would lower my head then and pinch my eyelids shut to pray for him. Only once did our eyes meet, and it was a terrible moment, as if I had been caught sneaking a shameful glimpse of his sex.

Three times a week we visited the Edgars for our English and math lessons, and each time Obāchan prepared a present wrapped in a *furoshiki* for us to take to them, some beancakes or English-style tea. She told us to behave. "Mr. Edgar is a very good man," she said on our first day. "He led me to God." Mr. Edgar was tall and old and had gotten used to stooping so much that he walked with one hand set in the small of his back. I do not know how tall he actually was, but in a Japanese house he seemed a giant, ducking his head under doorways. He was always cheerful and he always had presents in return, which he did not offer to us, but to Ojīchan. There were often books, and tapes—sometimes a Pirates hat or a sweater. The gifts made Ojīchan blush, always, and he politely refused them, but if the missionary urged strongly enough, he accepted.

I do not remember what Mrs. Edgar looked like, though it was she who taught us. I worked hard for her, my face close to the books and papers. I remember her thin, trembling voice. It was a lame voice, a pathetic voice, but I liked listening to it—I liked listening to any English at all.

"Your grandmother showed me the tea ceremony," she said once. "It was so beautiful, so complicated. She explained all the parts to me, like turning the cups. I love it when there are hidden meanings to things, little secrets."

Ame did not do so well. She made faces at Mrs. Edgar behind her back and smirked in her face and stared out the window. She chewed her pencils and pinched me under the table. She flummoxed Mrs. Edgar, who finally found a way to pacify her—candies. Ame sucked on them noisily.

As he drove us to and from lessons, Ojīchan would point out places in town linked to his life, repeating the same things almost every time. "This is the best golf course." "That used to be my father's farm: Chinese cabbage." "After the war, all of Karuizawa got its food here." "I used to ride my father's horse down this street."

The first time she heard about the horse, Ame, in the backseat, perked up. "A horse," she said. "That must have been fun. More fun than cars, anyway."

He smacked the steering wheel with a flat palm. "Your ass hurts!" he said. "When it rains you get wet. Nobody rode horses who could afford cars—and only Tokyo people had those, the princes and rich men. Look," he said, pointing. "That's where your mother used to go to school."

I turned and watched it go by and after it had passed Ame asked me, softly and with a funny face, "Can you picture her in school?" I shook my head, because I couldn't—I couldn't imagine her there, or anywhere in Japan. I couldn't really see her face anymore, though I remembered other things—the lilt in her voice, her fingers in my hair.

My grandmother never mentioned God in front of Ojīchan except to pray before meals. But privately, she told me she prayed for him every day. "You, too, please, pray," she said to me one day after a Japanese lesson, grasping my hand and shaking it. "We are old," she said. "We will die soon." I said yes, but then I said no, I did not mean they were old—yes, I would pray. Through the window we could see Ojīchan hoeing. He was bent over and the blade dropped and pulled the soil back. In truth, I hardly prayed anymore; standing there with her holding my hand, I was stricken with guilt. My grandmother bowed over her open Bible for an hour and a half, daily. Her faith was hidden and quiet and her strength was one of longing.

That night, lying in the darkness under the covers of the futon, I said my prayers. But Ame interrupted me. "What are you doing?" she asked loudly. I must have been whispering.

"I'm praying," I answered, quickly.

"Oh," she said. "I thought you were jerking off."

I wasn't sure where she had learned about that. I had never heard the phrase before, and I had not yet felt a need to masturbate, but I knew immediately what she meant somehow. The week before, Ame had been in my first wet dream, and since then I had been suffering immense guilt. I prayed for forgiveness. And yet I doubted my own sincerity.

Ojīchan had told us the first week that it was good for us to pray to God and go to church. "For me," he said, "it's just too late. I've committed many sins and I'm too old. I've already lived my life and it would not be fair." But every week he went to church with us, and

I wondered what he thought of it all—or what Ame thought, if she ever listened. The only one of us I was certain was assured of eternal rest was my grandmother.

"Come on," Ame said to me so often, "I know you know this." My grandmother's Japanese lessons were difficult for me. My throat would tighten from fear and ignorance. Ame, on the other hand, loved Japanese. She was better at it than I, and when my grandmother held up the flash cards of *kanji* she always responded first. She knocked them down, one by one, while I sat dumbly. "Autumn," she'd say. "East." "Temple." "God." "Phone." If she answered too many in a row, Obāchan would direct some questions toward me, holding out the cards with her arthritic fingers.

Slowly—excruciatingly slowly—I struggled through the strokes in my head, while Obāchan leaned forward with hope. I would think of all the words I could. She'd help by mouthing the beginning. I'd say the beginning, and then she'd mouth almost the whole word, the card shaking in her grasp, its meaning just beyond my tongue.

Sometimes I got one. More often Ame helped me along, giving me hints.

Often my sister was exasperated.

"Goddamn," she'd say. "You don't know this yet?" Her cursing shocked me, but my oblivious grandmother smiled. "Goddamn, it's car, it's car: car car car. You're a boy, you should know that one at least."

"Caaa," said Obāchan, opening her mouth too wide, too long.

We studied Japanese two hours in the mornings, with a half-hour break in between for *ocha* and sweets. Ojīchan came in from his garden then and told us his stories. Obāchan sat silently, pouring us the *ocha*. She sat on the chair like she sat on the floor: it was a western table with western chairs but still she sat on the seat of her chair as if she were on the floor—perfectly, knees together, her ankles crossed under thin buttocks. I soon found that Ojīchan's stories repeated themselves frequently, but with slight variations. He spoke of golf or the occasional eruptions of Mount Asama nearby, of high school baseball, and of the life of the surrounding farmers who went to Hawaii every winter. I couldn't always understand him because he spoke faster when he was excited, sometimes gesturing wildly. Often Ame laughed while I found myself smiling anxiously, wishing she would explain.

I liked stories of war best. He said he could not talk about it—and I never asked him to—but then he did anyway, by degrees. He spoke reluctantly, at first, and then without seeming to know we were there. The corner of one of his eyes leaked fluid sometimes, and he wiped it away with a handkerchief. He told us he had been in the cavalry and was trained in *kendo*. He had been shot twice. He had trained on Mount Fuji.

Ame craved tales of love. Obāchan grew up Japanese in Korea, in a wealthy family where she had learned to play the koto and perform the tea ceremony. During the war, Japanese women were mailed slips of paper with names typed on them, names of soldiers to whom they were instructed to write letters of encouragement about the war and the honor of war, about service worthy of the emperor. She got a poor farmer's son. He was in China and she was in Korea and they wrote back and forth like that, exchanging pictures. In the middle of war, and never having met, they decided to marry.

Ojīchan was telling the story. "Are you listening?" he asked Ame. But she was looking at Obāchan. My grandmother sat on her chair, silently, blushing, picking at cookie crumbs on the table with her napkin. "Oh," she said, almost whispering, "listen to your grand-father, Ame." Ame reached over and took her hand then. Ojīchan leaned over the table, eyeing me mischievously: "Women," he said, and I rolled my eyes as best I could. But then he and I sat awkwardly, with nothing to look at but each other, while my sister and grandmother embraced.

One night, Ojīchan rushed us through dinner. It was a Tuesday—Obāchan's samurai drama was on NHK.

"You were out too late," Ojīchan scolded us as we ate. "It's not good for you to eat this fast." He looked at Ame: it was her fault, she had kept us late, and he knew.

Ame beamed. She was radiant. She cocked her head and grinned. "Ken and I can clean up," she said to my grandmother. "You watch the show."

"No, no," replied Obāchan, hastily, as if Ame had suggested something shameful. My grandmother was rarely adamant about anything, but she never let us help in the kitchen.

"Please," said Ame, and then: "Okay." Though it made no sense, Ojīchan put us in front of the television, and my grandparents shuffled around from sink to cupboard to refrigerator until they were done.

The samurai dramas were the hardest for me to understand because the men often lapsed into long, guttural monologues, but I liked seeing the strange haircuts and the doomed samurais riding their horses through the villages, and I understood vaguely that honor and pride and sacrifice were underneath it all. Ame also liked them, I could tell, though she called them stupid.

"Isn't this boring to you?" my grandfather asked me, after they had finished the dishes and joined us.

"No," I said. "I like the sword fights." The fighting scenes were few, but I watched for them.

He laughed. "Oh," he said. "You would."

"I held a sword once," I said. "A guy in our church had one; he was from the Marines. He showed it to me once. It was heavy."

"Was it sharp?"

"No," I said. "It was just for show. They don't use them." I had not found that odd before. "Did you ever use your sword?" I asked him. "Or was it just for show?"

"No," he said. "Not for show."

Karuizawa lies cool in summer at the base of a smoking volcano. It lies hidden under forests of birch and hemlock and spruce. In the open spaces are meadows of sharp grass and butterflies and the squat, irregular portions of vegetable farms. In the forests are houses tucked into hills and along gravel paths, with thick, velvet moss-yards surrounded by short walls of volcanic stone. Ferns grow bright and the monkeys steal their way under them or perch high on branches, picking themselves clean.

On afternoons when we didn't go to the Edgars, my grandparents napped, affording us time to explore the countryside on cranky old bicycles with bells and baskets and streamers at the ends of their handlebars. We scrambled up the steep hills, stuck up like earthen thumbs, or we rode around them into town. We took our time or we raced the day, and afterward Ojīchan would pull out the map and we would show him where we had gone.

Ame liked the park best of all, though I found it boring. It was gray and dusty and when we went I didn't even bother with slides or swings, preferring instead to wander inside the community center where there were various board games, or to hunt along the rock walls for horned beetles—if you trapped two of them together they would fight to the death. Ame talked to kids hanging upside down from monkey bars and spinning on merry-go-rounds.

Those were the times I most felt the divide between us, when she had more fun than I did. For one thing, I was less confident, because of my hair color. Though adults found me adorable, children thought me strange. Some pointed me out to their mothers: *gaijin,* they said slowly and without guile, and their mothers would scold them with quick smacks that left them stunned. Once, dragging a line with my foot at the perimeter of the playground, I was pelted by small stones thrown by three boys hiding behind trees. I fled and they chased me until Ame ran them off, screaming Japanese. *"Buta buta buta buta buta!"* Pig pig pig pig pig. "You're running from a girl, you stupid pig boys, you stupid rock throwers!"

Ame grudgingly carried me along, but when she was making friends I was a dead weight that she dragged behind her like a knapsack heavy with schoolbooks. Those times, she didn't bother to speak to me much, and though I could hardly blame her, I resented it anyway.

But one day she brought me to a friend's house. It was a house like all the others in that part of town: three square rooms and sliding paper doors. They had something I had never seen before, in the way of video games. Nintendo, it was called. We spent hours navigating a squat mustachioed Italian through worlds of mushrooms and pelicans. Afterward, I nagged to be taken back.

A week later, when we returned from riding around on bikes, it was sitting there, in a box, on the floor in front of the television. Ojīchan puzzled over the directions. "Help me with this," he said.

It was a Nintendo set. "This is what kids like these days," he said proudly, as if he were helping us to be children. He sat back and watched with interest while I hooked it up. He handed me the directions but I didn't need them; it was simple, a few wires and plugs.

We showed him the game with the Italian. He seemed curious at first, asking hopelessly misdirected questions and frowning through my explanations. I wanted to thank him but I didn't know how. "Look," I kept saying. "Look at this part."

He chuckled that first day as we hopped across the cartoon world, but after that he only grunted or snorted at the game and was constantly turning down the volume. I was aware of his annoyance, but mesmerized as I was by the video world, I was reluctant to leave it. Ame tired of it easily, dropping it after a few times and leaving me there alone. I played in the afternoons while she went out and my grandparents napped.

"Get out there," Ojīchan said to me once, when Ame was about to go. "Go now. Leave. There's so much to see."

I answered slowly, blinking. "Not today," I said. "I think I'll stay here."

He narrowed his eyes, shook his head, and walked into his room for his nap, muttering.

He got me a new bicycle, another gift to get me going. It didn't work: Ame ended up with a boy's bike. She came back from her rides loud with stories, smug with adventure, smirking at me sideways. I consoled myself with the secret suspicion that she elaborated wildly and probably made up whole things, just to spite me. But Ame and Ojīchan would pore over maps in the evenings, while I rubbed away a dull headache. "When I was a boy," Ojīchan said loudly and without looking at me, "I went all over Karuizawa. The world is so big, when you're young."

Yesterday, Ame sent me an e-mail. "I call you," she wrote. "i call you tomorrow :)"

In the first week of August, they told us we would go to a Baptist boarding school in Pennsylvania. They would send money, and we could come back for breaks if we wanted. I suppose it was a difficult thing for them to decide, not knowing anything about America. I'm sure that it was more the Edgars' decision than theirs. But I wasn't thinking of those things at the time; I remember only my grandfather's voice, sober and punctuated by the slightest of head-nods—and the emptiness afterward.

That night I woke to Ame's weeping. I didn't say anything for a while. I just lay in bed and stared through the darkness, listening to her.

Finally I said: "Are you okay?"

"Yes." I could hear her wiping the sobs away. Everything stilled. "I'm scared."

"It will be okay." I wanted to reach out to her, in the dark.

"I don't want to talk about it," she said. I wanted to reach out to her, but I couldn't. I wanted to forgive her then for all the things I held against her—her Japanese looks, her smirk, her mischief and swank. I wanted to touch her, but, lying there, staring into darkness, I couldn't.

My grandmother cooked dinner for me on my birthday, August fourth, two weeks before we were to fly to Pennsylvania. We skipped the morning Japanese lessons and she spent half a day preparing, grating *dashi* and cutting cabbage and sending Ojīchan to the grocery. She worked slowly with her arthritic hands, slicing the shaking vegetables. Ame tried to help, but Obāchan would not let her.

Her meal was a feast. She broiled shark. She fried tofu dipped in eggs and *shoyu* and flour. She stuffed small pouches of *inari-zushi*. There was a dish with salmon eggs and one with *ika* and another with *ebi*. There were trays and plates all over the table.

She apologized. "The food is not good," she said. "I never learned to cook properly." But on the table it was overwhelming. My only regret was that I could never eat it all. Obāchan prayed and I lifted the chopsticks off the *hashioke* and filled my plate full of food.

Throughout the meal Ojīchan's sake cup stayed full. He offered me some, and I took it, and he offered Ame some, and she took it. It was warm and sweet and I didn't like it so much. But it made us giddy, Ame and I.

What I remember is that at some point I was picking through the spinach. I was spreading out the leaves with my *hashi,* separating a wet leaf out from the pile.

The bug was small and kind of mushed up, like a gnat.

"A bug," I said, and I made a face. I pointed at it with the *hashi.* Ame giggled. I didn't know what to do with it, since I didn't want to touch it with my *hashi.* I just looked at it there on the plate in the spinach.

Ame giggled again. Her mouth was closed with one hand cupped over it and she giggled through her nose.

Ojīchan slammed his hand down on the table, rattling the plates. I looked at him and there was fluid leaking from one eye and I thought that was funny. Suddenly, everything seemed funny. I joined Ame then, laughing.

"You apologize," he said. "Right now. Apologize to your grand-mother."

"I didn't mean anything by it," I said. "I was only pointing it out."

"You apologize," he said.

"Doesn't Ame have to?"

"You do it."

"But she laughed." He said nothing, but his eyes bored through me.

"The food is good. I didn't mean anything by it," I said. His fist stayed clenched on the table. I looked down at the leaf that was balled up like the wet, dead spinach, rolled up and puny. I took my napkin from my lap and picked up the bug, squeezing it between the folds of the napkin to kill it, but it was already dead.

I sighed. "I'm sorry," I said, into the table.

"What you say you say to her."

I turned to my grandmother. To my surprise she was weeping

silently. She said nothing. She just sat there and her tiny body shook and her hands at her face shook doubly, with arthritis and with sorrow. I had not thought it meant anything at all and now I saw it there, in those shaking hands, that it had meant everything, the whole world in fact. My throat was so dry I could not say anything. I opened my mouth but only a kind of hoarse gasp came out.

He slammed the table again. "You apologize!"

"Sorry," I said, and this time it was audible.

My grandmother raised her doleful eyes. "Don't," she said. "They didn't mean anything by it."

"No," he said. "There is no excuse. Your grandmother cooked all day for you. She is old and she is humble and shy about her cooking. She deserves respect."

"They don't know," said my grandmother quietly. "They're not Japanese."

He slammed the table. "It does not matter! It does not matter whether you are in Japan or America or China. Such disrespect for family." Under the table Ame grasped my hand. Our fingers locked together. It was the last time I remember her doing that; it seemed our hands would be joined forever. My grandfather's eyes darted across the room, across the cupboards and doors and chairs, across the table and away from me and away from my grandmother and off to the side of everything. He said: "Where I went to school you could not so much as step on the shadow of the teacher or you would be smacked. Where I was raised grandparents were treated as sacred. I do not understand the young people now. I do not understand what they wear and what they listen to and the games that they play but most of all I do not understand their disrespect. I do not understand how a daughter could dishonor her parents like your mother did. Obāchan was never raised to cook but when we married she learned. She is more refined than you two will ever be."

There was a silence, and food was turning cold, but no one dared to touch it.

"Now you eat that spinach," he said. "All of it."

I did not argue. I picked up the cold salted spinach, leaf by leaf, and thought of the bug in the napkin. The leaves in my mouth tasted like spinach, only worse.

Ojīchan rose then and cleared the dishes and he would not let my grandmother get up from where she was sitting. Ame helped him as I picked through the spinach. My grandmother looked at me with sympathy. "It's all right," she said. When the table had been cleared and I was finished, the sweets came out with the *ocha* as though nothing ever happened—but until we left, it was always there, behind what was spoken, though no one ever brought it up again.

I was late in losing my faith. I held on to it for the duration of boarding school, and then college, though at times it seemed so thin and useless as to be dangling from a thread. Ame lost hers early, or she never had it at all, I don't know. She played along, but she never really cared one way or the other.

She hated the Pennsylvania boarding school; she lasted only a year. My grandparents brought her back and sent her to a school in Tokyo. She has lived in Japan ever since. We visit each other occasionally, every couple of years.

As Video Ame, she is famous now, in Tokyo. In all of Japan, actually, though I imagine my grandparents have no idea what it means. She tells them that she works with computers, and that is true, mostly.

In Netscape I have her Web site address bookmarked, but sometimes I type it in just to type it—just like I dial her number manually sometimes instead of using speed dial: 011-81-3-3456-7976 instead of *1. There is something comforting about that, about remembering the actual number. So I turn on the PDP-11, and my fingers tap out this line: http://www.videoame.co.jp. I've visited the site many times, though in the past year I really haven't bothered to call much, maybe two or three times. We're both busy. Anyway that's what we tell each other—and there's always e-mail.

Video Ame is a new Japanese pop star. She has a popular album, with videos for two of the songs. She is featured on an advertisement for Pepsi: as part of a promotional campaign, a drawing will be held in 2001. Video Ame will draw a slip of paper with a name on it and the winner will ride in the American space shuttle. Video Ame fans, mostly young teenage girls, write letters of adoration. They say: I want to be like Ame. I want to sing like Ame, and live her life. I want to climb Mount Everest, like she did. I want to fly into space with her.

In reality, I guess Ame is quite busy; busier than I am at least. When I go to the Web site, it surprises me, without fail, how much Video Ame looks like my sister. The cheekbones are a little higher and the eyes are much bigger and wetter. She has my sister's thin lips, the small, angular chin.

But Video Ame is not my sister. Video Ame is a virtual creation, without a physical analogue. The image I bring up on the screen has long legs, stretched-out legs. The breasts are small, the neck white and smooth, and the face has been given a sprinkle of freckles. This does not describe my sister. The voice, too, is not hers. What is hers is the face, the imagination and strength, her fuck-all smile.

"Your sister is so hot," gushes a friend of mine. "Got her number?" I don't have a good comeback for these kinds of comments, though I get them a lot. "You can e-mail her," I say wryly. "Just click on the mailbox."

There is even a *manga* of her at another site in which Ame is practically naked. I called her when I saw that. "Don't you have any self-respect?" I was angry; I wanted to chastise. But she just laughed. "That's not me," she said patiently. "Think about it: it's a cartoon of a virtual girl who only has my face."

How could I argue with that? It only makes me wonder what my grandparents would think if they saw this. But at least, to her credit, she visits them often; whereas, for me, twelve thousand miles away, it's been—how long? Three years, almost four.

Ame calls me today, soon after I get home from work. "What is your problem?" she yells immediately, in English. "You're supposed to call me. Aren't you interested in the job?"

Just like her to jump right into it, like that.

"I don't know," I say. "I don't think so."

"I mean, what is it you do now?" she says. "Tell me. I forget, exactly."

"I've told you before, many times."

"Oh," she wails. "But Ame forgets. Ame doesn't get it. You just sit around playing with that time machine, that stupid PDP-thing." She stops, exasperated. I say nothing.

"Web design," she says, speaking quickly now. "Not the sexiest thing but you'd be doing good stuff, working with good people. And there's so many Americans in Tokyo now. Lots."

Still, I am silent. I think: I hate it, the way she can so easily make me unhappy with my life. I have no willpower with her, after all these years, even so far away.

"What's the big deal?" she says. "Ojīchan-Obāchan ask about you all the time and I'm sick of it. I just say things. I tell them whatever. 'Oh,' I say, 'Ken visits soon,' or 'Oh, Ken writes soon.' Just come, what's the problem?" She pauses.

"Ken," she says, quietly. "They are so old now. They just want to see you. And Ame just wants you to be happy."

The silence hangs there, padded by static. I am tired, just tired. "Okay," I say, defeated. "Tell me more about it."

Afterward, I go to the PDP-11. When you power it up it kicks and hums like a car. It *is* like a car, big and sexy, with quirks and switches that constantly need fixing.

And as I click through the Web—checking the prices on airline tickets, checking dates, checking my bank account—I realize that I don't know why I am doing this, who or what I am going for—Ame, my grandparents, a job. I take a deep breath, and click on.

It is still a bit of a mystery to me, why my grandfather finally decided to convert. The only clue I have is a message Ame sent me after he first converted. "Ojīchan likes the new pastor," she wrote. "He is young and Japanese and he is committed." Apparently, and though he had never said as much, he never liked Mr. Edgar, who died of a heart attack. Each day, she wrote, Ojīchan spends two to three hours copying verses out of his Bible.

I can picture him now, sitting at that kitchen table with the scroll smoothed out, each rolled end anchored by a paperweight. He is wearing glasses and he is perfectly groomed, as always. His Japanese Bible lies open to one side, open to Isaiah or Matthew or Psalms. He pours a bit of water into the dish, picks up the ink tablet, and scrapes it against the bottom of the dish, back and forth. He does this until it reaches the proper consistency and then he sets aside the tablet and mixes the ink with a toothpick. He dips his brush into the dish and smears a line across some newspaper. When he is satisfied with the consistency of the line and of the ink, he stops. He leans his head over to the side where his Bible lies open and reads the first line of the verse. He dips the brush into the ink dish.

For an instant the brush is poised over the paper. The paper is flat and white and pure and the brush above it is at an exact perpendicular. His hand is positioned upright as if he bears the offering of a single flower. Obāchan sits across from him with her own Bible open, reading silently, moving one shaking finger across the lines.

MARLAIS OLMSTEAD BRAND

University of Maryland

Closer Than You Think

Sven rolls the new mower to a stop in front of the garage and cuts the engine. Before climbing down from the massive John Deere, he tugs a soiled handkerchief from his back pocket. The job is done. He mops the back of his creased neck. Morning sun is strong. Three hours is what it takes to get it right, do it good. Sven can't take an overgrown lawn. Won't tolerate swaying wild grass, unruly weeds growing up so fast, infant popples choking, muddling what he's cleared.

He slips a Winston from the cool red soft pack in his breast pocket and lights a wooden match with the edge of his long nicotine-stained thumbnail. He should cut out the smoking, but it never did his daddy any harm. Lived to ninety-eight. Three packs and three boiler-makers a day. Sven's old nail is yellowed, almost translucent, same color as that elevated toilet seat—step ladder for the rear. Ina insists. Good for the knees, she says. Thing surprises Sven every time he makes to relieve himself. There it sits, like an inflated bedpan, gross and plastic, riding the cold porcelain. And it comes up fast! So fast, Ina had him plane a little pine board. He fashioned a small plaque and she painted in blue, yellow, and pink letters: IT'S CLOSER THAN YOU THINK! Then she added the little winking flowers.

His hand shakes intolerably as he holds the flame beneath the cigarette's tip. Ina says, No hassle getting on and off. But he always forgets about it until he has to go. He extinguishes the flame with a pinch of his blunt, calloused fingers and tosses the match into the grass. No way for a man to go. But he's an old man, ain't he? Bad knees—one plastic, in fact. Long line of stitches, like angry red railroad ties, from ankle to groin. S'where they slipped in the synthetic vein. Will it rot when he's done and gone? Plastic knee must be about the same color as the plastic toilet seat, but with pink flesh growing around it. The vein and the knee will melt if he's burned, if they cremate. He raps his left knee and then, clenching the cigarette between his dentures, he pushes his short sleeve up his hairy arm and makes a muscle. The old fella jumps to attention, Mr. Bicep. There. He grins, spits thick over his shoulder. Yes, but it's closer than you think. He shoves the wadded handkerchief back into his green dickies.

Sven dismounts and sways on bandy legs a moment before heading up the walk to the yellow house. Prefab, bought and put up after Ina's retirement. House came up all the way from St. Cloud on the flatbed of an eighteen wheeler. Makes him chuckle to think of it. After he retired from driving bus, they moved up to Ten Strike full-time. Nothing but Indian kids. All teeth and eyes, pizza parties in The Cafe. War whoops at the pinball machine. Every single one looking like a longhair. Ain't driving them kids.

Now the damn house has a full laundry room, pressure-treated deck off the back, slider, and even central air. Did it all with his own hands. And it's good to be back. Born next door in Black Duck. Grown up logging, pulling the weeds. Then Ina. Married. Went down to Foley for her. Drove a yellow school bus through flat farm-land five days a week. Tore down old farmhouses weekends, just for her. Good to be back.

High wavering voice comes out the screen door of Ina's little yel-low house. Too light to see beyond the shadowed door, but Ina stands behind it for sure. Smoke from her Carlton curls slowly through the wire mesh. Always with those Carltons.

"You forget something?"

Sven keeps on up the poured concrete walk, past the barrel of hot pink impatiens. "What?" He pulls the camouflage ball cap off his head and, still holding the Winston in his scraped knuckles, runs his large red fingers through his pomaded white hair. He's still got fingers like sausages.

"Sven, did you for-get some-thing?"

Being cute now. His knee pops, but he gets a little closer. He can make her out now. Shoulders slightly hunched, one arm lank at her side, trailing smoke. Up in her hand is one of those paperbacks, some Indian writer she's crazy about. Always with those Indians. She brings up the hand, cigarette in the tips of her fingers, and adjusts her glasses, the rhinestone numbers, with her thumb. Now she's old, too. Tiny and dry. Always worn the hair up, more bouffant than bun. Sven likes it, but likes to tease: Could I have a slice of that little loaf of bread up there, up top? Her lips purse now, typical schoolmarm. She thinks something's funny. "What in hell are you saying, Woman?" He smiles up the steps at her. "You talking to me, Young Lady?"

"Sven, you're slipping." She motions to something behind him.

He turns and looks at the mower. "Well I'ma gonna get something cool to drink first, if you don't mind, Boss."

She sighs and gives the old cat's eyes another nudge. "Not that." Her nose is too thin to hold up the glasses now. Again she motions. "Someone's growing a weed garden."

He leans against the railing and looks down the front lawn. Bottom of the hill, not far from the garage, down in the shade of the old cedar, lies an almost perfect rectangle of uncut grass, big as a grave.

He draws slowly on the cigarette. "Well I'll be damned. 'Bout two an' a half, maybe three, by six or so, wouldn't you say?"

"I would say so. Yes."

"I'll be damned, Ina." He replaces his cap, grips the railing in case the damn knee decides to pop again and proceeds up the steps.

"Aren't you going to finish?" Ina doesn't open the door, just stands pointing her chin at him.

"No, going to take a glass of lemonade, Boss."

He opens the screen door, squeezes past her—she ain't giving him much room—and eases fat red suspenders off his shoulders.

Sometime later, Sven is sitting on the elevated toilet seat. The red suspenders loop around his ankles. Ina gave him them braces, must be three Christmases ago now. Got a leather patch on the back that reads: BOSS. This is their joke, a joke on old Sven, because he's forever called the wife "Boss." He hears the Boss in the other room now, yelling out the kitchen window at that fat Mr. Bluejay. Steals all the feed, but she's fond of Mr. Bluejay. Won't let on, but he knows it. She stops scolding the cunning thing and begins to call for him instead. Not a moment is sacred. "Hang on, hang on. I'm coming." Maybe a skunk in her tomato patch. But she keeps it up and he thinks perhaps the bear again, and zips up quick.

"Sven, we've got company."

"Who's here, who's come a visiting now?" Sven makes for the kitchen window, his fingers already itching for the .22.

"No, no. Norb and Jo Ann and your grandson, plus his girl—today's the day, remember? That's their car."

Sven stops in the middle of the living room and feels a twinge as he remembers the grass, the mangy patch. Never has he kept such a yard, unkempt and ugly. They'll see. Right out front. The son'll rib him, once he hears. Three acres of yard, and it's got to be right out front. Jo Ann will see, and Anthony's new girl. But they're already up the walk. Outside the window a blond curly head, a smooth brown one bobbing behind. Injun. And quick: What if she's a Red Lake or somesuch? Don't make sense, not at all. The boy's been out East. But the thought drives right on through.

Ina peers through the curtains, whispers fiercely, "The boy, his girl, that's it, no Norb or Jo Ann out there."

Sven snaps up his suspenders as feet hit the stoop.

Ina has a big smile and a hug for the grandson, Anthony, and a handshake for the girl. Sven spies the lawn through the door, over the girl's shoulder. And she's busy cutting her eyes at him, cautious, sizing old Sven up. Anthony talking, introducing her, but the name goes and Sven pats her warm hand vigorously, then backs away from the gesture when he sees her eyes on his hands. Liver spots between the hairs. Oh yes.

Then Ina saves him, gives him the name. "Sven and I have heard so much about Elsie from your parents, Anthony."

They arrange themselves around the oak kitchen table. Elsie shadows Anthony, watches him for clues. Like an animal. Nervous, Anthony's girl laughs and smiles quietly, slightly, after the fact, as if she don't, for Chrissakes, speak the language.

Her dark eyes on his fingers, his cigarette, his mouth. Not much to look at, almost not there, like a dark little bird, a sparrow you could cup in your hands in church and not even the priest, not even the Holy Father himself, would notice. But she's not small, is she? Sven rises to dump the ashtray and it's an excuse to get a better look. Bare brown legs sticking out of shorts. Yes, solid legs. Looks strong, despite the bony chest, thin neck. Ain't any Indian though, something else. Anthony squeezes his girl's hand as Ina asks the questions about Theresa's wedding. He's a good boy. Too pale though, not enough sky out East. No good trees either to saw and haul and mill. And Sven interrupts the girl, not even thinking, starts telling the story about Anthony falling off the pontoon. She is bewildered, startled, and Sven feels ashamed for cutting her off, he does, but he goes on to talk fish—walleye and muskie. Sits back in her chair, not so much on the edge anymore, and begins to smile and nod again. What's she got to be afraid of?

Sven gets on to milling gin up the way, running to Canada. Anthony doesn't look like a booze hound. Sven talks mounties and the blizzards and Ina gives him a secret pinch for varnishing a bit, but she keeps it zipped. The girl can't keep her hands still; a little scratch here, smooth the hair there, they flit around her head involuntarily. So nervous.

She clears her throat and the listeners lean in. "My father's father used to run liquor, in the U.P., then into Canada." Her voice cracks.

Sven sees Ina out of the corner of his eye. He can tell Ina almost feels bad for this Elsie, the way Ina smiles, starts to say something. But then the wife stops and lets the silence roll in. Sven must admit, he's surprised. Old man up the U.P.? Well. Wonder did he ever get arrested, though? He won't ask. He hits on the game warden, Ole, instead. "When Ole first showed up he didn't know horseshit from shinola, an' he got himself lost out deer hunting and—"

Damned if she don't interrupt! "My dad got lost, too, jacking deer. Fell through the ice, wandered around for three days, nearly froze to death." Maybe she is an Injun then.

Ina says, "Well." She turns to Sven, raising her eyebrows, like she's impressed.

Jacking deer. "Jacking deer, huh? Well I jacked lotsa deer after I brought that Ole fella outta the woods. After that, I could jack anything I wanted." He laughs heartily, wishes for a beer. Ain't Sunday.

Anthony laughs, too, then sits up, taps his foot on the linoleum, looks at his Elsie, licks his lips. "Tell them, tell them about your dad and the pheasant."

She smiles, self-conscious. Sven looks away, thinks about Anthony instead. Norb's kid all right. Would've come out okay if he'd grown up here, stayed up here. And suddenly Sven remembers Ina whispering her agitation when the guests arrived. He says suddenly, "Thought your folks'd come up, too."

"Oh, Sven," Ina scolds. "We just went through that." She's genuinely annoyed. "They're at some kind of conference. The kids just told us."

"Too bad. Haven't seen 'em in a while. You tell 'em they're welcome any time now. Any time."

Anthony shifts uncomfortably but his girl doesn't move. Oh, Sven hasn't forgotten about her pheasant story, but he's bothered, too put out to ask for it. "Would you like to meet my talking bird?"

Anthony sings out, "Sure!" As trusting as a five-year-old. Ina rises for the stale pot of decaf. S'what you get when you show up out of the blue.

Sven sets down the stuffed, furry parrot, plastic feet glued to its perch. Cute fella. He slides it in front of Elsie, flicks the switch in its back. "Go on, talk to it. Go ahead, talk to Polly."

Elsie is bright red, full cheeks must feel hot, must burn up at her eyes. "Um—"

"Go on." Sven waves his cigarette at Polly and the girl sticks her face at the rainbow-colored bird, so shy. As if she'd get pecked!

"Hello?"

The wife fills up her own coffee cup and shuffles the pot back to the burner. She should offer some, at least.

Sven reaches across the table and flips the switch in the other direction. His voice comes out of the bird, boy-high, cartoonish, fast, "Go on, talk to it. Go ahead, talk to Polly."

Anthony laughs.

There is also the background rustle of Ina repeated, scratchily making her way to the decaf again. Then the tentative "Um," delivered even more girlishly by the parrot and followed by an urgent, Mickey Mouse, "Go on." And hearing her foolish salutation again, Elsie goes a new shade of crimson, almost purplish.

It's over quick, but she still looks like she wants to die long after they all take turns at Polly. Anthony holds Polly up to her ear as the stupid bird repeats, "Hi Elsie, Hi Elsie, Hi Elsie," until the words lose meaning. She catches his grandson's blue eye, looks straight into it, a cold heavy weight, a pressure that forces Anthony to quit abruptly. He places Polly on the table, swallows audibly, and searches his hands. Shouldn't have brought out the bird. Parlor tricks.

Ina sucks the last drop of Sanka from the cup labeled, HER CUP. "How 'bout a ride?"

Sven catches on. "Would you like to go see Eva's house? She's making a tepee."

They are all in the blue Caddy, rolling down the old spur to Eva's. Anthony and his girl look at the dirt road as if it's the surface of the moon. Sven explains how it was the old logging spur, how you can still see the old railroad ties in the road. They don't seem to believe him. When he spots one, he stops the car and buzzes down the power windows. Ain't the moon, for Chrissakes. But they still don't seem to see.

Sven catches Anthony whispering to Elsie, "Do your eyes bother you, the smoke?" He should pretend he doesn't hear. So he rolls the windows right back up. Air conditioning is on anyway.

No one home at Eva's when they pull around her nice circular drive. Course, you can half-expect this. Eva usually walks Val, the shepherd, afternoons. Her absence is fine though. Most don't quite understand Eva, her style. The little sister is unique. Best if he can keep her from the prying, ignorant eyes. But he can't help boasting about her. He knows Anthony will tell his mother all about the visit and that Jo Ann, in turn, will tell him and his girl all about Eva's stay at Wahkon Manor, but he can't help it. "See there?" Sven jabs his finger at the glass, pointing to a giant throaty pink ladyslipper painted on the side of a massive granite rock that stands in the yard. Purple hollyhocks, real, not painted, climb the squat bright blue house and swarm over the black roof. More evidence of her handiwork, too: old red dairy barn beyond has a parade of gigantic sunflowers on its weathered clapboards. So pretty. The flowers nod and dance far above her climbing snap peas and neat rows of corn. Up here there ain't no eyes. And the Indians sure as hell don't give a damn, one way or the other, not anymore.

"This is what she's been working on." A full-size tepee, right out front. Eighteen thirty-foot sticks of balsam, pulled from his own lot. Eva wouldn't let Sven skin them, wouldn't even take the adz he offered. His seventy-two-year-old sister says, I got an ax; I can do the job. And she did it, too. He supposes she's something of an Indian lover, too. "Yes, this is it." It's an art really.

Nothing but silence from the backseat.

Then the girl's voice, "It's really neat." Flat and dead, forgotten like an old wore-out dishrag.

Sven wants to tell her slow, so she'll understand: It's a tepee, made by hand, made by the sure hands of a very old woman. But he keeps the trap shut.

Anthony leans over to the front seat, head between Sven and Ina. There is an audible tightening in his throat and he says with a laugh, "But why a tepee?"

The wife has the presence to ignore this. Draws on her Carlton and touches up her hair, says, "Eva's really something."

They drive out and look at the old CCC camp. They go into Black Duck for a cup at the Ten Point Cafe. Sven keeps telling his stories; he points out racks of antlers on the knotty-pine walls, remembers the year, the weather, who took which buck, and once he looks at Elsie and says, "Jeez, you'll have to tell us old-timers to put a cork in it, so we can hear about you!" He swings his head from Ina to Anthony. "Don't think she's got a thin word in edgewise yet!" He ain't that old yet, not by half.

They also drive around the little lake, past the old cabin where they brought young Anthony so many summers ago. Anthony and his girl, they're tourists. Gawking at the sun setting over the golden lake, the wild rice. Expecting to see some damn fool in a birch bark number. They'll answer cheerfully to anything that Sven pulls out. He imagines them in their apartment. Making love. They must. Drinking cocktails, maybe even smoking and chatting over those highballs to other people with highballs. Onions and olives. Slick young men and women, people talking, talk shows, sitcoms, late night movies, talking about things he doesn't care to understand. Not anymore. Never did, for that matter. For a moment he thinks he might be a little afraid of them, and then he laughs out loud.

"Anthony, you still know your trees?"

The boy is walking behind, with his girl. Boy can't even let go her hand. They must notice what a chore it seems for him. Poor old man, they must be saying now. So old he can't get across his own lawn. Earlier, he showed Anthony his scars while she was in the bathroom. She had asked, ashamed of her need, if she could use the bathroom. She meant she wanted to be shown the whereabouts of the crapper. Ina obliged her and Sven called after them jovially, "It's closer than you think!" He should show her the scars, so she knows.

Anthony points out a cedar and an American elm and then loses steam. Sven tells them how he can't understand how people, some people, other people, go and pay thousands of dollars for school. "And what are they learning?" He knows he's baiting. Isn't a fool. But he's earned the right, hasn't he? "They learning anything useful?"

"I see Ina's reading Hillerman," says Elsie. "And I noticed that she likes Harjo and Marmon Silko."

He turns back to see her round face, make sure it was she who said the words, that he didn't imagine it. It's neither here nor there; they were talking trees, got a Reservation full of them over to Red Lake anyway. "Yep, lots of Indians, don't quite understand the mania. You've got a balsam there, a maple, and another cedar."

He leads them farther down the lawn. Anthony still mumbling about the trees, how many years it's been, apologizing really. Sven senses that Anthony has taken his words to heart and Elsie rubs the boy's shoulder, as if he's wounded.

"Anthony got a raise, he's doing really well." Her chin juts out. "It's tough."

She's tough, making the boy look like a kid. Not shy anymore, talking a blue streak.

He watches her carefully. They approach the garage and Sven suddenly remembers the mangy patch of grass as the John Deere comes into view.

"Wow," says Anthony, running his hand over the hood of the mower. "Wish Dad had had this kind of thing when I was mowing lawn. I'd have been out there all day, gladly."

Norb. His son had those kids mowing lawn at age five. Sat them up top of an old clunker of a ride-on. Amazing they all still had their hands and feet. And he'd scream bloody murder if they missed a spot.

Sven walks into the open garage and shows them his ice fishing jigs. He explains, for Elsie, about the ice fishing.

But she's nodding her head fast.

"Oh, I suppose you heard about it then, done it?"

She says, "Yes, I have." Prim as can be.

Sven rustles up his old coffee cans, carries them out into the light. Surely little Elsie's never seen this. He brings his hands, full of highly polished agates, up to her face, right up under her nose. "Know what them are?"

"Oh!" she says, fake surprise, little girl on her birthday. She leans over, hands clasped behind her back. "Anthony's mom has a ton of these; she loves agates, too."

"Got my own rock tumbler, see, makes 'em nice and shiny."

"Oh yeah," Anthony adds. "Mom's got one, but she makes Dad work it."

Sven turns away. He lets the agates slip through his fingers, clinking back into the can, and then he thinks better of it. He begins to sift through the stones again. He finds what he's looking for: a dark, bloodred one, small, peanut-shaped, with lots of grayish white figure eights all over it, a real rarity. "Here you go." Damn tremors. He drops the treasure into her steady, open palm. "Present for you."

She looks at it, turns it over. "Thank you very much."

She's blind. "Can you see 'em? Eights, look for the eights. How many do you see?"

Her expression is nothing. Then her face tightens up, and out cracks a painful-looking smile. She's in the woods.

"You want to look for the eights. There's tons of 'em."

Anthony leans in. "Oh yeah, these little things, shaped like the number eight." He handles the stone with grubbing fingers.

Sven wipes the back of his neck. Hot all of a sudden. Be nice to pull off the suspenders. He steps out of the shade of the garage anyway, looks up and blinks into the damn sun. He takes out his handkerchief and spits a thick mass into its folds. Moving in his chest now. He wipes his lips and looks down the yard. Mr. Bluejay flies into the cedar, screams at him. "That bugger."

"What's that?"

He turns. She is too close, frowning, shading her eyes. "Oh, that pesky bluejay—got a mind to shoot him."

"No, that. That patch of grass."

As Sven stuffs the handkerchief away he feels the disagreeable warm squish inside the material. His sickness, disgusting. He sighs. What else can he do? She watches him wipe his palm on his trousers and her nostrils widen and the skin under her nose, above her lip, stretches out into a smooth plane. Sign of revulsion, a cat sniffing at a decidedly rancid dinner. "Oh that." Looks at his boots, hikes his pants. "That there is a grave."

He begins walking down the slope to the cedar, leaving their hanging faces behind, knowing they'll follow like dogs. Soon enough.

"See that flower there? Little white one? That's what they used to plant on graves 'round here, back in my grandfather's time. How you can tell it's a grave. Mowed 'round it so I'd know where it is. Gonna have a couple fellas out next week, dig it up, see what's inside." Sven pauses, glances back at the house to make sure Ina is still inside, out of earshot. He lights a Winston. "Found a Chippewa couple years back. Dug him up while we were logging up past Black Duck. Fella was sitting up, sitting just like he's in a chair. Sitting Bull. Took him out, laid out the bones, seven and a half feet tall he was. Absolute truth." He stops to draw on the cigarette. "More'n likely this ain't an Indian grave though. More like it's some old-timer, forgotten." He pulls down his cap, to shade his eyes from the sun. The girl is speechless.

DAVID BENIOFF

University of California, Irvine

WHEN THE NINES ROLL OVER

> *SadJoe is a punk rocker, he rents by the week*
> *and if his landlord ups the bill he'll be living on the streets*
> *he's never had a run of luck, deuces load his deck*
> *his Rottweiler's name is Candy and she's tattooed on his neck*
> *his girlfriend sells tickets at the Knitting Fac-to-ry*
> *she gets him in to see the bands and every show for free*
> *so raise a glass for SadJoe, for SadJoe raise a glass*
> *he's going, going, going, gone but going with a blast!*

The singer had presence. She wasn't a beauty, and her pitch was imperfect, but she had presence. Tabachnik watched her. Lord, the girl could yell. From time to time he surveyed the young faces in the crowd. The way the kids stared at her—the ones in back jumping up and down to get a better look—confirmed his instinct. The girl was a piggy bank waiting to be busted open.

Tabachnik and a foul-smelling Australian stood by the side of the stage, in front of a door marked REDRÜM STAFF ONLY! Most of the kids in Redrüm were there to see the headliners, Postfunk Jemimah, but the opening act, the Stains, was threatening to steal the show. There was no slam-dancing or crowd-surfing or stage-diving— everybody bobbed their heads in time with the drummer's beat and watched the singer. She prowled the stage in a bottle green metallic mesh minidress so short that Tabachnik kept dipping his knees and tilting his head to see if he could spot her underwear. She crept behind the bassist—who had the bashful, goofy look of a born bassist—put her hand on the back of his neck to bend him forward, and mimed sodomy. The guitarist jumped on top of one of the giant black speakers and windmilled his strumming arm. He wore combat boots, camouflage pants, and a Nixon '72 campaign T-shirt. The bare-chested drummer furiously attacked his skins and brass, sweat leaping from his mohawked scalp. The crowd howled, stomped the floor with their bootheels. Tabachnik checked his watch.

He did not like young people. He hadn't liked them when he was a young person, and he saw no reason to start liking them now that, at thirty-one, he would never be young again. When the band finished the song Tabachnik turned to the Australian and asked, "What's that one called?"

The Australian had recently started an independent label called Loving Cup Records. The Stains were the first band he had signed. His head was shaved and his black tracksuit stank of sweat and cigarette smoke.

"It's good, huh? 'Ballad of SadJoe.' SadJoe's the drummer. He started the band."

"Who writes the songs?"

"Molly," said the Australian, pointing at the lead singer. "Molly Minx."

She didn't look like a Molly Minx. Tabachnik wasn't sure what a Molly Minx should look like, but not this. He guessed that she was Thai. Her hair was cropped close to the scalp and bleached blonde. A tattooed black dragon curled around her wrist.

Tabachnik had never heard of the Australian before tonight, which meant that the Australian did not matter in the music business. Whatever contract Loving Cup Records had with the band would be a mess, whipped up one night by a cocaine-addled lawyer who passed the bar on his third try.

Making money off musicians was so easy that third-rate swindlers from all over the world thought they could do it; they swarmed around talentless bands like fat housewives around slot machines, drinking free beer and exchanging rumors of huge payoffs. Third-rate swindlers were doomed to serve as dupes for second-rate swindlers—unless they were unlucky enough to get conned by a true pro. Tabachnik was a pro. He went out three hundred nights a year and he spotted the winners and he signed them. If they had bullshit contracts, Tabachnik snuffed the contracts. He got two points off every record his artists produced, versus the industry standard of one. He was so good at raping the talent that the talent thought he loved them—they invited him to their gold-record parties and asked him to usher at their weddings and called him in drunken misery when their albums slipped off the charts.

Tabachnik changed his phone number every three months to avoid getting those calls. Once the talent was signed—and signing with Tabachnik was a permanent condition—he wanted nothing more to do with them. He disliked musicians for the same reason he disliked young people: they were boring. They might have pentagrams branded on their ass, they might fuck goats onstage, but they were boring.

Most A&R representatives thought differently. They got into the business because they loved the idea of skiing in Telluride with Eddie Van Halen or eating sushi in Malibu with Björk or discovering the next Stevie Ray Vaughn in a sawdust bar in Austin. Then again, most A&R reps didn't even know what A&R stood for. They knew A was for Artists but couldn't come up with—or spell—Repertory. They tried to dress hip, tried to fit in with the scene they were scouting, but Tabachnik always wore a suit. Not a swinger's suit, not a zoot suit with broad lapels and a wallet chain—a business suit. Gray or blue. He wanted people to whisper, "That guy's with the label." He wanted to be called a "suit," because once they gave him a tag they thought they knew what he was, and that meant they would underestimate him, and that meant he would win.

After the Stains finished their set, Tabachnik retreated to the VIP room with the Australian. He expected the man to light a joint and offer him a hit; when it happened Tabachnik shook his head and took another sip of mineral water.

"I got you," said the Australian, leaning back in the overstuffed sofa. He sucked on the joint and kept the smoke in his lungs for so long that it seemed as if he had forgotten about the exhale part. Finally he released the smoke through his nostrils, two plumes curling toward the ceiling. It was an impressive gesture and Tabachnik appreciated it—Australians were always doing shit like this—but it was meaningless. He wasn't going to deal with Loving Cup unless it was necessary, and at this point he doubted it would be.

"I got you," repeated the Australian. "You want to keep a cool head for the negotiations."

"What negotiations?"

The Australian smiled craftily, inspecting the ash at the tip of his joint. He had told Tabachnik his name. Tabachnik never forgot names, but in his mind the Australian was simply "the Australian."

He was sure that he was simply "major label" in the Australian's mind, but eventually he would be "that fuck Tabachnik."

"Okay," said the Australian. "Let's just talk then."

"What should we talk about?"

"Come on, come on. Let's quit the gaming. You're here for the band."

"I don't understand something. You've signed Postfunk Jemimah?"

The Australian squinted through the haze of smoke. "The Stains."

"So what are we talking about? I'm here for Postfunk Jemimah."

"You like the Stains," the Australian said, wagging his finger as if Tabachnik were a naughty child. "I saw you checking on the crowd. Well, you want them?"

"Who?"

"The Stains."

Tabachnik smiled his version of a smile: lips together, left cheek creased with a crescent-shaped dimple. "We're having a conversation here, but we're not communicating. I came to see Postfunk Jemimah."

"Too late, man. They signed a six plus one with Sphere."

"Right," said Tabachnik, rattling the ice cubes in his glass. "But we're buying Sphere."

The Australian opened his mouth, closed it, opened it again. "You're buying Sphere? I just saw Greenberg two nights ago at Vel-Vet. He didn't say a word."

"Who's Greenberg?"

The Australian laughed. "The president of Sphere."

"Green*spon*. And he's required by law to keep silent about it. I'm breaking the law telling you, but," Tabachnik indicated the empty room with his free hand, "I know I can trust you."

The Australian nodded solemnly and took another deep hit. Tabachnik figured he would need forty-eight hours to get the girl.

The last thing he wanted was for this pissant label to sniff out his interest and put the chains on her, rework her contracts. If that happened he would have to buy out Loving Cup, and Tabachnik hated paying off middlemen. In the grand scheme of things, the musicians made the music and the consumers bought the music, and anybody in the middle, including Tabachnik, was a middleman. But Tabachnik did not believe in the grand scheme of things. There were little schemes and there were big schemes but there was no grand scheme.

"I can introduce you to Heaney," said the Australian, desperate for an angle. "He manages Postfunk Jemimah."

"Yeah, we went out for dinner last night. But thanks." Tabachnik gave another tight-lipped smile. All of his smiles were tight-lipped because Tabachnik had worn braces until a few months ago. He wore the braces for two years because his teeth had gotten so crooked that he bloodied the insides of his lips and cheeks every time he chewed dinner. The teeth were straight now, the braces gone, but he had trained himself to smile and laugh with a closed mouth.

He was supposed to get braces when he was fourteen, like a normal American, but his mother and father, who had split up the year before, kept bitching about who ought to pay for it. "Your only son is going to look like an English bookie," his mother would say into the telephone, smoking a cigarette and waving at Tabachnik when she saw that he was listening. "Excuse me, *excuse* me, I *would* have a job except you know why I don't? You know who's been raising our son for the last fourteen years?"

So when the money for the orthodontia finally came, Tabachnik told his mother he didn't want it. "Sweetheart," she said, "you want to be a snaggletooth all your life?"

Tabachnik found the negotiations over his teeth so humiliating that he refused to have them fixed. He never again wanted to depend on another man's money. He worked his way through college in New Hampshire, copying and filing in the Alumni Office, until he figured out better ways to get paid. He convinced the owner of the local Chinese restaurant to let him begin a delivery service in exchange for 20 percent of the proceeds; he hired other students to work for tips and free dinners and to distribute menus around town. Tabachnik made out well, until the restaurant owner realized he no longer needed Tabachnik. That incident impressed on Tabachnik the importance of a good contract.

He managed a band called The Johns, a group of local kids who worked as custodians and security guards at the college. The Johns always sold out when they played the town bars, and Tabachnik took them to a Battle of the Bands in Burlington, Vermont. The Johns came in second to a group called Young Törless. Young Törless became Beating the Johns and had a hit single remaking an old Zombies song. Tabachnik was reading *Variety* by this point, and he saw how much money Beating the Johns made for their label, and he thought, Jesus, they're not even good. And he realized that good doesn't matter, and once you realize that, the world is yours.

When Postfunk Jemimah began to play, Tabachnik and the Australian went to listen, and afterward they joined the band, its manager, Heaney, and the Stains for a postgig smoke session in the club owner's private room.

Tabachnik asked Heaney to speak with him alone for a minute; they huddled in a corner of the VIP room.

"Congratulations," said Tabachnik. "I hear you signed with Sphere."

"Yeah, they own us forever, but we're good with it."

"I need to ask you a favor..."

When they returned to the private room, the Australian stared at them unhappily. Heaney gathered his band and they went off, in high spirits, to eat pierogies at Kiev. Tabachnik stayed, as did the Stains and the Australian, who slouched with the discontent of the small-time.

"Well," said the Australian, passing a joint to SadJoe, "next year in Budokan."

There were no chairs or sofas in the room, only giant pink pillows. Everyone sprawled in a loose circle, and Tabachnik felt like an adult crashing a slumber party. Only Molly Minx sat with her back straight, very erect and proper. Her legs were propped up on a pillow and Tabachnik studied them: they were tapered like chicken drumsticks, thick with muscle at the thighs, slender at the ankles. She wore anklets, strung with violet beads and black slippers like the ones Bruce Lee wore in his movies. Her hands were clasped together in the taut lap of her green dress; her face was broad and serene below her bleached, spiked hair. Thai or Filipina? She smiled at Tabachnik and he smiled back, thinking that a good photographer could make her look beautiful.

The guitarist began to snore. The bassist was crafting little soldiers from paper matches; he had a pile of Redrüm matchbooks beside him and he arrayed his army on the gray carpeting. They were very well made, with miniature spears and a general on a matchbook horse, and Tabachnik watched, wondering when the war would begin.

SadJoe was still shirtless. His black mohawk was spotted with large flakes of dandruff. Just as the song said, a Rottweiler's head was crudely tattooed on his neck, the name *Candy* inked in green script below the dog's spiked collar. The air was rich with marijuana smoke and body odor. SadJoe puffed on the joint contentedly until Molly elbowed him.

"It's a communal thing, lover."

He grunted and passed her the joint; she smoked and passed it to Tabachnik; Tabachnik took a hit, let the smoke sit in his mouth for a moment, and breathed out. He passed the joint to the bassist and asked the drummer, "How'd you get the name SadJoe?"

SadJoe made a gun with his thumb and index finger and shoved it into his mouth. Molly said, "He's sick of telling the story."

If you're going to call yourself SadJoe, thought Tabachnik, you ought to expect a little curiosity.

"I'll tell it," said the Australian. The whites of his eyes were now mostly red. A strand of mucus was creeping out of one of his nostrils and Tabachnik started to say something about it but then decided not to.

"SadJoe grew up in New Jersey," the Australian began. "What town?"

"Near Elizabeth," said SadJoe.

"Near Elizabeth. Anyway, along comes a new family, with a little boy. This boy, unfortunately, was born a little off. Special, you call it?"

"He was a mongoloid," said SadJoe. Molly shot him a nasty look and SadJoe shrugged. "What's the nice word for mongoloid?"

Everyone looked at Tabachnik. There was something about his face that made people suspect he knew things that nobody else would bother to know. And he did. The word *mongoloid* reminded him of the word *mongo*. A mongo was a coin in Outer Mongolia equal to one-hundredth of a tugrik. Who else knew that? The words made him happy—*mongo, tugrik*—and they were his.

He said, "A kid with Down's syndrome, I guess."

"Mon-go-loid," said SadJoe, chanting the syllables into Molly's ear. "Mon-go-loid."

"But a sweet boy," continued the Australian. "Always smiling, always laughing."

SadJoe nodded. "When our ball got knocked out of bounds he'd chase after it and bring it back for us. He couldn't really play, you know, I mean the kid was pretty fucked up, but he would always chase after the ball for us. And we'd pat him on the back and he'd be so fucking happy. One time I knocked the ball into the sewer by accident and the kid was kneeling on the grate for hours. It was this bright orange street hockey ball, and he could see it down there stuck on something, and he started bawling. He was just kneeling on the sewer grate, bawling, for hours."

"But usually he was very happy," said the Australian.

"Right."

"Usually he smiled and laughed and was very affectionate."

"He used to kiss me on the lips sometimes," said SadJoe, scratching his armpit. "But I don't think he was gay. Sometimes retards don't know the difference between right and wrong."

"Jesus," said Molly.

"Well," said the Australian, "the boy's name was Joe. But the kids couldn't call him Joe, because our friend here already had the name. So they started calling him Happy Joe."

"He was a good kid," said SadJoe.

"And eventually," concluded the Australian, "if there's one Joe called Happy Joe, then the other will become SadJoe."

"Ta-da," said Molly, lighting a new joint.

"And they all lived happily ever after," said the Australian, gazing hungrily at the fresh weed.

"Not really," said SadJoe. "Happy Joe got run over by a UPS truck."

Everybody stared at him. He sighed and rubbed the palm of his hand over the stiff ridge of his mohawk. "First dead body I ever saw."

"You never told me that part," said Molly, frowning.

"Death makes me glum, baby."

Tabachnik smiled and repeated the line in his head. Glum!

The club closed down at four in the morning, but Tabachnik and the Stains stayed until five, when the manager came to say they were locking the doors. They shuffled outside and shivered on the street corner.

The Australian and the bassist and the guitarist murmured stoned good-byes, hailed a cab, and headed for Brooklyn. Finally, thought Tabachnik.

"If you two want to grab some coffee, there are things I'd like to talk about."

"Nah, I guess I'll go home," said SadJoe. "First train will be running pretty soon."

Molly stared at Tabachnik and then at SadJoe. "Maybe we should get some coffee."

"Not for me, pretty." He extended a hand for Tabachnik and they shook. The drummer had a firm grip. "Later, pilgrim."

"Why don't you invite him to the party," said Molly, staring at SadJoe purposefully.

SadJoe looked at her, raised his eyebrows, and then shrugged. "I'm having a party tomorrow afternoon. In Jersey."

"We can go together," Molly told Tabachnik. "His place is hard to find."

Tabachnik gave her a card from the hotel where he was staying, his room number already written on top in neat, square digits. "Give me a call. I'd love to go."

SadJoe watched this exchange in silence, chewing his lip. Finally he said, "Tell me your name again, man."

"Tabachnik."

"Yeah, all right. We'll see you."

SadJoe and Molly Minx walked away and Tabachnik watched them go, SadJoe's heavy black boots clomping on the pavement, the back of his old army jacket scrawled with faded words in black Magic Marker.

Tabachnik met Molly in the East Village and they took the subway to Penn Station. Tabachnik had not ridden the subway in years. He longed to be back in Los Angeles, where there were supposedly millions of people but you never really saw them.

Tabachnik and Molly Minx held on to a metal pole as the train shuddered and plunged through the tunnel. He wore black woolen pants, a black cashmere turtleneck sweater, and a full-length black peacoat. Molly wore a powder blue catsuit that zipped in the back. Winter wasn't over yet, and this is what she wore. She had what seemed to be a permanent wedgie. An old man chewing a potato knish stared at her ass, glanced at Tabachnik, and then resumed staring at her ass. Another guy pretended not to stare at her ass, pretended to look up only at appropriate moments—as when the conductor announced something unintelligible—and then sneakily stared at her ass. When Tabachnik caught him he would look away quickly, but Tabachnik *wanted* people staring at her ass. He wanted the whole world horny for Molly Minx.

When they got to Penn Station they boarded the 4:12 and sat in the smoking car. "The best thing about being a smoker," said Molly, indicating the empty rows around them.

When the train shot out from under the Hudson, the pale New Jersey sunlight seemed strange and hostile. They sped through the industrial flatlands, past smokestacks that pointed to the sky like the fingers of a giant hand. As the train began to slow down Molly said,

"This is us," and Tabachnik thought she was joking. People didn't live here.

It turned out that SadJoe had lost his weekly rental in Brooklyn, but instead of "living on the streets," as Molly's song had predicted, he had returned to his parents' house in New Jersey. It wasn't far from the train station. They walked past a sprawling chemical plant ringed with chain-link fencing topped with concertina wire to a small residential area that was normal and suburban—two parallel rows of ranch houses with aluminum siding—except that it was the only residential block in the entire industrial complex. In front of each house was a tidy lawn. Leashed dogs growled. Tabachnik and Molly walked below the outflung branches of leafless red maples.

SadJoe's house was the last on the block. Beyond his house the sidewalk abruptly ended and a high dirt hill, where bulldozers had dumped their loads, blocked further progress.

There was a barbecue party in the backyard. SadJoe stood at the grill, a bottle of beer in one hand, a pair of tongs in the other. He wore black sweatpants and no shirt, though the temperature was in the forties. Tabachnik noticed for the first time that SadJoe's chest and arms were crosshatched with fine, pale scars. Candy, the Rottweiler, sat by her master's feet. When SadJoe flung her bits of charred beef, the dog snatched them out of the air and licked her black lips.

A keg of beer sat in a red plastic tub of ice. A picnic table with a black-and-white checkerboard tablecloth held bowls of potato salad and coleslaw, bottles of cola, and a chocolate cake with the number 200,000! in yellow icing. Tabachnik had expected to see the other members of the Stains, but they weren't around. It wasn't a punkers' party. Most of the men wore work boots, blue jeans, and plaid flannel shirts. They stood in small circles drinking beer from Dixie cups and yelling at SadJoe to quit burning the goddamn burgers. SadJoe would give them the finger each time and the men would laugh and resume their conversations.

The women were sitting at the picnic table. They watched Tabachnik and Molly and spoke in low tones. Two of them held small babies. Other kids piled on top of each other in a hammock strung between two dogwood trees in front of a ten-foot-high redwood fence.

An older man, his eyes bright blue beneath savage strokes of white eyebrow, sat with the women. He wore a Jets football jersey with NAMATH embossed on the back, above the number 12. When he saw Molly he stood up and limped over to her. He kissed her on the cheek.

"This is SadJoe's father," she told Tabachnik. "We call him Old Joe."

"Not around me, you don't."

"And this is Edgar Tabachnik."

Old Joe grinned and shook Tabachnik's hand. His grip was as firm as his son's. "Help yourself to some beer, Edgar. I'm going to check on Joey's mom."

He limped to the house, opened the screen door, and disappeared inside.

Tabachnik turned to Molly. "Edgar?"

"You never told me your first name."

"So you came up with Edgar?"

"You seem like an Edgar."

Tabachnik wondered what that meant. He didn't like it. He followed Molly to the grill, watched her kiss SadJoe on the mouth, watched the drummer's bottle-holding hand slide over her ass. When they disengaged, SadJoe nodded to Tabachnik, gesturing with his tongs and beer bottle to indicate that he could not shake hands. Tabachnik nodded back and smiled. He shivered in the cold and wondered how long he would have to stay.

"Well," said SadJoe, watching the hamburgers sizzle above the coals, "welcome to the neighborhood."

There was a long silence until Tabachnik pointed at the scars on SadJoe's chest and asked, "What are those?"

"Huh?" SadJoe bent his head and studied his own skin. "Oh. Razor scars."

Tabachnik waited for the rest. When he realized it wasn't coming, he asked, "Why do you have razor scars on your chest?"

"From when I was in high school. How do you want your burger?"

Tabachnik shook his head and explained that he had eaten earlier. The conversation seemed to be over. The sky began to darken. Somebody turned on the floodlights and people ate their burgers and drank beer and cola and Tabachnik wondered if he was the only one about to die of exposure. It was the first week of March. Who had outdoor barbecues the first week of March?

After dinner everyone gathered on the front lawn. SadJoe and his father and several of SadJoe's friends were inside the garage. An engine revved and the crowd on the lawn cheered.

Molly smiled. "He's been looking forward to this for three years."

A black Ford Galaxie 500 rolled out of the garage, glistening in the floodlights with a fresh coat of wax. Everyone but Tabachnik whooped with pleasure. SadJoe sat in the driver's seat, his black mohawk brushing against the car's roof. His father sat beside him. Four other men were crammed into the backseat. All the windows were down and the car's speakers were blasting a song Tabachnik recognized, "The Ballad of SadJoe." Everyone else recognized it, too. People turned around and winked at Molly and then the whole crowd joined in for the final line of the chorus: *he's going, going, going, gone but going with a blast!*

SadJoe waved his friends over to his window and one by one

they came. Each leaned into the cabin, looked at something on the dashboard, and then shook SadJoe's hand. When it was Molly's turn she leaned in and kissed her boyfriend for a long time, and people started whistling and making smooch-smooch sounds. When she stood up she beckoned for Tabachnik. Tabachnik did not want to lean into the cabin and he guessed that SadJoe didn't want him to, either. But Molly kept curling her finger and everyone seemed to be waiting, wondering who he was, so Tabachnik went to the side of the car and crouched down until his head was level with SadJoe's.

SadJoe pointed at the odometer. "What does it say, pilgrim?"

Tabachnik squinted at the numbers, white on a black field. "Ninety-nine thousand nine hundred and ninety-nine."

"And nine-tenths. I've already flipped the first hundred. This is mile number two hundred thousand coming up."

"Wow," said Tabachnik. *Wow* sounded ridiculous, but what was he supposed to say?

He shook hands with SadJoe and backed away. SadJoe pulled himself halfway out of the window and called out to his assembled friends: "Everybody who's helped with this car over the years, Gary and Sammy and Gino, thank you. Thank you, Lisa, for the hubcaps. Molly, thanks for my song. Mom, if you can hear me in there, thanks for never complaining when I practiced the drums. And most of all I want to thank Dad for buying me this car when I was in high school, when it only had ninety thousand miles on it."

Everybody clapped and whistled and SadJoe put the Galaxie into gear and rolled into the street. He took a left and drove very slowly and all his friends walked behind him. Candy, loyal squire, trotted alongside the car. Tabachnik followed in the rear. He glanced at SadJoe's house and saw an old woman standing in the window, the curtain pulled back and gathered in her hand. She was watching the car's stately progress. She looked much older than SadJoe's father.

In the middle of the block SadJoe hit the brakes, leaned on the horn, and began yelling and pumping his left fist out the window. The four men in the back jumped out and high-fived each other as if the Jets had finally won another Super Bowl. The crowd cheered and started singing "The Ballad of SadJoe" a cappella. A few boys about high school age set off a round of fireworks. Everyone watched the rockets hurtle into the dark sky above the brightly lit street, higher and higher, disappearing into the blackness, everyone still watching, their faces upturned to the nighttime sky, waiting for the rockets to burst, for petals of blue flame to drift slowly downward. Everyone watched for a full minute, until it became certain that the rockets were duds.

On the train ride back to Manhattan, Tabachnik asked Molly if she loved SadJoe. It wasn't a question that he had planned on asking, and he didn't think it was a smart question to ask, but he wanted to know.

She was staring out the window. She said, "We went to this big party for Halloween. You know, big costume party. SadJoe wore some old pajamas and pink bunny slippers and he was carrying a teddy bear. And people would say, 'What are you supposed to be?' And he'd say, 'I'm sleeping. This is all my dream. I'm *dreaming* you.'"

Tabachnik nodded and studied the various New Jersey towns listed on the train ticket.

Molly kept talking. She said, "I guess there was a Shell station near where he grew up. And him and his friends, they had a rifle, and every now and then they'd get drunk and shoot out the S. You know, make it the Hell station. And the next week there'd be a new S up there and SadJoe and his friends would go over and shoot it out again. They got caught, finally. And the judge said, well, this is the first time you've been in trouble, and he let SadJoe go. His friends had records, so they were sent to a JD center. Anyway, a week later he shot out the S again. And they brought him back to the judge and SadJoe said, 'I want to be with my friends.'"

Tabachnik did not believe the story. It was too romantic, too perfect, but he thought if anyone would shoot the S out of the Shell station so he could join his buddies in the JD, it was SadJoe.

Tabachnik did not want to say any of this to Molly, so instead he said, "Hell is other people."

Molly turned away from the window and stared at him. "Really?"

"No, I mean, that's a quotation. I didn't make it up."

She rested her head on his shoulder and said, "I never heard that before."

Tabachnik stared out the window but it was too dark to see anything outside. He saw his own face reflected in the glass, and Molly's bowed head, and the empty seats around them.

They went to a Turkish twenty-four-hour restaurant on Houston, drank small cups of bitter black coffee, ate syrupy baklava. The Turk manning the cash register had the *Daily News* crossword puzzle on the counter between his elbows. He chewed on the eraser end of a pencil.

"I'm going to make you a star," Tabachnik told Molly. He never smiled when he said these words; he never made a joke of it. He said the line very simply, enunciating each syllable, looking directly into the listener's eyes. He knew that every kid in America was waiting to hear those words, or at least all the kids who mattered to him. They wanted to believe him. They needed to believe him.

Molly took a deep breath. She smiled and looked down at her fingers picking apart the layered pastry. She looked very young, very shy, a blushing girl on her first date.

"I'm going to fuck you anyway," she said. "You don't have to blow smoke up my ass."

Tabachnik made eye contact with the Turk at the counter. The Turk grinned.

"Check," said Tabachnik.

She had a small room in an Alphabet City apartment that she shared with five other musicians and actors. She led him by the hand through the shadowy hallways, guiding him past piles of dirty laundry, a sleeping dog, and a bong lying on its side in a puddle of bong water.

When they got to her room she closed the door and slid a deadbolt shut. She saw Tabachnik's raised eyebrows and said, "Weird things go on here. A guy got knifed on New Year's Eve."

He unzipped the back of her catsuit. Her skin was beautiful, the color of a cinnamon stick, and it flushed in the places where his mouth went. She shimmied out of the suit and stood naked before him, her hands covering her crotch with mock bashfulness. Tabachnik kissed her throat and her breasts and her belly, crouching lower and lower until he was on his knees.

"There's something I have to tell you," she whispered.

Uh-oh, he thought.

"I'm not a natural blonde," she said. Tabachnik laughed and proceeded below.

When they had finished they lay on their backs in bed and listened to the sleeping dog in the hallway moan in his dreams.

"I want to fly you out to L.A. and have you record a few demos."

"We have demos," said Molly, pointing to a black boom box piled with cassette tapes.

"I want them done right. We can fly out tomorrow."

"What about everyone else? I'm not just going to leave them."

Yes, you are, Tabachnik wanted to say, but instead he traced circles around her nipple with his fingertip and said, "I don't have the money to fly the whole band. We'll get you out there, have you meet a few people, send for everyone else later."

"SadJoe won't like it. The Stains are his band."

"I'll tell you what, Molly, the Stains might be his band but you're the one people want to see. You're the one writing the songs. I was watching the kids at the club. I was watching who *they* were watching, and it was all you. Nobody cares about the drummer."

"I care about the drummer."

Tabachnik had worked in this business for ten years and he'd come to believe that loyalty only existed when it was convenient for all parties. He'd never seen a band that he couldn't break up. He took no pleasure in splitting these people apart—he wasn't a sadist—but he felt no guilt, either. They all believed they were destined to be stars, and they were very sad to leave their friends behind, but they got over it quickly. They understood that not everybody could be a star.

Tabachnik looked at Molly Minx and saw that she was looking at him. She was waiting to hear the rest. She would argue with him, but not with much passion.

"You're the one with the talent," he told her. "I like SadJoe, he's a good kid, but you're the one with the talent."

"I don't even know what talent means," she said. She waited for him to speak, but he kept his silence; he wanted her to give it a little effort. She'd written a song for the poor kid, she could at least give him a mild defense.

"I don't think I *believe* in talent," she said at last.

Tabachnik believed in talent. A band he was scouting had opened for Buddy Guy in Atlanta and Tabachnik had stayed for the main act, had listened to Buddy Guy play guitar. On the drive back to his hotel, Tabachnik had thought, *I'll never be that good at anything.* It wasn't a big deal—most people would never be as good at anything as Buddy Guy was on the guitar. It was sad to realize you were lumped with most people, but it wasn't a big deal.

Still, he understood what Molly Minx was talking about. He wasn't trying to sign her because of her talent; she saw through that bullshit. He wanted her because she would sell records. That didn't mean she was talented and it didn't mean she was talentless. Talent was irrelevant to the equation.

"Listen," he told her. "Come with me to L.A. and good things will happen for you."

She stared up at the batik tapestry that was tacked to the ceiling and didn't say anything.

"Oh," he added, "do you have a copy of your recording contract lying around? I want to take a look at it."

"I think so."

She got out of bed and he sat up against the headboard and watched her squat beside a blue milk crate and rummage through a manila folder filled with receipts, bills, and certificates. When she found the contract he took it from her and studied it carefully. It had been printed on a dot-matrix printer with a dying ribbon. One page. A brown stain from a coffee mug neatly ringed the signatures. Tabachnik sighed. People were so stupid he no longer took pleasure in their stupidity.

"What's your real name, Molly?"

"Jennifer." She was sitting on the edge of the bed, watching him.

"Your whole name."

"Jennifer Serenity Prajadhikop."

"Where are you from?"

"Toronto."

"Really? Okay. Serenity. That's good. We'll need to retire Molly Minx."

He folded the contract and handed it back to her. She fanned herself with it and said, "I can do that. I was getting kind of sick of it anyway. I've been Molly Minx since high school."

The next day he took her out for lunch and then to the label's New York office. The receptionist sat behind a horseshoe-shaped desk sheathed in black granite. Behind her, twenty-foot-high windows stared out at the Hudson River.

"Good afternoon, Mr. Tabachnik. Good afternoon, Serenity."

Molly squinted at the woman as if trying to place her from grammar school days, and then she said, "Hey!" and tugged on Tabachnik's jacket sleeve. "They already know me!"

He took her into an empty conference room, left her staring at the platinum records on the wall and the giant photographs of smirking singers. From an unused office he phoned Steinhardt, the label's president, and waited for the assistant to patch him through.

"Tabachnik? How's our girl?"

"We got her. Schmucks, had the group signed to a two plus one, but they have her listed in contract *and* in signature by her stage name."

"Ha, I love it. Well, they might sue on breach of good faith."

"I already faxed a copy to Lefschaum. We're clear."

"Yeah, good faith my left nut. Now get her out here. Get her name on a six plus one and let's make this girl happen."

"It turns out she's Canadian."

"Uh-huh," said Steinhardt. "Everyone turns out to be Canadian. Listen, good job. You're my ace."

Tabachnik hung up the phone and stared out at the Hudson. A Circle Line boat was pushing north through the gray water. Tourists pressed against the starboard railing and snapped photographs of the Manhattan skyline. Tabachnik waved. Their flashbulbs flashed, pointlessly, and Tabachnik waved both hands, knowing he would never show up in any of the pictures.

Nothing went wrong. He flew back to L.A. with Molly Minx. She began introducing herself as Serenity—"Just Serenity," she told people—but he still thought of her as Molly Minx. He had one of the girls from the label take her shopping on Melrose, and that night she modeled her new outfits for him. He told her she looked good in vinyl and she said, "Are my breasts too small?"

He thought they probably were, but he shook his head and said, "Not for me."

They decided that she would stay in his apartment for a few weeks, until she learned her way around the city. He wasn't used to having a roommate. He hated sharing breakfast, hated having to say, "Pass the orange juice, please," hated to hear about her ornately symbolic dreams from the night before. But Tabachnik noticed that the apartment felt empty when she was out. They would put her face on television soon, they would put her face on CD sleeves and promotional posters and billboards, but right now he was the only one looking.

She signed a contract rendering exclusive recording services to the label for six records, plus a seventh at the label's option. When she received her advance she held the check between both palms as if she feared that the zeros might roll off like stray Cheerios. That night she took Tabachnik out for sushi on Ocean Avenue and forced him to drink shot after shot of sake with her. He got drunk for the first time in years. Later, at home, he knelt before the toilet, returning fishes to the sea, while she sat on the edge of the bathtub, writing lyrics in a spiral-bound notebook.

The next morning he was in a nasty mood. He left the apartment without waking her and went straight to work. His assistant was already there. She greeted him cheerfully and Tabachnik smiled his tight-lipped smile and closed the office door.

He skimmed the trades, glancing at each headline and noting names and dollar amounts. He paged through poorly written reports from junior A&R reps and then jotted a few comments on Post-its that he stuck to the appropriate demo tapes stacked on his desk: *pretty boys+good dancers; lead sing hot black chick; lead sing Marc Bolan's son.* He checked his e-mail quickly.

There was a message from a Joseph Paul Bielski. Tabachnik had never heard the name before. He opened it and read: THIS IS TABACHDIK HE GOT SHOT IN THE HEAD •:(THIS IS TABACHDIK AND THERES A SPEER STICKING IN HIS HEAD --->:(THIS IS TABACHDIK HE GOT SHOT IN THE HEAD BUT HES OKAY ABOUT IT •:) AND THESE ARE THE SPREAD CHEEKS OF MY ASS)*(SAYING KISS ME TABACHDIK! SEE YOU SOON, SADJOE.

He called for his assistant and when she came into the office he pointed to his computer screen and asked, "How did this guy get my e-mail address?"

She read the message and laughed. "Tabachdik? What is he, five years old?"

"I don't give this out to strangers. Did somebody call here asking for it?"

She closed her eyes and rapped her forehead with her knuckles. "Thinking, thinking...yes! Somebody called."

Tabachnik stared at his assistant and wished that he were a woman, a very large woman, so he could pound the little twit senseless.

"Who called?"

"Somebody from Loving Cup Records."

"Look, I've told you before, take a message and I'll contact them.

Okay? Assume that everyone calling is psychotic. All right, good-bye. And no more, okay? Next you'll be giving these fuckers my home address."

His assistant had the door halfway opened. She stopped and looked back at him, her mouth open in a small O. "Ooh," she said. "Uh-oh."

Tabachnik asked Molly if SadJoe still had the rifle he had used to shoot out the S's. She didn't know. He asked her if SadJoe was the sort of person who might plot a violent revenge. She pursed her lips, thought about it for a while, and then said, "No."

Tabachnik wasn't satisfied with that answer. If the kid cut himself with razor blades, what would he do to the man who stole his girl-friend and broke up his band? So Tabachnik shacked up with Molly in the Chateau Marmont for a week. He showed her the room where John Belushi overdosed and the lounge where the guitarist Slash fucked his girlfriend on a glass-topped table until the glass shattered and both of them had to be rushed to the emergency room.

They had drinks on the flagstone patio—Jack and ginger for her, mineral water for him—and she said, "And this is the patio where SadJoe murdered Tabachnik."

This struck her as extremely funny. Her hair was now fire-engine red.

When the week was over, Tabachnik decided he would not be in-timidated by a New Jersey punk who lived with his parents and had dandruff in his mohawk. He and Molly returned to the apartment in Santa Monica. He borrowed a pit bull from an agent who was going to Cannes for two weeks, but the pit bull pissed on the rug and chewed the heels off his leather loafers. He had a deadbolt installed on the front door. He took his name off of the building's intercom box.

SadJoe found them anyway. Tabachnik and Molly were lying in bed, smoking and watching an old episode of *The Jeffersons*. It was just after one in the morning. All the lights were out in the apartment. Tabachnik wasn't holding Molly's hand, but their shoulders and hips were touching. By this time, of course, she could afford her own place, but he kept forgetting to tell her that.

George Jefferson flew into one of his tantrums and was interrupted by a loud drum roll. Tabachnik frowned. The drum roll wasn't part of the show. The drum roll wasn't coming from the television. He looked at Molly and Molly looked at him and nodded.

They listened. SadJoe was playing from the sidewalk. He was loud. He was pounding on the skins, and the percussive thumps echoed down the quiet street. *Bud-a-bum-bum-BOM-bud-a-bum-bum-BOM-bud-a-bum-bum-BOM-BOM-BOM-bud-a-bum-bum-BOM.* It wasn't music; it was violence with a rhythm.

Tabachnik wondered if the kid was good. It was hard to tell. Who listened to punk rock drum solos? He found himself tapping the bedspread nervously with his palms, keeping time, and he stared at his hands as if they were traitors.

"That fucker," said Molly, laughing. "That little fucker."

SadJoe played so hard the windowpanes rattled. He played so hard he silenced George Jefferson. He played so hard every dog on the block began to howl, howling with the last traces of wolf blood remaining in their plump domestic bodies.

Tabachnik lit a new cigarette. "I guess it's a serenade."

Molly covered her face with a pillow and laughed. People were already beginning to yell at SadJoe. "Shut up!" someone yelled. "Hey! Asshole! Shut up! Hey!"

Tabachnik got out of bed and opened the curtains. He opened the sliding glass door and stepped out onto the narrow balcony that overlooked the sidewalk. Up and down the street, people were standing on their balconies or leaning out their windows to watch. SadJoe sat behind his kit in the middle of the sidewalk, ignoring the catcalls, pummeling the drums and toms. The bare scalp on either side of his mohawk shone in the streetlight. He was shirtless, and the muscles of his shoulders and forearms coiled and uncoiled beneath pale skin.

Tabachnik sucked on his cigarette and rested his elbows on the concrete parapet. The Galaxie 500 was parked in front of a fire hydrant. SadJoe's army jacket rested on its roof. Two golden arches—three-foot-high yellow McDonald's M's—leaned against the black car's rear bumper.

SadJoe looked up and saw Tabachnik standing on the balcony. He jumped off his stool and pointed toward his enemy with a drumstick. "FUCK YOU, TABACHNIK! FUCK YOU!"

Tabachnik tapped off his ash and sighed. SadJoe was the good guy in this situation. There was almost no way of reckoning the past events and coming to any other conclusion.

"WHERE'S MOLLY? MOLLY! MOLLY!"

Tabachnik turned and looked into the bedroom. "He's calling for you."

Molly pulled the pillow off her face and sat up in bed. "Tell him my name is Serenity, and he can go fuck himself."

Tabachnik stared at the burning tip of his cigarette for a long while before looking down at SadJoe again. "She says go away."

"FUCK YOU, TABACHNIK!"

Directly below Tabachnik the building's front door burst open and a big man in a white T-shirt, plaid boxer shorts, and black basketball shoes charged toward SadJoe and his drums. SadJoe saw him coming and said, "This isn't about you, pilgrim."

Tabachnik recognized the man as one of his downstairs neighbors, a stunt coordinator he'd spoken to once or twice before. The man had always seemed pleasant enough, but apparently he hated to be awakened by drum solos.

SadJoe said, "Wait a second, brother—" The stuntman wasn't listening. He dodged around the kit, grabbed SadJoe in a headlock, and started punching the drummer's face. Whack. Whack. Whack.

Tabachnik puffed on his cigarette and watched. The stuntman threw SadJoe into the drums and the kit toppled to the pavement, boom stands clattering on the concrete, brass cymbals ringing as they rolled back and forth on their rims.

Tabachnik winced. He turned and said to Molly, "He's getting his ass kicked."

She stared at him sullenly, her arms folded over her breasts. "Whose fault is that?"

Tabachnik wasn't sure. He stubbed out the cigarette on the parapet and walked back into the bedroom, pulled on a pair of pants and a sweatshirt.

"Where are you going?"

"I'm going out there before he gets his neck broken."

"Why?"

Tabachnik didn't know why. He left the apartment, jogged down the stairs, pushed through the building's front door and hurried over to the fight. Except the fight was over. SadJoe was lying on the sidewalk, bleeding from the nose and mouth. The stuntman was smashing the kit now, putting his shoe through the kick drum, slamming a floor tom against the pavement, breaking the stands over his knees.

"Hey!" yelled Tabachnik. "Enough!"

The stuntman glanced at Tabachnik and then walked over to the Galaxie 500, the broken end of a cymbal stand in his hand. He started swinging at the yellow McDonald's M's.

Tabachnik, barefoot, stepped around the shards of broken drum equipment and grabbed the man's arm. "Enough," he said.

The stuntman wheeled around and punched him in the nose. Tabachnik went down. He surprised himself by quickly standing up. He even swung. It seemed like the thing to do. He swung as hard as he could, got his whole body into it, hit the stuntman flush on the cheek. The stuntman frowned and punched Tabachnik again, and this time there was no getting up.

Tabachnik sat slumped against the fire hydrant. The stuntman surveyed the damage for a moment and then went back into the building, stomping on a snare drum on his way for good measure.

The curbside was littered with yellow plastic splinters. The golden arches lay facedown on the street; their backsides were burnished aluminum. Tabachnik heard police sirens in the distance. He looked over and saw SadJoe crawling through the wreckage of his kit.

"Are you all right?"

"Fuck you, Tabachnik."

"That's the first fight I've been in since fifth grade."

SadJoe wiped his nose with the back of his hand and stared at the blood. "You call that a fight? Usually I think of people fighting when I think of a fight."

"I got one punch in."

SadJoe sat cross-legged with the kick drum on his lap. He ran his fingers over the perforated skin. Blood leaked from SadJoe's nostrils, ran in rivulets over his chest, seeped into the waistband of his camouflage pants. He tilted his head back and stared skyward. "This kit cost me two thousand dollars."

"I'll get you another one."

"Hey, fuck you, man. Fuck your money."

People were still watching from their windows. A young man standing on a balcony across the street, wearing tightie-whities and a

Dodgers cap, recorded the scene with his video camera. Tabachnik checked his teeth with the tip of his tongue. They were all there.

"I want to talk to Molly," said SadJoe, his head still held back, the kick drum in his lap. "I want to give her the M's."

"The thing is, it's over. She doesn't want to talk to you."

SadJoe snorted loudly and spat a gob of blood and phlegm onto the pavement. He looked very tired, sitting beneath the flickering streetlight. Of course he looks tired, thought Tabachnik. His girl-friend abandoned him; his best shot at stardom was destroyed; he drove cross-country to win back his girl and got beat up by a stuntman.

"She didn't need you," said SadJoe. "She could have been a star in New York; she could have been a star in Toronto. She was going to be a star no matter what. The cream will rise to the top."

"No," said Tabachnik. "It won't." Whatever was floating on the top, it wasn't cream.

"She didn't need you," SadJoe repeated, slapping the side of the broken drum. "It was my band but she was the star and that was cool. I don't give a fuck if you don't believe me. I just wanted to sit back there and lay down the beat and watch her. You're going to put her with some studio guy who sounds like a fucking drum machine. Why, man? I'm not greedy. I just want to make a living—it doesn't have to be fancy. So why? I'm not good enough? Is that it? You think I'm not good enough?"

"It had nothing to do with you."

SadJoe laughed. "Jesus, Tabachnik, look at me!" He held up his bloody palms and waved them. "Look! I'm real. Real blood, see? A month ago, everything was okay. Not perfect, not even close to per-fect, but okay. Then you came along, and I don't know who invited you, and now I'm in Hell." He gestured at the demolished drums and cymbals around him. "Don't you have any fucking imagination? You think you turn the corner and I disappear?"

Tabachnik stared up through the palm fronds. The moon was nearly full and the clouds frothed like boiling milk. Closer to earth, Molly Minx stepped out onto the balcony and leaned over the parapet. She had put on an oversize hockey jersey. The red bristles of her hair looked like tiny flames rising from her scalp.

SadJoe saw her and scrambled to his feet. "Molly!" he yelled. And again, more quietly, "Molly." He pointed to the broken golden arches. "I brought you a couple M's, but that big guy busted them."

"It doesn't matter," she said. "My name is Serenity now."

"Okay." He nodded and rubbed his forearm under his nose. "Serenity's a good name."

"You need to go home, Joe. You can't keep stalking me."

"Stalking you? I'm not stalking." He looked at Tabachnik for support. Tabachnik shrugged.

"Go home, Joe." She walked back into the apartment and slid the glass door shut.

SadJoe stared up at the empty balcony for a long time. Finally he turned to Tabachnik and lifted his shoulders in a gesture of surrender.

"Molly Minx is dead," he said. He grabbed his army jacket, got into the Galaxie 500, and drove away, leaving behind the ruined drum kit and shattered M's. Tabachnik watched the car's taillights until they were out of sight. In a few minutes he would stand up and walk back into the building, climb the stairs to the second floor, return to his apartment, and lie down again with Serenity. But not yet. He wanted to sit for a moment and think.

All the street's balconies were empty now, the windows dark again. The show was over. He wondered how far SadJoe would drive, where he would pull over for the night. Nobody could drive straight through from Los Angeles to New Jersey, but Tabachnik couldn't imagine SadJoe stopping at a motel to sleep. He could only picture the drummer driving, his hands on the steering wheel keeping the beat of the radio's song. Driving past mountains and deserts and strip malls and farm fields, never stopping, never stopping, alone in his black Galaxie, the odometer ticking off each tenth of a mile.

MAILE CHAPMAN

Syracuse University

A LOVE TRANSACTION

It takes us hours to get everything cleaned up. I do the lighter jobs. He does the heavier ones—anything with lifting, anything with twisting, anything that I can't do because I am prone to having cramps around the baby-thing. The entire area is sore and lifting is bad—it provokes the pains down there. I have never told him about my health condition but I assume he must have guessed that I am not completely normal. I know he makes it easier for me, and in exchange I let him hurry me through. He has a standing plan for after work. It is probably a girl, I don't know, I almost don't want to know. I never ask and he never volunteers.

If he wants to know about it indirectly, he can find out from the office manager. She's the only one I've told, and I only tell her about my situation when it affects my job. Even then I don't tell her everything, not too many details. So far I have only told the minimum, that it pinches inside when I have to lift the metal gates and drag the hose out. I told her about the pressure from the baby-thing and the problems caused by the partial bones, because although they are small, and soft, it's uncomfortable when I have to bend down to do the gutters in the indoor runs.

We can have him do it for a while, she says. She seems sympathetic, but people don't really want to know the private story. I am sure it makes her want to go home and get away, get comfortable. She's got a husband. That's what she says, she likes to go home on time so that she can see her husband. But sometimes she stays a few extra minutes to check in with us—with me, since he's usually already started on something. He doesn't talk at all during the first part of the shift. He sweeps, then turns on the waxer and guides it away from her, pretends he can't hear when she says it's time to have a word. So I listen. She tells me whether there are any overnighters in the back, how many, what the special needs are. Someone puts a towel over their doors before we arrive so that we don't upset them with the equipment. We never even see them.

She slips on her belted raincoat while she goes over the details. She takes her purse out of the bottom drawer of the file cabinet, takes her keys off the hook. She wants to leave in her high-heeled shoes before the floors get wet. I have tried to get him to talk about her. I thought maybe there was an attraction there, I thought maybe that's why she made a point of staying around a little, to see him, to try to talk to him over the hum of the waxer. When I brought it up he looked at me like I was crazy. Which was an answer that made me happy.

We have a pattern of activity together. While he does the indoor runs and the floor I go out back and dump the small boxes of waste. I take the outdoor broom to the fenced area and flip any stools into the bushes. After a while he comes out to smoke and I stand there a minute because he might say something, now that the worst part of the cleaning is over. Then I go inside to bleach the exam rooms and do a general wipe-down. When I'm almost done he gets on the phone. He has a conversation with someone, with whoever it is that waits for him every night. When he hangs up he says, Are you almost finished? By then I am checking on the overnighters. He won't have anything to do with that. He won't go near the berths, doesn't want to get that close. I put an ear to each, making sure I hear the breathing. We get ready to walk out the door together. He waits while I set the alarm, and then we're done.

Depending on his mood, he will let me give him a ride somewhere. He likes to get out at a certain intersection midway between the clinic and where I live. He points and I pull over. At the intersection are a gas station, a tavern, and a dark apartment complex. He waits until I pull away before he starts walking. I'm sure he goes into the apartment complex. It is a poor-looking place. I think there's a girl in there, waiting. I know that he thinks I'm spoiled because I have the car. He doesn't understand the necessity. I can't do the walking that he does. I try to tell him this while we drive but I want to keep it vague. I always hope that when we talk he won't ask openly about my health. Saying too much about it would give the wrong impression, especially under the circumstances, he and I alone together in the darkness of the car.

I have appointments I need to get to, I say. I have to drive. I can't do the walking, for my medical reasons. I really can't.

He looks away out the window. He says, That's probably not any of my business.

I hope he won't make me say more. The best I can do is to think about my situation as hard as I can and hope he picks up on it. I picture the proteins, the spotty tissues all sealed together. The baby-thing with hair and teeth comprising twenty percent of it. I think about how much I don't want to describe it to him just then, how much I want to be natural and not suggestive with my details. He has mercy. I think he sees how it is with me. I think he knows that it isn't my fault, that it was a sterile happening, and that, despite everything, I'm still a very nice girl. By this I mean that he could ask me for anything, and I'd give it to him.

The office manager waits and talks to me in private. First she asks about my health, and I tell her that none of the doctors is telling me anything new, that it's going to be surgery eventually. But I don't want to take the time off. She says that I can cross that bridge when I come to it. Then she asks how it's working out to have both of us doing our shifts at the same time. I say that it works well. She asks whether it isn't too distracting and whether it isn't taking us too long to finish. Distracting? Did he say that? I am careful to be neutral. I ask her whether he has made any comments about me. Her kindness wavers and I see envy in her face. Not in so many words, she says. He's concerned with getting out on time.

We always get out on time, I say.

We'll talk again later, she says, getting ready to leave.

But I know that something is going on. He's been thinking it through on some level or he wouldn't have said anything about me, one way or another.

I stay out of his way, to make him wonder, to make him notice my absence when he goes out back to smoke. In the exam rooms I listen for him. I know he is right there. I know he is being careful not to think about me. My heart expands. The baby-thing shifts with excitement so that I have to stop and steady myself against the stainless steel table. I am almost sick with all of the possibility, all of the potential for happiness.

Nothing changes for several days, except that I avoid him. I find myself taking more time with the overnighters—adjusting the draping over the recovery area, repositioning the green mesh over the heat lamps.

Then I arrive and he is smoking outside in the parking lot. When I walk in he follows and goes into the back. The office manager is waiting. She says, He won't listen to me. Can you make sure that he knows there's a leak in the big room? He simply won't listen to me.

Runoff water is coming from somewhere. I can hear it hitting the floor.

She says, For God's sake get it mopped up.

The concrete walls are painted white. Water runs down them like glaze. I hear him turn on the waxer in the back.

He's going to be electrocuted, she says. I tell her I will take care of the water. I promise it will be taken care of. She wants to leave, and I want her to leave, to go home to her husband, to leave us alone.

When she is gone I bring towels from the utility room, dirty towels from the bin, I'm touching them with my bare hands but I don't care. The water slowly accumulates in the corners. I need more towels. Just leave it, he says. I'll do it.

There is a chill from the seeping water. I listen to the overnighters and check the controls on all of their heating pads. I turn them each up by one setting. Not too much, otherwise the overnighters who can't move will become dangerously overheated or even burned. Sometimes they are too weak to shift themselves off the pad. I hear him in the next room, moving toward the phone, making his usual call. I don't look under the toweling but I can hear stirrings behind the bars when I pause outside each berth.

He is on the phone. He says, Did you find out?

There is nothing but the sound of water, and then he says, I don't believe it.

There are jerky movements in the last recovery berth, the repeated sound of nails against stainless steel. I move the toweling a little. I make larger movements than necessary, to catch his eye and remind him that I am here. But he doesn't notice. He stares straight down at the phone. He says, Are you sure? His voice gets lower. Are you sure? Okay, he says finally. Okay, but stop. If you're sure then crying won't help now. He hangs up. I repeatedly adjust the toweling. It is light pink, frayed around the edges. I tuck it more securely around the frame of the door.

I keep my back to him. I am giving him the chance to make up his mind about something. My fingers are between the bars for a long moment during which I hear nothing from him in the room behind me. I try to maintain my calm. I hear the nails again faintly and I am afraid that the overnighter is about to touch my fingers. Maybe bite my fingers. But I know they are all delirious, not even aware of me.

He pulls the waxer away from the wall. Pauses.

Can you give me a ride somewhere? he says. It is the first time he has had to ask.

Of course, I say. Inside I feel a mounting pressure. I slide my fingers farther into the cage. Labored breathing. Delirium.

He puts the equipment away, the floors undone. He lines the corners and baseboards with rags to catch the seepage. He is on his knees.

I do the exam rooms, fast. He is waiting. He is nervous. He can't stand still and goes outside. I step out of the building, lock the door. Set the alarm. Push the buttons. He throws his cigarette into the gravel and we get into the car.

I drive him to a cash machine where he withdraws the maximum allowed. Then he asks me to take him to another cash machine nearby, where he attempts to make another withdrawal. He has reached his daily limit. He reads the screen, appears not to understand. He tries again but can't take out any money. He gets back into the car, waits, and then asks me to drive him to another cash machine. To try again.

By now it is dark out. I tell him it's no use, that no machine will let him take more. He says he has to keep trying. He won't look at me. I know he is thinking that I don't understand, that I can't understand the frustration.

How much? I say.

His hand twitches on his leg.

I don't know, he says. Anything.

I step out of the car with my purse, take out my debit card. It slides neatly into the machine. My fingers feel swollen when I press the numbers. I know what kind of gesture this is. I would take it all out, if it weren't for the limit, and so I go that far. I will give him crisp new bills. I get back into the car and sit beside him. Breathless. My hand touches his when he takes the money. His eyes look shiny and red. I feel a pulsing everywhere, a throbbing even in my throat, because now I know that eventually I will have him. Now I know the girl in the apartment complex will be easy enough to leave behind. It will only take money to fix that situation. And I never had to bring up the baby-thing directly. All of that has been left undescribed— there is still all of the telling to look forward to, all of the bonding. I'm thinking about the patience he will have to have, and the secret things he will do for me when we are alone together in a safe place. I have to sit and hold it in for a second before I can drive, before I can even turn the key, because of the movement, the excitement, the hidden cartilage twisting in anticipation of him.

MARTHA OTIS

University of Florida

AIDA SOUTH, FLOWER

I.

We are going to invent a death for Aida South Wiley, and let's make it magnificent, because I knew the real Aida South Wiley and she deserves a better death than the one she had. So let's say it comes with a few choices, with a nice smell, mysterious accoutrements, and some promise of an opening-up, not a closing down, at the end. A symphony rising at dawn. We can't be afraid to risk sappiness here.

The real Aida South Wiley died of a heart attack, conscious and terrified of it, far away from her family in a place where she barely knew anybody. She had come to Mexico, I supposed, to try to be happier.

We worked together, the only American women teaching at a private high school for rich kids on a hill in a suburb of the Port of Veracruz. We taught English as a Second Language, but she did it with a real academic degree, some grace, and slight-to-severe dismay at the students' disregard for her efforts, while I did it with a chip on my shoulder and not much else. Aida accepted five courses that first semester, even though I had warned her that under our working conditions, it would not be worth the money. To this day I wish I had tried harder to convince her, because I can't get it out of my head that overworking was part of what killed her. Those kids stressed her out, and she was afraid to say it.

So, if you please, the fictive Aida shall be a flautist, and if she teaches, it will be to appreciative, talented students whose language she understands implicitly. The fictive Aida South Wiley shall find a tangible happiness in sharing what she knows. Her gifts of communication will be met not with indifference, but with kindred spirit.

I got to know Aida only superficially, but was already beginning to admire certain things about her, to worry about others, and to guess at the rest. She was from Oklahoma City, and at the age of fifty-seven had completed her Ph.D., divorced her husband, and moved to Veracruz to begin professional life. Her husband, she told me on one of the occasions we lunched together, never understood why she had divorced him and she had no answer for him, really, except something like the old line that if he had to ask, he'd never know. I liked all this about Aida.

Aida had a tall, lanky frame that I found suitable to her plains origins, thick plastic glasses, and thin hair colored caramel blonde and permed into a soft fuzz. Her skin was so white that even on sunny days—that is, most days here—she had to cover it with long skirts and long sleeves. She wore the kind of powder you keep applying throughout a hot day to soak up the perspiration. Aida looked like a librarian, so it was hard for me not to be surprised to the point of rudeness when she reported one day that she had been driving through the city and the police had started following her, and rather than stop she had led them on a high-speed chase. And she had won. The extent of her boldness was so unexpected that I couldn't join her conspiratorial mood right away.

"You *what?*"

"They stopped me five times on the way down here," Aida said. "It's just not *right,* what they do." This was true. If she had stopped, she would have had to pay what were certain to be bogus fines or bribes, because foreign plates are bait to Mexican policemen.

A week later, when she parked in a no-parking zone and the police took her license plate, she wrote to the state of Oklahoma for the extra plates she was entitled to rather than paying the exorbitant fines to recuperate the original one. I approved of her self-righteousness in regard to Mexican police officers; Aida was becoming my ally.

I was glad she had come to teach, because frankly, being a lone expatriate had gotten to seem like a burden and I needed someone like a mother, one who would understand why one "goes south," whatever the consequences may be. I imagined that Aida understood why, and that she had similar reasons. This is why, not knowing her very well, I could complain to her about the completely erratic level of control an American woman could expect to have here over things like marriage and domestic and work arrangements. I felt particularly grateful when she offered me her house, any time I needed to get away from my Mexican mother-in-law, who had just moved in with my husband and me. I didn't get the chance to take her up on it, but I loved Aida for that.

Aida and I would walk through the guarded gates to the school and into the suburban neighborhood to find a restaurant where we could trust the hygiene—her stomach still had not adapted completely to the autochthonous amoebas—and while I whined and moaned about autocratic directors and arrogant students and how superior we were to all this, she would look at everything about her with her wide, owlish eyes. She would never say simply, "If you don't like it go home." She listened or didn't listen, but after a while would look down at me and tell me about the cheerful, odd, or precious thing she had seen that day. It was as if she'd just put a little tea cozy over her observations and waited for me to come along so that she could lift it off and share them.

I listened and nodded and agreed that you sometimes had to forget the big picture and concentrate on the really, really little picture. For example, Aida rode the public buses and was fascinated by the dashboard altars the drivers made with their different saints and baby shoes and offerings. She wondered actively who crocheted the curtainlike ruffle that hung around the upper edge of the windshield and that more often than not had the driver's name across the middle. Little stuff you notice when you first get to Mexico. We kept track together of the personal slogans painted on truck bumpers. Our favorite was one on the back of a dilapidated fruit truck that read, NO SOMOS NADA, *we are nothing*. These details of life in Mexico delighted her and more than made up for any disappointment the big picture—her students, loneliness—may have offered her.

No—already I am mixing up the real and fictive versions. I don't actually know if her observations made up for any discomfort or loneliness at all. I didn't know if she was happy when she died, or if she was trying to bluff it until happiness alighted. This angers me still. It infuriates me.

In the story, Aida will know exactly why she has moved to Veracruz, and we will permit her to find what it is she thinks she has come looking for. Maybe even what she truly needs. She will allow herself to be so moved by her own, late-arriving capacity to delight in novelty, that she confuses the moment of death with one very intense and delightful moment of life.

It was a weird semester when Aida South Wiley came to teach with us. There had been three divorces among our faculty members; I had come down with typhus; and I came back to work to discover that there had been seven bomb threats to our school, related, presumably, to the uprising in the southern states. The uprising itself and the political assassinations that followed became subjects for mandatory assemblies at which the students were asked to believe that the country, the state, the town, and the school were under control and that things would go on as usual. Then there was the student who had an argument with a classmate over whether or not faith in God actually saved us. They made a bet of some kind, but the nonbeliever couldn't have foreseen that to prove her point, that God protects believers, her opponent would jump from a third-story window.

I was walking back from teaching a class at the other end of the campus at the time and saw the Red Cross paramedics with a stretcher, running out the back of the main building. I thought they were doing some kind of drill. But later that day, when I taught class in the very room from which the girl had jumped, and my students were on edge and kept creeping over to the window when I turned my back to write on the board, I finally got the story out of them. They took me to the window and showed me the two holes where the girl had landed feet first. Her legs had sunk a foot into the soft, well-watered lawn. She had shattered both legs and gotten a severe case of whiplash, and the school would later expel her, but she did not die. The students were upset and a little confused about whether or not it had been a suicidal leap (rumors multiplied and burned through the school), and especially about who had actually won the bet. We had to stop the English class and carry on a conversation in pure Spanish about the nature of faith and God. I tried to get in a few words about the difference between faith and superstition, but to them the message lacked the drama suitable to the occasion. The gardeners behaved more appropriately, mowing carefully around the holes the girl's legs had made but not profaning them by filling them in. They are probably still there. All these events set the mood that fall. We remained on edge.

I didn't know Aida South Wiley had been having heart problems until finals week, when she died. On Wednesday she came to school feeling very weak and nauseated, but gave the exams to her classes anyway—two of them, back-to-back. Maybe she had insisted on coming out of pride in her new professionalism, or just fear of admitting she was in bad shape (a fear which the fictive Aida will not feel).

When I walked into the English office at eleven o'clock that morning, a very young nurse was taking her pulse and blood pressure and one of the teachers was translating everything that Aida said.

"It's gone now...Now it's back, okay, now it hurts, it hurts very much, it hurts even more, now it's fading..." She was sitting back in the chair at her desk, her blouse unbuttoned at the wrists and neck, her skirt waist drawstring loosened.

All the teachers were gathered around and I asked what was wrong. Someone said she was feeling chest pains. I went straight to the phone and called the Red Cross and told them emergency, heart trouble, come as fast as possible. I walked back to Aida and told her they were coming, she would be okay, and I really believed she would be, though she was extremely pallid under all that powder, her dismayed owl look wider and more endearing than ever. I wanted to take her in my arms to comfort her, but we were not melodramatic Latin women.

I found her purse and dug through it for an address book.

"What's your daughter's married name, Aida, just in case you have to go to the hospital? I'll give her a call."

"It's not in the book yet, she just got married." Aida gave me the number and I wrote it down.

"My right arm hurts," she said suddenly, rubbing it. "I always thought it would be my left arm. That's why I didn't worry." Then she became very silent and I thought the pain must be very severe.

The ambulance came and the paramedics carried a stretcher to her and she lay down on it. They secured her head between foam pads and strapped her in, and she smiled faintly and said the pain was less, and that she felt very foolish for all this fuss. The paramedics were small but strong. They lifted her up, carrying her out the office door, down the steps, and across a tennis court toward the ambulance. I walked beside the stretcher with our boss, Carmen, who directed the English language program. We smiled and joked with Aida, trying to take the worried look off her face. Then Carmen told me to stay and, with Aida's purse under her arm, she climbed into the back of the ambulance with the paramedics.

"Go teach," she said. I went back to my next class.

Carmen came back in a taxi an hour later carrying the purse. The principal and I met her and she crumpled into his arms. She could barely walk, she was so overcome. Moments after the ambulance had pulled away, sirens wailing, Aida South Wiley had had a massive heart attack and Carmen had watched her die.

"You know what 'massive heart attack' means?" another teacher whispered to me. "It means her heart exploded in her chest."

True to their nature, the school administrators skimped on everything concerning Aida's funeral that they could get away with skimping on. They paid minimal funeral costs from the rest of Aida's salary for the semester plus her Christmas bonus. It was a cut-rate funeral parlor, "Campos de Recuerdo." We went there that very night for the wake. Our secretary went calmly up to the open coffin and looked in, then reported that Aida looked like she was sleeping peacefully, but I didn't believe her and I didn't go look.

A day later, my husband and I went to meet Aida's daughter and son-in-law at the Mexico City airport, because the school wasn't going to send anyone, even though Aida's family did not speak Spanish and would need help. We sat with them and translated at all the U.S. and Mexican offices that they had to go to. They were so kind to us that I bit my tongue and didn't tell them it was all the school's fault (they didn't need that), but I felt a bitterness growing in me, the kind of bitterness I imagined could grow into my own heart trouble.

"The nurse wasn't even qualified—she flunked out of nursing school the first year!" I shouted to my husband later. I had found this out from the whisperings at the wake. "I could sue the school on their behalf!" I fumed. Of course I was wrong—you can't sue in a country like Mexico for the kind of thing that happened to Aida.

But a Mexican husband, even if you are mistaken, will defend you tooth and nail, zealously taking up your cause, if that cause does not concern getting his mother out of the house. Mine had even corrected papers for me when I was feeling unable to look this travesty of an educational system in the face. Now he narrowed his eyes and said, "Sue dem." It was the only moment of comfort I felt during the whole fiasco.

So let Aida's death be sweet. Let it come, loyal as a husband, handsome as Omar Sharif, decadent as chocolate, breathing rum and vanilla custard.

II.

We'll take it from the heart problems. When Aida South Wiley finally goes to the doctor with what she describes as "butterflies in her heart," she finds out that this organ is enlarged from all the trouble it has been having, for years, apparently, in pumping her blood through her body. Water has collected in the left ventricle and in her legs. Her long, angular form, her ladylike ankles, are experiencing a delicate swelling.

Enlarged heart. Aida will not be scared. No—a load has been taken from her shoulders. For the last twenty years, she has thought herself depressed, just one gray day after another. Now that she has been truly diagnosed, she knows that she has not been depressed. Her heart needs tending. That's all.

She comes home from the doctor's office to pick up her flute and play one of the passages requiring the most digital dexterity from, oh, let's say something really difficult: the bird from *Peter and the Wolf.* (Never mind that it was written for children.) Aida finds a note on her flute, a note she has never hit before, as skilled a player as she is. As if she has just found it in a dark, outer plain, she calls the note her "south star" and thinks of it up there, beckoning her. She pictures her name written in the sand on a tropical, moonlit beach. *Aida South Wiley.* A wave, alive with foam and phosphorous, washes over the last, married name, until she is no more, no less, than Aida South. *South.* It has been there all along, like a beacon. An imperative. She will drive south.

She says no encumbering good-byes but leaves discreetly one night in her white 1980 Lincoln Town & Country, easing, at fifty-five miles an hour, out of Oklahoma into Texas. Sitting on the seat beside her is her flute—a lightweight, solid silver Haynes with a silver and gold head joint. It is a flute that she saved for years to buy, a thing she paid for with a percentage of every paycheck she received from the music school between the ages of twenty-five and thirty-five. You can imagine how many times she wanted to pawn it to pay for toys and vacations for her daughter, but she could never quite bring herself to

do it. Whether she will find the occasion to play it down south is beside the point. She does not want to lose her embouchure or die far
from her Haynes, and we will let her have it.

Aida South stops in Brownsville and sleeps for ten hours in a
Holiday Inn, waking only once to the familiar butterflies. "Spring,"
she tells herself. "Butterflies are a sign of spring." She crosses into
Matamoros the next morning. She knows that the name of the city
means "Kill(s) the Moors." How is it that the dreadful phrase exhila-
rates her? She would like something tooled and leather and creaking, something curved and metal and dangerous, something robed,
hooded, dark, on horseback, something from the Orient, galloping
and violent. She drives past rambling wood houses, on stilts, above
the Gulf, past the expanse of bordellos and what else? Shrimp boats
with their complicated hoists and nets? Oil rigs? Refineries with their
flares and apocalyptic stage-set lights and sulphurous, plastic smells?
The *maquiladoras?* The shantytowns built beside them? Aida South
wants to open her window, she wants to ask each man, each woman,
what he or she is doing. She wants them to ask her. Her wants break
upon her like a wave. She is their breakwater—she wants and wants.

*Look at me, embrace me, spit on me, beat me, sing to me, play with
me, throw me on the ground, slit my throat, slip opium into my veins,
tell me where your children live, and how your mothers died. Don't forget to make love to me. Take me behind the walls of a convent and leave
me there. Let me taste the oil pumped like blood out of the earth. Bring
me out on your boats onto the highest swells of the ocean, so that I feel so
seasick you must tie me up so that I do not kill myself with the misery of
it. Oh, tie me to a lamppost in the eye of a Gulf hurricane and let it blast
me away.*

This is all excessive, and that is the point. Before this is over, Aida
South will need an emotional antihistamine. She takes the coastal
road south, feeling the Gulf to her left, a cup running over. She feels

shameless, risqué, but safe in her huge, leather-upholstered Town & Country. It is taking her where she wants to go, dreamland sedan. The world is literally hers, and nothing will happen except what concerns her. There is no one going north, no one going south. She is stationary, the road streaming past under the wheels of the car, bringing the tropic of Cancer closer and closer until it is behind her and she is in the state of Veracruz.

Somewhere outside of Ozuluama she looks in her rearview mirror and sees a patrol car advancing on her. She checks her speed—it is creeping up toward eighty. The patrol car follows her but its sirens do not wind up and the lights do not start spinning. *We* know, but she is not quite ready to know, that in this car rides her death: tall and handsome, of firm chin, smelling of the sweetest rum I know, which is Flor de Caña, but if you know of a sweeter one then by all means... On the seat beside Aida's death (who is not Death itself but really and truly only Her Death), and in a mysterious parallel to Aida's woodwind traveling companion, is an enormous remote control. We haven't decided yet just what it or this police officer controls. For now, Aida is in control, consciously, regally, riding into her future, now so fascinating and short.

Aida drives on, her mind on other things, and for a long time she sees no patrol car. Finally, halfway between Ozuluama and the Port of Veracruz, she glances in the rearview mirror. At first she sees nothing. She focuses on the road a split second, then looks in the mirror again quickly, as if doing a double take, or trying to catch somebody doing something he is not supposed to do. There it is, the black-and-white sedan, behind her white one. Her eyes meet the officer's eyes in the mirror, he blows a kiss, and it refracts into her gaze. Aida South steps on the gas. The Town & Country tears down the road, rocking and bouncing around the curves. Aida hits sixty, seventy, eighty, and then ninety miles per hour, but the patrol car draws steadily closer.

The lights begin to spin atop his car. She slows down. A half second before she makes the movement to draw the steering wheel to the right to pull over, he has already driven off the road and parked on the dusty shoulder. She pulls over and turns off the engine, presses the button to lower her window, and waits.

She watches out the side mirror as the officer climbs out of his car, one long, shiny black boot and then the next. Tamarind-colored, riding-style trousers, very becoming, hug his figure and the shirt covers the kind of strong, wide chest that suggests a delirious embrace. Aida feels the butterflies and a menopausal hot flash all at once. The officer stretches, taking his arms back like chicken wings and sticking his taut belly out, then takes off his hat, smoothes his hair, and with the hat under one arm strides up to the Town & Country. He bends down to look in the window and she can't quite look into his eyes. Instead she looks at the neat, clean ears, and then at his hair. His hair is salt-and-pepper, wiry—the kind of curly that you can't style. He can be no more than forty-five years old. He has a gorgeous cleft chin and the best clean jaw and five-o'clock shadow she has ever seen. Then the mouth comes toward her, full, curved, powdery purple red against the deep brown skin, the black mustache hanging over the upper lip. His mouth exhales the smell of vanilla custard. Aida is overpowered by her pleasure at this thick, sweet smell.

"Miss," he says, but it sounds like *Meese,* "can you sing 'Midnight at the Oasis'?"

"Vanilla custard?"

"'Midnight at the Oasis.' I can't get the song from my head. Who sing it? Dionne Warwick? Dinah Shore?"

Aida South looks up into his eyes. They are enormous, softer than she has ever thought these black Latin eyes could be.

"What is that?" The man is pointing a gloved hand at her flute. "Where do you think you go?"

"Why I thought that—"

"Never mind. Please sing the song. Come. Try."

Aida knows the song. She remembers driving back from working in her mother's vast vegetable garden in 1970 in a blue Oldsmobile. Her daughter was in the back because she wanted to eat the raw green beans from grocery bags on the floor. She was eating them and handing them up to Aida one by one. The black dirt clung to them and they tasted fresh and mineral, still bursting with the sun's energy. The deep golden fields flew by, the Oklahoma dust blew up behind them like the fumarole of a volcano. "Midnight at the Oasis" came on the radio and Aida and her daughter sang recklessly, right up to the highest notes. This moment was a perfect one, one that she has remembered often since her daughter moved from Oklahoma City to Galveston. Aida closes her eyes and remembers once again the sticky vinyl seats and the sweat under her thighs and her daughter's grubby hands around the string beans. How does this man know? She loves vanilla custard. She hums the first line.

"There!" the officer cries. He is still bent over in her car window, she can feel him, his wickedly handsome face so close to hers. "Go on! Now sing!"

Aida emits the first syllable of "Midnight," but her voice cracks and she slumps over her steering wheel, sobbing.

He sighs. "Just as I thought." Then he opens her door. "Your heart is so big and heavy you can hardly carry it. Come, I invite you for drink." He takes her limp arm off the steering wheel and holds her hand in his. "Your skin is very, very hot, Miss. Come, I have a wonderful rum. You feel better this way."

"Maybe just a sip." She lets him help her up and out of the car. They walk slowly back to his sedan and she looks in. She is pleased to see not only that there is no wire mesh between the backseat and the front, but that there is a full bottle of golden rum sitting on the front seat. Beside it is the remote control.

"What does that do?" she asks, pointing to the remote.

"I don't know," says the officer. He gets into the car and cracks open the bottle. "It is from Nicaragua," he says. "Very smooth. Sit with me. Have some. There is something I want to tell you."

"Where will you take me?"

"Nowhere you don't want go. Will you sit?"

"No."

"Then we must go somewhere in your car. You drive. We must eat some fish or something. Some *huachinango*. You must not get drunk too fast." The officer takes a swig and hands the bottle to her.

She takes the bottle and starts back toward her own car and the officer follows. They get in the car and Aida takes a swig and it tastes just as he promised. She has left the key in the ignition. She starts the car, revs the engine, and pulls onto the empty highway once again.

So, her death sitting beside her, Aida drives south with her left hand on the steering wheel and her right hand around the neck of the Flor de Caña bottle, handing it once in a while to the man she tells herself is nothing but an off-duty officer. Off-duty because the light is fading and these can't be his working hours. She feels very relaxed and comfortable after that cry, and the officer doesn't do anything to make her uncomfortable. It is almost like being alone, deliciously alone.

He stretches out in the ample seats. They both have long legs and there is plenty of room for them. His hat sits between them.

"Such a great car," he says. "It is almost as comfortable than mine. But older and more vulgar. With this you could be a drug dealer or a corrupt politician. I don't know but I like it. They don't make them like this now. So many things disappearing from your country. Telephone operator, family farm, card catalogue, letter-writing, and now you. And why don't they write another song like 'Midnight at the Oasis'? You know that song is a great one. The song the last gringa taught me (she was a real alcoholic) was about a little ball of yarn. She learned it from her husband and she taught it to me but I can't remember all the words. Some man in prison and he sings about his girl he got pregnant with his little ball of yarn. *In my jail cell I sit, With my shirttails in my shit... Ball of yarn, ball of yarn, and I rolled out my little ball of yarn...* After that I forget. That is another song I would like to remember. But I don't think you know it? My memory is notorious and disloyal."

He tells her to turn left on a sandy road about five miles down and they follow this to a tiny fishing town on the coast. There is a beachside restaurant with a palm roof and metal tables and chairs in the sand. The officer tells Aida to park on the south side, out of the wind. She thrills when he says "South," for he is pronouncing her name, unbeknownst to himself. The liter of rum is gone.

No one is in the restaurant, but the lights are on and they can hear a radio in the kitchen. They sit. The officer yells in the general direction of the kitchen.

"*Hola! Que pasa? Servicio, oye, servicio!*" He turns to Aida. "Hey. I wanted to tell you while we riding in the car that I think your hair is very becoming. The wash is perfect and the curl nice for your face."

"Thank you. That is very kind."

"*De nada.* Take off your glasses. Don't worry, I not that kind of man. I just want you to take off your glasses to see your eyes."

Aida takes off her glasses.

"Put on again... Oh, *much* better. Most American women don't look smart enough. My love, you are perfect for me. For my taste. I love your dress, for moreover."

"Skirt." She thinks it not impolite to correct him.

"Yes, your skirt. Moreover, I like your skirt."

"*Moreover* is a word we use in writing. Say, *for example.*"

"See what I mean? You are so smart. *For example,* I like the way the dress—I mean skirt—absorbs the travel stains." The officer leans over the table until his face is a mere six inches from Aida's. "Now, what do think you are doing here? Do you know how many of you there are? Every time I see a car like yours with gringo plates I say to myself, *here is another sad gringa.*"

"Look," Aida says, ready now to converse with the good looks that still take her breath away, "I am aware that I'm not the only one who comes south. I don't care. And I am not sad right now."

"Then do you think you could sing that song?"

Aida takes a deep breath and the whole first line comes out, clean and high:

"*Midnight at the oa-a-a-a-a-sis, sing your camel to be-ed . . .*"

Her voice pierces the air all the way into the kitchen and the young night guard comes out to interrupt them and to tell them that the cook, whose nephew has had a terrible accident, has gone home. There will be no food tonight. The officer pulls the boy aside and they whisper downwind for a few moments. Then he comes back and fills Aida in on what has happened in the town.

"If we want to eat tonight we have to go to a funeral."

"But we were having such a lovely time."

"You, a grown woman, can't handle a funeral?"

"Take me to a brothel if you must, anything but a funeral."

"Do you want to know what happened?"

"No."

"This young boy out on his fishing boat and he get out to check his nets and a shark got him. Some parts of him wash up on the beach in the afternoon."

Aida likes the way the present tense makes the body parts seem eternal. *And parts of the poor boy wash up on the shores of Veracruz every afternoon forevermore.*

"Which parts?" she asks.

"At this point I have to ask you what your name is."

"Why? You haven't given me yours. Are you working for the DEA? No, I think you do illegal things. I could call you something like 'the Pirate...'"

"Please, Miss."

"You say yourself there are so many of me, just choose any name you like."

"No, this calls for a real one."

"Aida South."

"Miss South, what kind of woman asks, 'What parts?' There are grieving people here. We stumble into their grief. What are we to do, walk away? Ignore it? He was a small boy and now he is even smaller. Think how his mother feel. You are not even in your own country, so I must tell you that protocol indicates we must stay and go to funeral. You have not deserved your fifty-seven years if this is what you are afraid of."

"How do you know that I am fifty-seven?"

"Just look at you! You are fifty-seven. So many things you think you are looking for and when you find them you are too afraid to take them. Why is it always like this? American women judge things from outside not inside. No. You are not afraid. You are shallow and selfish. All of you."

"What was that huge remote control in your car for?"

"I have told you I am not exactly sure, Miss South. Let's just say it controls sad."

"Sadness. Grief. Did you bring it?"

"No. Now get up and I will show you a good time, and afterward we will eat. Anyway the death was not natural and I am the closest thing to a mayor they have here. I have to do a report. Bring your purse. And your flute in case you get bore. But I don't think you get bore."

In order for Aida to follow the officer to the funeral, she extracts from him the promise that he will go back to giving compliments, not criticism. He understands, saying that this will be very easy. They walk arm-in-arm out of the palm-roofed restaurant and down to the water. Farther down the beach, under the dark sky, the townspeople have gathered outside the house of the deceased boy's parents. The yards of all the houses on the beach are planted around with coconut palms. The houses are small wooden shacks, and beside this one are piled as many crates of beer as there are in the town. Aida and her officer approach quietly, making their way into the crowd. *Perdon, perdon, buenas noches, mis pésames,* she whispers along with the officer. People are too busy and stunned to ask who they are. The officer sits Aida on a chair next to the front door from which a yellow light shines on the sand. The rest of the yard is full of dancing light and shadow from a bonfire twenty feet from the door. The officer brings Aida a beer and tells her to wait, then starts making the rounds and asking questions, writing on a small pad of paper. There is a small box on a long table in the middle of the sandy yard. Piles of flowers surround the box. Aida watches the officer approach the box, look inside, and back away. She pulls out her Swiss army knife from her purse to open her beer.

The officer sees her do this and comes running across the sand to tell her, "You are so practical!"

This is very meaningful to Aida.

"Stay here with your Swiss army knife. They need you. Do you notice, by the way, no one will look in the box! Why? They cannot say, 'He look so peaceful.' It is not true. It is disgusting, what is in the box."

Aida will sit here awhile like an ethnologist, just watching and noticing what happens, waiting for the moment she can be of use.

The mother is prostrate and bawling on the sandy yard. A group of women is around her, rocking and wringing hands. Bewildered children whimper, ignored, beside them. Four men are holding the father, who is struggling, trying to lash out at them. A man with huge biceps tries to pour beer from a bottle into the father's mouth. The father's left arm escapes and bashes the right eye of the man pouring beer, who reels and hits the sand. The father almost breaks loose entirely, but one of the men yells "Papaaa!" and sends a hard left to his jaw. He slumps forward as the man with the huge biceps gets up off the sand and finishes pouring what's left of the beer over the father's head. Then the group stumbles over to the house and lays the father in the sand next to the front door. He groans a little, then snores.

The father under control, the rest of the men begin to drink. Beers are passed around until even the children have them in hand. Aida South walks around opening bottles for people.

No one wears shoes.

On the smaller tables ringing the yard there are bowls of food. Large platters of fried fish. Boiled yucca. Fried fish cakes. Rice and beans. Sliced bananas. Hot tortillas. Raw onions in vinegar. Chickens roasted over open fires. Everything is still hot, the smells waft into the air and Aida thinks she can gather them around her in folds like a cloak. Some of the adolescent boys are there, raiding the table, scooping large spoonfuls of hot sauce on everything, rolling up the tacos and stuffing them in their mouths.

A priest comes running unshod down the beach toward the gathering. Heavy and short, he is huffing and puffing when he reaches them. He goes ungreeted to the long table in the middle of the yard, leans over the box surrounded by flowers, and shudders. He straightens, eyes pressed closed, crosses himself, and mouths something in earnest.

In a great galloping crescendo, three musicians on burros break through the trees and come trotting into the center of activity. The men pull up chairs for them. Like the priest, they are short, portly, and very dark. They carry stringed instruments, one the size and shape of a violin, the others similar but slightly smaller. "*Ya llegaron las jaranas!*" they cry. One carries a burro's jawbone and a stick, which he draws across the teeth of the jaw. The men play their instruments. They have a precise imprecision and their *jaranas* are precisely out of tune. They play in rhythms of three overlaying rhythms of four that meet at regular but always unexpected intervals, and when she hears the aching, minor chords, Aida wants to open her flute case and play with them. But she waits, rapt, listening. The music has brought the butterflies back. Her officer, done with his report, comes to sit next to her.

"Aida, my love. These are the *sones* and *gustos*," he says. "I knew you would want to be here. I am so glad I can give this night to you. I knew you had to hear this. This is the music of the region. We grew up with this."

"Thank you," she breathes.

Another man comes riding up on a burro.

The shouts go up. "Paganini! Paganini!" The man climbs down from the burro. He wears an elegant white guayabera and white pants. He carries a fiddle and bow and is drawing the bow across the strings before he even sits. His music is high, ornamental, very fast. His scales climb and descend, leaving Aida breathless. She feels as if he is drawing the bow across catgut strung through her belly, vibrating, full of beer.

The rhythmic strumming goes faster and faster, the fiddle and the *jaranas* working in complex and contrapuntal unison.

The father lying in the sand wakes up and asks Aida into the house for a drink. Aida understands his Spanish in the kind of intuitive and very profound way that she understands how and why the music moves them all. He shows her to a corner where, behind a big plastic twenty-gallon jug of water, he has hidden a one-gallon earthenware jug of *aguardiente.*

"Have some," he says. "You can drink this all night and get drunker and drunker but you feel fine in the morning." In fact Aida has already drunk five beers and does not feel drunk in the slightest, only excited with the music, the crowd, and her sudden and near complete comprehension of Spanish.

They leave the house again, passing the jug between them. They sit again next to the officer, beside the door. Two women who look like twins approach with plates full of fish—*huachinango*—and fried plantains and rice and beans and hot tortillas. Aida thanks them and devours her plate, and her officer and the father do the same. One of the twins brings three more and they devour these, too. When she finishes the third Aida asks for a fourth, but this time they bring her a plate of candied fruits—limes and figs and oranges and pineapple. A little cup of vanilla custard sits beside the fruits. Aida falls upon this first, with determined lust.

"Everything tastes divine," she tells the officer.

"I told you I would show you a good time," says the officer. "I sure this is the best funeral on planet tonight. I must sing, Aida." He stands, towering above all the funeral-goers, and despite the deep voice that Aida expects, he emits a sharp, plaintive howl that rises like a coyote's. Then, like Paganini's violin and its searching scales, his voice falls, and in its lower registers the officer declares himself:

Para expresar lo que siento,	To express what I feel
falta idioma falta idea	There's no language no idea
falta espacio y pensamiento	No space or thought

Exactly, Aida thinks.

"Exactly," says the father.

A woman shouts and whoops to hear the officer's voice, and this spurs him on. He continues, inventing verse after verse about himself:

Soy de la Huasteca, una región	Oh, I am from the Huasteca
donde se nace con gran corazón	There we are born with large hearts
Esta noche el mío está hinchado	Tonight my heart is swollen
Hinchado como un tobillo torcido	Swollen like a sprained ankle
Una infectada herida, mi querida	An infected scrape, my love
Es amor, amor amor,	It's love, love, love
Camino como charro con este amor	I am walking bow-legged with love

It is awful verse, but in Spanish it rhymes, and Aida admires the officer's cheek and metric agility. Other men stand up and begin to sing and their voices climb with the fiddle and throb with the strumming and the musician with the burro jawbone shakes it so its shrunken teeth rattle in their dehydrated holes. Everyone sings at once until one man's voice emerges stronger and more assured, and the others sit down to listen.

"*Tarima! Tarima!*" the women shout. The mother gets up from the sand for the first time since Aida and the officer arrived and drags herself past them into the house. She comes out with what looks like a large, flat crate made of wood. This she puts in the sand and knocks on it a few times with the knuckles of her right hand.

"*Aquí esta. Que bailen!*" she cries, and the wind carries her voice out across the waves. Two women come up to the crate, the twins who served Aida and the officer.

"*Dónde están nuestros zapatos?*" they shout into the small crowd. They are barefoot, sweaty, greasy from cleaning the fish and frying it, and tired from serving the platters all around. Their faces look hard and young and wild. A woman comes running out with the twins' shoes, and they put them on and stand face-to-face on the crate. One moves and the other mirrors her. The first one stamps her foot and the second stamps a foot. Then they begin stamping furiously to the music, staring each other down, issuing challenges, spinning, one-upping each other, fooling one another into false steps. Aida gets lost in their dancing. The people draw together around them in a circle and pretty soon the other women are running across the sand with their shoes and another pair of dancers replaces the first and dances with equal skill. The older children try a few steps in their shadows and the younger children clamor to be lifted into their mothers' arms to be bounced to the rhythm of the music.

It seems to Aida that the funeral party is getting drunker and drunker, but that in its frenzy, like her heart's butterflies, it has reached a kind of control. Sometime during the night, which lasts and lasts, the verses and the *aguardiente* and the dancers multiplying and repeating themselves and challenging each other again and again to greater innovation and stamina, Aida following along on her flute, going up and down like she has heard their scales go, to the great appreciation of the funeral-goers, sometime during all this, she is persuaded by her officer to rise and dance with the rest of them, and when she sits down again, she realizes, because it is time to realize it, and she is ready to realize it, that this will be her last night on earth. She is glad that she is here for her last night, even though she thinks she should be missing her husband and especially her daughter a little more than she does. She would like to shout across the Gulf of Mexico, shout all the way to Galveston some of this new music so that her daughter can hear it. But Aida's head is full of this novel, joyous grief. She knows that her daughter would not be interested in what she is doing now, she would not believe that her mother, Aida South, is in Mexico, has in fact run away to die. But it doesn't matter. There was a different, perfect moment that they shared once, driving through the late Oklahoma summer and singing, and she hopes her daughter remembers it as she does.

Then, amid the din, Aida notices the box abandoned on the table in its pile of wilting flowers. She dares to wonder now how the boy's death felt, where the blood bled from first, where the red stained the ocean. Aida slips away from the dancers and approaches the box, alone. She leans over, smelling her own perspiration, and looks in. What does she see there? A bloody thigh studded with shark teeth? The bag of the boy's empty torso? A pile of drying starfish? How about a gray heart, suspended in formaldehyde, which as she looks transubstantiates into a hungry shark? Or something the opposite of hungry: fruits so ripe their juices ooze from their thick skins? No, better: the round notes plucked live like fruit from Aida's flute. Or a little boy pressing the buttons of an enormous remote control. Sand.

Aida backs away, feeling as if there are pins and needles sticking into her body all over. They itch but they don't hurt. She is sweating profusely and wants to remove her long-sleeved blouse and long denim skirt.

"I am going back to my car," she tells the officer. "I want to change my clothes."

"Of course, I will accompany."

They make their way back toward the restaurant, letting the night guardian know as they pass. Aida looks into the trunk of her car for her duffel bag, where she has packed a looser gown. She goes to the restroom of the restaurant to change and the officer waits just outside the door.

Inside, under a harsh fluorescent light, she peels off the heavy clothes and pulls over her head a light, cotton dress with no sleeves, one whose hem comes just above her knees without being indiscreet. It doesn't matter now, there is no sun; she can't get burned. It occurs to her that she might want to go into a stall and use the toilet. She has drunk so much, eaten so much fish. She has stuffed and stuffed herself with *huachinango* and rice and beans and fried plantains all smothered with hot sauce. And then the candies! She opens a stall and cleans the seat with her handkerchief and sits down.

"How are you doing in there?" The officer's voice echoes off the tiled bathroom walls. The music reaches them from the funeral, hallucinatory. The light buzzes.

"Fine, fine, I'll be out in a second." Aida raises her voice a little to make sure he hears it through the wooden stall door. She is discovering that she can't go. She doesn't have to go. There is nothing in her bladder. There is nothing in her bowels. She feels light and comfortable and knows that the food and drink were truly divine, so easy to digest.

She comes out of the stall and catches a look at herself in the mirror. Is it the fluorescent light that makes her look almost green? She leans over the sink into the glass and pinches a hollow cheek. It feels just a little funny, as if she has lost a few nerves in her face.

"Aida, darling, you must come out now. It's time."

Aida pinches her cheeks some more to bring some color back into them and pulls away from the fluorescent light.

"I'm ready," she calls to the officer. She leaves her heavy clothes hanging on the stall door and her shoes on the dirty floor and walks out into the windy night.

"Oh, but you look beautiful, my Aida. How the night becomes you!" The officer smiles and holds out his arms, both to behold her and to invite her into them.

"You are being kind." Aida walks past him. "I thought tonight would never end. But here is the moon sinking toward the horizon."

"Come, let us go to the water."

"To the beach? Yes, the water would feel nice on my feet."

They walk down between the coconut palms to a place on the hard, wet sand and the officer invites Aida to sit.

She sits. He sits beside her.

"How do you feel?"

"I have butterflies in my heart."

"Tonight it has been a great pleasure. I hate to say, but tomorrow I will feel sad. Tomorrow I will mess you a lot."

"*Miss*. You will *miss* me."

"Tomorrow I will *miss* you. Now I want to ask you for something."

"I'll miss you, too."

"You won't miss a thing. You are a marvelous woman. Big heart. Nice big ladylike legs. Big car. You dance wonderful, too. And your flute is exquisite. And tomorrow, it is another woman for me and I will have forgotten you. My notorious memory. This is what I have to tell myself about tomorrow. And you know what? I pretty good liar. It is my talent. I believe me. Tomorrow I won't belong to you, you won't belong to me. But yours is a real talent, your flute. Aida, take off your dress. I am in love with Aida South and her flute."

Why did she not take the trouble to know her heart sooner? Aida looks down at the row of pearly buttons on the front of her dress. The officer's dark hand reaches out and begins to undo them. She reaches toward his uniform, feels for his shirt, and starts the elaborate unbuttoning. When the shirt and dress are off, Aida and the officer fall upon the pants and the underpants and when they are naked and gleaming, they lie down and let the waves wash over them. The officer writes her name in the sand. *Aida South.* They frolic like newlyweds.

"Aida, you outshine the moon," says the officer, and pulls her down on top of him at the place where the breaking waves become foam. His cleft chin looms before her, the soft mustache and full lips, purplish red, breathing rum and vanilla custard, thick, intoxicating. Aida surrenders to his embrace, her lips and tongue meet his, her heart blossoms.

JASON COLEMAN

University of Virginia

TEN SECRETS OF BEAUTY

She refused to leave the hotel room in Amsterdam, because she thought the buildings were going to fall on her.

"They can't just fall over." Scott's voice was gentle. He was trying to be patient. "They've been standing for hundreds of years."

"That's what I mean. They're so old."

He sat on the edge of her bed, next to all the magazines she'd bought at the airport in Phoenix and reread dozens of times. Used tissues littered the floor.

"But they're built in these long rows." He spread his arms wide, as if he were cradling a whole city block. "They're all connected. They sort of hold each other up, you know? If one fell down, they'd all fall down."

"Exactly," she said, and shuddered. He had entered her logic—which was as unsound, but as unyielding, as a dream's—and unintentionally conjured up a horrible image. The idea flickered in him that she was smarter than he was.

"Bev, do you *often* feel that buildings are about to fall on you?" he asked.

She shook her head.

He'd never dreamed he'd have to ask anyone such a thing. It was a newlywed's question: There was still a lot he didn't know about her.

"Has it occurred to you that you are *in* a building?"

She had no immediate response to this. She should have looked pitiful, but her beauty was laid on in thick coats that didn't crack, even in her worst moments.

"I'm still not feeling well," she said, and got up. He watched her go into the bathroom. From behind the door he heard the sound of running water: She always turned on the tap when she was in the bathroom. ~Insecure to be w/ him~

When she came out, he knew, the conversation would move on to her general illness, of which falling buildings was merely a subissue. Had it been a specific ailment—appendicitis, say, or mercury poisoning—they could have picked the proper course of action and laid it to rest. But it was a vague mixture of symptoms—headaches, some nausea, fatigue—and, thus, open to endless discussion. Three, four times a day she offered it up for conversation, and they laid into it like two mad scientists. The intricacies of her condition fascinated her far more than any mere city ever could. Amsterdam was nothing compared to the grand architecture of her unwellness.

He collected the tissues, stuffed them in his pocket. With Beverly a constant presence, the maid couldn't get in, and their room was going to seed. Used towels lay in heaps; empty Coke cans stood on the bureau, on the windowsill. The wastebasket spilled over. Their beds—which at the beginning of the week had felt like cotton fortresses—had gone thin and slack in the sheets and begun to feel like old newspaper. Hotel beds, Scott was discovering, have no stamina.

He had begun to see their room almost as a living thing—as a body that was trying to reject Beverly like a virus or a transplanted organ. Failing this, the room was dying before his eyes.

He glanced out the window at the costly view. It was still morning, but he sensed another day collapsing on him. The water continued behind the closed bathroom door. Waiting, he picked up one of her magazines. On the cover: "Ten Secrets of Beauty—The Things You Never Knew."

She would not have sexual intercourse with him until a minister had pronounced them married under the eyes of God and the State of Arizona. On this she had been firm. Their discussions on the matter were brief and focused, as if bound by mathematical law. She called it that, "sexual intercourse." The term always deflated him; it suggested something dry, complex. Something requiring the presence of an attorney, or an anesthesiologist. But Scott, who had his own word for it, could not continue much longer without it. And so, knowing he was beat, he married her.

She was, naturally, a beautiful bride. First, his own eyes registered this as a simple fact. And then people said so—literally told him, "Beverly is such a beautiful bride"—*whispered* it, as though they were warning him of something. Even people he didn't know, men and women, came up to him and, without introducing themselves, said, "Lovely girl you've got there." Said to him, "You're very lucky."

Like most great beauties, she narrowly missed homeliness. Her eyes were almost too large, her nose almost too long. *Almost.* He could see the same features going unchecked in the rest of her family, in whom these traits raced to their natural conclusions. Beverly's father had eyes so large you could imagine goldfish swimming in them.

She flirted with fatness, but just avoided it, and instead was ripe and full. She moved about the wedding hall, a great white float—a fistful of wedding dress in each hand—not so much walking as advancing. She threw her bouquet over her shoulder and hands shot up into the air. When she pulled up her skirt so he could remove the garter, the sight of her bare leg was so striking it was as if a small wild animal had entered the hall. He noticed a sudden quiet as he worked the garter down her leg, and when he looked up he saw a round of blank, concentrated faces on the crowd of bachelors. He fired the garter into the air; it lay on the floor, untouched, for a full second before the men collected themselves and raced after it.

A gray-haired man—married, too old to be chasing garters—leaned over to Scott and said, "You have a beautiful wife."

Wife, not bride. So wife it was now.

"You don't know me." The man smiled, stuck out his hand to shake. "I'm Bobby Gragg. I worked with your father for twenty years at Belton Chaney. That's my wife over there," he pointed, "and those are our daughters, Pam and Lois." They were speaking with the bride. Scott studied the broad white image of her. She looked huge, which she wasn't, but as she stood there, talking to Pam and Lois Gragg, it was easy to believe that the other two women had crept out from under her skirt—that, in fact, they all had, everyone here.

He ached to get her home.

Outside they threw birdseed instead of rice. Rice, the wedding director had explained, would explode in a sparrow's stomach.

At his home that night—not yet *their* home, not quite—she kept him waiting. She was a long time in the bathroom, then on the phone with her parents. Then with her sister. Another session in the bathroom: He listened to the tap running. It was very late when she finally got into bed. Her nightgown was thick, long-sleeved. She was cold, she said.

He touched her, then very gradually, like a tide moving in, enwrapped her. He'd had no idea he could move so slowly. A hidden talent.

He listened to her wedding dinner trickle down through her. He could hear it so clearly, he could almost see it, and he wondered if, inside, she was as perfect as she was outside. She lay very still. Wonderful, shattering thoughts visited him.

Then he noticed a certain rhythm in her breathing. He spoke her name in the dark, but received no answer. This was not poise; it was sleep.

Presently a small snore began to develop. It started as a periodic sigh. Then it built, gathered force, cultivated itself into a great, gaping sound. As if she'd been waiting all day to release it.

He moved into the living room, tried to read. Whole sentences failed to stick to his mind, so he picked up a book of baby names: fifteen thousand suggestions, with origins and variations. He had once looked up her name and found that it was Anglican and meant "beaver field." She hadn't enjoyed this, not even as a joke, and he'd decided against further informing her that it was originally a man's name.

He finally fell asleep in his chair, the names of fifteen thousand unborn children bothering his dreams. He woke up at dawn with all the lights still on.

A few hours later, they were on the airplane. Her parents saw them off. He had the window seat; she got up a lot and wanted the aisle. On the cheek facing him was the red imprint of her mother's kiss, the lips slightly parted, as if they were trying to tell him something. The airplane cabin produced its loud nonsound, and Scott wondered if on the return flight he would be able to tell the plane was pointed in the opposite direction.

Hours passed. Beverly fell asleep over Greenland.

A pen fell from her hand; a notebook lay open on her lap. There was no writing, only an elaborate doodle at the top of the page: a circle of stars enclosed a smaller circle of alternating black and white balls which in turn enclosed a slender rectangle whose sides waved like water and inside of which lay the scribbled-over writing from which the whole drawing radiated and which, before crossed out, had read: "Things To Do in Amsterdam."

They flew with the spin of the earth and missed an entire night. It was morning when they arrived. The room wasn't yet ready, so they left their bags with the desk clerk and walked through the city. Though summer, it was cool; the sun was white in a gray sky, and objects cast pale, bloodless shadows.

"Christmas lights," Beverly said. Scott looked away from her and saw that a line of red lights was indeed strung up in a row of trees running along the canal. His gaze went a little higher and came to rest on a woman standing at a window. Something tightened in his throat. She looked at him as if she knew him. What struck him even more was the fact that she wasn't wearing any clothes.

It had arrived like that moment in a Western, when the settlers suddenly realize they've been surrounded by Indians all along. They were being watched from dozens of windows, all framed by red neon tubing, deadened in the daylight. The glass was exceedingly clean. From behind it, women beckoned to Scott—fervently, as if a long-distance phone call waited for him inside. The sight went right through him and left him with a sick, sweet wound. And, though it brought him no pleasure, he could not take his eyes away.

Beverly drew her coat closer. Their pace quickened, as if they felt a downpour coming. On every corner they began noticing sex shops, the windows displaying pictures so anatomically explicit they suggested something more surgical than sexual.

And the Americans had not yet even had their breakfast.

She said she wasn't feeling well, and he guided her back to the hotel. She looked up at the buildings, painfully, the way you'd look at the sun. Inside the lobby she said she needed aspirin and went off to the hotel's gift shop. Scott took a seat in a leather chair facing two businessmen. One of the men glanced at Beverly heading into the shop and nudged his partner, who also looked. His bottom lip swallowed the upper as he nodded. *"Die vrouw heeft 'n lekkere volle kont,"* he commented.

The first man grinned. He turned to Scott. "Do you know what he just said about your girlfriend?" The other man frowned, turned to his newspaper. Scott looked at him dumb with jet lag. "He said she has a sweet fat ass."

That afternoon, as they slept off their flight in opposite beds, he dreamt of his wedding, the guests taking him aside one by one and repeating the Dutchman's words.

Scott dug the used tissues—stiff with snot—from his pocket and dropped them in a wastebasket just outside the dining room. For the third morning in a row, he ate alone.

He tried to work on his postcards, but they were as tough as algebra. He wrote without pronouns, to cover Beverly's absence. "Went to the Rijksmuseum." "Ate raw herring. Good!" Always mentioned how nice their room was. What could Beverly be writing on hers? He wondered how their postcards might be received back home. Like the wrong color smoke floating out of the Vatican.

He couldn't tell them that Beverly stayed in all day and at night retreated to her own bed—said she was exhausted, mouthed *good night* to him from across the room. Hid in her illness. He lay in bed, monitoring her sleep. Studied the rise and fall of her hip. He thought of pulling her blanket away, an inch at a time, but knew her eyes would snap open on him. Instead he lay awake, and in his mind Beverly said things to him she'd never said in life. Did things.

When he was done with his breakfast, he made a second tray of food, to take upstairs. The first morning he'd done this, he had actually asked permission. "Can I take food out of the dining room? It's for my wife," he asked the first hotel employee he saw—the hotel detective—who looked up from his coffee and told Scott in perfect English that he really didn't care where he took it.

The desk clerk noticed him on his way up. He looked soberly at the tray of provisions and told Scott he didn't have to take it up him-self—that the hotel paid people to do that sort of thing. Scott smiled, shook his head—held up one hand, international symbol for *Everything's under control.*

When he reached their floor, he saw the maid's trolley parked out-side a vacated room. The door stood wide open like the mouth of a dental patient. His step grew slower: He wanted to avoid the maid. She had taken her shutout as an insult; he often sensed her lurking in the corridor like a jilted lover. When he passed the room the maid's back was to him and she had the vacuum going. She eased it back and forth across the carpet in broad, even strokes that never covered the same ground.

When he reached his room, he could hear the television through the door. "By unhinging its jaw," a voice was saying, "the snake can open its mouth wide enough to swallow the egg whole. A special bone in the back of the throat fractures the shell, which is then ex-pelled in one swift motion." Down the hall, the sound of the vacuum cleaner snapped off.

When he opened the door he sensed a sudden humidity, which he took for shower steam, and observed two things he had never seen before—a snake swallowing an egg and, near the full-length mirror, Beverly naked.

Her finger grazed her throat; her eyes were fixed and calm. She was studying her reflection. ─ Insecure w/ herself

"Beverly," he said. In a different century he might have sung it.

When she saw him looking at her, she took a sweatshirt from the bed and held it up to her chest. Her bare hips were visible at the shirt's edges; in the mirror he could see the reflection of her tensed shoulders and buttocks. The sweatshirt was from an old ski trip, and read GO FOR IT!

"I'll be done in a minute," she said, not taking her eyes off him. When she didn't move, he knew what she meant.

She wanted him to leave. And he did. He couldn't stay—Beverly's stare was like a strong wind pushing him out. But he left talking. He told her she'd have to give all the wedding presents back, left her with words like *unconsummated* and *annulment,* words that he couldn't even spell, that felt hot in his own ears as he closed the door and felt as foreign in his mouth as *sexual intercourse.*

He didn't know how to return to her. He patrolled the city; every sight filled him with regret. By nightfall, he sat at an outdoor café, drinking beer brewed by Trappist monks.

A candle burned at each table. He shared the space with other bodies, people who rolled their own cigarettes and twirled them over the open mouths of the candles' glass chimneys till they caught fire. Clouds of cigarette smoke passed through him. How could their lungs hold so much? His mind was filled with the properties of the body.

The sight of Beverly without clothes, watching herself in the mirror, was still settling in him. He realized that, before that moment, he hadn't fully comprehended that Beverly could even *be* naked— hadn't quite believed it, in the same way that we can't believe we will die one day. He found himself imagining her just before he'd opened the door, and just after he'd left. These thoughts were breaking off the greater mass of his feelings and entering an orbit all their own.

He authored a dozen postcards in which Beverly magically rose out of herself. "She's having a wonderful time." It was what they wanted to hear. It was what he most wanted—was what they all wanted. Couldn't she see she was outnumbered?

The crowds thinned. The waiters blew out candles, began moving tables inside. They stacked chairs and chained them together. Scott finally left when he noticed them standing at the bar with their arms crossed, staring at him. He finished writing. "Beverly found a little café."

The city grew stark with moonlight and shadow. He saw two teenagers of undetermined gender necking in a phone booth. A car with German plates sped by, in reverse. Back in Phoenix, his electric lawn sprinkler would be starting up right about now.

Not far from his hotel he found a red postbox. He took out his postcards and fed them into the slot like he was stuffing a ballot box.

When he opened the door of his room, the moon was so bright he thought a light must be on. His eyes found no color, but outlines and surfaces stood out, and he saw quite clearly that the room had been cleaned.

More than clean, it looked vacated. He wondered for a moment if the wedding had ever really happened. Then he heard her speak.

"Where were you all this time?"

A shadow lay across her bed. He could just make out her form, sitting up.

He shrugged. "Amsterdam."

He went into the bathroom—the towels were off the floor now, the door swung open easily—and drew a glass of water. His path back was clear; there was nothing on the floor but the carpet that covered it. He set the glass down on the table next to his bed. No more used tissues, Coke cans all gone. Beverly in the corner of his eye. Still sitting up, watching him.

His clothes still smelled of cigarette smoke; even his shoes smelled of smoke. His blood felt like sour milk in his veins, and when he shut his eyes the bed commenced a slow, dull spin. He began to think she was right about falling buildings.

He could have passed out in his clothes, but he felt the bed dip with her weight. He opened his eyes and saw her sitting on the edge of the bed. She watched her own hands lying limp in her lap, and he watched them with her.

"You cleaned the room," he said.

"The maid. I asked her."

"What'd you do all day?"

"I was on the phone. My mother." She laughed, once, but it was mirthless and sounded like someone blowing out a match. "She said you were right."

"About what?"

She stared at him.

"She said you were right about the wedding presents."

Not since they'd been married had she looked so hard at him. He thought she was going to hit him; he even sensed a tingle rise to his face, anticipating where the blow would come. But instead, she raised her nightgown over her head. The air shrank around him as he witnessed it. → *She was comfortable w/ herself*

Moonlight glowed in the hollows under her arms with a larval paleness. She brought her arms down and held them close, as if through sheer posture she could be less naked. He wondered how long ago she had made the decision, how many hours she'd been waiting to do this. There was no expression on her face. What she must have looked like when she let the maid in, he thought. What she must have looked like when she got off the phone. He realized, joylessly, that he could do anything he wanted. The fact presented itself almost palpably, like a third person in the room.

There was still a chill in the air; when he touched her, her skin was cool. He held her breast—calmly, the way you'd feel a sick child's forehead. It lay in his palm with a dumb, simple heft, and he felt he could have stood up and carried it away with him, as easily as he might have carried off that glass of water standing on the table.

She didn't move, didn't touch him. But she would; there was no other way it could be. Later, and for the rest of their trip, she would stay close to him—sharing his twin bed, reaching for his hand across dining tables, in the backs of cabs, until he was almost embarrassed—presenting something new and strange to him, something residing in her weight, in her smell, in the air she exhaled. He would find he no longer knew if she was beautiful, ugly, what. But she would remain close. So close, in fact, that sometimes he wanted to get away. He would wake up in the middle of the night with her pressing against his back, his arm dangling from the bed, his knuckles meeting the floor's hardness. He would creep from the bed, glance back at her form, and he would find in the dark that he was unable to remember exactly what she looked like.

But for now, he watched her fold her nightgown and place it under the pillow. Something—a breast, an elbow—brushed him. She sat up straight. "What do you want me to do," she said.

"Help," he told her, for he didn't trust himself to get his own clothes off.

GABRIELLA GOLIGER

Banff Centre for the Arts

MAEDELE

On Tuesday and Thursday mornings Rachel's parents rise early to deliver their daughter to Professor Blutstein, with whom she's having an illicit affair. Of course, they don't know that's what they're doing. They think they're helping her get a head start on her research at the library. She's off to work in the reserve section, she's told them, before other students have a chance to monopolize certain texts. The new *Encyclopedia Judaica.* Yiddish authors in translation. Tales of the Hasidim. Rachel is both relieved and appalled at how easy it is to deceive her parents. Their daughter has developed a passion for Jewish studies and is on her way to becoming first in her class. Even her mother—a terrible snoop—appears to have only the most innocent of suspicions. Every now and then she wonders aloud if Rachel has a crush on some boy.

Deception comes easily, perhaps because the truth is so preposterous, so slippery. She's been singled out by a great Yiddish poet, a visiting professor from Jerusalem. She is having an affair with a married man old enough to be her father. She's receiving private lessons from a Holocaust survivor who saw children butchered, who was buried under corpses, who hid in a pit for almost two years. She is dreaming a grade B movie where too much happens, a calamity a minute, too much cliff-hanging for any one person. She is dreaming corpses, she is falling into a pit, she is buried under a professor.

And now here comes Hannah into the kitchen, to pad about and prepare her daughter's lunch. Rachel protests, but to no avail. Lunch must be made by motherly hands, otherwise her daughter won't eat properly. Hannah's brow furrows with ancient anxieties that can only be soothed through the preparation of food. And Rachel's father has a role to play, too. It is he and no one else who will bring his daughter to her special rendezvous. He insists. Why should she take the bus? He's driving downtown past the library anyway. He, too, could use an early start on the day.

Hannah bustles, slices, spreads, wraps, hauls yet another item out of the fridge. Thick sardine sandwiches to nourish the brain. Carrot sticks to strengthen the eyes. Slices of homemade *Apfeltorte,* made Viennese-style with butter, almonds, eggs, and cream. When she's finished the lunch, Hannah follows around after Rachel, ostensibly to help her get ready, but really to postpone their separation. It will be a long, lonely day in the empty apartment.

"Pink suits you," Hannah says. "That's what you should wear. A nice youthful color."

Rachel turns this way and that in front of the mirror, examining herself in her embroidered blouse and cameo choker, wondering if she's got it right. She's striving for a combination of innocence and sophistication, achieved by plenty of other girls on campus—the flower-child allure. Loose blouse, tight jeans, granny shawl, subtle eyeliner, pale lipstick. A look to drive a professor wild. A look to make his wife go mad. But maybe the choker makes her neck seem too long.

She shakes the eyeliner bottle, applies the brush with an unsteady hand, and ends up with a black splotch at the corner of her eye and a wavy streak above her lashes.

"You don't need that stuff," says Hannah. "It's grotesque."

Rachel dabs her eye with Kleenex and begins again, more successfully this time, but still an awkward, girlish face looks back from the mirror. A pale blob, unformed, and half hidden under a frizzy mop of hair sticking out from the sides of her head. She moves on to the eye shadow, a new cake of silvery mauve that looked good on the salesgirl at Ogilvie's. Then the lipstick, a delicate shade called Cherry Blossom. A sly smile spreads across Hannah's lips.

"So who is he?" she says.

Rachel freezes, holding the lipstick—a pink, exposed finger—in the air.

"He?"

"The boy you're trying to impress?"

Rachel's shoulders relax a notch.

"Don't you have a beau? A boy you admire? You can tell your mother."

Rachel knows exactly the kind of boy Hannah has in mind. Tall, handsome, shy eyes, polite manner, blue blazer, gold buttons. An adolescent, Jewish version of Oscar Werner. Her mother's eyes gleam and her cheeks flush as if she's knocked back a stiff drink. Wouldn't she just love to hear about this beau? And what would Hannah have to say about Professor Blutstein's craggy face against Rachel's belly? Rachel is almost tempted to throw this image at her mother but wills herself into a mask of calm.

"There's nothing to tell. Look, it's late." Rachel presses cherry blossomed lips into a Kleenex, snaps the lipstick case shut, and tosses it into the Mexican shoulder bag that serves as her carryall and purse.

At 7:15, her father strides down the hall, briefcase in hand, face still damp from Gillette aftershave. He helps Rachel slip into her coat and fusses with the scarf around her neck. The first snow of the season is falling. She mustn't catch cold. Hannah stands at the door with the lunch bags, shoulders drooping, face upturned. She looks like a piece of luggage forgotten at a train station. Ernst pecks her quickly on the forehead, muttering a gruff good-bye. Now that the moment of escape is at hand, Rachel thaws. She leans forward to give her mother a hug but Hannah hangs on, collapses against Rachel as if she wants to sink into her daughter. Rachel jerks away. Never, she vows, will she cling to anyone like that. And never will she be smothered under anyone else's need. She clatters down the stairs after her father.

They drive through gray, slushy streets in silence as the car heater puffs, the radio jabbers, and the windshield wipers snap back and forth, sweeping away fat, wet flakes. The announcer rattles through a long list of accident reports and then, in a more dire tone, warns his listeners to stay away from the downtown core over the lunch hour because of a huge antiwar protest being planned—a protest that may become violent, he says, an edge of excitement in his voice.

"Terrible," her father mutters, "Where will it end?" Her father thinks the Americans are bungling the war in Vietnam and wishes they would extricate themselves as quickly as possible, but he also believes the protesters are just pawns of the Soviets. This morning she doesn't feel like goading him with stories of atrocities, wants instead to sink into her coat collar and a blur of daydreams that will put her in the right state of mind for the rendezvous ahead. She needs calm. She needs languor. She needs her father to become a piece of unobtrusive, car-driving machinery, but he's unaware, as usual, of the message her hunched limbs and averted face convey.

"What are you working on now?" he asks, as they enter some stop-and-go traffic at Queen Mary and Côte des Neiges.

"I'm reading Martin Buber on the tales of the Hasidim. I'm writing a paper. It's for my Yiddish in Translation course." She hopes that these weighty titles will put him off.

"Ah. Yiddish." His head rocks back and forth, skeptical. "A funny language."

"You think so because you're such a *Yecke*." She meant to use a joking tone, but the word comes out harsh and stabbing.

"*Yecke!*" He rolls his eyes and emits a quick, forced laugh. "You are learning a lot."

Blutstein taught her the term *Yecke,* the German Jew. Stiff, formal, even arrogant, hiding his Jewishness under a jacket and tie, embarrassed by the *shtetl* Jew's caftan and beard. Her father's too self-effacing to be arrogant, she thinks, but he fits the bill in other ways. The *McGill Daily* would call him a model of bourgeois respectability. And both her parents look down their noses at Yiddish, which is bastardized German to their ears. To Rachel's, too, she has to admit. She tries to appreciate Blutstein's poetry, which he recites in class and which she can half understand. But she can't get beyond the outlandish sounds, the stretched-out vowels that are like fat, wobbling bubbles in the air. A great language, yoking heaven and earth, the sacred texts and the common man, Blutstein tells her. But she is poisoned against it.

"The tales of the great Hasidic masters were told in Yiddish. The language of the people," she informs her father.

"Rabbinic tales," he grunts. "You find that interesting?" To him, Hasidic mysticism and garden-variety religion are one and the same—all hocus-pocus, medieval superstition.

"Very," she mumbles into her coat collar, wishing she could explain as Blutstein does, even to herself. The tales seem both quaint and baffling until Blutstein reveals layers of meaning, including his own special vision. How does he put it? A mysticism based not on mythology but on real events: the here and now and the very present then. Jewish memory goes back and back and back, to Sumer, Akkad, three thousand years of Egypt, so that Greece and Rome are like yesterday to us, almost modern eras. The Jewish soul bears witness, suffers, has a destiny—to redeem the world by exposing the flip side of empires and to reassert Jewish sovereignty, which is happening right now, this very moment. We live in wondrous times. But her version of Blutstein's lecture would be feeble and make him sound like a crazed romantic, or worse.

Mercifully, her father doesn't probe further. He shrugs, peers through his bifocals at the line of cars ahead, swings the wheel, and they dart forward into the faster lane of traffic, avoiding a stalled taxi. He beams at this small victory.

"So when is this paper due?" he asks.

"Next Friday."

"And you're making progress?"

"Yes."

"Good for you."

So pleased because she brings home good marks and pleases the professors, his studious daughter, never mind what she studies. Her oblivious father. He is silent again, concentrating on the road ahead. A song floats out from the car radio. "Let the sun shine in, the sun shine in..." A song to make everyone feel better about the weather and the traffic and Vietnam.

Staring at a stubborn spot of ice that resists the battering of the windshield wipers, Rachel sinks down into her seat and drifts. She constructs a fantasy, beginning with a premise and adding details, a dab of color here, another there, until the vision wraps her in its fuzzy warmth. The premise is that Mrs. Blutstein's gone to Paris. A gallery there is exhibiting her work. Meanwhile Blutstein waits for Rachel on the front steps of his apartment building. He paces with impatience, then catches sight of her youthful figure up the street.

His eyes glow when he sees her, graceful, nonchalant, her hair streaming in the wind (it has lengthened and straightened itself by some miracle). He grabs her arm and guides her upstairs. No. He whistles for a cab, and they go to the Queen E. Hotel for a second breakfast. No. They drive to a resort in the Laurentians. That's it, a resort in remote, snow-filled woods. He reaches for her hand across a dining room table and his eyes, brilliant with all that he knows and feels and has a hold on, those eyes burn toward her, reduce her to cinders.

As it was that first time. She had come to his office late on a Friday afternoon, hardly expecting him to be there, conscious of the clack of her boots in the empty hallway. She'd been wrestling with a theme for her term paper and wanted help, but also—she sees it now—to catch a glimpse of the great Blutstein ensconced behind a desk. Would he become more ordinary, approachable, and slightly fossilized, like the other professors or would he still radiate that compelling energy as when he paced back and forth in the classroom, wresting truth from the air with tense, clenched hands? A short, stocky man with an oversized head and tiny feet, he should have looked cartoonish but didn't because of his restless, fluid movements and his breathless, excited speech. She was aware of listening, not to his words, but to the rise and fall of his voice, while she doodled a circus of amoebas in her notebook.

At her timid knock against the open office door he leapt immediately from his chair and came around the front of the desk.

"It's you," he said, beaming with undisguised delight. "Come in, come in."

As if he'd been expecting her, or someone he'd mistaken her for. She became flustered, blanked actually, and was unable to remember the little introductory speech she'd been planning. He looked straight into her eyes with unsettling intelligence, a sly smile on his delicate, almost girlish lips, forming her with his gaze. A girl with designs. That's what he saw, that's what she was, she realized, with a shock of embarrassment and pleasure. She was wearing a miniskirt and midcalf-length boots and clutched her coat and books to her chest, a gesture that put all the emphasis on her exposed, nyloned legs. She found herself smiling, too. An absurd, complicit smile. The moment stretched out for an amazing, outrageous length of time. He was not afraid to let the room fill up with silence and with what seemed to be deepening shadows. The lights in the room were off, she realized, and dusk was approaching. He continued to stare and smile and speak wordlessly with a lift of the eyebrow, a cock of the head, pantomiming wonder, invitation, and also that delicious undercurrent of mischief. She dropped her eyes and lifted them again, struggled to say something, while the chattering, doubting voice inside her was banished for once. Finally she collapsed into nervous laughter, and still he held her with his eyes. Had he mentioned right then that he was married, she would have stared at him in utter bewilderment as if he'd given her a complex algebraic equation to solve.

But Mrs. Blutstein is not in Paris. The professor will be tucked away in his fourteenth-floor apartment. And Rachel's approach will be far from nonchalant. She will dart through alleys, hunch her shoulders, afraid of being seen by the wrong Blutstein. The Mrs. has cat's eyes, Rachel is convinced. Wide and penetrating and inescapable.

At the corner of McTavish and Sherbrooke, near the Redpath Library, father and daughter part ways, he to continue to his office on Park Avenue, she to weave through the student ghetto until she comes to the street where the Blutsteins live. Unless, like today, she's early, which means she has time to poke about the campus and try to

soothe her jangled nerves. In the lobby of the student union building, the bulletin board accosts her. Pay attention, it says.

*Yellow Door Coffee House, Marxist-Leninists, ban the bomb, ride
to New York, guitar for sale, Jewish students meeting, Christian
Fellowship, we are, we are, we are the engineers, we can, we can,
we can demolish thirty beers, Marshall McLuhan in the Leacock
Theatre (bring lunch), learn to meditate, boycott California
grapes, fuck the fuzz, looking for crash pad, I have lost an earring
shaped like a crescent moon, massacre at My Lai, stop the killing,
march at noon.*

She shifts from foot to foot. Should she go on the march? She
imagines the turbulent, confident crowd and the angry or insolent
placards. "Burn pot, not people!" "End Canada's Complicity!" Stay
out of trouble, her father would say. It's not your concern. Blutstein
disapproves, too, but for different reasons. "Jews are on the front lines
of every revolution that turns against them," he once said with a
shrug, while his dismissive look told her that this business of marches
was a petty distraction, a game, not worthy of serious attention.

She feels awkward in demonstrations, like someone who can't
keep step in a dance. She watches her classmates—some of the girls
especially—their practiced, beatific smiles transformed into howls of
fury directed at the government, the system. They can let go, yell like
crazies, even shove and hurl stones, connected to and energized by
one another. She can't get angry enough or sure enough to yell. The
pictures and facts, all those facts about how many tons of bombs
dropped on villagers in paddy fields leave her numb or grieving but
don't translate into a demonstrator's ironclad conviction. She grieves
over the magazine picture of the huddled My Lai women about to be
shot—a teenager in the center with a grandmother's arms wrapped

around her—but at the same time strangely cherishes this image because it's the only thing she can hold on to in all the news reports, speeches, posters. When Rachel tries to chant, all that comes out is a feeble squeak. Is Blutstein right? But surely he, too, has seen the photo of the women.

At a little after eight she is in the laneway beside the high-rise on Hutchison Street. She hesitates by the side door to the parking garage, looks over her shoulder. No one. She slips inside. The air smells of car exhaust and rotten eggs but it is mercifully dark. The fire escape door is propped open, left so by the careless janitor. If not, she'd have to backtrack to the front entrance and run the risk of being seen. It's not just Mrs. Blutstein who worries her, it's anyone who might be in the lobby or elevator. She's afraid of suspicious glances—absurd, she knows, but it's a fear she can't shake.

She climbs up 182 stairs, arriving at the fourteenth floor breathless, armpits sweaty. She pokes her head into the hallway and looks for the newspaper on the mat in front of the door—their sign. If she sees it, all is well, she may tap on the door. If not, she must leave at once. Normally, by eight, Mrs. Blutstein's gone to the art college to teach her early morning class.

All these details and many others have been worked out by Blutstein. Signs, escape routes, contingency plans, and, if worst comes to worst, a story to tell to explain her presence in the apartment (she's late with a term paper and came personally to beg an extension). He's a master at subterfuge and escaping detection. He seems almost to relish it.

She smiles toward the peephole. The door opens a crack. She steps inside

"*Maedele*," he whispers in Yiddish as he pulls her toward him. More Yiddish endearments as he presses up against her and enfolds her. He is wearing the navy, cable-stitch sweater that makes him look distinguished, yet relaxed and almost young, the thick wool covering the folds of paunch below his belt.

Awkward and still blotchy from the climb, she struggles out of her boots, leaning on his shoulder, careful not to spread grit all around. The parquet floor is cold to her nyloned feet. His are sheathed in backless slippers that hiss along the floor when he walks.

He calls her *maedele* which means little maid, or little girl—a quaint term, something an aunt might say—although the way Blutstein croons the word it sounds melodic and plaintive. His first name is Mendel, but she can't call him that. It's too familiar. She's been taught to address her elders with titles of respect, and although Blutstein has his hands up her blouse, he's still her professor and more than twice her age. Besides, Mendel is a silly name, the name of someone in a comedy team. She calls him Blutstein in her mind and nothing to his face. Manages to complete sentences without using a name. He doesn't seem to notice.

He kisses her urgently. His eyes are shut tight, his eyelids quivering, she notices when she peeks through her lashes. The great Blutstein who chose her, created her, brought her out of the awkward girlishness in which she'd been stuck, now surrenders to his creation. Now, this moment, as they hover on the brink of possibilities, is the best time of all. He shapes her into a goddess with his eyes; she reads the poetry of his face and he looks exactly as an old-world poet should. Dreamy eyes under a bushy brow, sensitive lips, massive forehead, thick, wavy hair standing straight up like exclamation marks. If only they were together across a candlelit table. Or even in the living room, the beautiful living room that Rachel occasionally dares to enter, lingering over the fascinating objects that cancel out the bland rental furniture and dull winter light. Paintings of Jerusalem streets, a black-and-white photograph of a blind beggar feeling his way along an ancient wall, a copper Passover plate, a brass menorah, stones from the Judean desert, sun-bleached and pitted. Bits of Israel that the Blutsteins packed lovingly and brought with them to remind themselves of home. How different from her parents' house with its heathen clutter acquired during trips to Europe—the cuckoo clock, pewter beer steins, Dutch shoes, cow bells, and only one cheap, tin Hanukkah menorah, scratched from years of use, its base soiled with dusty wax from Hanukkahs past.

Blutstein nuzzles his face into her neck. His small warm hands run quickly over her body. He fumbles with her bra clasp until finally her breasts hang free and naked, although her arms are tangled in the straps. A breeze from under the front door blows against her ankles. What are they doing in the foyer? Someone passing by could hear. She pushes him toward the bedroom.

"Ah, *maedele,* you're in a hurry. Me, too."

They stumble toward the guest room at the end of the hall and fall upon the single bed, Blutstein tugging at his own clothes and hers. She is glad about the existence of this little room. She couldn't bear it if they had to lie in the bed that Blutstein shares with his wife, although she wonders if he would mind so very much. The guest room doubles as study and artist's studio, with an antique wooden writing desk near the window and an empty easel on a square of paint-splotched newspaper in the opposite corner. The long wall above the desk is lined, floor to ceiling, with bookshelves on which stand massive, leather-bound tomes, their spines emblazoned with gilded Hebrew script that Rachel can't read, as well as rows of more modern texts. A few drops from the ocean of learning that Blutstein swims in daily and that she is only just beginning to glimpse.

Now Blutstein is panting, his face almost purple, clownish. An embarrassed laugh bubbles near her lips, which he interprets as desire.

"*Maedele,*" he moans. He pushes himself inside her. It doesn't hurt because he's not too big. The first moment of strangeness passes quickly, and the thrusts become a dull rhythm, like falling rain. The lower half of her body is quiet and far away. But they forgot the towel. She should have a towel under her to protect the bedspread, which is beautiful—a rich heavy cotton, striped red, orange, mauve, and blue. It was purchased by Mrs. B. in the Old City of Jerusalem. Rachel dreams of such a bedspread for herself. If she isn't careful now, they will leave a chalky smear and a telltale smell behind. She will have to swing off the bed with her legs held together when he's done.

Propping himself up on his hands, he looks down on her and his face, pulled by gravity, becomes a slack mask—puffy, inflamed. A vein in his temple throbs, reminding her of his heart condition. What would she do...but she mustn't think. She doesn't want him to waste time with fondling and foreplay, although that's what the books say is supposed to happen. She becomes alarmed when he caresses her longer than usual and in places he doesn't normally touch, so she puts an end to his fumbling with a bold gesture of her own. She can't imagine writhing with him as she does by herself in her own bed at night.

The vein in his temple, the ticking clock, the hums and stirrings of the apartment—and any moment his wife might burst through the door to find them like this. She imagines Mrs. Blutstein's frozen eyes glaring down at her over her husband's naked back. In her mind Rachel pleads, *this is not what it seems.* Then what is it? A prelude. A preparation for the more important and devastating encounter that comes after the sex.

"Are you ready?" he gasps.

She smiles. He falls upon her, finished. Excitement drains out of him, his heartbeats fade, his body presses down on her chest. She doesn't move, takes shallow breaths, testing herself. How still can she be? How long can she bear his weight? The longer he crushes down on her, the more he will be restored, refreshed, grateful. The more of a woman she will be.

"Was it good?" he says, rolling over at last.

"It was," she lies. An unimportant lie.

Dressed again, the bed straightened, stray hairs and stains wiped away with a damp cloth, they prepare to sit at the writing desk near the window and drink coffee. She's less nervous now, even though danger still lies just outside the door. A step in the hall, a key in the lock, and her world would come crashing down. But he has fox ears, he reassures her, and cat's feet and a sixth sense. He knows everything there is to know about escape.

He brews the coffee double strength in an enamel percolator on the stove top. Rachel doesn't follow into the kitchen while he pours and stirs, because the pots, the potholder with the burnt thumb, all the domestic objects say *wife, wife, wife*. Instead Rachel waits by the writing desk in the guest room, her gaze drawn to the painting on the wall. An explosion of yellow dots against an expanse of blue sea and a signature in the corner. *Leah Blutstein*. Mimosa tree at Caesarea, it's entitled. The yellow balls wrap Rachel in sunshine, the cool blue invites her in. There is no reproach here, only kindness and wonder at yellow rapture and blue beginnings.

They hid together from the Germans. They've been married for twenty-seven years.

Blutstein enters with a rattling tray, cups of coffee, a plate with Rachel's mother's cake. He likes this *Apfeltorte*. It is buttery and bad for the heart. He chuckles as he eats, scattering crumbs across his lap and under the desk. He pats her knee at the alarm in her eyes. Don't worry, his chuckle says. I know everything there is to know about risk. This is no risk. This is child's play.

"*Maedele*," he says aloud, "How are you?" A question that requires no answer beyond a smile. He strokes her cheek, suddenly pensive.

"One of these days you have to find a boyfriend, a nice Jewish boy. I'm keeping an eye out, but those pishers in my class, they're not worth much."

"Oh, no," she says, alarmed, unable to read his face. Is he serious? She can see him as matchmaker, well-meaning and tactless, nudging her toward the same kind of clean-cut youth her parents would approve of, oblivious to the humiliation he's causing. She shudders, but he shrugs and hands her a steaming cup, his thoughts already elsewhere. The coffee is black and sweet, makes her jumpy if she drinks too much. On him, it has no effect except to deepen his gaze and prick his memories.

"In my hometown, at my Rebbe's court we drank coffee like this. No, actually, it was stronger. Twice as strong." He sits up, lips pursed in thought, eyebrows raised, listening for his story. His gaze travels far beyond the realities of this room, leaping past the walls, the bed, the cake crumbs, the painting, into a whirlwind of times and places. How magnificent his face is, she thinks. It justifies everything. The lines of concentration on his forehead, the electric hair, his mouth a small, tense seed about to burst open.

"You sniffed the coffee and your mind flew up into another realm. Coffee and the Hasidic Rebbe," he sighs. "Much more potent than your hippie hash." He pronounces it "hesh," but she doesn't smile. She clenches the chair as she leans forward to listen, knowing that he has stories like the sky has rain, and that they will soon break over her head.

"We talked of Talmud all night long. Amazing discussions. You think Talmud is dry and legalistic. No! It's alive, teeming with stories, questions, parables, great insights cutting down into the core of existence. The goyim had an inkling of the greatness of our holy books and they were envious. This is the source of European Jew hatred. They couldn't bear that we possess a greater wisdom than their own. Ah, you don't believe me, *maedele,* but it's true."

There it is again, goy and Jew, clear borders marked with barbed wire fences. What he says is too simplistic, like the words in the Bible "God hardened Pharaoh's heart," making the hatred inherent and preordained. The world is new, she wants to say. It's the Age of Aquarius. We're banding together to ban the bomb.

"There are other victims now. Vietnam."

He rakes his hair with his hands. "Can you possibly think there is any comparison? Wars are horrible, yes. But what I lived through was not a war with one side and another, one army and another. Let me tell you..."

He tells, reveals to her what he never does in class—the dark source of his brilliance.

It begins with a picture of a ghetto. Jews from the whole region have been crowded into the quarter, with sometimes ten people forced to live in one room, yet life goes on. Work, school, markets, even concerts. But then the roundup. The rooms with their careful partitions of curtains and cots ranged along walls spew forth broken glass, bedding, copybooks, bodies, and a shrieking stampede herded by men with whips and guns, and before long not a soul is left in the streets except the dogs licking the bloody stones.

She leans forward to listen, a greedy interest devouring his words and digesting none. She hears and doesn't hear as his eyes grow fierce and he shakes the air around him with both hands.

"They ransacked our town for the last of the Jews, yanked them out of chimneys, attics, pits. Children, mothers with infants, the old and the sick driven into the marketplace. Our great Rebbe sat on the bare ground and recited psalms. There was blood on his mouth where he'd been hit with a rifle butt. Blood dripped with every line of prayer."

She believes. She doesn't believe. She is a *Yecke,* a coward, clings to wishy-washy moderation. His stories are obscene. She lusts for more.

"...more and more people in the marketplace...no water...the blazing sun...hours and hours...the thirst...little girls offer themselves to the soldiers...mothers howl...then shots into the crowd...an infant is ripped from its mother's breast...and they played marching music...and they set up pots to boil for their pig's knuckle soup...and they ate and drank while we vomited and bled...until everyone was in the cattle cars or dead, every last soul, except for me under a heap of corpses. I clawed my way up through the dead."

He claws the air, his voice chokes, the vein at his temple throbs. Please stop, please stop. You'll keel over and I won't know what to do and she'll walk in and it will be my fault.

"I found a remnant of Jews in the forest. We bribed a peasant to let us dig a pit in his barn. We took turns keeping watch. Water-soaked straw, our clothes rotted, the lice, the worms. Quick, someone's coming...cover the entrance...stifling dark...no air...crushing our lungs...we cling to one another...her nails in my flesh, my nails in hers...hanging on for one more moment because they're here, the Germans, the peasants, the police, the partisans, to drag us out of the pit, to sell us to the Gestapo, one more Jew to kill. One more Jew to kill."

It is time for her to leave. Mrs. Blutstein's class ends at ten. She must escape out the door. Blutstein clasps her hand.

"Why did we stay alive after everyone dear to us was dead and when every moment of life was hell? It was a miracle, but not a pretty miracle. God bit into our hearts. Why were we spared? To bear placards for communist dictators who spit on the Jews?"

She rises to leave but he holds her down.

"*Maedele,* stay awhile, there's still time."

He has more to tell her, nicer stories. About the Holy Land that she soon must visit. How beautiful to walk in Jerusalem as the Shabbat begins, the traffic stills, the dusk descends, and voices flow out of the synagogues into the echoing streets, "Come let us greet her, the Sabbath queen."

A peace comes into his eyes. Now is the time to go—while he is calm and contemplative and she can slip out the door like a puff of air, leaving nothing of herself behind. But he kisses her again, a long insistent kiss, suckling her lips, then presses her face against his chest so that she can hear the irregular ka-thunk, thunk of his heart.

"So good with you," he moans. "You take me out of myself. You understand? I need this."

He holds her tightly so that they are welded together, become an unbalanced mass, swaying dangerously. She is afraid they will topple once more onto the bed, which is perhaps what he wants, to once again . . . quickly . . . his hands begin to search.

She jerks free and bolts for her coat and boots, flung into a corner behind the guest room door. Look at the time, she pleads.

"Ah yes, the time. My little *Yecke,* so conscious of the time." He sighs, rubs his flushed face, then whacks her a smart one across the bum, which is thrust out slightly as she struggles with her boots. But she's seen it coming and holds herself steady against the wall.

"See you in class," he grins and winks, opening the front door.

She runs, runs, down 182 steps, boots echoing up the stairwell, the stale air pricking her nostrils. Out into the fresh air of a winter's day where the cars still swish through the slush and the store at the corner still advertises Pepsi and Craven A. Nothing has happened in these streets of solid, blank-faced buildings, these stupid unmoved streets. A foul energy runs from the top of her head to the balls of her feet, crimping her toes in her boots. She wants to kick the metal garbage can set out neatly by the sidewalk and spill its contents into the path of oncoming pedestrians. All day, every day, images flicker beneath his eyelids, yet he grins and chuckles, eats cake and gropes for her breasts. She tries to hold on to just one image for an instant but it dissolves—*we clung together*...

She envisions the marchers with their signs, the boys with shoulder-length hair and beards—Jesus faces—the girls with beads and painted lashes. The righteous shouts, the cleverly worded placards, "Peace in the world, not the world in pieces." They lilt the words, link arms, hoot, holler, jostle, tumble together, sweep her aside. But she will burst upon them with a God-given fury, smash their signs, bash heads, kick and bite, bite, bite into their throats.

She leans against a wall outside the library, dizzy, nauseous, chilled with sweat. Buttery torte and coffee gurgle in her stomach. Rage has burst through her and left her empty, holding on to a wall of striated concrete. A good wall. It offers its indifferent support, asking nothing in return.

She sits in the carpeted stillness of the library, under cool fluorescent lights and neutral colors. Outside the window she can see the crowd gathering on the other side of campus, from this distance a small, gray swarm with placards the size of postage stamps half hidden behind the bare limbs of trees. They must have megaphones but she can't hear a thing; the double-glazing of the windowpanes muffling all sound. There's still time to join them if she chooses. The gathering and milling should continue for quite a while. She has time to decide whether one silent, unchanting marcher would add anything to the cause.

In the meantime, she writes notes in her exercise book, soothed by the clear blue rule lines and her own round script. "Hasidism," she writes. "Popular religious movement that swept Jewish communities of eastern Europe in eighteenth century. Led by master-teachers, wonder-workers. Taught piety, fervor, humility, joy."

Her hand wanders across the page. *Leah,* it writes. A strong name. She must be home by now and is bustling about the kitchen preparing his lunch, listening with half an ear to his chatter. She scolds him for the crumbs strewn all over the writing desk while he grins, shamefaced and sly. But she says nothing more. She *knows* though. Oh yes, she must. He may be a fox, but she is a cat, knows all the games of hide-and-seek as well as he does. She lived in a pit, just as he did. She lived in a pit with *him.*

After he leaves to teach his own class, what will she do? Cry? Howl into the empty air? No, no, she won't. She will grab hold of that old anger and disappointment, bring out canvas and easel, brushes and paints, and create a cascade of blossoms against an ochre-colored wall. "Bougainvillea in Jerusalem," she might call it. A brilliant purple bush, burning with a fierce inner light. Burning its presence into the room.

WILLIAM GAY

Sewanee Writers' Conference

THE PAPERHANGER, THE DOCTOR'S WIFE, AND THE CHILD WHO WENT INTO THE ABSTRACT

The vanishing of the doctor's wife's child in broad daylight was an event so cataclysmic that it forever divided time into the then and the now, the before and the after. In later years, fortified with a pitcher of silica-dry vodka martinis, she had cause to replay the events preceding the disappearance. They were tawdry and banal but in retrospect freighted with menace, a foreshadowing of what was to come, like a footman or a fool preceding a king into a room.

She had been quarreling with the paperhanger. Her four-year-old daughter Zeineb was standing directly behind the paperhanger where he knelt smoothing air bubbles out with a wide plastic trowel. Zeineb had her fingers in the paperhanger's hair. The paperhanger's hair was shoulder-length and the color of flax and the child was delighted with it. The paperhanger was accustomed to her doing this and he did not even turn around. He just went on with his work. His arms were smooth and brown and corded with muscle and in the light that fell upon the paperhanger through stained glass panels the doctor's wife could see that they were lightly downed with fine golden hair. She studied these arms bemusedly while she formulated her thoughts.

You tell me so much a roll, she said. The doctor's wife was from Pakistan and her speech was still heavily accented. I do not know single bolt rolls and double bolt rolls. You tell me double bolt price but you are installing single bolt rolls. My friend has told me. It is cost me perhaps twice as much.

The paperhanger, still on his knees, turned. He smiled up at her. He had pale eyes. I did tell you so much a roll, he said. You bought the rolls.

The child, not yet vanished, was watching the paperhanger's eyes. She was a scaled-down clone of the mother, the mother viewed through the wrong end of a telescope, and the paperhanger suspected that as she grew neither her features nor her expression would alter, she would just grow larger like something being aired up with a hand pump.

And you are leave lumps, the doctor's wife said, gesturing at the wall.

I do not leave lumps, the paperhanger said. You've seen my work before. These are not lumps. The paper is wet. The paste is wet. Everything will shrink down and flatten out. He smiled again. He had clean even teeth. And besides, he said. I gave you my special cock-teaser rate. I don't know what you're complaining about.

Her mouth worked convulsively. She looked for a moment as if he'd slapped her. When words did come they came in a fine spray of spit. You are trash, she said. You are scum.

Hands on knees, he pushed himself up, the girl's dark fingers trailing out of his hair. Don't call me trash, he said, as if it were perfectly all right to call him scum, but he was already talking to her back; she had whirled on her heels and now went twisting her hips through an arched doorway into the cathedraled living room. The paperhanger looked down at the child. Her face glowed with a strange constrained glee, as if she and the paperhanger shared some secret the rest of the world hadn't caught on to yet.

In the living room the builder was supervising the installation of a chandelier which depended from the vaulted ceiling by a long golden chain. The builder was a short bearded man dancing about showing her the features of the chandelier, smiling obsequiously. She gave him a flat angry look. She waved a dismissive hand toward the ceiling. Whatever, she said.

She went out the front door onto the porch and down a makeshift walkway of two-by-tens into the front yard where her car was parked. The car was a silver gray Mercedes her husband had given her for their anniversary. When she cranked the engine its idle was scarcely perceptible.

She powered down the window. Zeineb, she called. Across the razed earth of the unlandscaped yard a man in a grease-stained T-shirt was booming down the chains securing a backhoe to a lowboy hooked to a gravel truck. The sun was low in the west and bloodred behind this tableau and man and tractor looked flat and dimensionless as something decorative stamped from tin. She blew the horn. The man turned, raised an arm as if she'd signaled him.

Zeineb, she called again.

She got out of the car and started impatiently up the walkway. Behind her the gravel truck started and truck and backhoe pulled out of the gravel drive and down toward the road.

The paperhanger was stowing his tools away. Where is Zeineb? the doctor's wife asked. She followed you out, the paperhanger told her. He glanced about, as if she might be hiding somewhere. There was nowhere to hide.

Where is my child? she asked the builder. The electrician climbed down from the ladder. The paperhanger came out of the bathroom with his tools. The builder was looking all around. His elfin features were touched with chagrin, as if this missing child were just something else he was going to be held accountable for.

Likely she's hiding in a closet, the paperhanger said. Playing a trick on you.

Zeineb does not play tricks, the doctor's wife said. Her eyes kept darting about the huge room, taking in the shadows that lurked in corners. There was already an undercurrent of panic in her voice and all her poise and self-confidence seemed to have vanished with the child.

The paperhanger set down his toolbox and went through the house opening and closing doors. It was a huge house and there were a lot of closets. There was no child in any of them.

The electrician was searching upstairs. The builder had gone through the French doors that opened onto the unfinished veranda and was peering into the backyard. The backyard was a maze of convoluted ditch excavated for the septic tank field line and beyond that there was just woods. She's playing in that ditch, the builder said, going down the flagstone steps.

She wasn't though. She wasn't anywhere. They searched the house and the grounds. They moved with jerky haste. They kept glancing toward the woods where the day was waning first. The builder kept shaking his head. She's got to be *somewhere,* he said.

Call someone, the doctor's wife said. Call the police.

It's a little early for the police, the builder said. She's got to be here.

You call them anyway. I have a phone in my car. I will call my husband.

While she called, the paperhanger and the electrician continued to search. They had looked everywhere and were forced to search places they'd already looked. If this ain't the goddamnedest thing I ever saw, the electrician said.

The doctor's wife got out of the Mercedes and slammed the door. Suddenly she stopped and clasped a hand to her forehead. She screamed. The man with the tractor, she said. Somehow my child is gone with the tractor man.

Oh Jesus, the builder said. What have we got ourselves into here?

The high sheriff that year was a ruminative man named Bellwether. He stood beside the county cruiser talking to the paperhanger while deputies ranged the grounds. Other men were inside looking in places that had already been searched numberless times. Bellwether had been in the woods and he was picking cockleburs off his khakis and out of his socks. He kept staring at the woods where the day was fading fast. Dark was gathering there and seeping across the field like a stain.

I've got to get men out here, Bellwether said. A lot of men and a lot of lights. We're going to have to search every inch of these woods.

You'll pay hell doing it, the paperhanger said. These woods stretch all the way to Lawrence County. This is the edge of the Harrikan. Down in there's where all those old mines used to be. Allens Creek.

I don't give a shit if they stretch all the way to Fairbanks, Alaska, Bellwether said. They've got to be searched. It'll just take a lot of men.

The raw-earth yard was full of cars. Doctor Jamahl had come in a sleek black Lexus. He berated his wife. Why weren't you watching her? he asked. Unlike his wife's, the doctor's speech was impeccable. She covered her face with her palms and wept. The doctor still wore his green surgeon's smock and it was flecked with bright dots of blood as a butcher's smock might be.

I need to feed a few cows, the paperhanger said. I'll feed my stock pretty quick and come back and help hunt.

You don't mind if I look in your truck, do you?

Do what?

I've got to cover my ass. If that little girl don't turn up damn quick this is going to be over my head. TBI, FBI, network news. I've got to eliminate everything.

Eliminate away, the paperhanger said.

The sheriff looked in the floorboard of the paperhanger's pickup truck. He had a huge flashlight and he shined it under the seat and felt behind it with his hands.

I had to look, he said apologetically.

Of course you did, the paperhanger said.

Full dark had fallen before he returned. He had fed and stowed away his tools and picked up a six-pack of San Miguel beer and now he sat in the back of the pickup truck drinking it. The paperhanger had been in the Navy and stationed in the Philippines and San Miguel was the only beer he could drink. He had to go out of town to buy it, but he figured it was worth it. He liked the exotic labels, the dark bitter taste on the back of his tongue, the way the chilled bottles felt held against his forehead.

The yard by now was thronging with people. There was a vaguely festive air. He watched all this with a dispassionate eye, as if he were charged with grading the participants, comparing the spectacle with others he'd seen. Coffee urns had been brought in and set up on tables. Sandwiches prepared and handed out to the weary searchers. A crane had been hauled in and the septic tank replevied from the ground; it swayed from a taut cable while men with lights searched the impacted earth beneath it for a child, for the very trace of a child. Through the far dark woods lights crossed and recrossed, darted to and fro like fireflies. The doctor and the doctor's wife sat in folding camp chairs looking drained, stunned, waiting for their child to be delivered into their arms.

The doctor was a short portly man with a benevolent expression. He had a moon-shaped face with light and dark areas of skin that looked swirled, as if the pigment coloring him had not been properly mixed. He had been educated at Princeton. When he had established his practice he had returned to Pakistan to find a wife befitting his station. The woman he had selected had been chosen on the basis of her beauty. In retrospect perhaps more consideration should have been given to other qualities. She was still beautiful but he was thinking that certain faults might outweigh this. She seemed to have trouble keeping up with her children. She could lose a four-year-old child in a room no larger than six hundred square feet and she could not find it again.

The paperhanger drained his bottle and set it by his foot in the bed of the truck. He studied the doctor's wife's ravaged face through the deep blue light. The first time he had seen her she had hired him to paint a bedroom in the house they were living in while the doctor's mansion was being built. There was an arrogance about her that cried out to be taken down a notch or two. She flirted with him, backed away, flirted again. She would treat him as if he were a stain on the bathroom rug and then stand close by him while he worked until he was dizzy with the smell of her, with the heat that seemed to radiate off her body. She stood by him while he knelt painting baseboards and after an infinite moment carefully leaned the weight of a thigh against his shoulder. You'd better move it, he thought. She didn't. He laughed and turned his face into her groin. She gave a strangled cry and slapped him hard. The paintbrush flew away and speckled the dark rose walls with antique white. You filthy beast, she said. You are some kind of monster. She stormed out of the room and he could hear her slamming doors behind her.

Well, I was looking for a job when I found this one, he smiled philosophically to himself.

But he had not been fired. In fact, now he had been hired again. Perhaps there was something here to ponder.

At midnight he gave up his vigil. Some souls more hardy than he kept up the watch. The earth here was worn featureless by the ceaseless, useless traffic of the searchers. Like a world beset by locusts. Going out he met a line of pickup trucks with civil defense tags. Grim-faced men sat aligned in their beds. Some clutched rifles loosely by their barrels. They looked as if they would lay to waste whatever monster, man or beast, that would snatch up a child in its slaverous jaws and would vanquish prey and predator in the space between two heartbeats.

Even more dubious reminders of civilization as these fell away. He drove into the Harrikan where he lived. A world so dark and forlorn light itself seemed at a premium. Whippoorwills swept red-eyed up from the roadside. Old abandoned foundries and furnaces rolled past, grim and dark as forsaken prisons. Down a ridge was an abandoned graveyard, if you knew where to look. The paperhanger did. He had dug up a few of the graves, examined with curiosity what remained: buttons, belt buckles, a cameo brooch. The bones he laid out like he was a child with a Tinkertoy, arranging them the way they went in jury-rigged resurrection.

He braked hard on a curve, the truck slewing in the gravel. A bobcat had crossed the road graceful as a wraith, fierce and lantern-eyed in the headlights, gone so swiftly it might have been a stage prop swung across the road on wires.

Bellwether and a deputy drove to the backhoe operator's house. He lived up a gravel road that wound through a great stand of cedars. He lived in a board-and-batten house with a tin roof rusted to a warm umber. They parked before it and got out adjusting their gun-belts.

Bellwether had a search warrant with the ink scarcely dry. The operator was outraged.

Look at it this way, Bellwether explained patiently. I've got to cover my ass. Everything has got to be considered. You know how kids are. Never thinking. What if she run under the wheels of your truck when you was backing out? What if quicklike you put the body in your truck to get rid of it somewhere?

What if quicklike you get the hell off my property, the operator said.

Everything has to be considered, the sheriff said again. Nobody's accusing anybody of anything just yet.

The operator's wife stood glowering at them. To have something to do with his hands the operator began to construct a cigarette. He had huge red hands thickly sown with brown freckles. They shook. I ain't got a thing in this round world to hide, he said.

They searched everywhere they could think of to look. Finally they stood uncertainly in the operator's yard, out of place in their neat khakis, their polished leather.

Now get the hell off my land, the operator said. If all you think of me is that I could run over a little kid and then throw it off in the bushes like a dead cat or something then I don't even want to see your goddamn face. I want you gone and I want you by God gone now.

Everything had to be considered, the sheriff said.

Then maybe you need to consider that paperhanger.

What about him?

That paperhanger is one sick puppy.

He was still there when I got there, the sheriff said. Three witnesses swore nobody ever left, not even for a minute, and one of them was the child's mother. I searched his truck myself.

Then he's a sick puppy with a damn good alibi, the operator said.

That was all. There was no ransom note, no child that turned up two counties over with amnesia. She was a page turned, a door closed, a lost ball in the high weeds. She was a child no larger than a doll but the void she left behind her was unreckonable. Yet there was no end to it. No finality. There was no moment when someone could say, turning from a mounded grave, well, this has been unbearable, but you've got to go on with your life. Life did not go on. Life was parked somewhere before some cosmic traffic signal waiting for the light to change and there was a malfunction in the wiring of the world itself.

At the doctor's wife's insistence an intensive investigation was focused on the backhoe operator. Forensic experts from the FBI went over every millimeter of the gravel truck with special attention to its wheels. They were examined with every modern crime-fighting device the government possessed and there was no microscopic particle of tissue or blood, no telltale chip of fingernail, no hair ribbon.

Work ceased on the mansion. Some subcontractors were discharged outright while others simply drifted away. There was no one to care if the work was done, no one to pay them. The half-finished veranda's raw wood grayed in the fall, then winter rains. The ditches were left fallow and uncovered and half-filled with water. Kudzu crept from the woods. The hollyhocks and oleanders the doctor's wife had planted grew entangled and rampant. The imported windows were stoned by double-dared boys who whirled and fled. Already this house where a child had vanished was acquiring an unhealthy, a diseased, reputation.

The doctor and his wife sat entombed in separate prisons, replaying real and imagined grievances. The doctor felt that his wife's neglect had sent his child into the abstract. The doctor's wife drank vodka martinis and watched talk shows with an endless procession of vengeful people who had not had children vanish and felt perhaps rightly that the fates had dealt her from the bottom of the deck, and she prayed with intensity for a miracle.

Then one day she was just gone. The Mercedes and part of her clothing and personal possessions were gone, too. He idly wondered where she was, but he did not search for her.

Sitting in his armchair cradling a great marmalade cat and a bottle of J&B and studying with bemused detachment the gradations of light at the window, the doctor remembered studying literature at Princeton. He had particular cause to reconsider the poetry of William Butler Yeats. For how surely things fell apart, how surely the center could not hold.

His practice fell into ruin. His colleagues made sympathetic allowances for him at first, but there are limits to these things. He made erroneous diagnoses and prescribed the wrong medicines, not once or twice, but as a matter of course.

Just as there is a deepening progression to these things, so too there is a point beyond which things can only get worse. They did. A middle-aged woman he was operating on died.

He had made an incision to remove a ruptured appendix and the incised flesh was clamped aside while he made ready to slice it out. It was not there. He stared in drunken disbelief. He began to search under things, organs, intestines, a rising tide of blood. The appendix was not there. It had gone into the abstract, atrophied, been removed twenty-five years before. He had sliced through the selfsame scar. He was rummaging through her abdominal cavity like an irritated man fumbling through a drawer for a pair of clean socks, finally bellowing in rage and roiling his hands in bloody vexation while nurses began to cry out. Another surgeon was brought on the run as a closer, and he was carried from the operating room.

Came then the days of sitting in the armchair while he was besieged by contingency lawyers, action news teams, a long line of process servers. There was nothing he could do. It was out of his hands and into the hands of the people who are paid to do these things. He sat cradling the bottle of J&B with the marmalade cat snuggled against his portly midriff. He would study the window where the light drained away in a process he no longer had an understanding of and sip the scotch and every now and then stroke the cat's head gently. The cat's purring against his breast was as reassuring as the hum of an air conditioner.

He left in the middle of the night. He began to load his possessions into the Lexus. At first he chose items with a great degree of consideration. The first thing he loaded was a set of custom-made monogrammed golf clubs. Then his stereo receiver, Denon AC3, seventeen hundred and fifty dollars. A copy of *This Side of Paradise* autographed by Fitzgerald that he had bought as an investment. By the time the Lexus was half full he was just grabbing things up at random and stuffing them into the backseat, a half-eaten pizza, half a case of cat food, a single brocade house shoe.

He drove west past the hospital, the country club, the city limit sign. He was thinking no thoughts at all and all the destination he had was the amount of highway the headlights showed him.

In the slow rains of late fall the doctor's wife returned to the unfinished mansion. She sat in a camp chair on the ruined veranda and drank chilled martinis she poured from the pitcher she carried in a Styrofoam ice chest. Dark fell early those November days. Rain crows husbanding some far cornfield called through the smoky autumn air. The sound was fiercely evocative, reminding her of something but she could not have said what.

She went into the room where she had lost the child. The light was failing. The high corners of the room were in deepening shadow but she could see the nests of dirt daubers clustered on the rich flocked wallpaper, a spider swinging from a chandelier on a strand of spun glass. The dried blackened stool of some animal curled like a slug against the baseboards. The silence in the room was enormous.

One day she arrived and she was surprised to find the paperhanger there. He was sitting on a yellow four-wheeler drinking a bottle of beer. He made to go when he saw her, but she waved him back. Stay and talk with me, she said.

The paperhanger was much changed. His pale locks had been shorn away in a makeshift haircut as if scissored in the dark or by a blind barber and his cheeks were covered with a soft curly beard.

You have grow a beard.

Yes.

You are strange with it.

The paperhanger sipped from his San Miguel. I was strange without it, he said. He arose from the four-wheeler and came over and sat on the flagstone steps. He stared across the mutilated yard toward the tree line. The yard was like a fun house maze seen from above, its twistings and turnings bereft of mystery.

You are working somewhere now?

No. I don't take so many jobs anymore. There's only me and I don't need much. What has become of the doctor?

She shrugged. Many things have change, she said. He has gone. The banks have foreclose. What is that you ride?

An ATV. A four-wheeler.

It goes well in the woods?

It was made for that. Of course it goes in the woods.

You could take me in the woods. How much would you charge me? For what?

To go in the woods. You could drive me. I will pay you.

Why?

To search for my child's body.

I wouldn't charge anybody anything to search for a child's body, the paperhanger said. But she's not in these woods. Nothing could have stayed hidden the way these woods were searched.

Sometimes I think she just kept walking. Perhaps just walking away from the men looking. Far into the woods.

Into the woods, the paperhanger thought. If she had just kept walking in a straight line with no time out for eating or sleeping where would she be? Kentucky? Algiers? Who knew.

I'll take you when the rains stop, he said. But we won't find a child.

The doctor's wife shook her head. It is a mystery, she said. She drank from her cocktail glass. Where could she have gone? How could she have gone?

There was a man named David Lang, the paperhanger said. Up in Galletin, back in the late eighteen hundreds. He was crossing a barn lot in full view of his wife and two children and he just vanished. Went into thin air. There was a judge in a wagon turning into the yard and he saw it, too. It was just like he took a step in this world and his foot came down in another one. He was never seen again.

She gave him a sad smile, bitter and one-cornered. You make fun with me.

No. It's true. I have it in a book. I'll show you.

I have a book with dragons, fairies. A book where hobbits live in the middle earth. They are lies. I think most books are lies. Perhaps all books. I have prayed for a miracle but I am not worthy of one. I have prayed for her to come from the dead like Lazarus, then just to find her body. That would be a miracle to me. There are no miracles.

She rose unsteadily, swayed slightly while leaning to take up the cooler. The paperhanger watched her. I have to go now, she said. When the rains stop we will search.

Can you drive?

Of course I can drive. I have drive out here.

I mean are you capable of driving now. You seem a little drunk.

I drink to forget but it is not enough, she said. I can drive.

After a while he heard her leave in the Mercedes, the tires spinning in the gravel drive. He lit a cigarette. He sat smoking it, watching the rain string off the roof. He seemed to be waiting for something. Dusk was falling like a shroud, the world going dark and formless the way it had begun. He drank the last of the beer, sat holding the bottle, the foam bitter in the back of his mouth. A chill touched him. He felt something watching him. He turned. From the corner of the ruined veranda a child was watching him. He stood up. He heard the beer bottle break on the flagstones. The child went sprinting past the hollyhocks toward the Rorschach bushes at the edge of the yard. A tiny sepia child with an intent sloe-eyed face, real as she had ever been, translucent as winter light through dirty glass.

Her hands laced loosely about his waist, they came down through a thin stand of sassafras, edging over the ridge where the ghost of a road was, a road more sensed than seen that faced into a half acre of tilting stones and fading granite tablets. Other graves marked only by their declivities in the earth, folk so far beyond the pale even the legibility of their identities had been leached away by the weathers.

Leaves drifted, huge poplar leaves veined with amber so golden they might have been coin of the realm for a finer world than this one. He cut the ignition of the four-wheeler and got off. Past the lowering trees the sky was a blue of an improbable intensity, a fierce cobalt blue shot through with dense golden light.

She slid off the rear and steadied herself a moment with a hand on his arm. Where are we, she asked. Why are we here?

The paperhanger had disengaged his arm and was strolling among the gravestones reading such inscriptions as were readable, as if he might find forebear or antecedent in this moldering earth. The doctor's wife was retrieving her martinis from the luggage carrier of the ATV. She stood looking about uncertainly. A graven angel with broken wings crouched on a truncated marble column like a gargoyle. Its stone eyes regarded her with a blind benignity. Some of these graves have been rob, she said.

You can't rob the dead, he said. They have nothing left to steal.

It is a sacrilege, she said. It is forbidden to disturb the dead. You have done this.

The paperhanger took a cigarette pack from his pocket and felt it, but it was empty and he balled it up and threw it away. The line between grave-robbing and archaeology has always looked a little blurry to me, he said. I was studying their culture, trying to get a fix on what their lives were like.

She was watching him with a kind of benumbed horror, standing hipslung and lost like a parody of her former self, strange and anomalous in her fashionable but mismatched clothing, as if she'd put on the first garment that fell to hand. Someday, he thought, she might rise and wander out into the day-lit world wearing nothing at all—the way she had come into it, with only the cocktail glass she carried like a used-up talisman.

You have break the law, she told him.

I got a government grant, the paperhanger said contemptuously.

Why are we here? We are supposed to be searching for my child.

If you're looking for a body the first place to look is the graveyard, he said. If you want a book don't you go to the library?

I am paying you, she said. You are in my employ. I do not want to be here. I want you to do as I say or carry me to my car if you will not.

Actually, the paperhanger said, I had a story to tell you. About my wife.

He paused as if leaving a space for her comment but when she made none he went on. I had a wife. My childhood sweetheart. She became a nurse, went to work in one of these drug rehab places. After she was there awhile she got a faraway look in her eyes. Looked at me without seeing me. She got in tight with her supervisor. They started having meetings to go to. Conferences. Sometimes just the two of them would confer, generally in a motel. The night I watched them walk into the Holiday Inn in Franklin I decided to kill her. No impetuous, spur-of-the-moment thing—I thought it all out and knew it would be the perfect crime.

The doctor's wife didn't say anything. She just watched him.

A grave is the best place to dispose of a body, the paperhanger said. The grave is its normal destination anyway. I could dig up a grave and then just keep on digging. Save everything carefully. Put my body there and fill in part of the earth and then restore everything the way it was. The coffin, if any of it was left. The bones and such. A good settling rain and the fall leaves and you're home free. Now that's eternity for you.

Did you kill someone? she breathed. Her voice was barely audible.

Did I or did I not? he said. You decide. You have the powers of a god, you can make me a murderer or just a heartbroke guy whose wife quit him. What do you think? Anyway I don't have a wife. I expect she just walked off into the abstract like that Lang guy I told you about.

I want to go, she said. I want to go where my car is.

He was sitting on a gravestone watching her out of his pale eyes. He might not have heard.

I will walk.

Do whatever suits you, the paperhanger said. Abruptly he was standing in front of her. She had not seen him arise from the headstone or stride across the graves, but like something in a jerky splice in a film he was before her, a hand cupping each of her breasts, staring down into her face.

Under the merciless weight of the sun her face was stunned and vacuous. He studied it intently, missing no detail. Fine wrinkles crept from the corners of her eyes and mouth like hairline cracks in porcelain. Grime was impacted in her pores, in the creped flesh of her throat. How surely everything had fallen from her—beauty, wealth, social position, arrogance. Humanity itself, for by now she seemed scarcely human, beleaguered so by the fates that she suffered his hands on her breasts as just one more cross to bear, one more indignity to endure.

How far you've come, the paperhanger said in wonder. I believe you're about down to my level now, don't you?

It does not matter, the doctor's wife said. There is no longer one thing that matters.

Slowly and with enormous lassitude her body slumped toward him, and in his exultance it seemed not a motion in itself but simply the completion of one begun long ago with the fateful weight of a thigh, a motion that began in one world and completed itself in another one.

From what seemed a great distance he watched her fall toward him like an angel descending, wings spread, from an infinite height, striking the earth gently, tilting then righting itself.

The weight of moonlight tracking across the paperhanger's face awoke him from where he took his rest. Filigrees of light through the gauzy curtains swept across him in stately silence like the translucent ghosts of insects. He stirred, then lay still for a moment getting his bearings, a fix on where he was.

He was in his bed, lying on his back. He could see a huge orange moon fixed beyond the bedroom window, ink-sketch tree branches raking its face like claws. He could see his feet bookending the San Miguel bottle that his hands clasped erect on his abdomen, the amber bottle hard-edged and defined against the pale window, dark atavistic monolith reared against a full moon.

He could smell her. A musk compounded of stale sweat and alcohol, the rank fish-market smell of her sex. Dissolution, ruin, loss. He turned to study her where she lay asleep, her open mouth a dark cavity in her face. She was naked, legs outflung, pale breasts pooled like cooling wax. She stirred restively, groaned in her sleep. He could hear the rasp of her breathing. Her breath was fetid on his face, corrupt, a graveyard smell. He watched her in disgust, in a dull self-loathing.

He drank from the bottle, lowered it. Sometimes, he told her sleeping face, you do things you can't undo. You break things you just can't fix. Before you mean to, before you know you've done it. And you were right, there are things only a miracle can set to rights.

He sat up, still clasping the bottle. He touched his miscut hair, the soft down of his beard. He had forgotten what he looked like, he hadn't seen his reflection in a mirror for so long. Unbidden, the child's face swam into his memory. He remembered the look on her face when the doctor's wife had spun on her heels—spite had crossed it like a flicker of heat lightning. She stuck her tongue out at him. His hand snaked out like a serpent and closed on her throat and snapped her neck before he could call it back, sloe eyes wild and wide, pink tongue caught between tiny seed-pearl teeth like a bitten-off rosebud. Her hair swung sidewise, her head lolled onto his clasped hand. The tray of the toolbox was out before he knew it, and he was stuffing her into the toolbox like a rag doll. So small, so small, hardly there at all.

He arose. Silhouetted naked against the moon-drenched window he drained the bottle. He looked about for a place to set it, then wedged it between the heavy flesh of her upper thighs. He stood in silence watching her. Philosophical, he seemed possessed of some hard-won wisdom. The paperhanger knew so well that while few are deserving of a miracle, fewer still can make one come to pass.

He went out of the room. Doors opened, doors closed. Footsteps softly climbing a staircase, descending. She dreamed on. When he came back into the room he was cradling a plastic-wrapped bundle stiffly in his arms. He placed it gently beside the drunk woman. He folded the plastic sheeting back like a caul.

What had been a child. What the graveyard earth had spared the freezer had preserved. Ice crystals snared in the hair like windy snowflakes whirled there, in the lashes. A doll from a madhouse assembly line.

He took her arm, laid it across the child. She pulled away from the cold. He firmly brought the arm back, arranging them like mannequins, madonna and child. He studied this tableau then went out of his house for the last time, the door closed gently behind him on its keeper spring.

The paperhanger left in the Mercedes, heading west into the open country, tracking into wide-open territories he could infect like a malign spore. Without knowing it he followed the selfsame route the doctor had taken some eight months earlier, and in a world of infinite possibilities where all journeys share a common end perhaps they are together, taking the evening air on a ruined veranda among the hollyhocks and oleanders, the doctor sipping his scotch and the paperhanger his San Miguel, gentlemen of leisure discussing the vagaries of life and pondering deep into the night the inevitability of miracles.

MAILE MELOY

University of California, Irvine

TOME

For eight months, I had been telling my client he had no tort claim. Sawyer had worked construction for thirty years, building houses for people with Montana fantasies, until he was putting up a roof and one of the trusses fell, collapsing the others and taking him down with them. He started to have fainting spells and memory loss and couldn't work. We got a settlement, not a great one but not bad. The contractor was clearly negligent, having failed to brace the trusses, but workers' compensation precluded the tort claim—we couldn't sue.

Sawyer had worked outside all his life, and suddenly he could do nothing. It seemed to be the idleness, more than the brain damage, that made him crazy. He couldn't read, because the words came out scrambled, even when he could manage to sit still. He phoned me three times a day. My secretary stopped putting his calls through, so he came to the office, on foot because they wouldn't let him drive. He was a big, graying blond-bearded man, my father's age, muscular but getting fat without his work. He treated me like a daughter, scolding and cajoling me. He wanted to sue, demanded to sue. His wife was sick of his moping at the house, and his friends had been the men he worked with; he'd lost everything he liked about his life. I knew workers' comp and I tried to explain: he'd gotten what he was going to get. There was nothing more I could do for him.

Finally I found a tort lawyer in Billings, four hours east, who was willing to give him a second opinion. I had to be in Bozeman anyway, halfway there, so I drove over and met Sawyer and his wife at the lawyer's office. I didn't think Sawyer, frustrated and hair-triggered as he was, should be making his case alone, with his wife jumping in and correcting him. The lawyer was a thin man in a dark suit and a big leather chair. There were antelope heads on the walls, bear claws as bookends. We explained the situation. The lawyer said, "You have no tort claim."

Sawyer said, "Okay."

I thought, *That's* what it's like to be a man. If I were a man I could explain the law and people would listen and say, "Okay." It would be so restful.

We went back outside. The lawyer's office had a view of the cliffs. We had been in Billings fifteen minutes and had nothing to do but drive home. My client shook my hand, and his wife, a small curly-haired woman who had been pretty once, gave me a quick motherly hug. She smelled like roses and cigarettes. When I stopped at the mall for a sandwich, they pulled up in the parking space next to mine. Sawyer got out of the car screaming at his wife about her fucking attitude, grabbed his coat from the seat, and slammed the door.

He said, "I'm going in your car." His wife peeled out of the lot and turned toward the highway.

We stood alone a minute in the parking lot, my client and I, and then I told him I wasn't going yet, and he climbed into the passenger seat to wait. His head touched the ceiling of my car. I offered to get him lunch and he shook his head like a great, sulky child. I left him there and walked the length of the mall twice, eating my sandwich. When I returned, he hadn't moved: coat in his lap, eyes on his knees, he waited for his ride.

Before we were out of Billings he said the only thing to do was get a machine gun and kill everyone. I stopped the car. I said I wouldn't have him talking like that, and told him to get out. I knew that no one knew where I was, and Sawyer weighed twice what I did, but I wasn't afraid—I was only tired of him. He promised not to do it again.

At the first sign for the turnoff to Red Lodge, outside Laurel, Sawyer said, "I wish my wife would roll over on the highway."

I stopped the car on the shoulder and said, "I swear, I'll leave you in Laurel."

Twenty miles on he began a low, keening rant about his negligent boss, about his negligent wife, about how no one understood how miserable he was. I told him if he opened his mouth for the rest of the drive I would let him out wherever we were. He didn't bridle. He didn't say anything at all. I found a country station to fill the silence, and Sawyer began to weep. He sobbed in the passenger seat all the way home, without saying a word.

A week later my phone rang in the middle of the night. I was sleeping alone then, and there was nothing to do but answer it. A call in the night could mean anything. What this one meant was that Sawyer had a hostage and a gun at the state fund building and wanted me to look at his workers' comp file. The hostage specialists in town, such as they were, said I didn't have to go in. But I was afraid of what they might do to him, so I stood in front of my closet deciding whether to wear lawyer clothes or not, then pulled on jeans and left the house in the sweatshirt I'd slept in. In the parking lot behind the building the cops had the bureau chief from the office and a big thermos of coffee. They had Sawyer on the telephone and said he'd been crying earlier, but now he was calm. The hostage was a night watchman, a Samoan kid who'd come here to play football at the college. I'd known his name once, something long with A's and N's in it, but everyone called him Big Man. I was impressed, just for a moment, that my client had taken Big Man down.

I drank the coffee while the bureau chief drew me a map of the office. They gave me his keys and a cop gave me a heavy bulletproof vest to wear under my sweatshirt. I changed awkwardly in the back of a squad car, trying to keep myself covered, the vest cold against my skin. The officer who helped me fasten it had written a report for a child-support case of mine, including the line, "The defendant instructed me to consume feces." I'd always liked him. He socked me on the shoulder and told me to do good, and I went in.

The building was four stories, dark brick, at the end of the old gold-rush main street. It was dark inside, and the bottom floor was all cubicles, the burlap-faced dividers hung with calendars and cartoons. I found my way to the stairs by the light of screen-savers and exit signs and walked up to the third floor, where my client was keeping Big Man.

"Sawyer?" I called, as I came out of the stairwell into another dark maze of cubicles. "It's me. I'm here to find your file."

I heard a rustling noise, but no one answered.

"Should I come to you or go get the file?" I asked.

Sawyer's voice came out of the gloom, hoarse and tired. "Go get the file," he said.

I couldn't tell which cubicle the voice came from, but it was on the east side of the building, to my right. The cops had told me to engage him in conversation. "Is Big Man okay?" I asked.

"His name is Amituana," Sawyer said. "Did you know he's a member of the Samoan royal family?"

"I didn't," I said. I followed my office map to the big beige file cabinet where they kept the dead files. The lock on the cabinet had a tiny six on it, and I flipped through the ring of keys until I found the one with the six. I asked, "Does that make him a prince?"

Two low voices conferred. Then came a voice an octave lower than Sawyer's. "Sort of," Big Man said. "If fourteen people die, I will be king."

I found Sawyer's file, a fat brown accordion, under S. "How likely is that?"

There was another pause. "Not very," Big Man's voice said.

I could see the room well now, by the exit signs and the streetlights. "I have the file, Sawyer," I said. "What should I do?"

"We're in the third cubicle from the door," he said. "Near the windows. With the horse calendar."

Big Man sat cross-legged on the floor, hands tied behind his back with orange baling twine, and Sawyer sat in a chair designed to support the lower back, by a computer screen with changing photographs of the sea. He rested a hunting rifle on his knee, and seemed to have hung up the phone on the police. The two men filled the entire space.

"We've been talking football," Sawyer said.

"He played both offense and defense in college," Big Man told me. He had close-cropped hair and a narrow mustache attached to a goatee. He seemed genuinely impressed.

"It was a junior college," Sawyer explained. He looked at me in my sweatshirt bulked by the Kevlar vest underneath. "Sorry to get you out of bed," he said. "Sit down."

I sat in the remaining floor-space next to Big Man, and he nodded to me. He was carrying himself beautifully: no dishonor to his family or his future subjects.

"Read me the file," Sawyer said. "Not the stuff I said, just the stuff they said about me. I want to hear all the letters."

"That'll take all night," I said.

"So start."

I began to read in the dim light. One of the computer's ocean scenes was darker than the others, and each time the dark one came around the reading was harder. I read the letters from the insurance adjuster to the bureau chief, the memos from the chief's secretary to her boss, the letters from Sawyer's employer's attorney. I read letters by me, dictated too quickly, sounding too lawyerly, typed up by my secretary and flung into the afternoon mail. What wasn't embarrassing was sad, and what wasn't sad was stultifying, but Sawyer sat riveted. I looked up from time to time to see if I could stop. He gestured me on with the rifle in his right hand. I read through the neurologist's account of what Sawyer could do and through the settlement. I read the figure Sawyer was to receive for the loss of his work.

"You got screwed," Big Man said.

"Thank you," Sawyer said, with no irony in his voice, only relief that someone else could see the injustice. "What can I do now?" he asked me. "Tell me, now, what can I do?"

"Give yourself up," I said.

"No, I'm serious here. I mean about the claim."

I looked at the heavy stack of papers in my lap. "I don't think you can do anything," I said. "Go to physical therapy, be nice to your wife."

"She's gone," he said. "No, that's all over. This is over, too, isn't it? It's a wrapped-up case."

I nodded. It was in with the dead files. And finality was the effect of the letters, read together: it was a thing done. Sawyer could hear it, too.

"I'm letting Amituana go," he said. He helped the kid to his feet, which was a struggle with the rifle in one hand, the kid's wrists tied, and both men so heavy. Amituana staggered back against a cubicle divider and it shuddered, and then they were both upright. "He's got a country to rule," Sawyer said. "Fourteen people could die, easy."

He brushed off the kid's clothes with his free hand. "If you get to be king of Samoa and I show up there," he said, "you'll have a job for me, right? You'll remember I got screwed and I let you go."

"Sure," Big Man said.

"Okay," Sawyer said. "You take the stairs and go outside, and tell them if they try anything I'll kill the woman. She's my lawyer—I've got reason to kill her. Tell them that."

I looked at Sawyer to see if he was serious, but I couldn't tell.

"Okay," Big Man said.

"Okay." Sawyer turned him around and clapped him on one of his great halfback shoulders, and the kid nodded at both of us like he was leaving a party. He walked off toward the staircase, trailing orange twine from his bound wrists.

"He's a good kid," Sawyer said to me as we watched him go. The heavy, careful steps died away on the stairs below. Then Sawyer turned to me.

"There's nothing for me here, I can see that," he said. "But you can still help me."

"If you turn yourself in," I said, "we can gin up a mental distress defense, get you a good lawyer for it."

"Nope," Sawyer said. He checked his watch. "I'll slip out the front, where they don't expect me. You go out the back, to the parking lot where you came in, and keep them busy. Stand in the door and pretend I've got the gun on you, and relay messages to the cops like I'm hiding there. Say I want a car, and I want three thousand dollars, and I want an hour's head start. Okay? Afterward, they'll never know I wasn't there with the gun. Just give me a chance to get out the front and get away."

He was calm and seemed sane, even with the rifle in his hand. He was just my client, still in a bad spot, still wanting me to help him, and I was trying.

"Aren't there cops out front?" I asked.

"I've been watching," he said. "They've all stayed out back, where I told them I'd come out. So will you do it?"

I said okay. There was no arguing with him, and there was nothing else I could say. He called 911 and we waited while the operator figured out how to patch him through to the squad cars below. I asked him again to give up and he said no. He told them we were coming out. We went downstairs with both my wrists in one of his hands behind me, his grip warm and damp but not tight. Then he took the office keys and told me to wait a minute before I went out. Crouched down, he dodged through the cubicle dividers to the front door. I heard a deadbolt scrape. Blue streetlight outlined his body, and he waved to me to go.

The back door was a fire door that opened without a key, and I pressed the bar and put a hand out to wave so they wouldn't shoot me, and then I stood with one hand behind my back, the door barely cracked. I thought I was going to do it, to play the part Sawyer had scripted for me, and then somehow it seemed impossible, a thing that was plausible back in the dark but now was not. He was a man with a gun. I stepped out with my hands up and said, "He's in front," but my voice cracked and I had to say it again, louder. "He's in front."

Sawyer wrote me a letter from prison. He said,

> *It would sure be great if you came by. Tuesdays from 2–4 I can have visitors and it would be really something to see you. Or if you wrote a letter. You wouldn't believe how great it is to get a letter from the real world. On good days I can read okay now, and I can write back, and on bad days someone will read it to me. No one writes to me except my defense lawyer, and he's an asshole, and hardly writes anymore anyway. (Don't tell him I said he was an asshole. I know all you lawyers are tight.) And don't feel too bad about what happened. Of course they were out front. You did what you could do.*

I kept the letter on top of my in-box for weeks, always moving it to the top, keeping it where I could see it, but I didn't write back. Whatever I could say to him would be so inadequate I couldn't imagine it on paper. I settled one case, started another, and the rest plodded along, piling up on my desk, while Sawyer's note kept floating to the top.

Finally one cold blue Tuesday when the roads were dry, I left everything in the mess it was in and drove out to Deer Lodge. I called a warden I knew and got permission to bring food, picked up burgers on the way, and parked at the prison at two. They brought Sawyer into the visiting area and let us sit at the same table, no barrier at all. He'd lost the weight of the idle months, but he didn't look healthy. He looked pale, a little gray in the face, and older. We looked at each other awkwardly, like neither of us knew what we were doing there.

The paper bags, still warm and smelling of fried things, felt heavy and wrong in my hand.

"I guess you've just had lunch," I said.

Sawyer gave me an appraising look. "Is there a shake in there?" he asked.

Sometimes I have a little luck—I had a chocolate shake and a vanilla one, still mostly frozen. We unpacked the bags and sat at the table, and Sawyer ate happily and talked about the inmates, using first names, telling stories that sounded like he'd planned them in his mind for someone to come from the outside and listen. He washed down burger with chocolate shake, sucking noisily through the straw.

"You know my wife's gone," he said finally. "You know where she went?"

I shook my head.

"When I stopped working, and started getting crazy, she got a pen pal. A guy in prison in Wyoming. They wrote back and forth all year and I never knew. Then he got furloughed and she went to live with him. She sent me a letter that says they're living on a farm and have forty cats and she's never been so happy. Can you believe that? She mailed the letter from another town so I couldn't find her."

"Would you want to find her?" I asked.

"Yeah!" he said, then, "No. I don't know. A guy in prison. I can't believe she found a guy in prison. I'm a guy in prison. What's wrong with me? But she would have left anyway."

"What did the guy do?"

"She won't tell me. Probably an ax-murderer. It's Wyoming." He grinned, and his face stretched into wrinkles he hadn't had before, but the grin was charming. Sawyer was still game.

"So, you never wrote to me," he said, picking at the last of his fries. The bags and boxes and cups were strewn between us, empty now, an embarrassment of grease.

"I meant to," I said. "I kept meaning to."

"It wouldn't be so hard," he said. "You know?"

"I know," I said.

"Man, you wouldn't believe how good mail feels. I think I told you that."

"I will, I'll write," I said. "I didn't know what to say."

"That's the thing—you don't have to say anything special," he said. "I told you it's okay, about what happened. They would have got me anyway. I fucked up. But I mean this, you could talk about anything, talk about the weather, talk about your day. Just so you put it in an envelope and put it in the mail."

"Okay," I said.

"It doesn't have to be a tome," he said.

I drove home as the sky was beginning to darken. A sign in Deer Lodge advertised dinner theater: The Old Prison Players performing *Arsenic and Old Lace* at eight o'clock in the old prison building. I wondered where they found their audience, but I didn't wonder enough to be in it.

I was not sleeping alone then, the only news in my life since I had last seen Sawyer, but I might as well have been. The guy was a prosecutor who never left the office before midnight, and sometimes then he'd stop by. So the evening stretched before me: long blue-gray clouds on the horizon, the abandoned work on my desk, my empty house. I could go back to the office, maybe catch my secretary locking up, say good night and stay to work until I was hungry again and could get a bite to eat and a bath and go to bed. I would maybe be awakened to news of my prosecutor's militia case, and to sex, and then go back to sleep with another body in the bed.

It was a tolerable plan, but I couldn't focus on it. What I did was watch the sky. As it changed, as the clouds stretched out and the orange flared up and pink reached out to meet the blue, I started thinking of it as a description, a letter, not a lawyer-sounding one, and not a tome, but a start, an account for Sawyer and for me on what the day did out here, and what it was like.

ADAM JOHNSON

Florida State University

CLIFF GODS OF ACAPULCO

My father is dying in Zaire, though I don't necessarily know that yet as I drive to Vegas with Jimbo. I do know my dad is a Rover driver for Mobil geologists and, instead of seismic surveys, he carries two ammo clips and a military discharge that's semiautomatic. This is 1985, and I'm going to Vegas because I'm still in those hazy couple years after high school when I read a lot of racing magazines, drink with secretaries at Bennigan's every night, and take things at face value. I'm failing Mythology, my lone course at Riverside Community College, and Jimbo and I test diodes all day for Futron, an electronics firm that makes black-market cable boxes and will shortly be shut down by the FCC. Between us, we have 244 TV channels.

My favorite viewing is always the live coverage on the Canadian Motorsports Network. Jimbo prefers the Playboy Channel, whose only movie I remember liking is *The Black Box,* a soft-core in which, following an emergency landing on a desert island, naughty stewardesses screw survivors on inflatable rafts, yellow escape slides, galley carts, and even a 30,000-horse pulse-injector tail engine. What the crew doesn't know is that the sex is being transmitted by the flight data recorders, which leads to hilarity when the Coast Guard comes to "rescue" them. Getting the Playboy Channel free for yourself is simple—just connect two parallax converters in tandem with a P-9 capacitor, then bridge the diode with an alligator clip.

Jimbo's from Vegas, and we make the hop every couple weeks, though our thing is usually to get a United flight that leaves us about eighteen hours of solid bingo-bingo before we sleep on a flight home to six hundred transistors waiting for the green light. On United, I fly free. For Jimbo, the best I can do is drink coupons. Today, we drive instead of fly because of FAA rules: You can't take poisonous animals (scorpions) on commercial airliners. Jimbo has a whole box of them, a ridiculously large cardboard box for the dozen red scorpions the label says are within. They're a special gift for a friend who has a "death thing," Jimbo says. The box doesn't have airholes, and is so light I don't believe there's anything in there—there can't be. Jimbo's excited to see what's inside, keeps talking about opening it, though he wants me to do it. But the trick to life, it seems to me so far, is learning to tolerate the not knowing. I can take that box or leave it.

Jimbo's big into thrills, and our hotfoot to Nevada is all him describing this new indoor skydiving attraction we're going to try when we get there. I don't tell him my Mythology teacher says thrill rides are a mix of sky worship and disaster simulation, both primitive kinds of foreplay. I can't explain it the way my teacher does, so outside the state line, I just tell Jimbo, "Let's piss already."

Detouring over Hoover Dam, Jimbo leans hard into the canyon curves, chuting the two-lane fast enough that the scorpion box slides back and forth in the hatch, cornering tight enough that we flirt with guardrails and great heights. Such driving does not appeal to me. The thrills I go for are more predictable—a pistol kick, a sudden loss of cabin pressure, the way a secretary or nurse at Houlihan's will try to lay you by chewing ice from her drink and saying things like "Grrr." Thrilling driving takes place on oval tracks, especially thousand-lap endurance races that stretch late into night—tight, boxy circuits— spinning long after you turn off the TV and go to bed, races in which the victor is a mystery until the last lap, when you're crashed already and dreaming.

Entering the shadows of great saguaros and graffiti-covered rock-faces, we pull over to take a leak in the bluffs above Lake Mead. The outcrops are like lava, and we walk through the shoulder's gravel and ground glass to stand among barrel-chested Joshua trees. "My old man used to take me up here when I was a kid, to see the bomb tests," Jimbo says, unzipping. Jimbo keeps his dope in his jockeys, so he holds the Baggie in his teeth as he points. I look up through out-stretched cactus limbs to the bluffs, which are low and don't offer much of a view, then scan the distant scrub plains and tawny hills below.

"You'd need some L-5 optics for that," I say, using a testing term from Futron.

"We're talking about nukes," Jimbo says, "which tend to be large events, and our binoculars were Bushnells, the best." Speaking through the Baggie, he goes on to describe how the military would build a little dummy city for every explosion, complete with town halls and fire stations. "My old man would flip. Some of the houses were two stories, with yards and barns. He'd look through those Bush-nells and ask, 'Is that a Cadillac in the driveway? Tell me that's not a Caddy they're gonna cook.' But the white flash always shut him up."

Talk of the white flash, which I imagine too clearly, shuts me up as well. We do not go on to discuss either bombs or fathers here among the Joshua trees; we just piss into their hairy arms and leave.

What would I have to say anyway?

Actually, I will never know if my father is pulled from his Rover and shot in a sorghum field in West Africa. My only confirmation comes from a man who arrives out of nowhere one day and claims to be my father's best friend, who begins seeing my mother, and finally convinces her to move from Michigan to Acapulco with him. His name is Ted, and all I know about the whole deal is the sketchy portrait he paints of guarding Mobil interests from tribal warlords, and the general fact that Acapulco is a place where, in long streaks of flashing skin, people throw themselves from cliff tops into the frothy abyss.

Before Ted takes my mom to Mexico, the only time we see her is in LAX on Sunday mornings. Ted and I both find ourselves at the SkyLounge cocktail rail, eating prepopped popcorn and watching people go by until my mother's red-eye comes through, a point at which we have thirty-five minutes with her before she stows tray tables and passes out pillows all the way back to her base in Detroit. The first time we meet, Ted tells me he and my father really took some heat from the local screws in Africa. "Things are different on the continent," he says, and I watch his teeth. Ted has knuckles for teeth. "Those screws were coming at us from all sides. There was no dealing with them."

I have yet to watch enough cable movies to know "screw" is prison talk.

Ted is going to become a saga, but that's not a concern right now. It has no bearing as Jimbo and I drive to Vegas. This story is about amputation.

For these couple years I am unshakable, so the back roads through Vegas speak nothing to me. I do not think about the people who wander the edges of sidewalkless causeways, the cars that shift and float as if unused to daylight, or the particular strains of Vegas trash that string wire-lined gullies. The power lines simply sink and rise above us, the sky is only October blue, and it seems perfectly natural that people hitchhike in the dips, where freshly blacked streets wash over with sugar sand.

The plan is to get stoned and ride a new attraction called Fly Away, which basically consists of indoor skydiving in a room shaped like a padded tube. There's a wire net at the bottom that keeps you from falling into the DC-3 engine below. Actually, it's Jimbo's plan. I don't smoke dope, and I'm a big guy. I don't believe I will fly.

Key to the plan is going to see Jimbo's old friend Marty. He's the one the scorpions are for. The whole ride out is Marty this and Marty that, an old-school parade of Marty memories, but what's important is this: Marty's girlfriend Tasha is the preflight girl at Fly Away, the one who suits you up, so we're headed to Marty's to get some good dope and the VIP from his girlfriend.

"Wait'll you get a load of Tasha," Jimbo says as we crest the foothills outside Vegas. He's pretty stoned, and from his description of Tasha, I know she's the kind of thank-God-it's-Friday secretary I'd work at Bennigan's.

"Tasha's seen the other side," he said.

"The other side of what?"

Jimbo just raises his eyebrows, and we drive for a while.

"Maybe I'll show her the white flash," I tell him.

Jimbo doesn't quite know what I mean by this, but he likes the sound of it. He smiles and steps on the gas, sending us full tilt through the newly paved scrub desert leading to the suburbs. "White flash," he repeats.

Closing my eyes, I let the road's g-force take me. I feel this Tasha woman cinch me into a billowy nylon flight suit, her hands folding Velcro, running zippers, jerking my straps tight. I hear her knock my helmet twice, meaning A-OK, thumbs-up, as I follow her into Fly

Away's engine room. It is a more modern version of this engine, the DC-9, that kills my mother's best friend Tammy, climbing out of Dulles International. You've seen the footage, the one that goes into the icy river. I say this because Tammy is a fox, too, a woman I stare at endlessly as she and my mother sit by our condo's swimming pool in white bikinis.

Marty's house is on a pie-shaped lot at the end of a cul-de-sac in west Vegas. It's long and low, hard-lined and brown, the kind of house John Wayne would've lived in, if he'd never gotten famous. Beyond the sprawling roof rise two jagged outcrops of stone, one with a five-story radio tower that flashes red strobes bright enough to make us wince a bit, even at noon. The light's glow pattern is two fast and one slow, which warns overhead airplanes that this particular hazard's in the approach lane.

On the front steps, we stare into twin, rough-hewn doors and Jimbo rings the bell again. "Like I said, Marty's a soap-opera case," he whispers. "Don't say anything about his face. He's sensitive about his face."

I'll tell you this. Jimbo's not a good friend. He's shallow and deceptive, and there's a hole in him that will make him say anything. I'm not a good friend either. I am asleep in an essential way, and I will not begin to wake up for several years, not until I learn the meaning of the word *loss,* until I am in Acapulco and Ted hands me his favorite pistol, a chrome Super-25.

A woman finally answers the door in a UNLV Runnin' Rebels T-shirt she's adorned with glitter and spangles. She is clearly not happy to see us. I'm six foot four. Jimbo has no neck, and he's holding a box labeled LIVE ANIMALS POISONOUS.

It takes her three full seconds to place Jimbo, then she turns and walks away.

We let ourselves into a room carpeted in cream wall-to-wall, with a black pumice fireplace and a ranch-style bar made from dark wood and warbled green glass. There is an elaborate seventies intercom system, with talk stations on every wall. Jimbo heads straight for a Wurlitzer and works its silent keys. "We used to play Ozzy on this," he says. The walls are covered with photos of Marty, blond-haired, blue-eyed: Marty in football uniform, Marty in a powder blue prom cravat, Marty midair in front of a white '66 Mustang, which it turns out is the crash vehicle in question.

The Marty that rounds the corner, though, is hard to look at. He is tall, slightly stooped, with long jet hair that curtains his face. One eye points down and in a bit, making him seem half interested in something just beyond the tip of his nose. He looks almost sad, which is not what I expected after all of Jimbo's descriptions of the crash scene on our drive up—"They found the steering wheel in the tree, a fucking tree, man"—the amnesia's peculiar effects—"He doesn't even know his dad's name but he walks right to his locker and wheels out the combo"—horrific surgeries—"The third time they sewed it on it stuck"—and high school dramas—"Tasha and I stood by him at the pep rallies; we were the only ones."

Jimbo and Marty do an elaborate handshake that ends with a knuckle punch and slips into a last toke off an imaginary joint; "fff," they inhale. There are a lot of *wow*s and *dude*s in their reunion, and after neither notices that I am standing right next to them, I imagine as sort of a joke that they walk off without speaking to me, which they do.

I follow clear carpet runners down the hall, where there are two white doors. I open the wrong one. Inside sits a boy of about fourteen. His swing-arm desk lamp is on, and he leans back in a blue director's chair, his feet up on the white laminated desk, reading a racing magazine. He looks at me, looks back at the page. But I know this chair, the way canvas webbing gathers under your shoulder blades after a certain amount of nothing. I know how long it takes your ankles to go numb from propping them on a desk like that. I see years of airplane models and electric cars, a thousand magazines read atop tiger print sheets—all the things anyone would see, if they'd just open the door.

The kid sets down his issue of *PitCrew*. It's the one featuring Rick Kreiger's 500 win. Then he does a strange thing. He takes his desk lamp and swivels its armature so the hard bulb shines in my face.

This is where one story could become another.

This other story I could tell would be about the following years when your father doesn't open the door. It would have to do with the after-school jobs you pick up to kill time, about the GM family-sedan proving ground behind Futron's industrial park, how you can spend whole lunch breaks without taking your eyes off circling cars that stop only to change the drivers who will run them into the ground. This different story would have to do with a Mythology class in which you discover the gods are all-petty and their names are hard to remember, or the endless chain of nature shows about Africa a skilled TV viewer can find from midnight on, or the place your mind goes while waiting for a diode to finally light reject-red.

A *woo-hoo* high five sounds in the next room, and this boy and I look toward the source, our eyes landing on a poster of the space shuttle. There is a white plastic intercom next to my shoulder that surprises me when it comes to life. "What's your ten-twenty, copy?" a man asks over a hail of barking—the kid's dad, I assume. When there is no answer, the father says, "Roger this: the griddle is firing up. The Runnin' Rebs won the toss, and they're taking the field."

The boy returns the light to his magazine. "Please," he says, with an air of boredom and indifference aimed at me, his father, and life in general. I have nothing deep to add, so I go.

When I open Marty's door, there is a giant snake, but I try to act cool. The room's darker than I expect, though I can clearly see the snake cage takes up a third of it, framed floor to ceiling with studs and chicken wire, and there is a faint smell of cat piss. Marty is shaking the box of scorpions. He holds it to his ear, his eyes roaming the room, looking right past me as he listens. He squints some, smiles. Satisfied, he sets it on a junk-strewn desk without opening it. Marty doesn't need to look in that box just yet, either.

Jimbo reloads the bong and holds it out to me. It hovers between us, and I do not take it. In less than a year, after I fail Mythology and the doors of Futron are chained shut, Jimbo will kiss me, awkwardly, on the neck, in a secretary stable named Fuddrucker's. Even now, I look at him suspiciously. He knows I don't smoke, so this stoner's etiquette is only for Marty's benefit. The snake hangs from a ceiling beam at the edge of my vision, its skin the felt green of a Vegas gaming table.

"Go for it," Marty says. "Bong up."

Again, one eye points down, and the way he has to look out of the top of it humbles him in a way I don't expect.

Over the intercom, the dad says, "The Rebs are kicking off." Marty ignores him, even though the barking in the background makes it sound like his father is being eaten by wolves or something. With the static on the intercom, I imagine a man on a radio in Africa. Or a pilot with hydraulic trouble, cutting up with the tower.

There is a Polaroid taped to the wall, and I know this must be Tasha. She's everything I hoped she'd be: posed in a skydiving drag suit, her chi-chis perfect, even through billowy orange nylon, as she stands above a dark and sleeping DC-3.

I nod toward the photo. "Who's the fox?"

"That's Tasha, the love of my life. We almost died together."

"That when you messed up your face?"

Jimbo looks at me like, *You fuck, we had ground rules.*

"Car crash," Marty says.

"Rough deal," I tell him. "Jimbo says you can't remember most stuff."

"Some stuff."

"At least you had Tasha." We glance at the wall. "You couldn't forget her."

Marty's not sure if I'm dicking with him or not. "She says we were just dating before the crash, but I know it was more than that. On the outside she was a stranger, and I couldn't say much about her life, but I knew her, you know?"

Marty says this, and my head wanders across eight time zones, a continent away. I find myself looking through the snake cage to the wall beyond, thinking about the boy in the next room.

"It doesn't bite," Marty says.

"What?"

"Its mouth is open to check you out. It has glands that can see your heat."

Sure enough, the snake's mouth is open. It has three loops around a pine ceiling beam, and it screws itself down some, tail sucking up into the coil of its square trunk, head unreeling to arc closer to my heat.

"What's with the snake?" I ask.

"It's hard to explain."

"Let's feed it," Jimbo says.

"No, it ate last week."

Jimbo lifts his eyebrows. "Meow," he says.

"Meow," Marty says.

"What about the caiman—you still got the caiman?" Jimbo asks Marty, then looks at me. "Wait till you see the fucking caiman."

I think of the Cayman Islands, which my mom says is the worst route there is. After Tammy dies, my mother covers her schedule there for a while, but she won't even speak of the layovers. *They don't have any laws down there,* she says. *You will never know* is all she tells me. But after a couple years with Ted my mother changes her tune, and they even pop over to beach bum a time or two. Tammy is never pulled from under the D.C. river ice, and Mom likes to say Tammy's really just laying low in the Caymans, high on piña coladas and that special light they have down there, playing baccarat with the boys at the Royale.

Marty sees the confusion on my face. "A caiman's a kind of crocodile," he says, "from Central America."

"You have a crocodile?"

"It's a kind of crocodile."

"Bullshit."

Jimbo smiles.

We go out back to see the caiman. There is a blue pool with green patio furniture, all surrounded by silver fencing that leads to the base of the bluff above. Everything looks cool; my hands are in my pockets, and the sun is bright in my eyes. Then the wolves come at us, sprinting across a triangular yard of close-cropped yellow grass with their long necks down, their rolling haunches kicking out behind them. The chain-link fence between us isn't even chest high—four, four and a half feet at best. When they reach the fence, they are coming over, I know it, and the assault at hand is something I feel first as a rattle in my breath and then as a loosening in my veins. Instead, they plunge to the base of the fence, legs splayed, and snap at us out of the sides of their mouths as if they are chewing the metal sprinkler heads.

"Shut those damn wolves up," Marty's father says from the patio. He is shirtless, in swim trunks, basting a mounded platter of meat with a sauce-stiffened brush, the kind you use to paint a house.

"They're only half wolf, Dad. Half Mackenzie, half malamute."

"I'll kill them, Marty. I swear," his father says in a soft way, speaking to meat he dabs with care.

For now, though, the wolves are barking machines, vicious and ceaseless, noxious as tire fires. Marty walks, arms crossed, past the pool, until he stands looking down over the short fence in admiration at their snarling faces, as if big, mean animals were a rarity in this world.

Jimbo follows suit. He kneels before the fence and touches their wet noses whenever snapping teeth catch in the chain-link. In a sweet, childlike voice, he insults them. "Come to Daddy, you iddle widdle teethy fucks," he says, and pinches a nose, prompting one wolf to reel back and pop the other's folded ear.

"Christ," Marty's father yells. "Leave the damn things be. It's Saturday. The Rebs are playing." The woman who first answered the door slides a blue-screened TV out the kitchen pass-through, and Marty's father turns all the knobs on the intercom, shouting "Game time" into every room.

Because of all the *Wild Kingdom* episodes I talk about, my mom tells Ted I'm a big nature fan. One Sunday morning at the SkyLounge, he brings me the gift of a "Safariland" snow globe he says is from Africa, though there's something like Safariland in Florida, too. The globe features plastic cheetahs, giraffes, and gazelles in brown grasslands, racing full tilt into a surprise blizzard. It is *Hecho en Mexico*.

So I'm suspicious of the wolves, which are at once completely unreal in this Vegas backyard, yet so obviously dangerous I feel it in my toes. To a lesser degree, I feel the same way about a family barbecue, which is something I've never been to.

Somehow satisfied with the wolves at hand, Marty stares up at the imposing rock formations above. Out in the bright light of day, the scars on Marty's face pronounce themselves with the clear slickness of sexual skin. I follow his gaze up to the communications tower, and the hard throb of the red light on top hypnotizes me. It's the red light I look for with my current meter all day at Futron, and this red seems right. I know it the same way that, after looking into a million circuits, I can just feel when one's going to go reject on me.

Above the tower, a jet splits the October sky, wavering and adjusting on approach to LAS. Its nose floats much lower than a DC-9. This is a Lockheed L-1011.

I know the outlines of airplanes because, at sixteen, I spend a weekend making marker drawings of jetliners and quizzing my mother as we sit on a gold-comforted hotel bed in Michigan. When she gets all the flash cards right, I know she will pass her United test in the morning and move to Detroit the following week. The L-1011 is an easy one: Its wingtips curve up at the ends, so from below they look cut off.

Ted tells me he can fly a jet, if push comes to shove, if that's what it comes down to. I don't have much to say to that. The statement somehow implies my father doesn't have what it takes, when it comes down to it, which is why he may or may not be dead. I tell Ted there's a god of flying. Rickimus maybe. Rick something or other. Something-something-rus, for sure.

Marty's father tries a softer tone. He is standing at the grill with a long fork, and the heat from the coals is enough to distort the edges of things, to make the brown of the roof and the blue of the sky trade places for an instant. "Come on, Marty," he says, "bring your friends over for some grub. The Runnin' Rebs are playing. They're your favorite. They're playing Arizona. Remember that big game against Arizona a few years back? You loved that game."

"We're just going to look at the caiman, Dad."

"Why can't you leave that gator alone?"

"It's called a caiman, Dad."

With a fork in one hand and the platter in the other, Marty's father lifts his arms in a shrug of indifference. "Whatever. I don't see the attraction. You tell me the appeal."

He throws the meat on a grill so hot the steaks bounce; they squeak and whine. The wolves go crazy over this. They, too, let out short, high moans, like children.

The sounds remind me of a nature program I see one night that sticks in my head for reasons that will remain unclear until I eventually meet Ted. On the show, a man walks into brown savanna chewgrass to reconstruct a takedown. From the dirt, he collects whitened ribs and hocks and knuckles. He examines them, noting teeth and claw marks. A horn, he decides, is an important clue. A sound track of feasting hyenas plays as he points at trees and hills, deciding how many predators, direction of attack, strategy, and carcass distribution. Then this man looks into the camera. *There's no rest for the hungry,* he says. *So come, let's see what the lions are up to,* and we watch his Jeep drive off into the plain, the bumper folding down tall grass that springs up behind him, and he is gone.

Ted tells me he has my father's binoculars, which are all that's left. He's been meaning to give them to me.

Marty nods a forget-him look toward his father and leads us to the caiman. Jimbo's eyes light up at the prospect, and we walk, hands in pockets, in our natural order—indifferent, disruptive, and doubtful—along pool decking bordered by chain-link and wolves that cut their faces trying to take our ankles.

In the other corner of the yard is the most ridiculous thing I have seen. Another chain-link fence, complete with posts and gate, stands a foot and a half tall. I mean, it doesn't even come to your knees.

"You're kidding me with this," I say.

"It's all you need," Marty says. "Caimans can't climb."

"This is such bullshit," I tell him and make a show of stepping over the fence, rather than through the tiny gate. Jimbo follows my lead. We cross tan gravel that crunches under our boots, stop in front of a lone blue kiddie pool. There is no shade, just brown and blue.

"There it is," Marty says.

"Did I fuckin' tell you, or what," Jimbo says.

Inside the pool floats a four-foot reptile, motionless, with a thin, tooth-rimmed snout. It can't weigh thirty-five pounds. Its eyes are cataract black, and it doesn't even seem to breathe.

In life, some things will come clear to you. There are the knowns—the exact video-feed frequency that unscrambles pornography, for instance, the foot-pounds of lift inside the hot, distorted edge of air cutting over a 737 wing, the speed at which your mother endlessly circles the city in her gold Cadillac after your father leaves, or the way young dictators are known to buy stewardesses drinks in the lounge of the Cayman Royale.

And then there are the others, the things that aren't so easy. There's the boxy loop of youth, a decade that leaves your ears ringing with television and loneliness. There is the way Tammy's body becomes one of the "unrecoverables" beneath the D.C. ice. Then there's an overbright morning at the SkyLounge when Ted mentions that, technically, I might have a younger brother in Africa. Eventually comes a moment you accept the not knowing, like a first step into the blue, when you must trust the shifty cliff gods to see you down.

I stand and stare at the reptile. Reflected in the water is the tower above, the deep ruby strobe seeming to beat from the caiman itself. "That's totally fake," I say.

"Come on, look at it," Jimbo says. "There it is."

"Fumble," Marty's father calls out to us. "Check it out. Rebs're first and goal." He is sitting in a folding chair strung with nylon webbing, beer and fork in the same hand, but he's watching more of us than the game.

The wolves still sprint along the perimeter of their run, frothing and clipping, their legs tripping them into balls that tumble, roll, and emerge as charging blurs.

"The Rebs are going to reverse. Hundred bucks says it. Remember when I taught you the reverse? You weren't even ten."

"Sure, Dad."

"The Rebs are gonna go for it. Bring your friends over and check out the game," he says, and when we don't respond, he stands up. "I'm telling you to leave that stupid thing alone."

Marty and his father have a moment when they eye each other across the pool. Jimbo leans in close to me, his mouth hovering by my ear. "I dare you to touch it," he whispers. Signals I don't understand pass between father and son. Marty's father then heads for us, walking barefoot and stiff-legged around the pool with his beer, throwing dirty looks at the ceaseless wolves. He, too, steps right over the fence and walks gingerly, arms out, over the rocks. He comes to stand beside me at the edge of the kiddie pool, so that he has to yell past me and Jimbo at his son. "What's the fucking deal with this thing," he says. "Show me the appeal. It doesn't do anything. It just sits there."

"I think it's fake."

Drinking his beer, he glares at me like I'm an idiot. "What's the point? What's the big deal? You got a car and a girl and a family. Your favorite game's on. There's steaks and beer. You do fucking remember what steak tastes like, don't you?" He stops and turns toward the wolves. "Shut up," he yells.

"Dad, I'm not hearing you now, not when you're like this."

I stare at the caiman that hovers in the water, unblinking, legs out, heartbeat red.

"I'm with him," I say. "What's the point?"

"There is no point," Marty's father says and kicks the side of the kiddie pool. The sides yaw and wow with the waves, and the caiman, frozen, rides up and down. "See?" he says. "It doesn't do anything."

There is no motion from the caiman, nothing.

We look from the pool to Marty's father as he knocks back the last of his beer. "Watch this," he says and leans out to drop the can on the caiman's back. There is only a hollow sound when it bounces off. "Boy, what a barrel of fun this thing is. I'm glad it takes up a third of our yard. I'm glad I can't sleep for those fucking wolves, too."

"That's it. We're leaving," Marty says, as if this isn't really our plan.

I look at Jimbo, who shrugs. "It's fake anyway," I tell him.

Without taking his eyes off us, Marty's father shouts "shut up" over his shoulder. "Where do you think *you're* going?"

"To Fly Away."

"You're going to Fly Away?"

"Yeah.

"Well, the rest of the family will just pal around with the gator then." He leans out, dips his toes in the pool, and splashes water on it. "I *know*, 'It's a caiman.'"

"You don't know anything about me," Marty says.

Marty's father puts a hand on my shoulder for balance. With this touch, things suddenly become real for me, and my eyes shift from the hand that grips me to the bare leg below it, swinging back into the blue of the kiddie pool.

This is how a toe comes off. When it happens, it is simple: A sound seems to come before the water even moves, the cracking of a wet sheet maybe, and the caiman rises in motion, turning, too fast to take in. The light changes on the water, there is the popping sound of a hock joint, and I feel fingers grip deep into my shoulder. Then Marty's father turns from us.

We all just stand there as he hobbles across the gravel, and we watch what is to be one slow lap around the pool, alone. As he moves past the pool's shallow steps, the blood starts in earnest, and when he rounds the deep end, we can see his big toe is hanging by a flap.

He moves slowly, foot and heel, foot and heel, looking up at the sun. We have never seen so much blood, and as he passes the wolves, they go crazy with it, heads pressed against the chain-link, eyes rolled back, rear legs digging in place.

He says something through his teeth, something we can't make out, and looks back at us. He comes to the diving board, but instead of going around, he labors over, arms out, in hard-placed steps. Up, off balance, he stares down his yard, the charring meat, the Saturday this is. He looks back at us again.

"Who are you?" he asks. "What are you doing here?"

He comes down hard, half stumbling, and this is when Marty and Jimbo rush to him. But I don't rush. I look at that caiman, the red strobe warping across its back and the curve of the blue bottom. It sits motionless, rocking in its own wake, and it looks more fake than ever. I get the urge to kick it, too, but I don't have the guts.

When I catch up, they are in the garage, lowering Marty's father into the Chrysler. The goal is to elevate his pumping foot on the dash, but they are forced to settle for the open throat of the glove box. Jimbo turns to me. We are standing by the trunk, giving room, and I really think I will be invited along with the family to pace and fret in the emergency room. Instead, Jimbo unzips his pants and spreads the ears of his fly to reveal the white of his jockeys. When I realize he doesn't want to take his dope to the hospital, I just shake my head and unbuckle my pants, looping a thumb in the elastic of my underwear in anticipation. Jimbo reaches deep into his groin and fishes out the sweaty bag of weed just as Marty's mother rounds the fender. Her shirt reads: RUN, REBELS, RUN!

They all load up and drive away, leaving me looking from the dark garage out into the overbright harrows of sharp-cornered tract homes, and I am alone in a stranger's garage. On the wall are spray-painted silhouettes of missing tools—wrench, hammer, plane—just the empty hooks, and I become aware of the cool air on my legs, pouring from an open door, past me through the garage and out into the world.

"They gone?" a voice asks. I'd forgotten about the boy.

There is a white plastic intercom near the garage door, and I push the button. "Yeah," I tell him, "everyone left."

Out back, I find him balancing a plate of burned meat as he drags a patio chair around the pool, where he parks it in front of the wolves. Except for deeper pockets in the pool decking, the blood is turning dark and colorless, the dull metallic of high photography or the platinum black of some fish—a bullhead or drum, maybe—that you see on *Freshwater Sportsman*.

I pull up a chair and join him, our feet outstretched to the edge of the fence, a move that leaves the wolves insane with rage, slathering each other's necks, roaring at our faces. The boy throws a piece of meat over the fence, and it just disappears. I, too, grab a fillet and loft it over the short fence. All you see is the sudden white of upstretched necks and the falling punch of the throat that gets it.

We lean back in our chairs then, staring straight at those wolves with our heads cocked in a lazy, curious way.

"What'd you do yesterday?" I ask him.

"I don't know," he says.

There are gods who were raised by wolves, but I don't recall the details. It was one of the seventy-three questions I missed on the midterm.

"You'd think they'd get tired of this."

"I think it's the waves from that thing." The boy nods toward the tower. "That's what drives them crazy."

Above, I hear another bird on approach. Wobbling in, it seems to nearly clip the tower.

"Bird" is a term my mother first picks up from Tammy when they're flying the Cancún-Kingston-Cayman triangle eight times a week. It is outbound from Jamaica that my mother's bird, an MD-80 wide-body with bad fuel lines, drops 17,000 feet over Cuba. Tammy, with her overtan skin and tired blue eyes, tells my mother that drops happen, that you can learn to love the thrill.

I look up at the flashing tower, and this boy's radio-wave theory makes a certain kind of sense, but the mystery I'm trying to solve is what in the world keeps these wolves from coming over the fence.

The stupid part of this story is that the next day we all still go to Fly Away, Jimbo, Marty, and me. It is late afternoon when we arrive, the sun setting over the Vegas strip as we wait before a big muraled door out back by the Dumpsters. Its painting depicts a free-falling woman, limbs out, hair rushing up like fire, and, knowing this must be her, I study the tight body and thin scowl until the door opens to reveal its model, Tasha in the flesh, looking bored and irritable in yellow goggles and a signal orange jumpsuit. I see the artist captured nearly perfectly the sullen indifference in Tasha's eyes, which can't be easy when you're painting in big jugs and winking lashes.

She eyeballs Marty and shakes her head. "You owe me."

We follow her in the back way, where we sit in preflight until the last paying customers of the day leave and Fly Away is ours. Between rows of echoing lockers, we strip to our underwear in front of her.

Marty still has a quarterback's body and Jimbo's an ottoman of a man, but at the sight of me Tasha shakes her head, hands on hips, and decides I'll need a red drag suit, extra large.

"Where'd you get the scar?" she asks, eyeing my sternum.

"I was a kid," I tell her. "I took a tumble."

Jimbo and Marty bake the last of their dope through a toilet paper tube while suiting up slowly and without conversation. Tasha sits on a metal stool, watching as I strap into that red suit. She fixes her earplugs, removing then replacing them.

"You don't talk much," she says, licking the tips of the plugs before screwing them back in. "Not that that's bad."

"What's there to say?"

She leans forward, points at her ear. "What?" she asks.

Finally, she leads us to the control room above the flight chamber, where she presets the engine with a bank of digital switches and relays. With little fanfare, we follow her downstairs to a round chamber, where, in a 200-mile-per-hour wind, I fly. The padding on the walls is red vinyl, rolled and tucked, like the choice upholstery of an old Cadillac. Hovering over the wire mesh that separates me from the motor, I don't try any flips or fancy moves. I just float eye-level with those who hug the sides, waiting their turns while I take too long, as I am held transfixed, staring straight down the maw of a DC-3.

For the others, there are stunts and bloopers, amazing vaults and gymnastics from Tasha, but I don't really see any of it. After thirty minutes, the engine winds itself down, and we wiggle off our helmets to reveal sweaty, matted hair. Marty and Jimbo compare flight stories, gesturing with their hands like fins, their voices echoing with the strange sound in there, and I don't feel so hot.

Tasha comes over and places two fingers on my neck, clocking my pulse on her watch. The move surprises me at first, but there is purpose in her fingers, and I sense she knows what she's feeling for. She leans in close for her reading, and at this height I can watch how her ribs finger her suit when she exhales.

"You take everyone's pulse?"

"Only ones that look like you. They gave us a course on it." She nods at the motor below. "You know, heart attacks."

"Nothing's wrong with my heart," I say. "How do I look?"

"I've got that same scar on my chest, so save the story."

"From the crash?"

Marty just hears the edge of this but pipes in, "Don't get her started on that crash."

"Shut up," she says to him, and then turns back to me. "You're okay. You look good." She adjusts her fingers on my neck, pushes harder.

"We're going on a smoke run," Marty says, stripping his flight suit clean off, right in the chamber.

"Sure," she says. "Whatever."

Jimbo comes up to me. "Right back," he says and tries to do the complicated shake with me, leaving my hands fumbling to keep up. Jimbo punches the air and tokes an imaginary joint before the two of them cruise, half-naked, out the padded door.

Tasha slides her fingers from my neck to my helmet, which she pats. "Your pulse is strong, rising some, but fine."

"That scar—really, I was a kid. I fell on a rake."

Tasha sits next to me, throwing a leg across the padding. "Mine was heart massage. You know what that is?"

"That must have been some crash."

"I used to be a cheerleader. Can you believe that? What was I cheering for? I don't even see the point now."

"'Cause you saw the other side?"

"The other side of what?"

"Jimbo says, you know, you saw the light."

" 'The light'? What an asshole."

We hear Jimbo and Marty bang a locker closed in preflight, and Tasha and I stare at each other. In our minds, we are both mentally following the dopey boys through the corridor, down the stairs until they pass a painting of Tasha that will wink them through a self-locking door, and we almost hold our breath listening for the sound of the exit's electric deadbolt.

"You wanna see the light? I'll show you light," she says.

Using a time delay, Tasha programs the motor for top-speed, 240 miles-per-hour, to get us off the ground together. On the wire mat, she lies face down, arms and legs out, and tells me to lay on top of her, so that we are stacked and spread-eagled, both with a view down into the DC-3. I immediately begin to swell in my dragsuit, and I know she can feel me harden. The pneumatic starter motor whines into life, and as the radial cylinders choke and sputter before firing up with authority, the lights turn out, leaving us in absolute blackness, something she must have programmed, too. With the sudden dark, Tasha says yes, and, given the earplugs and air pressure, it is more a vibration through our ribs than a sound.

There is no noise or light as the propeller claps up to a fast throttle. The ground simply falls away, and we rise, riding a column of air like a life raft on roiling, black breakers. Tasha does the balancing with her arms and I just hold on, wrapping around her, letting my fingers interlock her ribs, run the raised line of her breastplate scar. Mostly, I just hold on, but as my eyes start to adjust, I begin to see a faint light. From the dark engine below comes a coppery fire, the green black glow of its hot cowls, and into this I look for a first glimpse of the future. In air hot and black as jet, this minor light speaks loud to me, winks at me as I feel Tasha reach back through the dark to unsnap the crotch flaps in our suits. She yells something I cannot hear.

I enter her without ceremony, and we screw spread-eagled, through wind-whipped nylon, the rattle making Tasha's flesh feel hard and fibrous inside, like the slick white, gumlike meat of coconut. In the wind tunnel below, the motor's buttery fire is the only light we have to guide us, and we fall endlessly toward it, like the path-dangling shimmer of a tree viper's heat pits, the golden Isis beetle burrowing beneath the Valley of Kings. I am a cliff diver, held midleap. I am between engine and ice, green felt and craps, hovering between the untrue city and the coming flash. Close by is my father, night falling, high on endorphins, somewhere after the bullet but before the hyenas, the constellations overhead forming themselves not into giant bears or crabs, but silver Jeeps, celestial banana clips, a great gavel. Of the hard, wheeling lights above, my father's eyes make out Ladder, Lariat, Fleece, and Sickle. From the stars of Serpens, Scorpio, Leo Major, and Lupus, he sees the Burning Chariot, the Lesser Wing, the False Book.

Tasha has her feet looped around my ankles, and she's elbowing me in the ribs, to fuck harder, I figure, so I jostle my hips as I am supposed to, yet I feel nothing. Losing my senses, I drift closer to my essential state: coupled and bound with someone I cannot see, hear, or feel. It is in this state—floating, hungry, tethered—that I have a moment of clarity, a vision: I see a resort permanently frozen in glass, like a "Wish you were here" diorama in a snow globe, with plastic figurines of those who people my life, while around them whips a constant category-three storm. If there is a heaven or hell for Tammy, it is the same place—this hot tub she reclines in, with enough chlorine to burn her hair blonde again, while above tumbles a sky of yellow masks, complimentary Tanquerays, and wheeling black boxes. On a white towel, my mother sleeps under this sun, margarita gone warm. Of Ted, there is only the red tip of his snorkel as he examines bright fish trapped in clear blue plastic. And driving blind through a storm of seismic charges, MP badges, and Togo masks is my father, one hand on the wheel, the other holding binoculars focused so that everything near him is overblown and blurry, so that all beyond is bathed in tempting, miraculous light.

The storm around me, however, begins to subside, and our column of air becomes unsteady as the engine tires down. While I'm still inside Tasha, we slowly settle on the wire mat, lightly bouncing from its spring as we begin to gain weight. I don't know if I came in her or not. I thought there'd be that white flash, the divine light, so to speak, but I may have missed it.

Finished, we strip out of our sweaty suits, and, naked, our skin red-streaked, we lie facedown together on the mesh, letting our forearms dangle through the squares of wire. We let it go quiet, and above the smoldering engine the aluminum sounds of our breathing echo from its turbines, mingling together, so that it whispers back.

Tasha shifts so her breasts swing through, and above the pale ticking blue of hot manifolds we both let our bladders go, our ears following the urine as it dribbles to crackle and hiss in the blades below. The glowing steam that lifts, a fog of pissy vinegar, drowsily mumbles to us with our own breath, and it is the first true ghost I have seen, though there will be others.

"There it is," she says. "There's your light."

This is the point in the story where I'm supposed to tell you how everything works out and then hit you with the big picture. I'll give it a shot.

It turns out that, after three operations, Marty's father loses half the foot to infection and later he sways when he stands. Jimbo shakes his head as he tells me this on the last night I see him, when I go to his house to watch *Speedweek*'s coverage of Le Mans. *Speedweek* puts me in a bad mood because there are too many commercials. There are no breaks or second halves in the real world. You can't call time-out at

200 miles an hour. Around lap four hundred, Jimbo returns from the kitchen shirtless, holding two Millers. Smiling, he asks me if I'd like a beer with head.

The Runnin' Rebels go on to win the conference title.

Mythology isn't for me. Right before I fail, though, as an aside, the teacher says something I remember. *Of course there are no gods, really,* he tells us, which surprises me, because I'd gotten used to the idea. But it makes sense. I know there's no great hand that shuttles jets safely down or suggests to scavengers that they find other meals.

Ted says he hears from somebody who hears from somebody that my dad is caught bartering military radios for low-grade emeralds in Tanganyika and is deported by the British. They say he makes it out of Africa A-OK, but the more I get used to Ted, the less I trust him. Back when we first meet, when I am nobody in his eyes, the truths come hard and fast. Now I see Ted often, and he no longer says things like *Tough break* and *Face it.* Assuming he's ever even met my father, which is still in question, Ted's little stories suggest a bigger truth: He's begun to care enough to lie.

Some days, sure as the sun, I know my father is dead. Others, I hear his Rover circling the oil-field perimeter wire full throttle. I see him on a drilling platform set in a sea of chewgrass, scanning heat waves for signs of motion between the drilling towers, his fingers running in and out the focus of his brassbound marine binoculars. Maybe he studies the sky, impossibly blue, or eyes distant villages, rising phoenixlike from the tawny rose savanna clay. Of course, he sees women, bronze from this distance, hair dyed like inky wine in the evening sun, as they move their burdens silently along the horizon.

The best version of things I won't be able to imagine till later, when I am alone in a way I didn't know people could be. I move to Acapulco, where cliff diving at night is all the rage, and on Friday evenings, Ted and I sit with tourists in silence as we follow bodies that drop through darkness into a pumice-colored sea. On some Sundays, Ted teaches me target-match shooting on the brown plains just beyond the brochure-beautiful mountains of coastal Mexico. Ted's pistols are of tournament quality, quiet and firm in your hand as they snap and ring the distant silhouettes. On these mornings we leave the church bells and take his Jeep up the winding mountain roads, past Chidiaz and El Agujero, to the high, grassy plains that extend into the heart of mid-Guerrero. The fields whip in the wind, and we shoot into the brown waves whenever the red targets flash through the grass. Ted never produces my father's binoculars, but it doesn't matter. We walk into the scrub to see what we hit. We examine the targets, decide angles, hit-and-miss ratios, and then walk out of the brush together to the Jeep, parked on a ridge that divides our view of the world in three: a khaki run of grass, a thin strip of indigo ocean, and the sky, palest of blues.

Ted thumbs the indentations our bullets make in silhouettes of pronghorns and lions and boar. He looks at me hard, in a way he has never done before. He squints. In Africa, Ted tells me, gods live in animals and trees, even in things like tables and radios. There is a big problem over there of gods taking human form and sleeping with women. The god then changes back, and the woman is alone, but for the boy that is born things are worse: He's a semigod, with small powers he doesn't understand, and, like his father, he's a roamer, with one wing in heaven, one foot on earth, doomed to wander toward every distant mud city that appears golden in his half-divine sight. His real father might be a bird or storm, sea-beast or lion, so this typical young man, Ted says, must learn to find his fathers where he can.

This story Ted tells me is a good one, though I'm sure he's probably making it up. I don't remember my Mythology teacher lecturing on this topic. Ted does have a point, though. You can't go around talking to trees and radios. You must learn to live with the unknown, never taking your eyes off it, but not growing used to it, either. For instance, from this vantage, it looks like these cliffs deadfall straight into the ocean's abyss. But there's a strip of land between the ledge and the surf that you can't quite see from here. You'd have to listen for the church bells or smell for the meat smokers in the market to know this stretch of shore is below. You'd have to use all your powers, because in life you can count on the most important things being beyond your knowing, like a decade you can't remember, a lost younger brother, or this hidden beach where your mother's villa is, where she sleeps late after flying all night through turbulence.

CONTRIBUTORS

SCOTT ANTWORTH is a three-time PEN Prisoner Writing Award winner for fiction. He graduated, with distinction, from the University of Maine at Augusta while at the Maine State Prison. After making his debut in print in Biddle Publishing's *Trapped Under Ice,* he has since gone on to appear in numerous journals and anthologies, including *Doing Time: 25 Years of PEN Prison Writing*. He remains at a minimum-security work farm and is currently finishing his first novel.

DAVID BENIOFF was born and raised in New York City. His first novel, *The 25th Hour,* will be published in January 2001 by Carroll & Graf.

MARLAIS OLMSTEAD BRAND lives with her husband in Maryland and teaches in a private high school in Washington, D.C. She was born in Maine and her first novel, which she has just completed and hopes to sell soon, is set there. Brand received her MA in English from SUNY Stony Brook and completed her MFA in Fiction at the University of Maryland.

MAILE CHAPMAN is a fiction writer and playwright whose stories have appeared in *Stand* magazine, *Third Bed, Minimus,* and others. She lives in Syracuse, New York, and is writing her first novel.

JASON COLEMAN attended the School of Communications at the University of Texas. Following his graduation he lived for three years in the Netherlands. He recently earned his MFA from the University of Virginia, where he currently works in public relations.

MERRILL FEITELL was born and raised in New York City. She completed her MFA at Columbia University and dutifully and joyfully served as a waiter at the Bread Loaf Writers' Conference. She has just finished her first collection of stories and is currently working on a novel.

WILLIAM GAY is the author of *The Long Home*, a debut novel published last year to critical acclaim. His story "The Paperhanger, the Doctor's Wife, and the Child Who Went into the Abstract" was nominated by the Sewanee Writers' Conference, where the author was a 1999 Tennessee Williams scholar. He makes his home in Tennessee.

GABRIELLA GOLIGER grew up in Montreal and now lives in Ottawa, Canada. Her first collection of short stories will be published in 2000 by Raincoast Books. In 1997, she was co-winner of the Journey Prize for short fiction, Canada's biggest prize for a single story by a new writer. In 1995, she was short-listed for this prize and, in 1993, she won the Prism International award for short fiction. Her work has also been published in *Parchment: Contemporary Canadian Jewish Writing, Canadian Forum, Coming Attractions 1998, Quintet,* and *Tide Lines: Stories of Change by Lesbians.*

ADAM JOHNSON was a Kingsbury fellow at Florida State University. His stories have been published in the *Missouri Review, New England Review,* and the *Virginia Quarterly Review,* as well as *Esquire, Speak,* and *Orion* magazines. His stories also appeared in all three editions of *Scribner's Best of the Fiction Workshops.*

MAILE MELOY was born in Montana. She received an MFA from the University of California, Irvine, and is finishing a book of short stories.

ANA MENENDEZ, a former reporter for the *Miami Herald* and the *Orange County Register,* recently finished a *New York Times* Fellowship at New York University. Her work has also appeared in *Capital Style* magazine, *Zoetrope: All-Story,* and the *New Republic.*

LISA METZGAR is a graduate of the MFA program at Colorado State University and the daughter of a mouse biologist. She lives and writes in Golden, Colorado, and she doesn't have any cats.

MARTHA OTIS grew up in Minnesota. She has published poetry and translations, as well as journalism and academic articles. The story in this anthology is her first published fiction. She lives with her husband and daughter in Chetumal, Mexico, where she teaches at the University of Quintana Roo.

MARGO RABB was born and raised in New York City. Her stories have been published in the *Atlantic Monthly, Zoetrope: All-Story, New Stories from the South, Seventeen, American Fiction,* and other magazines, and have been broadcast on National Public Radio. She received the grand prize in the Sam Adams/*Zoetrope* short story contest, first prize in the *Atlantic Monthly* student fiction contest, first prize in the *American Fiction* contest, and a Syndicated Fiction Project Award. She has an MFA from the University of Arizona in Tucson.

LADETTE RANDOLPH is currently an acquiring editor at the University of Nebraska Press and formerly managing editor at *Prairie Schooner.* Her fiction has appeared or is forthcoming in *Prairie Schooner, Passages North, The Clackamas Literary Review,*

South Dakota Review, Writers' Forum, and *Blue Mesa Review.* She is the author of an unpublished collection of stories, *This Is Not the Tropics,* and is finishing a memoir.

KATE SMALL is the recipient of the 1999 *Chelsea* Fiction Prize, the 1999 *Other Voices* Fiction Prize, the 1999 *Sonora Review* Fiction Prize, the 1999 *Madison Review* Fiction Prize, the 1999 *Evergreen Chronicles* Novella Prize, and a 1998 AWP Intro Journals Award. She is currently at work on a novel and is completing an MFA from San Francisco State University.

SHIMON TANAKA was born in Tokyo in 1971 and moved to the United States in 1977. This is his first published story.

JENNIFER VANDERBES is a graduate of Yale University and the Iowa Writers' Workshop.

MONICA WESOLOWSKA received her education from Reed College and in 1998–99 was a fiction fellow at the Fine Arts Work Center in Provincetown. Her fiction has appeared in *Beach: Stories by the Sand and Sea* (Marlowe Books, 2000) and *The Writing Path II: Poetry and Prose from Writers' Conferences* (University of Iowa Press, 1996). She lives in her hometown of Berkeley, California, where she supports herself working as an environmental activist.

TOBIAS WOLFF is the author of many books, including *This Boy's Life, Back in the World,* and *The Night in Question.* Tobias Wolff has been the winner of the Rea Award for excellence in the short story, the *Los Angeles Times* Book Award, and the PEN/Faulkner Award. He currently directs the Wallace Stegner Writing Program at Stanford University. Previously he was writer-in-residence at Syracuse University.

DAVID WOOD is serving a forty-year sentence in a Florida prison, where he works as a GED tutor and studies computer drafting. He has a bachelor's degree from the University of South Florida, and since his incarceration began twelve years ago, he has been published in *State Street Review, Black Ice, Poetic Space,* and the *Florida Times-Union.* He is presently working on a novel about wolves in Minnesota, titled *Legend.*

PARTICIPANTS

Colorado State University
Department of English
Fort Collins, CO 80523-1773
970/491-6428

Columbia College Chicago
Fiction Writing Department
600 South Michigan Avenue
Chicago, IL 60605
312/663-1600

Columbia University
Writing Division
School of the Arts
Dodge Hall
2960 Broadway, Room 400
New York, NY 10027-6902
212/854-4391

DePaul University
MA in Writing Program
Department of English
802 West Belden Avenue
Chicago, IL 60614-3214
773/325-7485

Eastern Washington University
Creative Writing Program
705 West First Avenue
MS #1
Spokane, WA 99201
509/623-4221

Emerson College
Writing, Literature, and Publishing
100 Beacon Street
Boston, MA 02116
617/824-8750

Fine Arts Work Center in
Provincetown
24 Pearl Street
Provincetown, MA 02657
508/487-8678

Florida International University
Creative Writing Program
English Department
3000 N.E. 151 Street
Biscayne Bay Campus
North Miami, FL 33181
305/919-5857

Florida State University
Department of English
Tallahassee, FL 32306-1036
850/644-4230

George Mason University
Creative Writing Program
MS 3E4
Fairfax, VA 22030
703/993-1185

Georgia State University
Department of English
University Plaza
Atlanta, GA 30303-3083
404/651-2900

Hamline University
Graduate Liberal Studies Programs
1536 Hewitt Avenue
MS A1730
Saint Paul, MN 55104-1284
651/523-2047

Indiana University
MFA Program
English Department
1020 East Kirkwood Avenue
Ballantine Hall 442
Bloomington, IN 47405-6601
812/855-8224

Johns Hopkins University
The Writing Seminars
135 Gilman Hall
3400 N. Charles Street
Baltimore, MD 21218-2690
410/516-7563

The Loft Literary Center Mentor
Series Program
1011 Washington Ave., S.
Suite 200
Minneapolis, MN 55415
612/215-2585

Louisiana State University
English Department
213 Allen
Baton Rouge, LA 70803
225/388-2236

Loyola Marymount University
Department of English
326 Foley
Loyola Boulevard and West 80th
Street
Los Angeles, CA 90045
310/338-3018

Manhattanville College
Master of Arts in Writing
2900 Purchase Street
Purchase, NY 10577
914/694-3425

McNeese State University
Program in Creative Writing
Department of Languages
P.O. Box 92655
Lake Charles, LA 70609
337/475-5326

Miami University
MA Program in Creative Writing
Department of English
356 Bachelor Hall
Oxford, OH 45056
513/529-5221

Minnesota State University, Mankato
English Department
P.O. Box 8400
Mankato, MN 56002-8400
507/389-2117

Mississippi State University
Drawer E
Department of English
Mississippi State, MS 39762
662/325-3644

Naropa Institute
2130 Arapahoe Avenue
Boulder, CO 80302-6697
303/546-3540

New Mexico State University
Department of English
Box 30001, Department 3E
Las Cruces, NM 88003-8001
505/646-3931

New York University
Graduate Program in Creative
Writing
19 University Place
New York, NY 10003
212/998-8816

Ohio State University
Department of English
164 West 17th Avenue
Room 421 Denney Hall
Columbus, OH 43210-1370
614/292-6065

Oklahoma State University
English Department
205 Morrill Hall
Stillwater, OK 74078-4069
405/744-9469

Old Dominion University
Department of English
BAL 220
Norfolk, VA 23529
757/683-3991

Pennsylvania State University
MFA Program in Writing
Department of English
22 Burrowes Building
University Park, PA 16802
814/863-3069

PEN Prison Writing Committee
PEN American Center
568 Broadway
New York, NY 10012
212/334-1660

Purdue University
Office of Admissions
1080 Schleman Hall
West Lafayette, IN 47907-1080
765/494-1776

Rivier College
Department of English
South Main Street
Nashua, NH 03060-5086
603/888-1311

Saint Mary's College of California
MFA Program in Creative Writing
P.O. Box 4686
Moraga, CA 94575-4686
925/631-4088

San Diego State University
MFA Program
Department of English and
Comparative Literature
5500 Campanile Drive
San Diego, CA 92182-8140
619/594-5443

San Francisco State University
Creative Writing Department
College of Humanities
1600 Holloway Avenue
San Francisco, CA 94132-4162
415/338-1891

Sarah Lawrence College
Office of Graduate Studies
1 Mead Way
Bronxville, NY 10708-5999
914/337-0700

The School of the Art Institute of
Chicago
MFA in Writing Program
37 South Wabash Avenue
Chicago, IL 60603-3103
800/232-7242 or 312/899-5219

Sewanee Writers' Conference
735 University Avenue
Sewanee, TN 37383-1000
931/598-1141

Sonoma State University
Department of English
1801 East Cotati Avenue
Rohnert Park, CA 94928-3609
707/664-2140

Southampton College/Long Island
University
MFA Program in English & Writing
English Department
239 Montauk Highway
Southampton, NY 11968
631/287-8420

Southern Illinois University at
Carbondale
Creative Writing Program
Department of English
Carbondale, IL 62901-4503
618/453-5321

Southwest Texas State University
MFA Program in Creative Writing
Department of English
601 University Drive
San Marcos, TX 78666
512/245-7681

Syracuse University
Program in Creative Writing
Department of English
College of Arts & Sciences
Syracuse, NY 13244-1170
315/443-2174

Temple University
Creative Writing Program
Anderson Hall, 10th Floor
Philadelphia, PA 19122
215/204-1796

University at Albany, SUNY
The Graduate Program
in English Studies
English Department, HU 334
Albany, NY 12222
518/442-4055

University of Alabama
Program in Creative Writing
Department of English
P.O. Box 870244
Tuscaloosa, AL 35487-0244
205/348-0766

University of Alaska, Anchorage
Department of Creative Writing &
Literary Arts
3211 Providence Drive
Anchorage, AK 99508-8348
907/786-4330

University of Alaska, Fairbanks
Creative Writing Program
Department of English
P.O. Box 755720
Fairbanks, AK 99775-5720
907/474-7193

University of Arizona
Creative Writing Program
Department of English
445 Modern Languages Bldg.
Tucson, AZ 85721-0067
520/621-3880

University of Arkansas
Program in Creative Writing
Department of English
333 Kimpel Hall
Fayetteville, AR 72701
501/575-7355

University of California, Irvine
MFA Program in Writing
Department of English &
Comparative Literature
435 Humanities Instructional Bldg.
Irvine, CA 92697-2650
714/824-6718

University of Central Florida
Graduate Program in Creative
Writing
Department of English
P.O. Box 161346
Orlando, FL 32816-1346
407/823-2212

University of Cincinnati
Creative Writing Program
Department of English &
Comparative Literature
P.O. Box 210069
Cincinnati, OH 45221-0069
513/556-3946

University of Colorado at Boulder
Creative Writing Program
Department of English
Campus Box 226
Boulder, CO 80309-0226
303/492-7381

University of Denver
Creative Writing Program
Department of English
Pioneer Hall
Denver, CO 80208
303/871-2266

University of Florida
Creative Writing Program
English/4008 TUR
Gainesville, FL 32611-7310
352/392-6650

University of Georgia
Creative Writing Program
English Department
Park Hall 102
Athens, GA 30602-6205
706/542-2197

University of Hawaii
Creative Writing Program
English Department
1733 Donaghho Road
Honolulu, HI 96822
808/956-7619

University of Houston
Creative Writing Program
Department of English
Houston, TX 77204-3012
713/743-3015

University of Idaho
Creative Writing Program
English Department
Moscow, ID 83843
208/885-6156

University of Illinois at Chicago
Program for Writers
Department of English MC/162
601 South Morgan Street
Chicago, IL 60607-7120
312/413-2229

University of Iowa
Program in Creative Writing
102 Dey House
507 N. Clinton Street
Iowa City, IA 52242
319/335-0416

University of Maine
Master's in English Program
5752 Neville Hall
Orono, ME 04469-5752
207/581-3822

University of Maryland
Creative Writing Program
Department of English
4140 Susquehanna Hall
College Park, MD 20742
301/405-3820

University of Massachusetts,
Amherst
MFA in English
Bartlett Hall
Box 30515
Amherst, MA 01003-0515
413/545-0643

University of Michigan
MFA Program in
Creative Writing
Department of English
3187 Angell Hall
Ann Arbor, MI 48109-1003
734/763-4139

University of Minnesota
MFA Program in Creative Writing
Department of English
Lind Hall
207 Church Street, S.E.
Minneapolis, MN 55455
612/625-6366

University of Missouri, Columbia
Creative Writing Program
English Department
107 Tate Hall
Columbia, MO 65211
573/882-6421

University of Missouri, St. Louis
Master of Fine Arts in Creative
Writing Program
Department of English
8001 Natural Bridge Road
St. Louis, MO 63121
314/516-6845

University of Montana
Creative Writing Program
Department of English
Missoula, MT 59812-1013
406/243-5231

University of Nebraska, Lincoln
Creative Writing Program
Department of English
343 Andrews Hall
Lincoln, NE 68588-0333
402/472-3191

University of New Hampshire
Creative Writing Program
Department of English
Hamilton Smith Hall
95 Main Street
Durham, NH 03824-3574
603/862-3963

University of New Mexico
Creative Writing Program
English Department
Humanities 217
Albuquerque, NM 87131
505/277-6347

University of New Orleans
Creative Writing Workshop
College of Liberal Arts
Lakefront
New Orleans, LA 70148
504/280-7454

University of North Carolina,
Greensboro
MFA Writing Program at Greensboro
134 McIver Building
P.O. Box 26170
Greensboro, NC 27402-6170
336/334-5459

University of Notre Dame
Creative Writing Program
355 O'Shaughnessy Hall
Notre Dame, IN 46556-0368
219/631-7526

University of Oregon
Program in Creative Writing
Box 5243
Eugene, OR 97403-5243
541/346-3944

University of Pittsburgh
Creative Writing Program
526 CL
4200 Fifth Avenue
Pittsburgh, PA 15260
412/624-6506

University of San Francisco
MA in Writing
Program Office, Lone Mountain 340
2130 Fulton Street
San Francisco, CA 94117-1080
415/422-2382

University of South Carolina
MFA Program
Department of English
Columbia, SC 29208
803/777-5063

University of Southern Mississippi
Center for Writers
Box 5144 USM
Hattiesburg, MS 39406-5144
601/266-4321

University of Texas at Austin
English Department
PAR 108
Austin, TX 78712-1164
512/471-4991

University of Texas Michener Center
for Writers
J. Frank Dobie House
702 East Dean Keeton Street
Austin, TX 78705
512/471-1601

University of Utah
Creative Writing Program
255 S. Central Campus Drive,
Room 3500
Salt Lake City, UT 84112
801/581-7131

University of Virginia
Creative Writing Program
Department of English
Bryan Hall
Charlottesville, VA 22903
804/924-6675

University of Washington
Creative Writing Program
Box 354330
Seattle, WA 98195-4330
206/543-9865

University of Wisconsin, Milwaukee
Creative Writing Programs
Department of English
Box 413
Milwaukee, WI 53201
414/229-4511

University of Wyoming
Writing Program
Department of English
P.O. Box 3353
Laramie, WY 82071
307/766-6452

Unterberg Poetry Center/Writing
Program
92nd Street Y
1395 Lexington Avenue
New York, NY 10128
212/996-1100

Vermont College
Master of Fine Arts in Writing
Montpelier, VT 05602
802/828-8840

Virginia Commonwealth University
MFA in Creative Writing Program
Department of English
P.O. Box 842005
Richmond, VA 23284-2005
804/828-1329

Washington University
Writing Program
Department of English
Campus Box 1122
St. Louis, MO 63130-4899
314/935-7130

Wayne State University
Creative Writing Program
English Department
Detroit, MI 48202
313/577-2450

Wesleyan Writers Conference
Wesleyan University
Middletown, CT 06459
860/685-3604

West Virginia University
Creative Writing Program
Department of English
230 Stansbury Hall
P.O. Box 6269
Morgantown, WV 26506-6269
304/293-3107

Western Illinois University
Department of English and
Journalism
Macomb, IL 61455-1390
309/298-1103

Western Michigan University
Graduate Program in Creative
Writing
Department of English
Kalamazoo, MI 49008-5092
616/387-2572

Wichita State University
MFA in Creative Writing
1845 N. Fairmount
Wichita, KS 67260-0014
316/978-3130

Woodland Pattern Book Center
720 E. Locust
Milwaukee, WI 53212
414/263-5001

The Writer's Voice of the
West Side YMCA
5 W. 63rd Street
New York, NY 10023
212/875-4124

Canada

Banff Centre for the Arts
Writing & Publishing
Office of the Registrar
Box 1020-28
107 Tunnel Mountain Drive
Banff, AB T0L 0C0
800/565-9989 or 403/762-6180

Concordia University
Department of English
Creative Writing Program
LB 501
1455 de Maisonneuve Boulevard West
Montreal, PQ H3G 1M8
514/848-2340

University of Alberta
Department of English
3-5 Humanities Center
Edmonton, AB T6G 2E5
780/492-3258

University of British Columbia
Creative Writing Program
Buchanan Building, Room E462
1866 Main Mall
Vancouver, BC V6T 1Z1
604/822-0699

University of Calgary
Creative Writing Program
Graduate Studies
Department of English
Calgary, AB T2N 1N4
403/220-5484

University of New Brunswick
Department of English
Box 4400
Fredericton, NB E3B 5A3
506/453-4676